ALSO BY MEGAN CHANCE

Susannah Morrow

An Inconvenient Wife

The Spiritualist

Prima Donna

City of Ash

Bone River

INAMORATA

MEGAN CHANCE

LAKE UNION
PUBLISHING

Published by Lake Union Publishing, Seattle

www.apub.com

Amazon, the Amazon logo, and Lake Union Publishing are trademarks of Amazon.com, Inc., or its affiliates.

ISBN-13: 9781477823033
ISBN-10: 1477823034

Cover design by Cyanotype Book Architects

Library of Congress Control Number: 2013922577

Printed in the United States of America

For Kany,
who has always believed

Omnia Mundi Fumus et Umbra
All in the World is Smoke and Shadow

–Latin motto

PROLOGUE

PARIS—1878

Though it was only a few hours until dawn, it was not quiet. It never was in this part of town, which was not among the best in Paris. Talk and laughter from a nearby cafe murmured through my open window, along with the soft cries of whores calling from doorways as they tried to eke the last bit of profit from the night. Some things even two hundred years did not change.

I searched the shadows of the street below. He had not found me yet, but he would, and it would all begin again. He had learned too much in Barcelona, and I did not think he would give up now.

I didn't know whether to welcome or dread his arrival. It had already been a year, much of which had been spent in darkness and shadows and fear, hiding from the world. Twelve months, and now, here I was, myself again, only to find I was no longer very good at living.

I sighed and turned away, leaving the window open for the scents of the city to drift inside. Sometimes it was only the smells that told me where I was—what place, what time. Whenever I stepped off a steamer or out of a carriage, I stopped and inhaled deeply. *Ah yes, this is Paris. Or London. Or Madrid or Rome or Vienna.* Though I would not have been able to describe before that moment what smells were uniquely theirs.

I took a deep breath of Paris now. It was not quite my home—there was no place I called that anymore, though Paris was as close as any, and this hotel belonged to my past and so was comforting, despite its cheap pretensions to grandeur. I was no longer accustomed to anything less than the best, but I'd wanted a place to heal after the months of hiding. This last incident had shaken me greatly, and I was exhausted at the thought of starting again, of seeing his face and knowing what he meant to do. To fight again—had I the strength for it now?

Slowly, I went to the flecked mirror near the bed and put up my hair, which was a thick and heavy brown with a great deal of red. My crowning glory, some said. Others had written poetry of my graceful neck and my smooth shoulders. My naked breasts graced dozens of canvases. Music celebrated my laughter and my frowns. *Your beauty will be your fortune,* my mother had said to me once, so long ago now I wasn't certain it was my own memory, or just something I'd been told.

I undressed, and reached for my portmanteau, taking out the narrow razor case. The blade inside gleamed. I turned down the lamp to a tender glow, and then I stepped into the bath. I took my time, lowering myself inch by inch, sighing at immersion, letting the warm water lap my body for a moment, relaxing within it.

Then I raised my arm from the water. I glanced down at my wrist, at the thin pink scar that marked it already, the vein pulsing beneath it, a blue line beneath my pale skin making an easy map to follow. I brought the razor to my wrist and cut, wincing at the pain, waiting for—I don't know . . . *something*, some feeling I didn't know, something real even if it wasn't new—as the blood bloomed beneath the blade, as I slit deep and long, tracing the old scar.

But there was nothing but pain and that familiar ennui. Even this was not enough.

Well, I'd known that would be so, hadn't I?

I turned to the other wrist, cutting it just as deeply, and then I let the razor fall to the floor. The water stung as I submerged my arms again. I watched the blood wisping like smoke as it was drawn from my wrists, curling in beautiful patterns as it followed the weave and weft of the faint current set by my breathing and my pulse, and then there were no more pretty patterns; only clear water fogging into homogenous pink and then red. I embraced the lassitude when it came; I was weightless and strange, no longer myself but someone else, that long ago me who had watched a brilliantly bejeweled woman across the room and felt an unyielding, unhesitating affinity.

I heard her voice in my head still. I heard her laughter. I felt the way her breath trembled the hair at the nape of my neck, the way the diamonds circling her wrist had pressed hard into my arm. I remembered how I'd lost myself in their seductive, tempting sparkle.

What do you most desire, Odilé?

I looked down at the water, very red now.

I leaned my head back, and waited for the sunrise.

3

ONE

LONDON—APRIL, 1879
NICHOLAS

I cannot explain how it begins, or why it happens, what strange alchemy puts such things in motion. Whether it is a whisper on the wind or the whiff of a strange perfume that has people stopping in their tracks, caught by a curious caprice as they barter with merchants or test the firm heft of an orange, caught by a desire they'd never thought to have.

I cannot tell you how she does it, only that she does. She is the cause and the urge, and all things move to her pipe and drum. I have followed her for years, long enough to recognize when it happens, when everyone begins to talk of Paris, or all thoughts turn to Rome or Vienna or Madrid.

But now my timing seemed somehow off. Lately I found myself always a step behind, arriving always just after she'd left. I was not the most patient of men, and this inability to find her had me twisting with frustration. I could not afford to let her out of my sight for so long. It had already been two and a half years since Barcelona. The clock was ticking; she must make her choice soon. The knowledge was both the curse that had set me on this path seven years before and my solace now. She could not stay hidden for long. Her very nature forbade it. I would find her. All I could do was hope it wouldn't be too late when I did.

I knew she was in London—or had been—and it was there I knew I would hear of her next step. But I'd heard nothing yet, and I was restless and short-tempered, for once abandoning the salons I frequented nightly to seek peace and solace in a city tavern. I was cutting into one of the heavy steak pies my countrymen consider to be edible when an old friend of mine, Giles Martin, an artist of little renown and less talent, happened in.

He seated himself at my table without delay, reached across the table for a chunk of my pie and shoved it into his mouth, his eyeglasses tipping crookedly on his long patrician nose. He straightened them automatically, saying excitedly as he did so, "I've had the idea, Nick. I know what I shall do next!"

"Who is it this time?" I asked wryly. "Have you finally convinced that pretty redhead at the fish market to take off her clothes for you?"

"Not yet," he said, completely unfazed. "But she's not to be, I fear. I've moved on. I've made a decision—I know at last what will make my career: *plein air!*"

I regarded him skeptically. "Landscapes? You?" Giles hated weather, preferring most of the time to shut himself up with his newest "inspiration," which usually lasted only as long as it took him to get between her thighs.

"Not just any landscape, Nick. Imagine this if you will: picturesque decay. Crumbling buildings. Gorgeous poverty—"

"*Gorgeous* poverty? Here? Good God, what have you been drinking?"

"Not *here*," Giles said impatiently, reaching for another piece of my dinner. "London's exhausted her charms for me."

"Then where? Paris?" I gave him the rest of the pie, which was only greasy shortcrust and gristle. He scrabbled at it with his fingers.

"Venice," he said.

"Ah, Venice. And just how did you come to that?"

"It's all anyone's talking of lately. Whistler's planning to go. I heard Duveneck might abandon his students in Vienna for it as well."

That caught my attention. "Both of them?"

"They say now is the best time." He stared out the tavern window as if he saw the Rapture. "You know, I've never felt so strongly about anything in my life."

That look in Giles's eyes—I knew it. Everyone talking; men abandoning their former plans to rush off. The hush in Giles's voice when he uttered the word *Venice*, as if he were consumed with the thought of it, as if all the charms of the world—including that pretty redhead he'd been obsessed with only days before—were subsumed in its thrall.

My waiting was over.

I tempered my excitement. As casually as I could, I said, "Venice? You know, I wouldn't mind going there myself."

"Come with me," Giles said. "Hell, we could get rooms together, share expenses, that sort of thing. I don't see as how a poet might not gain as much inspiration from the city as an artist."

"And no doubt there will be plenty of Venetian maids lingering in 'gorgeous poverty,' in need of a coin or two," I teased.

He laughed, and I ordered another ale. Though I joked with him the rest of the evening, I was too distracted to remember later what we talked of. Venice. How had I not considered it before? The city of pretense and duplicity and decay. It was perfect for her.

She was Venice personified, with her immortal agelessness and her beautiful, mysterious eyes that promised deliverance and salvation, her mouth that had spoken a hundred promises.

All of them lies.

It was the perfect place for the task I'd been given. I had heard of no new artistic geniuses, and no one was yet speaking of new works to inspire the ages, and so I believed she had not yet chosen. There were only six months left in this cycle—not much time, at least for her—but it meant I was close. The horror of the last time I'd made the attempt to destroy her still haunted me, but now I knew what to expect. Now I had a plan. This time, I would have what I wanted at last.

TWO

VENICE—SEPTEMBER, 1879
SOPHIE

E very book I'd read said that Venice was at her most beautiful come upon from the sea, at sunrise or sunset, and that we *must* see her first that way. So naturally we did not. My twin brother and I first encountered Venice in the dead of night, and not from any romantic gondola, but from the windows of the train racing across the railway bridge from dismal Mestre.

I leaned close to the glass, pushing the veil of my hat impatiently from my face to better see, but there was nothing to look at. The train itself seemed suspended in darkness. Sparks from the engine glowed bright and fleeing, fluttering away into ash, the only thing to show we were moving. I had the strange impression that we were completely alone in the darkness, only Joseph and me in our dimly lit compartment, floating on nothing, disappearing into nothing.

I said, "We're almost there."

My brother gave me a sleepy smile, his dimples parenthesizing his wide mouth, stunning even in half sleep. "You've no need to worry, Soph. I promised it, didn't I?"

"You did."

He squeezed my hand. "This will work. We'll have everything we want. You'll see."

I nodded and looked back into the abject darkness. It was too early for the moon. It was disappointing. I *had* so wanted to come upon Venice as in a novel, watching the campaniles and the top-hat chimneys come into view against a pink-and-lavender-tinted sky as I listened to the soft plashing of a gondolier's oar. I'd read the Murray guidebook cover to cover, over and over again—it was within easy reach even now, shoved into the outer pocket of my carpetbag, which nudged gently against my feet. I'd described how it would be to Joseph a thousand times, though he'd just laughed at me and said, "Only pretty words. They'll never show what my brush will."

Once we had decided to flee New York City, I had thrown myself into travel preparations. I had made lists of everywhere we were to visit, all the things we should pay attention to, no matter that I knew such effort was pointless. Joseph had not opened a single book, and had only listened to my itineraries with amused detachment, but he would be the one who truly knew the city once we stepped foot in it. He would know it in that strange way he had of taking in everything, of seeing what was important, of finding things I did not even know to look for. All my words from Murray or Ruskin or Byron or Howells would be as naught.

But I couldn't just leave it all to chance, could I? So much depended on this. Everything, as he'd said.

You're not leaving it to chance, Soph. You're leaving it to me.

It was true; Joseph's talent and confidence had opened doors for us before. But I was never so easy as my brother, and I knew what lay beneath his confidence. I could not help feeling nervous and afraid. I wanted so much for him—Venice *must* be the answer we'd hoped for.

"You're worrying," he leaned close to whisper. I felt the warmth of his breath against the bare skin below my ear, and I turned to give him a quick kiss.

"I'm not. Truly. Or . . . not much. Oh, when *will* we be there?"

"Now," he said, glancing toward the window, nodding for me to look. Then I saw it. Little pins of light that grew larger as I watched, a city that seemed to bloom from the darkness, spreading and spreading so that I couldn't tell what was real and what was only reflection. But before I could truly grasp it, the train plunged into the station, and shuddered to a halt. A cloud of smoke fogged the window, momentarily obscuring everything, and then it was only bustle. Joseph rose, grabbing my bag and his own, teasing, "You intend to stay here all night?"

I followed him, grabbing on to his arm as he led us into the station, where people raced to and fro, jostling with luggage, and Italian officials in their worn gray-and-green uniforms called for passports. Joseph shifted both bags to one side and reached into his pocket for ours, which were offered and glanced over so quickly we were moving on before I knew it, maneuvering around piles of trunks and luggage and carts, people squeezed in so tightly I did not dare release my grip upon my brother's arm.

We were running a gauntlet now—porters and *valets de place* and men trying to get us to look this way or that, gesturing and shouting in Italian I barely understood—it sounded nothing as it had in Rome, though surely those were the same words? Joseph approached a porter—a small man with very large brown eyes and an official-looking badge—who asked us in perfect French where we would like to go, and I answered in kind before my brother could say a word, "The omnibus. We're to look for the omnibus."

The porter nodded and began to turn. But Joseph said, "No omnibus."

The porter halted. I looked at my brother in confusion. "But the guidebook says the omnibus is cheaper."

"We're in Venice, Soph," he said.

I stared at him, not understanding, and he said to the porter in French, "We'll have a gondola."

In a low voice, I said, "But Joseph, the cost—"

"You wanted to see it from the lagoon at sunset," he said softly, for me alone. "Instead we'll have it from the Grand Canal at night. Our first night in Venice, under the stars. It will be like one of your stories."

How well he knew I would find such a thing irresistible.

"To where, monsieur?" The porter asked.

Joseph looked questioningly at me, and I knew a moment's exasperation that he hadn't remembered the name of the hotel. I said, "Albergo Beale Danieli."

The porter nodded. He glanced at the bags Joseph held and asked if we had luggage, and Joseph motioned toward the small trunk we shared, sitting forlornly among the mounds of other trunks. I saw the way the porter looked at us again, askance this time, as if he knew we hadn't any money. I felt myself grow hot, and it wasn't until he arranged for the trunk's delivery and led us through the crowd and out of the station, where the water of the Grand Canal lapped right up onto the steps and the golden dome of San Simeon loomed across, and the whole glittering, otherworldly spangle of the city burst into being, that I forgot to be embarrassed. I halted, jerking Joseph to a stop and causing the people behind us to stumble and curse.

"Oh," I breathed, and Joseph laughed and pulled me gently toward some man who offered us a piece of paper with the tariffs for the gondola printed upon it.

Joseph didn't even look at it. He took me with him to where a row of gondolas waited, the strangely shaped funereal boats bobbing gently with the current, the toothed projections of their bows alien and vaguely threatening. My brother handed our bags to a tall, broad-shouldered gondolier whose face I could not see well in the darkness, and glanced up at the sky. "The stars are out. Look."

He was right. Glitterdust across a broad expanse of blue. Before me, the water unfurled like dark swaths of shadowed silk, colors muted, reflections cast by the lamps hanging from the prows of the gondolas rippling, and my heart swelled at the beauty and the romance of it.

"You're spoiling me," I told him.

"Don't you deserve it?" His dark blue eyes looked black in the darkness, glowing. "Don't we both?"

He passed me off to the gondolier. The man's long, strong fingers wrapped mine, warm even through my gloves as he helped me into the boat. I arranged myself as comfortably as I could upon the pile of black-leather-covered cushions in the middle, but they were made for lounging, and I could not lounge in a corset and tight skirts.

Joseph settled himself beside me, stretching out his long legs. The white of his trousers glowed in the darkness. White, in spite of the day of travel and dust, but one could not see the dirt on them now. He put his arm against my back, a bolster, something solid to lean against, and I gave him a grateful look.

The boat pushed off into the Grand Canal, and we were plunged into a world of impressions, other gondolas like shadowed hearses gliding past, the bouncing halo of their colored lamps lending an enticingly mysterious air. Abandoned palazzos in dilapidated splendor rose from the water, together with the reflections making a strange sort of labyrinth that melted and dissipated constantly, always changing so I was never quite certain of what was real and what was just an image. A shadow might become a man who disappeared through a silently opening door, a quick shaft of light slanting, washing away, gone, the candles and tiny oil lamps from little street shrines seemingly floating in an endless dark. We caught smatterings of music or conversation as we passed beneath balconies, the sounds carrying distinctly on the water.

It smelled of elusive perfume and river water washed by a sea tide and ancient stone. Joseph and I were silent with wonder as we were swept farther down the Canal. It seemed to go on forever, and I was glad for that, so perfectly stunning it was, and then suddenly there was the Campanile, the pillars of the Molo, St. Mark and his winged lion, the pink-and-white glimmering pattern of the Ducal Palace, all so beautiful and unexpected in spite of the fact that I *had* been expecting them. Only . . . not this way, not in darkness and not in enchantment.

The boat turned into a narrow canal, stopping only a few yards beyond a low, arched bridge. "Danieli," the gondolier said in a deep voice.

Joseph got to his feet and helped me from the gondola onto the slippery stone steps. He arranged to have our trunk brought in, and then hefted our bags, and together we went inside the hotel.

I had never been in a place so fine. I felt an imposter as I took in the marbled floors and walls, the Moorish arches and Oriental-styled pillars. The lobby was opulent, with multi-tiered gilt stairs leading into an atrium. We could not possibly afford to stay here—how had I made these arrangements? I was certain, as Joseph went to the desk and checked us in, that the man there would say, "Oh, monsieur, I am so sorry to tell you that the price is not what was quoted you. I am afraid you must pay a good deal more." But the man only handed Joseph a paper to sign and then we were going up those impossibly narrow, beautiful stairs, past more galleries and more gilt. Gaslight blazed brightly from sconces everywhere, and there was so much heavy marble I wondered that the whole thing didn't sink into the lagoon.

When we finally reached our room, and the porter left us, I leaned back against the door and said, "Did you check the price? Did I make a terrible mistake?"

Joseph had gone to the window, and was pushing aside the slate-blue velvet drapes. He looked over his shoulder. "It's cheaper than you remember. And we're only here until we can find something else."

"There were others I could have chosen. I'll look into it tomorrow—"

He motioned for me to come to him. When I did, he drew me close, my back to his chest, and wrapped his arms around me, resting his chin on the top of my head. "Look out there," he whispered, his voice rumbling. "It looks like the setting of every story you ever told me."

I followed his gaze. The Canal glimmered before me, the towers of San Giorgio Maggiore looming shadows in the near distance. The Molo stretched to the right with its dozens of gondolas moored for the night, black and jagged shadows against the lamp-lit glow of the *fondamenta*. It did look like a fairy tale.

"It's beautiful," he said, and I heard his reverence; I felt it in him as he held me tight and close. He leaned forward, his dark hair brushing my cheek. "You did this perfectly, Soph. I won't let you regret it."

I took a deep breath. "And tomorrow?"

"Tomorrow I'll discover who we must see. I'll find the way in. It will take a few days at most, I promise, while you look for a place to rent. All right?"

I gripped his arms, holding him in place, and nodded, my hair coming loose from its pins where it caught on the stubble of his cheek. "All right."

Gently, he pulled away. I let him go. "Now go to bed," he told me. "You're tired."

"You must be just as tired."

"Not yet. I want to look for a while."

He was right; I was tired. I unbuttoned my coat and took off my hat and my gloves. I went to him to undo the myriad fastenings of my gown and petticoats and corset, which he did, his deep blue gaze focused on the view outside.

I undressed and put on my nightgown, and then I let down my hair, brushing it before the mirrored dressing table. When I went to braid it, Joseph said, "Leave it," so I knew what he meant to do. I left it falling about my shoulders, dark and curling, as he liked it, and went to the bed. The room was chilly and damp, and I was cold. There was neither fireplace nor stove. I lay down—the mattress was thick and comfortable. I asked, "Might I have a blanket?"

Joseph shook his head. I didn't protest. I lay there on top of the bedcovers and waited. But he only stood at the window, and I was too tired, and so I closed my eyes. I felt sleep hovering, no matter the cold, and I was back on the Canal again, swaying in a gondola beneath the stars while the water lapped against the sides in a soothing, quiet rhythm, and it was only then, in some distant part of my mind, that I heard Joseph go to his bag at last. I heard the *shush* as he took what he needed from it, the scrape of a white-and-gilt chair as he pulled it across the floor, next to the bed. I heard the hush of his breath and the quiet rustle of paper, the scratch of charcoal. I didn't open my eyes, and he didn't ask me to. I let the lap of water and the familiar rhythm of his drawing rock me to sleep.

THREE

NICHOLAS

I watched her in the Rialto strolling among the fishmongers and the peddlers, a vision of grace that caught every eye she passed, so beautiful it made one ache to see her. That was one thing that had never changed: despite everything I knew of her, the desire I felt for her remained, and I feared it always would, my own wasting disease. No one could compare to her as she hovered over pyramids of speckled plums and pressed an elegant finger to test the freshness of a tunny. She laughed with a produce seller as she weighed a bright pepper in her hand, those perfect lips parting, flashing white teeth. She wore dark blue that accentuated the red in her hair, the gray of her eyes. Jet buttons. A hat with a black feather sweeping to brush her cheek.

I stayed out of sight. I would show myself soon enough, but for now, I only waited in the shadows as she bought a bit of red mullet, a loaf of bread, a melon—she had a particular fondness for it—though none of these things would appease her real hunger.

I followed her like the devotee I was as she made her way to a small cafe and took a seat at one of the tables on the street. I hid myself behind a stall selling spicy *sguassetto*, watching as her gaze darted from one thing to another. As always, I felt the draw of her, stronger now, as it always was toward the end, and I knew others felt it as well—a juggler had staggered as she passed, dropping one of his pins; an organ grinder stuttered over his keys. But she was not hunting, I realized. She was waiting, which meant she had already found her next victim. I wondered how much talent he had, if she thought he might be the *one*, or if he was only easing the pain of her hunger while she searched.

My senses sharpened as a man approached her, and she broke into a charming smile. He was tall and blond, though not so blond as I, his hair straight where mine was curly. He sat down at the table and pulled his chair close to her, touching her familiarly—already her lover, then—and as if he could not help himself, something I remembered. His hair was too long; his coat frayed at the hem. I thought I'd seen him before—at the salon, perhaps, though not for some time. He was an artist of some kind, of course. And young as they all were. Pretty as she liked them. She was always so predictable.

I leaned back against the wooden post of the stall and waited impatiently through ordered coffees and sweets, fawning and rather nauseating public intimacies. Then at last, he rose, leaning to kiss her before he left.

I hurried after him. I could almost smell the tang of his sweat as I followed him out of the Rialto. The vision of that little room in Barcelona flashed through my mind, strengthening my resolve. I had spent the last seven years doing exactly this, trying to save these men as I wished someone had saved me, but more importantly, keeping them out of her hands. This one, and hopefully the next and the next and the next. And when the cycle was permanently broken . . . I hoped—I believed, I prayed—that the talent she'd stolen from me would return. Then, I could become again the poet I'd been on my way to becoming. Then I could take back my life.

This man did not go far. Only to the Campo San Bartolomeo, where he sat at the wellhead, pulling out his notebook and a pencil. I expected him to begin scribbling frenziedly—the inspiration she provided was like a fever—but he only sat there, staring blankly at the page. After a few moments I stepped up to him, casting a shadow. He looked up, frowning and squinting at me where I stood in the sun.

"Hello," he said, cautiously polite. He was as English as I was, too distracted even to try for French, which was widely spoken here, a clean substitute for the incomprehensible Venetian dialect.

"Oh, thank God you speak English," I said. "I've spent the whole morning looking for a countryman in this wretched maze."

He lifted a hand to his eyes to shield them from the sun, and smiled. He wore a great deal of cologne. I smelled it from where I stood, even in the open air. "You must be new to Venice."

"A veritable babe," I lied. "I arrived just yesterday and already I've been lost three times. How does one navigate?"

"Getting lost is part of the experience." He motioned to his notebook. "I've written my best poems playing Wandering Jew among the *calli*."

"You're a poet?"

He ducked his head humbly. "I make some claim to it."

"Well so do I! Imagine, a fellow poet *and* an Englishman! You must let me buy you a drink. There's a cafe just over there. Come with me and regale me with your impressions of Venice."

"I would, but—"

"And if you're a poet, surely you'll know Katharine Bronson? She's a good friend of mine; in fact, she's who I came to Venice to see. I'm to go to Ca' Alvisi tonight for her salon, assuming I can find it."

"I've been there. Though . . . not for a while."

"So you can point me in the right direction."

"Oh, certainly."

"Perhaps you know another friend of mine too. Odilé León?"

I saw the friendliness in his expression melt away, replaced by suspicion tinged with jealousy. "You know Odilé?"

"I've known her for years."

"Really? I confess I've only known her a short time, but . . ."

"A moment with Odilé is worth a thousand lifetimes, isn't it?"

"Yes." His expression turned to one of such longing and adoration it was almost embarrassing. It was like seeing myself in a mirror, as I'd once been.

"Ah, the stories I could tell you," I said. And then I waited.

The opportunity to speak of her with someone who understood was what hooked him, as it always did. It was one of my better strategies. He nodded and offered his hand. "I'm Nelson Stafford. Perhaps we should have a drink."

I shook his hand. "Nicholas Dane. And I would be delighted."

He rose, tucking away the notebook and pencil, and I led him to a cafe across the campo. But I didn't stop at one of the outside tables. Instead, I took him inside, to a table in a dark back corner, away from prying eyes. He was so eager to speak of her that he didn't question why I might choose gloomy darkness in lieu of bright late-summer sunshine. I ordered a bottle of wine, though it was barely past noon. When it came, he gulped down the first glass in moments. Now, with time to observe him more closely, I noticed the signs of her demolition. He'd been with her at least a week, I thought. Perhaps two. He looked famished, like someone who could not eat or sleep for thoughts of her. It was hard to tell if this was the best time—too early, and they wouldn't listen; too late and . . . well, too late.

"When did you know her?" he asked me fervently. "How long ago? Where?"

"I met her when I was twenty-three," I said, sipping my own wine. "Nearly seven years ago. In Paris."

"Ah . . . to think of her in Paris!"

I gave him a thin smile. "Do you imagine she fails to bewitch any city she visits?"

"Were you—"

I shook my head, trying to put him at ease. He would listen to nothing if he thought I was a rival, past or present. "We were friends only."

"How could you resist her?"

"She's the one who chooses, like any woman. Haven't you learned that by now? Surely there's not a man in the world who wouldn't be with her, given the chance. I would have done anything for her once, but she didn't return my interest, more's the pity."

He poured more wine, drinking it thirstily. "She is . . . she is beyond anything I've ever known. Such inspiration . . ."

"Yes indeed. It's what she does, you know. Inspires. Until she doesn't."

He was in the middle of taking a sip, and he paused, frowning over the edge of his glass. "Until she doesn't?"

"Your poetry was what caught her eye, wasn't it?"

"She saw me writing at Florian's. She sat down beside me and I found myself reading lines to her aloud. She said it was sublime."

"You've written odes to her?"

"Yes. Yes, who wouldn't?"

Idly I played with a spoon, watching how the gaslight glinted upon it. "Have you written a great deal?"

"I did, but . . . but lately—"

"Lately you've been too distracted to write."

His gaze leaped to mine. "How did you know?"

I shrugged. "It's what happens. You'll get over it. Unless you're *lucky* enough to be chosen."

"Chosen?"

"Then, why, you'd write an epic for the ages. She is the muse of all muses, and if she chose you, she would inspire a poem that would give you a fame you've only dreamed of."

He was watching me closely, with a fevered light in his eyes, never doubting. No, of course not. He'd already felt the pull of her, the exhaustion of such a rapacious appetite.

I went on. "But such a thing has a cost. That poem would be the last you ever wrote. Except for doggerel, perhaps. Rhymes for children to speak as they learn their letters. Mother Goose. 'Daffy down dilly has come into town . . .' 'Little Tom Horner. . . .' Whatever genius you once possessed would simply disappear." I snapped my fingers, and he jerked as if the sound startled him. "You'll go mad or take your own life. But dying of a peaceful old age . . . no, my friend, you can't hope for that—unless you do one thing."

"What's that?"

"Leave her now. Walk away from her and live. Or stay and die in madness and frustration."

He stared at me in stunned amazement. "Leave her? How could I possibly do that?"

I poured his next glass of wine. "You said you're having trouble writing. You haven't eaten, unless I miss my guess—"

"I've no appetite."

I lowered my voice. "You're desperate to have her. You can hardly think of anything else."

He went red. "You said you were never her lover. How do you know these things?"

22

"My friend, I have known this woman for years. I know what she is capable of." I leaned back in my chair. "Do you think you're the only one? There have been dozens before you. Hundreds, even. I have seen it again and again."

"Hundreds?"

"Hundreds. She will destroy you. She will drain you until you are nothing but a shell, and then she will discard you, the way a spider discards her prey once she's sucked the fluids dry. And if that is the worst of it, you will be fortunate indeed."

He reached for his wine and drank convulsively.

I cajoled, "You don't understand what's happening to you. You're afraid and desperate in the same moment. Shall I tell you what happened to the others she *inspired*?"

He nodded, wide-eyed as a child.

"Suicides. Slit wrists or poison. Some hanged themselves. I personally saw one pulled from a river with his pockets full of stones. At least two of her victims went mad—one says nothing, but only stares into space and drools onto a bib tied around his neck. The other raves in an asylum. Do you know what he talks of? Demons, my friend. He claims to see serpents in every shadow. That padded room has become his own Garden of Eden, where he faces Satan's temptation every moment of every day. Do you know what he dreams of? Odilé. He wakes screaming."

"That's absurd," Stafford said boldly, but I heard his uncertainty.

"Is it? Ah, well, I suppose you know best. But I'll just say this: the last place I saw her was in Barcelona. She had seduced a violinist. He played like an angel, truly. I tried to warn him, just as I am warning you, and he reacted just as you are now. Do you know where I saw him next?"

Nelson Stafford shook his head.

"Dead on the pavement outside her door. He'd shot himself in the head. He was only eighteen."

Stafford paled. "But . . . how . . . I wouldn't know how to leave her."

"Simply walk away. She won't pursue you. I promise."

"I can't."

"Then I'll see you next at your funeral. For God's sake, man, think about it, at least. You know in your heart that what I say is true. Listen to me. I'm trying to save you."

"Save me?" He went to pour the wine; the bottle was empty. He dribbled the last few drops into his glass and grabbed it with trembling hands, draining it. "Why would you care? You don't even know me."

"No, I don't. I could just leave you to drown. I have no idea how big your talent is, or if you matter in the least to this world, or if she will even consider truly choosing you. But I find I have no stomach for madness and despair, especially when I have the power to stop it." I gripped his arm and said softly, "Please, I beg of you. At least consider my words. Think about it. Meet me here tomorrow afternoon. If you can't tell me then that you believe me, at least give me another chance to convince you."

He looked fearful, but he nodded. "Very well. I'll . . . think about what you've said. And I'll meet you here tomorrow."

I was relieved. He'd been easier than I'd expected; perhaps the timing had been what I'd hoped. But then again, the real task lay before him still. It was premature to think I'd made any difference at all. "That's all I ask. You'll meet me here at three?"

"I will," he assured me.

"Good," I said, smiling. "I want to show you just how good a friend I can be."

FOUR

ODILÉ

I heard him behind me, his sigh and the faint creak of the mattress, the soft *ssshhh* of the fine mosquito netting as he pushed it aside. I drew my dressing gown closer and looked down at the Grand Canal outside my window, the early morning sun pearlescent, soft where it caressed the barges loaded with brightly colored fruits and vegetables making their way toward the Rialto market, fish shining like fine metals in their baskets, glittering tunny and sardine, the amethyst of octopi, Venetian chains of dark eels.

The Canal was crowded now, the early mornings and twilight the busiest times. I closed my eyes, breathing deeply of the morning: bitter coffee and toasty polenta; the greasy, smoky oil from a fritterer's; the garlic of sausage and the pungent, salty broth of the *sguassetto* the gondoliers ate by the bowlful; along with the familiar reek of algae and seaweed in a low tide, the river smell of the Canal, wet stone.

And of course, his cologne. Too heavy again.

I opened my eyes and glanced down at the windowsill, at the little Murano glass dish the color of blood, the mound of white ash from a burned pastille within it. I stirred it with my finger, raising the noxious stink of camphor meant to keep off mosquitos, burned off now but still lingering. I was glad the summer was nearly over; there would be no need for pastilles for a time, or the nasty, heavy smoke that was nearly worse than the bites, nor for mosquito netting. I would soon be able to leave the lamps on with windows open to smell the city without being bedeviled.

A sharp stab of pain made my fingers spasm in the little bowl, spilling ash.

I heard him slap and curse. "Damn these cursed bugs. How do you bear it?"

"Autumn's nearly here," I said, knowing I must tell him to go. The hunger never left me now. It was gnawing and relentless. *One every three years,* she'd said, the words both a promise and a curse, and now I felt the curse, the dark terror that waited restlessly for me to fail. Less than a month left to choose, and I was no closer to finding the one I searched for. I had been so certain Venice was the place. Paris had not held him. Nor Florence, though perhaps there had been one or two there who might have done, had they not been taken from me too early.

It was desperation that had driven me here, to the city that had always served me well, that had nurtured Byron and Titian, Veronese and Tintoretto and Canaletto. But the days passed so quickly. The darkness within me was growing. It was harder now to command. My appetite devoured everything, just as it was devouring this one. He'd been complaining of headaches; often he struggled for breath. He was not the one; I knew it already. Two hundred and fifty years of immortality had taught me what I needed, and he was not it. I knew he must go before I lost control and drained him completely, which I didn't want to do. I must find the right one before it was too late.

Too late. I felt a cold little clutch of fear. No, it wasn't too late. I would not fail again. Each time I had, the terror had stayed longer; it took more victims and more time to remake myself. How long would it take to survive it the next time? Or would I?

I still had time. The three years mandated were not yet over. I had until the fifteenth of October to find him.

But first I must release this one. I turned from the window. He looked up from pulling on his boots. He was shirtless still; when he straightened, the morning light brought out the red in the curls on his chest. "Tell me you want me to stay and I will," he said urgently. "God knows I don't want to leave."

"I thought you had an appointment."

"I've changed my mind. I'm not going." He strode over to me with an odd clopping gait, one boot on, the other foot bare. He pulled apart my dressing gown and buried his face in my breasts. I felt the rough stubble on his cheeks against my skin. "The only appointment I want to keep is with these," he murmured, and suddenly I was overcome with weariness. I was so tired of this. A thousand times I'd taken men to bed. A thousand thousands. All to feed my hunger, all in search of that singular, momentary rapture that came when I made the choice, when the bargain was agreed to and sealed. I lived for that moment. But there was no reason to take this one to bed or let him touch me again. I raised my hands to push him away.

But just then, he lifted his face. He looked ravaged, gaunt and restless, his blue eyes reddened, his pale skin ruddy. My hunger was tearing at him, and it raised a sadness and pity in me I could not suppress. I did not want to hurt him. I did not want to hurt any of them. But I always did.

Let him go, Odilé. It's better done now. He is not the one.

"I'll write odes to your breasts," he said hoarsely. "Sonnets. Rondelets. I promise it."

"Or perhaps an elegy," I suggested.

"An elegy? God no! How could such exquisiteness inspire sorrow?"

As gently as I could, I pushed him away. "Write whatever poems you wish. But you have an appointment, and you should not let me keep you from it."

"How can you stand to be away from me, when I cannot bear a moment apart from you?"

I felt what was left of his talent feeding the harsh, hungry maw of my craving.

"Why do you tremble?" he demanded. "Please, God, let it be from fear of losing me."

He had fallen to his knees. His arms encircled my hips. He pressed his face to me, kissing the curls between my legs. I must end it now. Swiftly, ruthlessly. I must be out hunting again before I lost control.

But pity was my downfall, as always. A few more minutes before I set him loose—what harm could it do? I gripped his hair, tangling the soft honey of it in my fingers, pulling until he gasped—something he liked. He looked up, hopeful as a puppy pleading for scraps, eyes big and blue and heavily lashed. I liked his eyes best of all, I thought. Those, and his poetry. He had written so prettily.

I let him crawl up me, a monkey on a tree. I let him press me to the wall. He lifted me, fumbling with his trousers even as I wrapped my legs around him. I let him pound me into the crumbling plaster wall as I grabbed for purchase, and as he moaned and panted into my throat, I felt my dark and ceaseless appetite sink its teeth into him and the bliss of momentary relief. It could not last, but oh it was something; it was sweet. He groaned with agony, collapsing even as he came, releasing me hard, falling to his knees, shaking with combined ecstasy and terror. He looked up at me.

"God, I adore you," he gasped. "What's happening to me?"

I knelt down, taking his cheek into my hand. He surged toward it, my very touch an addiction. I kissed his forehead softly. "You should have gone to your appointment."

I left him gasping in a ball of weakness on the floor, and called for Antonio to throw him out into the street.

FIVE

SOPHIE

When I woke the next morning, Joseph was already up, shaving at the washbasin. A pale, watery light filled the room; reflections danced over the ceiling, sun-cats shifting and playing.

I stretched and got out of bed. "Did you sleep?" I asked him.

He glanced at me and flicked shaving soap from the razor into the basin, where it skimmed like a tiny cloud. "A little."

I went to his sketchbook where it rested on the gilded dresser, pushing away the little pile of broken charcoal sticks he'd left upon it, to see the sketch he'd done while I was sleeping. Though I was pretty enough, my brother made me beautiful. In the drawing, I looked voluptuous and sensual, my hair alive and shining where it curled over my shoulder, my pouting mouth not caused by a faint overbite, as I knew it to be, but because he'd made my lips full and plump and . . . alluring. Which I knew wasn't true. Pretty enough, but not alluring.

"It hardly looks like me."

"You say that every time. It looks exactly like you." He drew the razor over his jaw with experienced precision. "At least how I see you."

"Perhaps you need spectacles."

He made a face and rinsed off the razor. "You should get dressed. We've a full day ahead of us."

I felt again that rush of nerves, which I worked to hide as I pulled on my chemise and corset, going to him to tighten the laces. He helped me slip on my gown, and as he was buttoning it, I said to him in the mirror, "There's no time for the Piazza today, Joseph. Not St. Mark's nor anything else. Not yet. You do understand me?"

He slanted me a glance as he slipped the last button through its loop. "You don't think it will be full of artists?"

"Tourists, yes. Not that they might not be helpful, but you won't know, will you? Especially if you get lost studying a Titian for two hours. The Accademia first. There will be a dozen copyists there. One of them must know someone who could get us in. Promise me."

He reached for his shirt. "I promise. I won't linger in the Piazza."

"I don't care how beautiful the light is."

"It will still be beautiful tomorrow," he agreed. He pulled on his shirt, buttoning it before he ran a hand through his dark brown hair—his idea of brushing it. I was envious again of how perfectly it fell in artful disarray, waving and curling at the ends, brushing his collar.

Suddenly I was afraid to have him out of my sight. We didn't know the city; so much could happen. He was all I had. "Your hair's too long," I said, my fears erupting in quick criticism.

He only smiled and knotted a crumpled tie about his throat.

"And there's still dust on your trousers."

31

"I won't be talking to rich tourists, remember?" he teased, taking up his coat. "D'you really think anyone would trust an artist who was well put together?" He was so good at carelessness that even I forgot sometimes that it was a lie, something he cultivated. It helped allay my fears; it was a reminder of whom we meant to be here. He would do what he had to, what he'd promised me he would do. For today, he would ignore the beauties of Venice, and look for the man—or woman—who could get us into Katharine Bronson's inner circle. We had a plan, and he intended to follow it, and I must do the same, no matter how fragile I felt away from him.

Joseph went for his sketchbook, tucking it beneath his arm, shoving the charcoal sticks into his pocket. Then he came to me, chucking my chin before he leaned to kiss me. "Just find us a place to live, and leave this to me. And Soph, I don't want you thinking I need a studio the size of a stable. I expect to do most of my work out of doors anyway. This is Venice, remember. If I don't paint the view, we might as well have stayed in New York."

"We didn't come here for the view," I reminded him.

"Oh yes we did." Though he smiled, ambition glittered in his eyes. "Don't forget it." He went to the door and opened it. "I'll arrange for a gondolier to take you around—"

"No, please. The expense—"

"I insist on this, Sophie. For now I want to know you're safe without me. And anyway, we want to set the right impression, don't we? People sense desperation. We won't get what we want if we appear to want it too badly."

I gave him a pert smile. "Of course. Why, I wouldn't think of going about Venice without an escort—how scandalous! I am the very respectable sister of Joseph Hannigan, after all."

He laughed and gave me an admiring look that warmed me. "Why, you make me half believe it." Then, before he ducked out the door, "Not on your own, Soph, not to save a few francs. Take the gondolier. I mean it. Or I'll spend the whole afternoon at the Doge's Palace just to spite you."

"Very well," I promised.

Once he was gone, I forced my uneasiness away and made myself think of what I must do. We had enough money for only a few days at the Danieli, which meant I had to find us something else quickly. I finished with the rest of my toilette, and then I pulled on my hat and my gloves, leaving my coat behind. The day was beautiful, the damp chill of last night already a distant memory.

As I went downstairs and stepped again into the opulent lobby of the Danieli, I was struck once more with that sense of imposture. Two well-dressed women, one wearing a frighteningly expensive-looking fringed silk shawl, talked near the desk. I remembered what Joseph had said about impressions, and summoned my confidence. Pretending that the elegance of the Danieli was not just something I expected, but my due, I gave them my best smile. Their glances turned curious and measuring, and I felt a frisson of fear that I'd made a mistake, that they somehow knew of me. But then they looked away. There were several other people about, a gentleman sitting negligently in a silk-upholstered chair, smoking a cigar that filled the whole lobby with its stink, an older couple, another man with a woman who looked to be his sister, but I avoided meeting any other eyes and went to the desk. "I'm Sophie Hannigan," I told the man there. "My brother was to make arrangements—"

"Your gondolier awaits, Miss Hannigan," said the man with a smile. He rang a little bell, and when a porter came hurrying over, he directed, "Please show Miss Hannigan to Marco."

I was led out to the water steps, to the gondolier Marco. He was as tall as my brother, though Marco's shoulders were broader, his forearms corded with muscle beneath the rolled sleeves of his shirt. He was bronzed and smiling, with such an air of good health and amiability that I trusted him immediately.

He held out his hand for me, flashing adorably crooked teeth, and introduced himself as "Marco, who will soon be your favorite gondolier in all of Venice."

"Sophie Hannigan," I answered with a smile as he helped me into the boat. Like last night's gondola, the cabin on this one had been removed, but in its place there was an awning striped white and blue. Beneath that was a seat of black leather cushions, with two other smaller seats on either side, and a gray carpet below. Marco moved to his spot at the stern while a boy pushed the neck of the prow from the mooring post.

"Where will you go, *padrona*?" Marco asked. "I am yours all day."

He made it sound almost indecent; I had to resist the urge to look at him again, and I was glad he couldn't see my face. I remembered what my research had told me, that the gondoliers were the best source for information in the city. "I'm looking for a more permanent lodging, a place to rent for my brother and myself for a few months. Nothing too expensive."

"Ah, you must leave it to me." He immediately swung the huge oar in its lock so we turned about, and we moved away from the sparkling Bacino, slinking into a narrow canal. It seemed to lead us into a strange and mysterious land, where the gilded, rococo beauty of Venice faded away to reveal charmingly quaint pale-pink walls stained so romantically with mildew it was as if an artist had put it there for the best effect. Reflections sank into the water and bloomed out again, wavering and dancing as we passed. Ripples cast by the gondola's prow lapped against steps and narrow *fondamentas*. Crabs scuttled at the edges, a cat or two dodged into shadows.

I was struck by how rustically beautiful it was. Laundry strung from the balconies overhead fluttered in the slight breeze. A fig tree poked its head over a garden wall. The dichotomy of feeling lost in time while at the same time moving through it was hard to shake. Once or twice, I saw a woman leaning pensively over a balcony railing, or a group of girls laughing as they hurried down a *calle*. Although I saw few people, it wasn't the least bit quiet. Sounds carried down the *calli* and over the canals, footsteps and the calls of gondoliers and from somewhere someone singing, someone else shouting. The singing of birds— canaries and parrots—hanging in cages from the balconies among the laundry was a perfect accompaniment.

Marco took me to palazzos among the regular brick and pink homes of peasants and merchants, helping me out onto slippery steps, speaking to the owners in that strange Venetian dialect. He escorted me with a dignified pride—almost possession—as we went into narrow courtyards with their elaborately carved wellheads in the center, statuary picturesquely blackened with mildew and clothed in moss, up stairs onto terrazzo floors that undulated gently with the settling of the house, vast empty spaces and aged frescos running the lengths of walls.

Many palazzos had been broken up, no longer serving families, but instead boarders who rented by the floor, or by the room, which were separated by a common hall or stairway. The upper floors, most coveted and decorated by those who had lived there, were still beautiful with their pillars and marble and arched windows, plaster carvings and impossibly high, elaborately painted ceilings. Many had recesses where once had hung immense frescos done by Titian or Tiepolo or countless others— artists had been a dime a dozen in Venice when the nobility had built these palaces, and there was no place I saw that didn't either still have them or had empty spaces where they'd once been before they were sold off.

But each place was too expensive or too small or dirty or dilapidated, and I was growing frustrated and tired. As much as I had enjoyed the day, the sun was lowering in the sky, and I had a nagging headache behind my eyes from the glare of the sun on the water.

I told Marco, "We should go back. My brother will be returning."

"We are very close to one more, *padrona, ai?*"

I nodded wearily and put my hand to my eyes, and we turned down another narrow canal. He brought the gondola to a stop at an arched doorway set in a facade of beautifully detailed plaster. He moored to the brown *palo* and helped me out onto stairs so coated with algae that I had to grab his arm hard to keep from slipping. I glanced up at the darkened passageway leading from the stairs, which was so wonderfully mysterious it somewhat restored my temper.

The courtyard was paved with cracked slabs of Istrian stone, half of it hidden behind a spreading fig tree and a set of stairs that led to the main floor. At the top was another arch, which opened into a wide *portego*, with huge paned windows at the other end letting in the sun, glowing upon the pale terrazzo floors, filling the room with light. Frescos lined each wall— some bacchanalian revel I was just turning to look at more closely when a rather large, florid-faced woman emerged from a doorway. She was middle-aged, with graying hair nearly falling from its chignon.

Marco fell into a flurry of Venetian. When he was done, she burst into a smile and fluent French, "Welcome, mademoiselle. You are looking for rooms?"

"For my brother and me," I answered in kind. "I'm Sophie Hannigan. My brother, Joseph, is an artist. He's come here to paint, and so—"

"You're looking for a studio," she broke in. "And bedrooms. A sitting room too, perhaps? And a kitchen, of course. Well, I have the upper floor available now, though you must split it with my other young man. He's a writer, so perhaps he and your brother will suit."

She turned, gesturing for me to follow her to the end of the *portego*, and then up another staircase to a set of doors, which she flew open with a flourish—and without knocking, I noted. We entered an empty *sala* with the same bare spaces on the walls I'd noted in other places, where paintings or frescos were gone. The ceiling bore evidence of having been removed as well, and each corner had holes where carved plaster cornices had been taken out and no doubt sold. But the space was huge and high ceilinged and lovely, and the rooms she showed me were equally so—a sitting room and one bedroom overlooking the canal, another overlooking the courtyard, though the view was blocked by the fig. There was a third large and well-lit room that would serve well as Joseph's studio.

"All for only forty francs per month."

An amount I could afford, and rooms I liked. My headache eased.

"Who is the writer living here?" I asked her when she finally paused for a breath.

"Mr. Nelson Stafford. Do you know him?"

I shook my head. "Is he American?"

"English, I believe. But he's a fine boy. Very handsome too." She nudged me with a wink. "I'm certain you and your brother will like him exceedingly. He's very quiet. I never have a moment's trouble with him. Would you like to see the courtyard? We all share it, but I can arrange a time for you to have it alone if you like."

It was perfect. "I would like to see it, yes."

She took me back down to the main floor, Marco following quietly behind, and then down the stairs into the courtyard. The sun gilded the top of the fig tree; from the stairs I could smell some fragrance I had missed on the way up, something like gardenia, rich and lovely. I could imagine living in these huge rooms and coming down into the courtyard of an evening, breathing deep of that lovely scent, posing for my brother beneath the shining leaves of the fig, telling him the stories he loved deep into sunset.

When we reached the bottom, she skirted the corner, past a statue of a faun, moss-covered, half-blackened. A huge urn nearly half my height held some bushy, viney plant. I heard a strange buzzing beyond, a low hum. Bees, I thought, or perhaps a cloud of gnats.

"Mr. Stafford rather enjoys it in the morning," she said, pushing aside a wildly tangled vine to pass into the courtyard proper. "He's always saying to me—"

She stopped short so suddenly I crashed into her. She yelped, a little scream, and her hand went to her chest, and it was a moment before I realized that it wasn't my stumbling into her that caused her outburst.

"Mr. Stafford!" she gasped.

There, in the middle of the courtyard, near a marble wellhead, lay a man staring vacantly at the sky while a pool of black blood congealed beneath him, covered with darting, buzzing flies.

SIX

NICHOLAS

"Aren't you tired of drawing that yet?" I asked Giles, glancing over his shoulder at what must have been the four hundredth sketch he'd done of the Ponte dell'Accademia—an iron monstrosity of a bridge, to put it kindly. I had no idea what he, or any of the dozen or so artists in the Campo della Carita that afternoon, found so intriguing about it, though most of them, admittedly, were painting the view of the Salute.

"I can't get it right," he said, pushing his sliding spectacles back into place. "I'll keep trying until I do."

I refrained from saying what was true—that Giles would never get it right, and that even if he did, the bridge was so ugly that only someone with egregious taste would ever buy a painting of it—and glanced impatiently away. Art held little appeal for me right now. Nelson Stafford had never appeared for our appointment, and I feared that I'd been too late to save him.

"So where is this girl you want me to see?" I asked.

"She'll be here," Giles said implacably.

"I don't have all day, you know."

Giles chuckled. "No? What else have you to do?" Then he stiffened. "Oh, oh—there she is. No, for God's sake, Nick, don't stare!"

"You sound like a ten-year-old," I said, following his gaze to where his Giulietta wandered off the bridge and onto the campo. She was, as far as I could tell, the typical dark-eyed, black-shawled Venetian girl, and like them all, she had that way about her that said she expected men to fall at her feet. I suppose men like Giles did, but then, they'd never known true beauty.

Which only reminded me again why I couldn't linger. I turned back to Giles. "She's quite pretty. No doubt she'll pose for a centime or two. God knows they all will."

"It's tiresome how cynical you've become."

"Or perhaps just realistic. There isn't a Venetian girl these days who doesn't know her worth as a model."

He made a face. "How would you know? I haven't seen you with a single girl in months. You've been like a monk."

I glanced toward her again, and that was when I noticed the man crossing the bridge into the campo. He had the kind of presence that caught one's attention, a confidence to match the kind of looks that even I recognized as stunning. His hair was dark, and he wore no hat. His white trousers were creased and grayed in places with dust. He carried a large sketchbook beneath his arm.

"Who's that?" Giles asked, frowning.

"How would I know? I'm not the one who spends all day here."

"I've never seen him."

Nor had I, and it was true that Giles and I knew almost every artist in Venice by now. They all gravitated to the same places: here at the Accademia, the *fondamenta* of the Riva near the Public Gardens at sunset, the Zattere for its views of the Lido. They came, they went, almost all of them at one point or another wandering into the salon Giles and I frequented at the Casa Alvisi. So it was strange that neither of us had seen this one.

The man made his way through the campo. Not arrogant, but self-possessed, unlike most of the artists here, who seemed to cower beneath the weight of Venice's past masters. I found myself watching him, curious. He smiled at those he passed, murmuring a hello here and there. One artist caught him with a word as he went by, and he paused, leaning over the man's shoulder, pointing at something on the easel, making a comment. The artist exclaimed and laughed, and the man moved on and took a seat on the paving stones. He pulled his sketchbook from beneath his arm and a stick of charcoal from the pocket of his deep blue coat.

There was no hesitation in him, no stopping to consider a line or a shadow. He drew as if he knew exactly what should be on the page and how he should put it there. I found myself envying his surety—I'd never had such confidence with words. But I told myself it could be only that he was very bad, unlearned enough not to know he *should* hesitate, and I was wondering if in fact that was the case when I realized that little Giulietta was sauntering over to him, having just noticed he was there.

Giles dropped the case with his pastels on the pavement, cursing as he raced to stop her, waylaying her not three steps from where the man in white trousers sat sketching. Giles said something to her, and everyone in the vicinity heard her call Giles a dog in that distinctive Venetian cantilena. She shoved him hard in the chest, sending him stumbling over the man and his sketchbook. Giles fell, the sketchbook flew from the man's hands to skitter across the pavement, and Giulietta stalked away.

I hurried over and hauled Giles to his feet. He was red faced, sputtering, "What did I do to her? You saw it. What did I do?"

"For God's sake, Giles, she's a peasant," I said. "What did you expect?"

He dusted himself off, glaring at me before he turned to the man he'd fallen over, who had risen now, and was giving us both a bemused look. "I'm sorry. You aren't hurt?"

"Not the least bit," the man said. "Startled only."

I stepped to his sketchbook, and as I picked it up to hand it over, I saw what he'd been drawing. I paused, struck. He had managed to capture the languid bustle of the campo in only a few strokes. It was more than impressive. "This is very good."

He smiled and reached for the sketchbook, which I gave to him. "Are you an art critic?"

I laughed. "Hardly."

"An artist yourself then?"

"Not that either, I'm afraid. Giles here is the artist. I'm merely a poet."

"A poet? Are you famous? You must pardon me for asking; I'm not much for reading. My sister would know better."

"I've had a few successes," I said, not at all modestly; there was so little to celebrate. "But as yet, true fame eludes me."

"Are you looking for it in Byron's footsteps, then?"

I ignored the twinge the name brought, the memory—not as faint as I might wish. "I've had quite enough of Venetian debaucheries and excesses."

Giles laughed. "Debaucheries? Why, Nick hasn't debauched at all since we've been in Venice. Perhaps that's your problem, old boy. No debauching. I'm Giles Martin, by the way, and my poet friend is Nicholas Dane."

"Joseph Hannigan," said the man, shaking hands all around.

"Have you been in Venice long?" Giles asked.

"I arrived last night." Hannigan glanced across the campo, toward the Accademia, shielding his eyes from the sun. "I've been trying to determine the best places to see. Is it worth going inside, do you think? I've heard there's a good Veronese."

"Dwarfs and dogs," I said wryly.

He laughed. "I take it you don't care for Veronese."

"I haven't the eye, I'm afraid," I said.

"Nick's being modest. He might not be Ruskin, but he's got a very good eye. Everyone comments on it." Giles looked at me with a kind of vague pride that startled me. "Why, Henry Loneghan himself asks for his opinion before he buys anything."

"Henry Loneghan?" Hannigan asked.

"An art collector who lives in the city," I explained. "An expatriate. And Giles exaggerates. Loneghan hardly needs my help choosing art."

"But he asks for it anyway," Giles said.

I was more aware than ever of the passing time and where I needed to be. "It's a pleasure to have met you, Hannigan. But I'm afraid I must hurry off. Perhaps we'll meet again."

"I hope so." As he reached out his hand to shake mine, the sketchbook in his other tilted and fell, crashing again to the paving stones, pages splayed. "Clumsy," he said with a smile, bending to pick it up, flipping the pages as if to reassure himself they were all fine, letting it stop not at the page he'd been working on, but another, a sketch of a woman—though to call it a sketch was to do it a disservice. She was sleeping, her dark hair curling and spreading over a white pillow, her pouting mouth slightly parted, her nightdress fallen down one shoulder, revealing a round, pertly nippled breast. It was beautiful, so exquisitely rendered and erotically charged that I felt stunned. Dear God, he was a singular talent, perhaps more so than anyone I'd yet seen in Venice. He was exactly what Odilé was looking for.

Giles gasped. "Good God, man. Who is that?"

Joseph Hannigan glanced down at the sketch. "Do you like it? It was the first thing I drew when I got here."

"You mean she's *here*? In the city?" Giles asked.

I heard myself say, as if from far away, "Given that sketch, I think you'd be wasting your time with Veronese."

"Well then, what should I look at instead? Where should I go? I've been hoping to find a guide—not one of the *valets de place*. I've no interest in shopping or restaurants. I'd like to find someone who can show me something new. Do you know of anyone who might serve? I can pay. Not much, but if a few centimes would do—"

"Something new?" I managed. "For what?"

"Inspiration."

"I would think you'd already found it in those arms."

Something I couldn't read flickered through Joseph Hannigan's eyes before he said with a quick smile, "She's my sister. My twin, actually."

"Your sister?" Giles was obviously as surprised as I.

Hannigan nodded as if he saw nothing odd in it. "She often poses for me. She's a good model, don't you think?"

"Most assuredly," Giles said with fervor, and I knew he'd already forgotten his Venetian girl. "She's here with you?"

"Yes. And she's as anxious as I am to discover Venice."

That the model was his sister only made his skill more amazing; the sensuality he'd managed to invent spoke to an imaginative talent of the kind Odilé was always searching for—now more intently than ever. Less than a month left . . . she needed a man like Joseph Hannigan. Young. Attractive. Charming. And with such talent . . . she would sniff him out in moments, and once she did, she would choose him. If I was ever to get my life— my talent—back, I could not fail again. If she were to get what she needed from Joseph Hannigan, her strength would be fully restored and the cycle would begin anew.

I could not let it happen. Not now, not so close to an end. Which meant I must keep Odilé from finding him. I must keep him too busy to wander the city. He wanted inspiration, and I would make certain he found it—in the places of my choosing.

"Giles and I could show you what there is to see in Venice, couldn't we, Giles?"

Giles nodded with alacrity. "Oh, absolutely we could. What we haven't seen isn't worth seeing. And we'd be happy to show your sister about too."

Joseph Hannigan smiled, obviously pleased. "I don't wish to impose."

I smiled back. "It is no imposition. Truly, we're happy to do so."

We made plans to meet later that evening, and I hurried off in search of Stafford, but Joseph Hannigan did not leave my mind. It seemed fate was smiling on me at last.

SEVEN

ODILÉ

There are moments in Venice so sublime you cannot breathe for the sheer beauty and weight of them. The mournful pas de deux of the gondoliers' songs is one of those things, a phenomenon of melancholy summer nights. Though this time, as I stood listening at my open balcony door, unable to sleep, it had a different effect. My hunger was raging and restless now in a way that I dreaded and feared, and I was unsoothed by the beauty of "La Biondina"—no matter how lovely were its echoes and harmonies, one line sung close, another answering from far away, back and forth, until it faded and was gone. I remembered the woman it had been written for—the Countess Benzoni—who had charmed and beguiled her way through Venice. But though the melody stayed with me all that night and into the next day, it wasn't Benzoni I was thinking of. It was Paris.

And Madeleine Dumas.

Some memories fade to tender nostalgia, and some fade altogether, and after living nearly three hundred years, I had forgotten so much. But my memory of Madeleine never dimmed. To think her name was to see her standing as vibrantly before me as she had all those years ago, splendid in jewels and silks. It seemed she sparkled even in the dimmest light. She was the one who'd told me that what I most wanted was in reach. *You can have it all,* cherie, *but you must have the will to take it.*

By then, I'd been on my own for many years—since I was twelve, in fact. But twelve was not so young then, and I'd been trained to tricks and pleasure long before my whore of a mother sold my virginity to an old, rich man. I had thought to treat him as any pretty adolescent treats older men—as if I could enchant and beguile my way to anything, as if he were too stupid and addled to see my manipulation.

I had been disabused of that idea within moments. He was inside me nearly before he'd cleared the door, holding me down, saying through clenched teeth as I screamed at the pain of it, "Shut up, little dove. I've just paid a fortune to fuck you first, and I mean to enjoy it."

He hit me then, over and over, savoring my cries and moans. He took me twice more that night, finally leaving me half dead on the floor and sick with the knowledge that I was nothing— less than nothing. He was gone without a backward glance—I was not worthy of a second thought.

It should not have been a surprise. I'd been born in a brothel and raised among whores, and I knew how ephemeral was such a life. Women often disappeared in the hours between twilight and dawn without explanation. They were never thought of again. I had always believed I was not meant for such a fate, as did my mother, a Belgian farm girl who'd run away to Paris and ended with an opiate-sotted life of pain and degradation instead of the exciting one she'd hoped for. On the days she remembered I was even there, she would comb my thick hair with her graceful fingers and whisper to me, "Your beauty is your fortune, my love. You won't be like the rest of us. You will be something fine."

But that terrible night, as I stared up at a stained ceiling, gasping with pain, tears wet on my cheeks, I knew it wasn't true. I knew I was no different than the rest of them, and in the end, my beauty would not save me.

My mother died two months later. She was found in a ditch in the backstreets of Paris, strangled. No one ever investigated her death. No one cared. I only knew what had happened because I'd gone looking for her. We always checked the city morgue first in those days, and there she was, pale and cold on a slab. I did not even claim her body—what would I have done with it? As far as I knew, she was buried in a potter's field along with a hundred other nameless, faceless souls. I was the only evidence she had existed, and even I chose not to acknowledge her at the end.

The fear of such a destiny haunted me. I tried to tell myself she was right, that my beauty must mean something. Why else had it been given to me? Surely I *was* meant for something fine. Surely I could not die unseen and forgotten, just another anonymous body in a pauper's grave.

In those days there was only one real way for a woman like me to be known in the world. It was a hard ladder to climb, but I was determined. I meant to become one of Paris's famous courtesans. I meant for the name of Odilé León to linger forever, to never be forgotten.

By the time I was fifteen, men vied for my favors. They sent me candy wrapped in franc notes, jeweled toys and fine perfumes. By seventeen, I held the lease on two houses. I had caskets of jewels, silks and expensive laces. I had my own carriage with four matched gray horses. At nineteen, I was the most coveted courtesan in Paris. It was rumored that I was an exiled princess, an aristocrat in hiding, a slave escaped from an Oriental harem, stories it pleased me to never deny—in fact, I planted some of them. Mystery and allure were all-important. Rich men needed to feel as if they possessed something of unique value.

I decorated my rooms in Byzantine splendor long before it was fashionable to do so. I scented it with exotic incenses and served the best wines and foods that were aphrodisiacs. I was said to have skill enough to bring back any man's vigor. I taught young men how to be good lovers, and now and then a young woman hired me to teach her the ways to please a husband. I chose my patrons well; I became a luxury only a few could afford, a prize that only the most well-connected could win.

I thought I had beaten my fear at last. Surely my name would be remembered now? And for years, I had no reason to think otherwise. I was the best and the most expensive. Everyone knew who I was. But time is no woman's friend. I began to notice the fine wrinkles at the corners of my eyes, the faint sag at my jaw. Strands of gray began to appear in my dark hair; I could not go to sleep at four a.m. and rise at eight without looking as if I'd done so. I began to lose my favorite lovers to younger women whose eyes sparkled guilelessly, whose breasts were more pert, whose skin was whiter and more fine.

I began to feel afraid again—and that, too, showed. Men sense desperation; they are like animals, wanting always to be at the top. I was thirty-six. My influence was waning, and they felt that too. I was no longer the prize I'd been, but a fading symbol of another time. I began to notice the way men looked past me when I came into a room, and I realized I had not beaten my fear after all. In a few more years, it would be as if Odilé León had never existed. It was too late to change the path I'd taken—I was destined for my mother's fate, for the one I'd seen as I lay bleeding on a barren floor.

But then I met Madeleine Dumas. The great courtesan, Ninette, held a salon to showcase an artist everyone was talking about—his newest canvas was scandalous and brilliant, and it was rumored that he meant to bring with him the woman who'd inspired it. I wanted to meet her. I wanted to know what she had done to win such immortality. But when I arrived, the artist was alone. There was no woman hanging on his arm and none he seemed to adore, and so I did not suspect that his lover and his muse was Madeleine, though I should have known the moment I saw her across the room, sparkling and smiling, jewels bedecking every inch. That night, she'd worn a gown so crusted with tiny rubies and beaded with pearls that I wondered how she could walk in fabric so heavy. Golden combs had glittered in her blond hair, but her eyes . . . her eyes had been dark as obsidian. Eyes I'd been drawn to, unable to look away from. I thought I saw something strange in them, something captivating and exciting. She'd smelled of confidence and lilies. She was my age, and yet she had what I did not—a lack of care or fear.

I wanted to be her, which was something I had never felt before—why should I have ever felt envious of another woman? The singularity of the emotion brought me up short, the sheer, brutal longing.

She gestured to me as if she'd seen me staring at her. I went as if compelled. She smiled at me and asked me who I was, and when I told her, her smile broadened. She tilted her head in amusement, though all I'd told her was my name. "I know you, don't I?"

"I think we've never met," I said. "I would have remembered."

"Perhaps not." She glanced across the room, to where her artist-lover was engaged in animated conversation with some other man, and she leaned close to whisper to me, "I am the one who made him everything he is. Do you believe me?"

"Of course."

"How he loves to ignore me in public."

"But he will not be ignoring you when you are home," I reassured her.

"No, not if I am there, which I have not quite decided yet."

"You mean to leave him?"

She shrugged; it was a pretty, elegant gesture. "I leave all of them. It is *my* life, is it not? Mine to live. Mine to manage. Why give it to them to squander?" She paused. "What do you think of his talent?"

"I think he will be very famous."

"Oh, I mean for him to be famous. That is never in doubt. But I wonder: do you think he will *last*? Will men laud him centuries from now?"

I considered her question. "I don't know. Perhaps. But while he is very skilled, he is showing nothing truly new, so perhaps not."

Madeleine sighed. "So I have thought. I wonder if perhaps it is a flaw in me."

"What do you mean?"

"I have done this before. So many times. Before him, there was a musician. He was just the same. He had a great deal of talent, but he was penning songs for school children. I took him up. I was his muse, his inspiration. His new compositions were well received by the church, published in psalters, and for a time, he was very famous indeed. And quite rich."

"He must have been glad," I said.

"For the money?" she asked.

"For fame," I said, unable to keep the envy from my voice. "People knew his name. They remembered him."

She looked at me, and I saw something in those black eyes, a piqued interest. "You wish that for yourself?"

"To not die in obscurity? Yes, of course. Who does not wish to leave a mark on the world?"

Her gaze slid away. "Ah."

I didn't know what I'd expected from her, but her response disappointed. I felt I'd lost her attention, and I wanted nothing more than to call it back. "What happened to him? The composer?"

"His songs have fallen out of favor. He has not had the influence I thought he should." She leaned close again. "I think I do not have the eye. Do you think you could do better, given the chance?"

"Me?" I laughed. "I hardly know."

Her words lingered throughout the nights that followed. I had been enraptured and ensorceled. Madeleine had shown me how small was the world I'd lived in. She had shown me how much more there was, how much to be had.

What do you most desire, Odilé?

Even as I stood on my Venetian balcony and smelled Venice, it was Paris that was in my head. Paris, and Madeleine. I thought of everything she had given me, the years as I had known them, but I no longer felt a sense of wonder. Only exhaustion. There were times, like now, when the curse of my nature overwhelmed everything. It was too late in the cycle for joy. My hunger cramped, squeezing tight and painfully. Time was running out. Somewhere in this city must be the man who could inspire a world. Somewhere. And if I did not find him—

Barcelona flashed through my mind. A vision of waking from a nightmare only to discover that it was no nightmare at all, but real. Real and terrible, and I was nothing but darkness writhing, a vortex of need, and him standing in the doorway, haloed with sunlight, a look of horror on his face, the monster I had become reflected in his gaze. . . .

I closed my eyes, forcing the memory away. He was not even here. He had not found me. I had days yet to make a choice without fear of his intervention. He could not destroy me, but what he *could* do, what he could force me to become. . . .

Another stab of pain, worse this time. Enough of memories; it was time to hunt. Usually I liked the Rialto—it was one of the busiest places in Venice, and I never failed to find someone there—if not true and lasting talent, then at least someone to ease my hunger for a time. But today I had something else in mind. I remembered the faint strains of music I'd heard coming from a church last week, sweet and alluring. The sound of possibility.

I called for Antonio to ready the gondola, and I was just stepping into the boat when he said, "He is dead, *padrona*."

For a moment I had no idea whom he was speaking of. I'd already forgotten the writer, you see.

"Signor Stafford," Antonio said.

"Oh. How do you know this?"

"He was found in his courtyard."

Gossip in Venice never lacked speed. The gondoliers knew everything nearly the moment it happened.

Antonio made a slicing motion across his wrist. "Suicide."

Another one. I did not have to manufacture my dismay or my sorrow. I had not wanted this. I never did. I thought of the poet as I'd seen him last, collapsed on the floor. The tears in his eyes when he realized I was banishing him. My appetite surged at the memory. Antonio put his hand suddenly to his heart, frowning—and I felt a rush of nourishment and remembered with a start his gondolier's songs. A bird calling from a nearby cage went suddenly silent.

With all my strength, I forced the darkness back. Antonio took a deep and shuddering breath, and I said, "Take me to San Maurizio. And quickly, before mass begins."

He nodded, still looking puzzled, and it was all I could do to control the gnashing inside me. When we arrived, the organ music was already drifting from the simple white stone edifice, and the campo with its huge square wellhead was nearly empty. I went to the door of the church, peering into darkness. I heard the creak of the organ bench as it was pushed aside, a few words exchanged, a pleasant voice, and then footsteps.

The man who came out was red haired, blue eyed, pale and lithe and lovely. I saw the expression I loved on his face—startlement, then awe and desire—as I stepped into the light.

"Was it you who played?" I asked him.

"Y-yes," he stammered.

I smiled. "It was wonderful. I knew I must come and discover who had such talent."

He flushed. I felt a sudden stab and bit back a gasp as I put out my hand. "I'm Odilé León."

He took my fingers in his, caressing my hand as if he'd waited his whole life to do so. "Jonathan Murphy."

In the end, for me, there was only this: desire and addiction and hunger, a craving that made the world look hard-edged and brutally lovely.

"Would you have a glass of wine with me?" I asked Jonathan Murphy.

EIGHT

SOPHIE

The police kept me for two hours, though I had nothing to do with the body or with the place it had been found. The landlady was hysterical, and I was not much better. Marco was the one who sent for the police, and Marco was the one who drew me gently away from the courtyard after they'd asked their questions, firmly ending the interview, leaving them with my name and situation in the event they had need to contact me again.

But as I watched the oily, dusky reflections on the water glide by on the way back to the Danieli, I could not shake the vision of that body in its pool of blood, or stop hearing the buzzing of flies.

Marco frowned as he helped me disembark. "You should rest, *padrona*."

I smiled at him—I felt how strained it was. "I will. But you must promise to come back tomorrow—I won't take that place after all, you know. I couldn't bear it."

He looked alarmed. "No, you must not, of course! Not with such an angry ghost."

"An angry ghost? But it wasn't a murder. It was a suicide." That was what the police had decided. The pool of blood was from his wrists, which had been neatly and fatally slit. The landlady had said, *He looked ill, that is true. I begged him yesterday morning to eat more. He said he had no need of food, that love kept him alive.*

Not anymore, the inspector had said in distaste.

"An unhappy ghost then," Marco said to me now.

"Whether there was a ghost or not, I would never be able to go into the courtyard," I told him. "You will be here tomorrow? There are other places to show me?"

"A hundred places, *padrona*. You can rely on Marco."

I managed to keep my composure as I left him and walked through the grand lobby of the Danieli—full now with people returning from their day trips, looking to rest before they went out again for the evening—but I couldn't manage to smile or talk to anyone. By the time I finally reached our rooms, the day had caught up with me; I could not stop trembling.

Joseph was already there. He was lounging on the bed, barefoot, sketching, leaving charcoal dust all over the coverlet. When he saw me, he looked up, smiling. "I think I've found the way in."

I swallowed, trying not to show my distress. "Have you? So quickly?"

"I told you I would. I met him this morning. A poet. He's been in Venice for a while. He knows Henry Loneghan, Soph. *Loneghan.* They're friends."

"Loneghan? Oh . . . that's very good." I sat on the edge of the bed, drawing off my gloves, which stuck to my sweating palms. My fingers fumbled with the hat pin.

"He's amusing. I think you'll like him."

I dropped the pin; my hands were shaking too badly to keep hold of it. I lifted my hat from my hair, pretending it didn't matter. "What is this paragon's name?"

But Joseph had seen—he always did. He put aside his sketchbook. "What happened? You're white as a ghost."

A ghost. I couldn't help it; I laughed. Even I heard the edge of hysteria in it.

"Sophie, for God's sake . . ." He moved to sit beside me. "Tell me."

"It's nothing to worry about. The police said it was a suicide—"

"A suicide? What do you mean? Who was a suicide?"

"Mr. Stafford. Oh, Joseph, it would have been so perfect! The *sala* was so bright and your room was to overlook the canal and he was a writer—"

"Sophie. Look at me." As he spoke, he turned me firmly to face him. "You're not making sense. Who is Mr. Stafford? What *sala* are you talking about? Start from the beginning."

He reached for my hands, gripping them hard, stilling my trembling, and I felt myself regain my composure, moment by moment returned to myself.

I explained it to him, the search for lodgings, the landlady. But I could not bring myself to leave it so bare and ugly and meaningless, and so I tempered it, my imagination painting it in different colors, ones I could bear. "She said he died for love. It's so romantic really, don't you think? Something kept them apart, perhaps, and there was no way to be together. He couldn't live without her. Or perhaps . . . perhaps there was a reason she had to leave him, but she refused to be parted, and so he made the most honorable of sacrifices. For her. It was all for her."

Joseph gave me a thoughtful look, and then he said quietly, "You've had a shock. Let me get you something—chocolate, perhaps?

Would that help? Or no . . . sherry." He released me, getting to his feet. "Damn me, but there's nothing in this room, is there? I'll have to go downstairs—"

I grabbed at his arm before he'd gone a step. "No. No, please, I don't want anything. Don't leave me."

I thought he would protest, but then he looked at me, and his expression softened. He sat beside me again on the bed, drawing me into his arms, pulling me back with him until we were leaning against the carved, gilded headboard, my head on his chest. Gently he smoothed a loose tendril from my cheek.

"We'll stay in tonight," he whispered, brushing his lips across my forehead. "I'll have someone bring food up."

"It's too expensive," I murmured.

He ignored me. His caress was mesmerizing, soothing. "We'll save Florian's for tomorrow. I wanted you to meet Dane, but it can wait."

It was what I wanted to do. To lie here and be comforted and think of nothing and go nowhere. To not have to pretend at something I did not feel. But a whole night, wasted. . . . We could not afford it. I pushed myself away. "No. No, I'll be all right. We should go to the cafe."

"A night won't change anything."

"You say he can help us?"

"I think so."

"Then we shouldn't lose him."

"Are you certain? We could stay here. I don't mind it. I could send him a message. It's not much of a delay."

"But I do mind it. I want to go," I told him earnestly, and it was what I wanted just then; the specter of poor Mr. Stafford drifted away for the first time since I'd laid eyes on his corpse. "We haven't a choice. Our money won't last long. We *have* to take every opportunity. You've found him; now I must do my part."

Joseph was quiet for a moment, measuring me. He sighed. "Very well. If you insist."

"I do," I said firmly. "Now, tell me all about him. Is he handsome?"

"You'll find nothing to complain of, I think. And it shouldn't be difficult to snag him. He's half in love with you already, thanks to me."

That too had been part of the plan. A man was mine to manage; a woman belonged to Joseph. "And the Bronsons' salon?"

"If he knows Loneghan, it's a safe bet he knows the Bronsons, don't you think? Besides, Loneghan's got the money for patronage. He's the more important one." He leaned his head back, looking dreamily at the ceiling. "I never thought there would be a chance at him. Not in a hundred years."

"It seems fated, doesn't it?"

"I told you it would work out, didn't I? It's what we're meant to have. It could be no other way. But now it's up to you, Soph. You'll need to reel him in."

By the time we left for Florian's, I was well prepared to meet Nicholas Dane. I knew of the cafe, of course; everyone did. It had been there forever, one of those that served the greatest drawing room of all, the Piazza of St. Mark's, and in the evening it was at its most brilliant. The setting sun gilded the herringbone pattern of the pavement and sent a rosy golden glow over the basilica and the pink and white of the Doge's Palace. When Joseph and I arrived, the tables crowding the Piazza were already nearly full; the supposedly ubiquitous pigeons had mostly retired for the evening, though one or two strutted about, scattering beneath a careless foot.

There was no band tonight; but it was noisy. Talking and laughing; flower girls calling out; vendors crying, "Caramel! Caramel!" as they bore their baskets of shining candy; boys performing tricks for pennies; a man with an accordion and a ragged girl with a pretty voice singing whatever anyone would pay her to sing. Promenaders circled the square and dodged into the arcades, waiters hurried about bearing ices and syrups, coffee and the occasional chocolate. It seemed nearly everyone in Venice must be here.

Joseph pulled out a chair, then waited for me to sit. "Let him find us. It wouldn't do to look too anxious, would it?"

I took my seat, but I was never so confident as my brother, and I worried that Nicholas Dane might even now be at another table, waiting the evening away for us. But Joseph seemed perfectly at ease. He ordered a lemon ice for me and a coffee for himself, and when they were brought, he leaned back in his chair, stretching his arm along the back of mine, lounging and looking for all the world like a man at his leisure.

I picked at the ice, taking only the barest of tastes.

"You look ready to shatter," Joseph said in a low voice. "Shall we give it up for tonight and go back to the hotel?"

Before I could answer, his gaze leaped past me, his worry for me disappearing in a quick smile. "Dane!" he said, rising. "I'd wondered if we'd missed you."

"Oh, it's early yet, isn't it?" said a voice—smooth and British, and I looked over to see two men standing there, one very tall, with lank brown hair, who kept poking at the round spectacles sliding down his long nose, and the other, shorter and more compact and quite handsome, with a chiseled face and wavy blond hair cropped short, a high forehead and very blue eyes.

Joseph said, "Sophie, may I present Nicholas Dane and Giles Martin."

I held out my gloved hand and smiled. "I'm Sophie Hannigan, and I'm very pleased to meet you both."

Mr. Martin gaped at me like a fish. "So very pleased, Miss Hannigan," he said, grasping my fingers a bit too tightly before he released them.

"As am I," Mr. Dane put in smoothly. "You look very like your brother. Hannigan said you were his twin?"

I said, "Yes, but even so, I've never thought we looked much alike. Beyond our coloring, I mean."

"Fortunately Sophie escaped Papa's nose. I was not so lucky." Joseph touched the tip of my nose affectionately, teasing.

We sat again, and Giles Martin looked at me hungrily, but I already knew, given what Joseph had said, that Mr. Martin wasn't the one I had to charm. Still, I wasn't certain how important he might be, so for now, I included him in my smile.

Joseph said, "We almost didn't come. I'm afraid Sophie's had a bit of a scare."

"Is that so? Nothing too bad, I hope." Mr. Dane motioned to the waiter for coffees. It gave me a moment to survey him. He looked well put together, in his deep-brown coat and fashionably checked trousers, though I suspected he wasn't wealthy—I saw no watch chains dangling from his waistcoat pocket, and no rings or studs at all. A poet, Joseph had said, but there were no ink stains on his fingers either.

I was so busy studying him it was a moment before I realized they were all waiting for me to say something. I struggled to remember what the question had been—my scare. "Oh. Oh, well, yes it was bad, I'm afraid. Terribly so."

"She stumbled upon a body today," Joseph said.

"A body?" Giles Martin asked, clearly shocked. "A corpse, you mean?"

I nodded. "Yes, though the police assure me it was a suicide and not a murder, which is what I thought at first."

Nicholas Dane raised a sandy brow. "A suicide?"

"He was a poet, like yourself, Mr. Dane. His name was Nelson Stafford."

He took a hard breath. "Dear God."

"However did you manage to stumble upon him?" Mr. Martin asked.

"It was not nearly so difficult as it might seem," I said wryly. "I was looking at lodgings. He was in the courtyard of one."

"I hope you didn't lease it!" Giles Martin said.

"I nearly had. But then . . . well . . . of course I couldn't."

The coffees were brought. Mr. Dane played with the handle of his tiny cup, saying thoughtfully, "I had not heard. It's strange. Venice lives for gossip. And a suicide. How tragic."

"We only found him a few hours ago," I said softly. "I don't think there's been time for word to get around. Did you know him?"

Giles Martin shuddered. "No, though we'd seen him about once or twice."

Mr. Dane brought his cup to his well-shaped mouth. His eyes met mine over the rim. "A horrible thing for a gently bred young lady to see," he said when he'd taken a sip. "I cannot imagine you're recovered, Miss Hannigan."

I reached reflexively for my brother's hand, which dangled near my shoulder. He gripped my fingers tightly, reassuringly.

"Why d'you suppose he did it?" Mr. Martin asked meditatively. "God, I hate suicides. They always make me think there must have been something I could have done."

"But you said you didn't know him," Joseph said.

"Well yes, but still . . . I hope he doesn't take it into his head to haunt you, Miss Hannigan."

"You're as superstitious as any Venetian," Mr. Dane said dismissively.

Joseph laughed lightly. "Well, it's easy to be so here, isn't it? Last night, coming to our hotel . . . it felt as if time stood still. All that history . . . Venetian spies, murders around every corner. The place feels full of ghosts."

"Oh, I'm certain it is," said Mr. Dane. "And I imagine those with a sensitive disposition feel it most keenly."

"Spirits in the water and in the wind," murmured my brother, staring off into the soft glow of the arcades.

"Is that what brought you here?" Mr. Dane asked. "Searching for those elusive spirits?"

I saw the familiar haunted look come into Joseph's eyes—a brief moment, but enough for me to despair at what he was remembering. I tightened my hand on his, and the motion seemed to call him back to himself. He gave me a faint, wistful smile and said, "I've no wish to go looking for spirits. But I feel them just the same. Don't you?"

Nicholas Dane said, "One would have to be numb not to. And Venice loves a mystery, doesn't she? The place seems made for it. It's what brings artists here in droves. It's what brought Giles. Something in the air calling, an unstoppable force—"

"You make it sound like idiocy," Mr. Martin protested.

"Well, half of genius begins with an idiotic whim," Mr. Dane said affectionately. "Yours not the least of it. Is it what you felt as well, Hannigan?"

"I wouldn't call it idiocy," my brother said reflectively. "But it was a dream that brought me here."

"A dream . . . like a wish, you mean? You'd always wanted to see Venice?" asked Mr. Martin.

"A dream like a dream." Joseph's smile was sleepy and fine, the smile I loved best. "I was dreaming of Venice and thought I should come to see why."

It was a lie, of course. It was the kind of whimsy people expected of artists, and my brother was clever enough to be what was expected. But Joseph had never dreamed of Venice. He'd only listened to the talk of its salons held by expatriates and the sublimity of its light, and he and I had seen the opportunity we needed. Venice was the perfect place to escape to, a place to lick our wounds and hopefully find the fame and fortune Joseph felt we were destined for.

But leave it to my brother to make our flight sound romantic and artistic.

"Well," Mr. Dane said. "I hope Venice lives up to the dream, my friend, and doesn't turn into a nightmare instead."

"You think it could?" my brother asked.

Mr. Dane shrugged. "I've seen it happen. There are those who will warn you not to stay very long here. They'll tell you foreigners often discover that Venice's legacy is despair."

"Look at poor Stafford," Mr. Martin agreed.

"That would never happen to Joseph," I said ardently. "We've come here to escape despair, not to find it."

I felt my brother's warning in the tightening of his grip, nearly painful, on my fingers.

I tried to smile. "What I mean is . . . Joseph has a great deal of talent. No one with talent like that should ever despair."

"Nor should any lady so beautiful as yourself," put in Mr. Martin a bit too earnestly. "Have you seen Venice's Public Gardens, Miss Hannigan?"

The change in subject, as well as his too-obvious compliment, disconcerted me. "Oh . . . oh no. We've been here too short a time."

"Nick and I promised your brother the best views in Venice, and the Gardens have several. It's truly the only bit of green in the city. We've agreed to go tomorrow. I, for one, would be delighted if you would join us."

I'd meant to spend the day looking for a place to live. But Joseph squeezed my hand, and I knew what he wanted me to do. I looked at Mr. Dane. "You'll be going as well?"

"I'd thought to," he said.

Giles Martin said, "Perhaps there you'll find the inspiration you've been searching for, Nick."

I said to Mr. Dane, "How is it that inspiration has eluded you in a place like Venice?"

He gave me a languid look. "Who knows? Words are my trade, Miss Hannigan, but Venice sweeps them all away."

"I keep telling him he simply hasn't found the right muse," Mr. Martin said.

Mr. Dane laughed shortly. "Oh, I've had enough of muses, I think."

He said it with a bitterness that told me he'd been unlucky in love, and no doubt recently. It was a bit dismaying, but not fatal. There was too much at stake to let it matter. We needed Nicholas Dane to like us. To like *me*.

"Oh, but perhaps you'll find one more to your taste in the Gardens," I said.

Nicholas Dane bowed his head slightly in acquiescence. "Perhaps so," he said, but when he looked at me, I saw only politeness, and I thought of the bitterness I'd heard in his voice, my sense that he was a man who'd been thwarted by love. But love was not what I required from him.

Don't forget that. I could almost hear Joseph's voice in my head. *Any man can be led by desire, Soph. But desire isn't love. Don't make the mistake of thinking it is.*

I knew that better than most, didn't I?

NINE

NICHOLAS

She was as stunning in person as his portrait had made her out to be. She was not quite beautiful, but there was something in her more interesting than beauty, than blue eyes and dark hair and pale skin. It was what her brother had captured in his sketch, a deep, almost primal carnality, some occult attraction. . . . He had not invented that eroticism, as I'd thought. It was there. It was real.

I'd known only one other woman who possessed that quality, and while Sophie Hannigan could not possibly be so dangerous—in fact, I would have said she was completely unaware of just how bewitching she was—I knew enough to be wary.

There were a hundred reasons to stay away from Sophie Hannigan—not the least of which was her relationship with her brother. What he'd seen in her, well . . . it was strange that a brother had noted it, though I told myself it was obvious enough that he no doubt saw other men's reactions to her. But even beyond that, there was another strangeness about them. While

Joseph Hannigan was compelling on his own, the two of them together were curiously irresistible, as if each enhanced the other. It made it impossible to stop looking at them. I was not the only one so captivated—Giles was as well. Perhaps it was only that they were twins and so shared that womb-deep connection I'd heard about but never before witnessed. Whatever it was, I didn't quite understand it, though it was perversely fascinating, and it only served to feed the desire I'd felt for her since I'd seen that sketch. Such desire was reason enough to keep my distance; it was a complication I couldn't afford. To keep Sophie Hannigan's brother in my sights while I worked toward destroying Odilé would take concentration. I could not be distracted by another woman, no matter how tempting the package.

I resolved to be friendly to Miss Hannigan, but to hold her at arm's length. Later, perhaps, when her brother was safe and Odilé was gone, I could reassess.

The Gardens were a swath of green at the very end of the Riva, a sudden crowding of leafy trees and winding walks dotted with statuary. One came out of Venice's crowded, close *calli* and canals, a city of water and stone, and stepped into a different world, onto paths lined with hedges and roses and vines. The day was warm, the sky cloudless, the Euganean Hills blue and the Alps dappled with snow in the distance. There were several people walking the paths, reclining in the shade of the trees, lingering at tables by the balustraded wall overlooking the lagoon, San Giorgio Maggiore and the Lido.

After an hour or so of wandering about, we sat at one of those tables. The Hannigans had brought lunch: wine and sausage, bread and melon. Hannigan cut big chunks of the orange flesh with a knife, and I did my utmost not to notice the sensuous way Sophie Hannigan ate it. She had peeled off her gloves, and the juice dripped over her slender fingers, trailing down her wrists to disappear in the somewhat yellowed lace edge of her sleeve.

Giles was obviously equally enraptured with her. "To inspiration," he said, raising a glass to her, his gaze fixed upon her plump lips.

"As elusive as it may be," I added.

Joseph Hannigan bent to pick a bright pink rose from a bush twining near our table. He snapped off a thorn and then tucked it behind his sister's ear, smiling broadly. "The pink becomes you. Don't you think so, Dane?"

It did, of course. That shocking pink against her hair, bringing out the pink of her cheeks touched by the sun. I kept my voice as blandly polite as I could. "Indeed. It's quite your color, Miss Hannigan."

"You should be covered in pink," Giles said fervently. "From head to toe in roses!"

"I should think the thorns would make such a thing quite uncomfortable," I said wryly.

Hannigan tore off a chunk of bread and leaned back in his chair, studying his sister the way I'd seen a hundred artists study their subjects, a critical, assessing eye that depersonalized her completely. "Hmmm. Maybe not head to toe. But a few here and there, I think. Maybe against white, to highlight your skin. Perhaps we'll try it. What do you think, Soph?"

She gave a little shrug, taking up another piece of melon. "Whatever you like. You've the eye, not me."

"My God, it sounds beautiful," Giles said. I thought I detected annoyance in her expression, but it could have been only that I was annoyed myself, despite the fact that by now I was used to Giles's ardent attachments. He was never more foolish than when he was infatuated with some woman or another.

But I understood it too. The spell of her closed the space between us, touching and then drawing back. Her smile, along with that small overbite, was so sensual one was led immediately to thoughts of lovemaking. It didn't help that her brother found myriad ways to bring her to our attention—the rose had been only one of a dozen or more little gestures, as if he himself was so taken with her he couldn't help himself.

She leaned her chin upon her hand and gazed out toward the lagoon. "Such a beautiful day, isn't it? It seems impossible to believe there could be anything but days such as this here."

"Thus far I haven't seen a bad one," I said. "But I've only been here the summer."

"The lagoon is magical," Miss Hannigan went on dreamily. "Before we came, I read so much about it. Everyone spoke of the first sight of Venice from the lagoon. But that was before the train bridge was built. I suppose no one first comes upon it that way anymore."

"No, probably not," I agreed. "But even coming from the train station, Venice has its charm. Especially after Mestre."

Joseph Hannigan laughed.

Giles said, "Such a dismal, dusty town."

"It has its moments." Hannigan turned to his sister. "Tell them, Soph. Tell them what we saw in Mestre."

She smiled, that dreaminess in her eyes becoming more pronounced, impossible to turn away from. "We had an hour wait, and we were sitting there on the bench outside the station when a train came in. One of the cars had a carriage strapped to it. It shone even in the dust. It had a gold emblem painted upon the door, and its windows glittered in the sun like diamonds." Her voice took on a lovely vibrance, a storyteller's opulence, transitioning us into a fairy tale before I'd realized it.

"The train stopped so suddenly that the carriage jerked and the straps holding it broke. It rolled onto one wheel and hung there long enough that I thought it might stay that way, suspended. But then it crashed to the ground. The trunks on its roof broke open, and jars and bottles and wooden boxes rolled everywhere, cracking apart as if the violence of the world had been cast upon them, releasing butterflies and moths and bugs. The air shivered with shining, vibrant wings and the ground shimmered with all the colors of the rainbow. It was so beautiful we could not look away.

"The man and woman whose carriage it was ran about, trying to gather them up again, desperate to keep them safe. Because you see, they weren't really insects waiting to be dried and pinned to mats in museum exhibits, but fairies who had been transformed by a wicked demon and locked in a mummy's tomb. They had spent hundreds of years in darkness, and that man and woman had rescued them, and meant to return them to the ancient gardens of Rome, where they belonged.

"But now the fairies were bathed in sunlight, and laughing because they would never be in darkness again. They would not go back into those bottles and boxes. We could feel their joy and hear them singing. The man and the woman let them go—what else could they do? They could protect them no longer. They could only hope that the fairies would find their own way to the gardens. Some of them have made it there already, I know. And the rest will as soon as they find the path the others have left for them to follow. I shall never forget the magic of Mestre."

Her voice trailed off, but the vision she'd conjured for us lingered, impossible to forget. I had heard singers who could charm the world with their voices, and actors whose sonorous tones left one in weeping awe, but Sophie Hannigan's skill with a story left me staring at her in wonder. It wasn't just her words, it was her way of putting them together, the voice that seemed to gain power with each one, so that my head had been filled with images so magically vibrant it was as if I had seen them with my own eyes. She changed the world into something fine. She made one *believe*.

We were all dumbstruck, but Hannigan . . . Hannigan's gaze was so full of love and yearning—such a fatal and somehow *wrong* combination—that I was momentarily distracted. I had no idea what to make of it.

"Did that really happen?" Giles asked, breaking the silence that had fallen over all of us. "The bugs and the butterflies? I mean, they *were* going to a museum for display, of course?"

Sophie Hannigan's smile faltered—for a moment a darkness came into her eyes that only confused me more, and I wanted to throttle Giles for asking the question, for marring the magic of the tale, but it was Joseph Hannigan who said gently, "Sophie's is the story I want to believe, don't you?"

The shadows left her eyes. She gave her brother a grateful smile.

The moment held, lingering between them in a way so private I felt as if I were intruding, and I had to look away. But then Hannigan sighed, and I looked up again to see him rising. "Come along, Martin. Perhaps we should try drawing the view instead of simply talking about it."

Giles frowned. He looked ready to protest, but then he rose reluctantly and followed, glancing back at Miss Hannigan as he did so, obviously loathe to leave her.

"That was quite a story," I said when they were gone.

"Did you like it?"

"You've a way with words. And quite an imagination. Have you written it down?"

"Me? Oh no, I'm no poet. I like telling stories, but I'm not very good at writing them. You can have it if you like. Write it for me. I shall sit back and quietly admire the view while you do so."

71

I looked away, up into the leafy canopy, and heard myself say, quite unexpectedly, "'For she was beautiful—her beauty made the bright world dim and everything beside seemed like the floating image of a shade.'"

"Why, that is lovely," she said with a smile. "A pity it's not yours, but Shelley's."

That she knew it surprised me, though it shouldn't have. She was obviously educated, and she and her brother had either come from money and fallen on hard times, or had been at the lower echelons of society. Or perhaps her parents had disowned her artist brother and she had followed him. There could have been many reasons why the gown she wore—good quality silk, unless I missed my guess—was not quite the current fashion. Or why I'd seen it twice now. Last night at Florian's, and today, though she wore a different hat and shawl as if to disguise the fact. I found myself wondering about her history, her relationship with her brother, and where she'd learned to tell stories. I fiercely quashed the urge to ask her. I did not want to be so involved, I reminded myself.

She said, "Tell me one of your poems. Joseph said you'd published, though I confess I didn't recognize your name. But there are so many writers we don't know in America. I suppose you must be famous in London."

I took a sip of wine, ignoring the resentment—very old now, and very familiar—I felt at her words. "I think even London doesn't know me. At least not most of it. There's nothing like publishing to humble a man." Or to show the extent of his insignificance.

"Well, I expect Venice to do her best by you, whatever you think. Perhaps it's as Mr. Martin says, and one day you'll discover inspiration standing right in front of you."

She was still leaning her chin upon her hand. Her eyes were bright, and fastened on me as if she found me fascinating. It was heady, I had to admit. "Perhaps. But thus far I haven't been as lucky in my inspirations as your brother."

I said it deliberately, hoping to tell something from her reaction, but she only blinked and said lightly, "You never know what the future will bring."

"You're another optimist, I see."

"Another?"

"Well, Giles is one too. Or he's mad—I can't tell which. Is it optimism or madness that keeps one forging ahead despite failure after failure?"

"Faith, I think."

"Oh? Faith in what?"

"I don't know. God. Or fate."

"Or symmetry," I said unthinkingly.

Sophie Hannigan's forehead furrowed. "Symmetry?"

"It was something an old . . . friend . . . used to say. That the world liked balance. Symmetry."

"Oh." She looked puzzled. "Well, I suppose that's like fate. Everything works out for the best, doesn't it?"

"Does it? You saw Nelson Stafford in that courtyard. There are plenty of horrors out there fighting for one's soul, Miss Hannigan. Sometimes they win. Is that best? For whom?"

The brightness in her eyes dimmed, replaced by the shadows I'd seen before—and for a moment these were so dark and haunting that I was taken aback; I realized suddenly that whatever was the story in Sophie Hannigan's past, it was much different than the one I'd imagined for her.

But then she glanced away, out toward the lagoon, to her brother, and that expression disappeared, leaving me uncertain of what I'd seen.

"I think beauty has more power than horror, don't you?" she asked softly.

"Like your story of Mestre."

She nodded. "I'd rather have the magic. I want to see the world the way Joseph does—he sees so much beauty in everything."

"He's fortunate to have the talent to show that vision to the world. I suppose we're all luckier for it."

"Yes. I don't know what I'd do without him."

"From the looks of it, he feels the same about you. He seems quite devoted."

"We're devoted to each other," she told me frankly. "We've no other family."

That didn't surprise me. "Your parents—?"

"Died in a carriage accident when we were very young."

Here it was, I thought, the reason for the haunting shadows in her eyes. "How tragic. Who raised you?"

"Our aunt was our guardian. Have you any family, Mr. Dane?"

I was too good at this myself not to notice her deflection. "A full one, I'm afraid. No unfortunate deaths or illnesses to blight it. My mother and father are well on their way to a distinguished old age. My brother and sister are both married. My sister has proved to be excellent at breeding, which removed from me and my brother the need of providing grandchildren, though I suppose he could have obliged by now. It's been some time since I visited, so I don't really know."

"You don't? How strange."

"Not really," I said. "We've no real interest in each other. And my father and I don't get along. He had other aspirations for me."

"He doesn't like your being a poet?"

"He thought I should pick a profession that might actually make me a living. I suppose he wasn't wrong."

Again, that smile. "Well, I have great hopes for you, Mr. Dane." She leaned forward; the movement sent her perfume wafting—violets, I thought, and desire rose unbidden, unfettered and intense.

Just as it had with Odilé.

The moment I had the thought, Giles called, as if the universe had put him in place to save me, "You shouldn't monopolize Miss Hannigan that way, Nick! You'll bore her to death with your cynicism. Come over here a moment, Miss Hannigan. Tell me if I've truly captured the color of that rose."

She hesitated; I thought I saw disappointment, and I was struck by the realization that she had wanted to be alone with me, which made me a little too glad. Deliberately I summoned control, which brought a chill to my voice I didn't quite mean when I said, "Please don't let me keep you."

It took her aback, I saw. She colored and rose, going over to Giles, and I watched in interest as he stood back to show her whatever it was he was painting, trying to imagine what words she might find to compliment Giles's true lack of talent for landscape. Whatever it was she said, it was the right thing, because he exclaimed with pleasure.

He pointed to the balustrade, and as she wandered over to it, I realized that he was asking her to pose for him. I felt a stab of annoyance. It was too late in the afternoon for it; he would have her standing there for hours, and I would be caught up in it, and I'd had enough of the day. There were still things I must do before the sun set. I rose, wandering over to them, saying as I approached, "For God's sake, Giles, don't burden her with posing."

Sophie Hannigan tendered a hesitant smile. "Oh, I don't mind it. I'm used to it."

"What else have we to do?" Giles asked.

His words reminded me of the reason I had come to the Gardens today. To keep Joseph Hannigan in my sights, too busy in my world to wander about in Odilé's. There was a poetry reading at Katharine Bronson's salon, and Giles and I had promised to attend.

I said to Giles, "We're supposed to be at Katharine's tonight, or have you forgotten?"

Giles winced. "Oh yes, I did forget. Well, it won't matter if we're late, will it? It's only Johnson's verses."

"Oh no, please, not on our account," Miss Hannigan said, and there was a stillness to her now, disappointment or restraint. "Neither Joseph nor I would keep you from an appointment."

I said, a trifle disingenuously, "It's not an appointment, not really. More of a longstanding engagement. Katharine Bronson's salon at the Alvisi. You know, you and your brother should come. Yes, you absolutely should. I think the two of you would enjoy it."

"Whistler was there the other night," Giles said. "And Frank Duveneck."

"Oh it sounds wonderful. But I shall have to ask Joseph—"

Giles shouted, "Hannigan! Come here!"

Hannigan jerked as if he'd just awakened from a reverie. He closed the sketchbook, rose from where he sat against a nearby tree, and came over to us. I said, "You've no plans for tonight, have you?"

He glanced at his sister, who said, "Mr. Dane has just invited us to Katharine Bronson's salon."

"A salon?" He seemed barely waking from his distraction.

"It's not so boring as it sounds," Giles said. "At least not usually."

I said, "No indeed. They'll love the two of you. Fresh blood, as it were."

Giles laughed. "The only requirement is that you be entertaining. They put a great store on that. If you can't be entertaining, you must at least be a good audience."

"I am the best of audiences," Sophie Hannigan said. "Isn't that so, Joseph?"

"But you're already destined for entertainment, Miss Hannigan," Giles said. "You'll never get away with being in the audience tonight."

She frowned. "Why is that?"

I expected Giles to prattle some compliment about her loveliness or something equally inane, but he said, "By tonight, Stafford will be all the gossip. They'll want to hear your story."

"Oh," she said. "I'm not certain I'll want to talk about it."

"They won't forgive you for withholding," I said quickly. "You'll be the guest *du jour*, after all. I give you fair warning: you'll make no friends with reticence. Not in this crowd. And you should embellish too. They love detail. They expect lies. You'll be very good at it, if your tale of Mestre is any indication."

Sophie Hannigan's smile caught me unexpecting; I had no defense.

She said, "Of course. I shall tell them anything they want to hear."

TEN

SOPHIE

We went back to the room to dress before Mr. Dane and Mr. Martin were to fetch us at six. We were no sooner through the door than Joseph turned to me, taking my face in his hands, kissing me hard. "Mrs. Bronson and the Alvisi, Soph!" he said, ebullient. "I told you, didn't I? I knew he had the connection."

I wrapped my arms around him, holding him tight. "You were right, as always."

"And now, thanks to you, we're in."

"Thanks to me? Oh, I don't think it's thanks to me at all. It's more thanks to you."

"To me?"

"He's taken with you. I don't think he's attracted to me at all."

Joseph sobered and frowned. He stepped away and went restlessly to the window. "No. He's interested in you. The sketch and . . . yes, I *know* he is. I saw it."

"Well he didn't seem so today."

"When I left you alone—"

"He seemed quite immune."

"What did you speak of?"

"I hardly remember. God, I think. Or fate. His lack of inspiration. He was envious of yours, though. He asked about our family."

Joseph turned, ghosts in his eyes. I felt the ragged edges he worked so carefully to hide calling to mine. "What did you tell him?"

Quickly, I said, "Enough to show him it wasn't very interesting. Dead parents, raised by an aunt, nothing more."

I was relieved when his ghosts fled. My own settled in response. Joseph sighed. "Did he touch you? Your hand or your arm?"

"Not once."

"Did he smile? Or laugh?"

"Yes, but not as you mean. Perhaps you're right and he is interested, but if that's so, it's obvious he means to do nothing about it. I can tell."

"Martin said he had no other girl. You just need to flirt with him a bit more. Remember what I taught you?"

"Yes of course. I tried. Truly I did. He hardly looked at me."

"Give him time," Joseph said dismissively. "He's cautious is all. He liked the story as much as I did. It was . . ." he trailed off. I saw the memory of it in his eyes, the world I'd made for him that we both wished to live in, where nothing hurt and no one troubled us. And I saw the desire it raised too, that mirrored my own, that made me feel powerful and miserable and helpless. He blinked it away and said a bit roughly, "Believe me, he wants you as much as Martin does."

I drew off my tight gloves, wiggling loose one finger at a time. I remembered the bitterness in Nicholas Dane's voice, my thought that he'd been hurt before and meant not to be hurt again. "Perhaps. Though he's drawn to you too. He couldn't stop watching you."

"I'll remember that."

"Why does it matter now? Why should either of us keep trying? We're to go to the Bronsons'. What more do we need him for?"

"We'll need his support a while longer, at least until we establish ourselves there. And there's still Henry Loneghan."

"Yes," I said on a sigh, setting aside my gloves, pulling out my hat pin. "Loneghan."

"You know his reputation. People listen to him. They follow his lead."

"I know." I lifted my hat, shaking loose the strands of my hair that clung to the veil before I threw it to the chair.

"Dane won't be able to resist you for long, even if he wants to. Trust me. You're irresistible."

I only looked at him.

My brother's eyes softened. "You don't have to do it alone, you know, Soph. I'll do my part."

I nodded. "I know."

Joseph looked back out the window. Quietly, he said, "They won't have heard of us at Bronson's. Don't mention Roberts, whatever you do."

A pall settled over me. "Why would I mention him?"

"I didn't say you would. I'm just warning you not to. You get nervous sometimes, and things just come out."

That stung, no matter how true. "I wouldn't talk about him. I've forgotten him already."

"You're certain he wouldn't have spoken to them of you?"

That pall grew heavier. "I meant nothing to him. It was only you he cared about."

Joseph let out his breath. "Then we're fine," he said with satisfaction. "There was no reason to speak of me."

I went over to him. "It was such a very little scandal, Joseph," I whispered. "Hardly anyone knew of it. No one was hurt."

"Only you," he said gently.

I nodded. I laid my cheek against his back, the soft, worn cloth of his suit coat, and put my arms around him. He gripped them tight. "Only me."

ELEVEN

ODILÉ

I stood at the window and watched the late afternoon sun play upon the currents of the Grand Canal, sparkling and settling and spreading to the strains of the pianoforte he played. It was a concerto I knew well. I had heard it as it came to life, each note set fast upon the one before it, a flurry of notes like a blizzard, racing and tumbling from a hand shaking with the urgency to get them down, to not lose them.

I closed my eyes, remembering, savoring. I remembered how he'd finished it, nearly collapsing from exhaustion, sweating with the heat of composing, staggering to me, falling into my arms and bringing me down to the floor, where those notes of his tangled in my hair, twining around our contortions and contractions, convulsions of pleasure, cries that echoed his song.

Now, the playing came to an end, the last chord lingering in the warm afternoon, fading slowly, dissipating into separateness, settling like dust upon the floor. Neither of us said a word—this new musician of mine was as appreciative as any of a predecessor's talent. It was my favorite characteristic of musicians. They were competitive and jealous, but unlike poets or writers or painters, musicians borrowed and built upon old foundations and acknowledged the genius of before. They *used* it. One discovered, and others embraced, embroidered, and embellished, twisting and shaping it into something that was quite their own, even as it held echoes of the past. In this way, every melody and harmony felt part of some vast universe that belonged not just to man, but to every other creature—worldly and otherworldly.

It was music that had saved me once upon a time. Music that assured me I still had a soul—otherwise how was it possible to be so affected? During those times when my appetite was appeased, and I was left numb and waiting, it was music that reminded me that I had felt something once. Smells anchored me, but music . . . music told me that whatever else had been taken from me, my soul remained. Even when the dark craving possessed me, and I was nothing but appetite and rapture tangled together, I was still—somehow—Odilé. And that was what I was most afraid of losing now.

I heard the shuffle of papers, the soft closing of the lid, the creak of the stool as he rose. I opened my eyes, glancing toward him. He was wild with playing, his pale face flushed, his red hair falling over his forehead, his eyes bright. My appetite leaped the space between us, drawing upon him, making him stumble. He frowned a little in confusion and looked at the floor as if accusing it of meaning to trip him. Then he came up behind me, wrapping his arms around me and pulling me against his chest.

"Odilé." He whispered each syllable—Oh-de-lay—into my neck, just below my ear, stirring the fine hairs there, sending a shiver down my spine. "You look so beautiful and sad I can't bear it."

"It was the music," I said. "Do you know who wrote the piece?"

"Schumann," he said without pause.

"They say he was inspired by angels. But he wasn't, you know."

"His wife, I heard."

I resisted the pull of hunger for the moment, letting the pain—almost exquisite now—build. "No, not his wife, though he loved her. There was another woman. One no one knew of. He called her his angel. He thought she had come from another world, and in a way, she had."

He nuzzled my neck, breathing deeply of me—I felt his bewitchment in my pulse, my hunger opening wide to swallow him. For now, I denied it, savoring.

"He met her on an icy street in Düsseldorf." I remembered the way Robert Schumann turned a corner, sliding on the ice with the suddenness of his stop. He caught his fall with a gloved hand pressed to the wall. He had intense, burning eyes, and longish dark hair beneath his hat. "He told her later that she had been silhouetted against the winter sun when he first saw her, so it seemed she was haloed, as if she'd been an angel sent to him by God, and he'd thought for a moment that she wasn't real."

The musician murmured something. I felt his lips move upon my skin, warm and moist, the press of his kiss.

"He was desperate. He loved his wife, but he was jealous of her. Her fame eclipsed his, and it tormented him. He felt he could write nothing. He said he heard voices that told him to stop composing, and others screaming to be let free. But when he was with his angel, the music flooded from him. He could not write quickly enough. It was she who made him see his own genius. It was she who brought him the fame he longed for."

My musician had gone still. "Who was she?"

"No one knows. Only that he wrote *The Ghost Variations* for her. Some think he dedicated it to his wife. But he didn't. It was for his angel, though he never revealed her name. He rewarded her with obscurity and insignificance."

"I remember that he was obsessed with angels. He went mad, didn't he?"

I turned to face my musician, wrapping my arms around his neck. "Yes. It was the price he paid."

"The price? For what?"

"For inspiration." I smiled at him. "For fame. Do you think it was worth it?"

The musician stared at me as if I'd bewitched him—the same look I'd seen in Robert Schumann's eyes on that frosty street, the black glove poised upon the wall, a moment in time frozen, arrested, a breath of fog on the air.

"Yes," Jonathan Murphy murmured. "He's the one we remember now, isn't he? Not his wife."

"Indeed." I went up on my tiptoes to kiss him. His mouth was like honey. He staggered against me like a drunk.

"But what of the woman?" he insisted, slurring, weakened. "Was she really an angel, as he said?"

"An angel? Oh yes." I pressed my mouth against the pulse in his throat, feeling it jump beneath my tongue. He gasped and shuddered with pleasure, already cresting, a willing prisoner, begging to be taken, and I felt a frisson of exhaustion, and relief too, as I ran my hand through the fine thick red of his hair, murmuring, "Yes, she was his angel. But can't you guess, my love? She was his demon too."

TWELVE

ODILÉ

I was obsessed with Madeleine—I can see that now, though at the time I knew only that I was fascinated. For months, I followed her like a hapless puppy, and was grateful that she seemed to want me about. I know now it was because my insistence bewildered her. *You are something new,* she said to me, and I didn't understand until much later exactly how much of a novelty I was. She was used to leaving, and I would not be left.

She had abandoned her artist, as she'd told me she would do, and he went into a decline soon after, a depression that ended with his suicide. She seemed unmoved by it, unsurprised. When I brought her the news, she said only, "Ah, very sad," as if the sadness were simply something to be acknowledged, a fact like *that dog is black,* but not something she felt. She was quiet and reflective in those first days—she liked to listen to me talk, and I found in her a listener who was always interested, if not empathetic.

"What is it you want with me?" she asked me one day, those black eyes sharp, and I felt the question held weight and import; I felt oddly that my future depended on what I might say.

"I want to be like you," I told her.

"You want this, you mean," she said, gesturing to the room, which was almost cloying in its opulence—scarves and pillows, golden statuettes, lamps inlaid with jewels, plush carpets.

I shook my head dismissively. "I have enough *things*."

"You want lovers then."

"No. I want to be what you are."

"What I am?" she asked, and there was a wariness in her voice, a stillness I had not heard before.

"These men you've inspired will never forget you. You've made your mark upon them. They say you are unforgettable." People knew her *name*; they wanted to be with her. Since she'd left the artist, there had been letters, pleas, visits from other artists: poets and painters and musicians, all begging for a moment with her, all hoping for more. Madeleine did something I had never before seen in a woman alone: she chose whom she liked without regard for money or prestige, and her choice transformed. She whipped her lovers into an artistic frenzy. She moved them and inspired them, and I wanted to know how she did it. No one ever looked past her. No one ever looked away. They remembered her. I wanted what she had with an intensity that sometimes frightened me.

I never wondered about the strange things I saw in her, though I should have. I never wondered at how quickly she went through her lovers—sometimes only in days. Now and again I came to her rooms in the morning to see them staggering away as if they'd been weakened by a fever. I found one or two of them collapsed on her carpet. She would say only that it was nothing—he was ill, he'd forgotten to eat, the night had been exhausting—and the servants carried them away. In those first months, two killed themselves over her, one jumping from a balcony and another hanging himself. I didn't wonder at it—why would I? I understood it. I would have been devastated had she cast me aside.

I put off the few lovers I had, not caring when they grew so impatient with my lack of attention that they left me for others. I cared only for her. Her influence was astonishing; she told me stories of the men she'd inspired, and I was stunned at how much she'd done in her life, how many works of art owed their existence to her. The realization only increased my own sense that she held the answer to my every dissatisfaction. I believed she alone knew how to make me stop *wanting*.

Tell me how to be you. I must have said such words, or variations of them, several times, and she always put me off. *You don't know what you're asking,* cherie, or, *Be happy with your own life.*

But I was not, and over the next six months, it became more and more evident. She took up with a composer, and I watched in envy as she cajoled him into writing his best opera—a stunning enough piece, but nothing to thrill the ages. I began to realize that what she'd said before was true, that she had an eye for talent, but not for brilliance. I began to think that she was not utilizing her abilities to their utmost.

"Do you never wonder what the world could be if you chose to inspire the best?" I asked her one day.

She frowned. "What do you mean?"

I shrugged. "This composer has talent, but he is like your artist. He will be famous for a time, but he will be forgotten. Do you not wish for more? You could be known as the muse to genius, Madeleine. You could change the world. Choose the best, instead of the middling talents you take up."

She turned a critical eye to me. "Do you think you could do better?"

"Yes. Let me find someone worthy of you."

She went thoughtful. I felt the magic of her dark eyes as I always did; there was something truly astounding within them. She said slowly, as if she were trying to decide something, "Very well, find him. Bring him to me and we will see if you are right."

It was the only thing she had ever asked of me, and I was determined not to fail her. I still had some cachet, and I used what was left of it to attend the suppers and balls that had once been, for me, de rigueur. I went to the theater, to the gambling halls where artists gathered looking to change their luck.

When I found him, I knew. He was not pretty. His hair was dark and wild, and he had been crippled in childhood, a bad hip that required the constant use of a cane. He was also nearly sixty, but in those days neither Madeleine nor I shirked from age. He had a gnarled face, but it was not unpleasant, and his eyes were sharp. I found him reading his poetry at a small supper, and I knew the moment I heard him that he was touched with genius, though I think no one else at the gathering noticed. They chatted through his reading, laughing among themselves, paying no attention, and I could tell by his sighs that he was discouraged at the end of it.

Afterward, I brought him a glass of sherry to ease the rasp in his voice. I think he was surprised I deigned to notice him. I was still beautiful, after all, and he was not a man used to such attention. I said, "Come with me. There is someone I would like you to meet."

I took him to Madeleine's. When I brought him through the door, she raised her eyebrow and I said, "Trust me."

He was struck immediately, as they all were. When she invited him to have wine with her, he stayed. I left them with a smug sense of satisfaction. Because I was right about him. His poetry still is lauded, though he went mad soon after Madeleine left him. It was a small price to pay, I thought then. I think it now.

Although Madeleine was grateful for what I'd done, something changed after that. I often caught her watching me when she thought I wasn't looking, and the expression on her face made me uneasy.

One day, as we strolled the halls of a private art exhibition, Madeleine stopped short, as if arrested, before a portrait of a young man. He was dressed in velvet finery; his hair hanging in dark curls to his shoulders, his eyes so black they were only pools of opacity.

Madeleine shuddered. "Those eyes."

I frowned. "What of them?"

"How they follow me. They seem . . ." She let the words fall away as if she could not wrangle them.

I glanced at the portrait. The eyes were badly done, with no depth, and I saw no real reason for them to have so affected her. I started to move on. She touched my arm to stop me. Her gaze had not left the portrait.

"What do you know of demons, Odilé?"

It was the painting, I knew. It was obvious that it troubled her. "It's only that the artist did a poor job of capturing dark eyes. I hardly think him a demon."

"How little you know of the world."

That stung—it was unlike Madeleine to be so dismissive. "I'm hardly an innocent."

"No, but there is so much you don't know. You're like everyone else, believing things because you've never questioned them."

"Why would you say such a thing to me?"

"Because it's true." She seemed hardly aware that she'd offended me. "You talk as if you would know a demon if you saw it."

"I believe I would," I said coldly, thinking of the man who'd taken my virginity and left me bleeding on the floor. "One rarely mistakes malice and cruelty."

"And you think those things the province of demons alone."

"No, of course not. But I think it is how you know when you are dealing with one. The man who ruined me had a demon's eyes. I see them in my nightmares."

"And yet, had it not been for him, you would be a common whore like your mother, instead of one of the preeminent courtesans in Paris."

"No longer preeminent," I said softly, feeling the pinch of it.

"But you are better off than you would have been otherwise, are you not? He forced you to do what you had only dreamed of before. He was not your ruin, but your savior."

"I hardly think of it so rosily."

"No, you are like everyone else. You would like to think that things are easily categorized. Mankind likes little boxes. Everything in its place. And yet . . ." She moved close to the painting, reaching out, pointing to the boy's painted eyes. "You say the artist hasn't the skill to paint dark eyes. I say you are not looking closely enough."

She laid a finger upon the eyes. I looked, and suddenly those blank painted orbs sprung to life. They seemed to glimmer, as if her pale skin and the rings on her fingers caught the light and reflected them into the paint. Though I was looking only at heavy impasto, I thought suddenly of the compelling nature of her gaze, those times when its darkness seemed to pull me in, to capture me in an endless orbit, and I saw the same thing now, in the eyes of a painted boy.

"Do you see, Odilé?" she whispered. "Do you not see the light, even in such darkness? Now that you are looking for it, do you see what is beyond a first glance?"

She drew her finger from the painting. The boy's eyes went black again, black as eternity, endless, and yet . . . I saw that glimmer in them, as if the reflection she'd put there had somehow stayed. Ah, but that was impossible, wasn't it? It was only an illusion.

When she turned to look at me, I saw that glimmer in her eyes too, something that spoke of hidden things, of a knowledge beyond what anyone could or should possess—a knowledge I yearned for.

She said, "You told me I should use my talent to change the world."

"Yes," I agreed. "And I was right, wasn't I? His poetry was stunning, and everyone knows who inspired it. It will last. And so will you."

"You know this?"

"How can anyone know for certain? But yes, I think it will."

She looked back at the painting. I heard sounds in the hall beyond, footsteps, the swish of skirts, the low murmur of talk and laughter.

"And if you had such a talent for inspiration, what would you do?"

"What I advised you to do. Inspire the world. Leave a *mark*."

"No matter the cost?"

"Is there a cost?" I asked. "I confess I fail to see it. And even if there were, surely such an outcome is worth it? To change the world *and* have your name be known and remembered? Yes, I think it must be worth anything. Now come, shall we move on? I'm beginning to feel the boy's eyes as you do."

She nodded, but before I could take a step, she said, "How glad I am to have discovered you, Odilé."

The warmth of her smile was a balm on my irritation. I forgot everything but her. I forgot what we'd spoken of. I forgot the confession she'd wrought from me; I failed to see its meaning. I was glad only to be with her.

Later, I realized how true were the things she'd said. I *was* blind. I had no conception of the world beyond my pleasure, and so I did not see how it tilted and bent. I did not see the door I was walking through, nor how it would change my life. I did not realize we weren't talking of figurative demons at all.

THIRTEEN

NICHOLAS

It was mid afternoon by the time Giles and I left the Hannigans at the Danieli and returned to our own rooms off the Campo San Fantin, but there were still a few hours before the salon.

I told Giles I had to run out for a bit, and he didn't question me; he was too busy looking over his canvas, where he'd scratched in Sophie Hannigan's form leaning over the balustrade. It was decent enough, though if Giles had any gift at all, it was for allegory. Something about overly muscled, winged gods and fantastical creatures called to what talent he had—perhaps it was simply that no one had ever seen such creatures except in books, and so he didn't have to make them look real.

I left him there making endless alterations, and went out the door and down the stairs. Our place was small; no palazzo, this, but just a merchant's house, with a shop selling relics on the ground floor, owned by a Jew whose constantly circulating inventory of saint's parts suggested a connection either to the occult or a cemetery. He preferred his home in the Ghetto, as did his wife, apparently, because he rented out the rest of the house. There was a German couple on the middle floor, and Giles and I had the upper, reached by two flights of stairs leading from a courtyard that was mostly a repository of junk, and which included a well with a constant layer of greenish scum that neither Giles nor I would drink from, and a tumble of old black-smithing tools—don't ask me why; I don't know. I never saw anyone even look through them.

The chief attraction of the place was a roof garden, which was the reason we'd taken the rooms to begin with, and which only Giles ever visited in his constant search for the perfect land-scape—which apparently was an endless array of tiled roofs and the top of the Teatro La Fenice. Venice's most famous and beloved theater was closed now until the start of the Carnivale season, though Carnivale itself was nearly extinct but for a few costume balls given by those wishing to keep the old decadence alive.

I hurried out into the campo, and made my way to the Casa Dana Rosti. There, I drew back into the shadows of an upturned boat on the *fondamenta* of the adjacent palace and waited.

I was lucky—it was only an hour before I heard the squeak of her door, swollen in the humidity, scraping against the stone floor above the water stairs. The gondolier stepped out, leaving the door open behind him. A man—red haired, young, with that anxious exuberance she always inspired, at least in the begin-ning—emerged, adjusting his suit coat as if he'd just thrown it on. He glanced behind him as he walked toward the waiting gondola; his yearning obvious.

Behind him, I saw a flash of white, ephemeral as a ghost, and then she was there, her hair falling loose and heavy down her back, her gray eyes hooded. Venetian chain glinted at her wrists, coils and coils of fine gold, but other than that she wore only her chemise, and she was obviously naked beneath it. Her breasts jiggled as she embraced the red-haired man and then drew back, leaving him with a lingering kiss.

I forced myself to remember Barcelona, the things I'd seen in that darkened room, the horror. I watched as she smiled at him, as he left her reluctantly, climbing into the gondola. I burned his features into my memory until I knew I would not mistake him when I saw him again. He settled onto the cushions; she lifted her hand in farewell as she stepped back into the shadows, closing the door, and the gondolier plied his oar, gliding away.

I lurched from my hiding place, racing until I reached the *traghetto* station, just in time to see the glint of the sun on the man's red hair as the gondola made its way down the Grand Canal. There were gondoliers loitering about as always, waiting for fares, and I hired one quickly, saying, "You see that one there? I want to know where it goes."

He only nodded, setting off almost before I was aboard, and we followed, into the Rio de Ca' Corner, another turn, past San Anzolo. It came to a stop at the Campo San Maurizio, and the red-haired man got out. I disembarked quickly, hurrying to catch up.

But in just those few moments, he had disappeared—not a difficulty in Venice. I ran to the various *calli* that led from the campo, searching each of them. He was either moving more quickly than I'd thought, or he had taken none of them. Frustrated and annoyed, I went back to the campo. I stood beside the ubiquitous wellhead, staring down at its black stone cap, and wondered how it was possible to lose someone I'd been nearly close enough to touch.

He had to be somewhere around the Campo; he had disappeared too quickly for it to be otherwise. I sat on the stone steps of the wellhead, staring at the little church of San Maurizio. Tomorrow I would be better prepared; I would have a gondola waiting. I would be ready to follow him now that I knew for a certainty she'd found someone new.

I glanced up at the sky. It had to be close to five, and I still had to wash and dress. Wearily, I stood, meaning to make my way back to the rooms I shared with Giles, which fortunately were not far away.

And then I heard the organ music coming from the church, and I knew where the red-haired man had gone, and why she'd chosen him.

Slowly, I made my way up the shallow, narrow steps and walked through the open doors into the nave. There he was, sitting at the organ, his hands moving over the keys, shoulders rising and falling, feet pumping with a seemingly boundless energy.

I knew how that felt.

I closed my eyes, letting his music wash over me for a moment, listening to the things that had obviously called to her. There was no one else in the church—he was only rehearsing—and so I waited for the piece to end before going to stand beside him. As he leafed through a sheaf of music, I said, "Your playing is very good. Where did you train?"

He started as if he hadn't realized I was there, though I'd been standing right beside him. I saw the distraction in his expression—something else I recognized. "Oh. Oh, thank you. Thank you very much. I learned in Dublin."

An Irishman. And as pretty as she liked them. Strong features to go with a strong accent. I smiled. "You've given me several good hours, listening to your music. Perhaps you'd allow me to buy you a drink in thanks."

He hesitated. "Thank you, but I really must—"

"We have a friend in common, I think."

"We do?"

"Odilé León," I said smoothly.

"Odilé," he whispered, reverently.

I said, "I could tell you a hundred stories of her."

I saw the leap of curiosity in his eyes, his fevered longing. "A drink, you said? Well, why not?"

I got back to our rooms to find Giles waiting anxiously for me. "Hurry up, will you?" he said as I came through the door. "Did you forget the time? We told the Hannigans six."

After my conversation with San Maurizio's organist, I was more than ready to think of something other than Odilé. It never took much to reinvigorate my desire for her, and talking about her for an hour had been more than enough. I hated that she was still so hard to resist, even after everything. Odilé made my desire for Sophie Hannigan seem a paltry, ordinary thing compared to what I'd experienced before.

Or so I thought. But when Sophie Hannigan made her appearance in the lobby of the Danieli, followed closely by her brother, I did what I'd thought was impossible: I forgot Odilé.

Gone was the tightly corsetted, respectable-looking woman who'd spent the day with us in the Gardens. Tonight, Sophie Hannigan seemed to more properly belong to the bohemians. She wore a draped, full gown of a bluish-green color with medieval sleeves, her hair loosely gathered, looking ready to fall at the slightest touch. She looked as if she'd stepped from a Rossetti painting—some Pre-Raphaelite Lilith come to life. Giles was struck dumb, and I was not much better.

Joseph Hannigan wore the same dark blue coat he'd worn since I'd met him, but with it he wore a vest and brown trousers with a thin black stripe. He hadn't bothered to oil his hair, though it was swept back elegantly from his broad forehead. "Do you think us presentable enough? We weren't certain if tonight required evening wear."

The two of them were captivating; their strange alchemy hit me anew. Giles opened and closed his mouth as if his words had completely left him. I worked to gather myself.

"You'll fit in perfectly." I motioned to the door. "Shall we?"

We went out to the waiting gondola and settled ourselves, Hannigan and his sister on the center cushions, Giles and I perched awkwardly on the sides.

"Tea began at five," I told them as we started off. "But people will come and go all evening. It's a very casual sort of thing."

Hannigan nodded. "Who will be there tonight, do you think?"

I said, "Whistler probably. And the Curtises and their son—they're expatriates. Out of Boston, I believe. Mr. Curtis especially can be a bit tiresome."

"Prepare yourself to *not* defend your country," Giles put in. "He despises America. They both do."

"Why?" Miss Hannigan asked.

Giles said, "Something about your long-over War. I stopped listening to him weeks ago. Don't bring it up if you want to save your ears. And the rest of us from having to listen to it again."

"We'll remember," Hannigan said with a smile.

I went on, "Possibly Robert Browning. They're expecting him any day. And Frank Duveneck no doubt." I looked at Hannigan. "They'll want you to draw something in the guestbook. They like caricatures the best."

Hannigan's blue eyes sparkled with amusement. "Caricatures? Well, I can do that."

"What should I do?" Miss Hannigan asked.

"As I said this afternoon, simply be engaging."

There wasn't time for more conversation; we were there. Ca' Alvisi was square and plain, not so adorned as many of the other great palazzos of Venice, with a single row of balconies across only the main floor—the piano nobile. Our gondolier pulled up to the blue and white *pali* and let us off. A servant waiting in the archway said, "Welcome to the Ca' Alvisi," as he helped Miss Hannigan on the slippery, water-splashed steps.

He left us to make our own way through the darkened receiving court, with its paving stones and pillars and faint gaslight sputtering against pale walls and shadowing the corners, toward the stairs that led to the main floor, and the salon. Giles led the way while I followed behind the Hannigans. Miss Hannigan had her hand in the crook of her brother's arm, and he leaned close to whisper something to her, an intimacy that felt odd, off-putting and alluring at the same time. As we entered the *portego*, the tinkling music and laughter and smoke-filled rooms of Mrs. Bronson's salon met us full on.

The long, well-lit *portego*, with its glowing terrazzo floors, ended at the main balcony, which was outfitted with soft cushions, and looked out directly upon the glowing white dome and statues and porticoes of Santa Maria della Salute. It was crowded, as always, and as we entered, conversations paused, every eye turned to look at the Hannigans. So Giles and I weren't the only ones fascinated with them. I'll admit I liked the attention. I swelled a bit as I led them past the smaller drawing rooms—one of which had been made into a permanent miniature theater for our many impromptu dramas or readings—to the *sala* where Katharine Bronson held court.

It too had windowed doors that opened onto another narrow balcony, but even the air coming off the canal could not dissipate the cloud of cigar and cigarette smoke fogging the room, hovering near the exquisitely molded and painted ceilings and wisping around the dark velvet drapes.

There was the clinking of cups against saucers, tea poured from a silver service, sherry from Murano glass decanters. Arthur Bronson, Katharine's husband, stood talking to someone in the corner. I was surprised to see him; it was rumored he was ill, and he rarely made an appearance. Near the balcony, against a frescoed wall, was a settee upon which sat Katharine Bronson, resplendent in deep green silk, her brown hair artfully arranged above a kindly, animated face.

She was speaking to a small woman in delicate blue and a bewhiskered man in an ancient brown frock coat—the Peabodys—but she was situated facing the door. Katharine was a flawless hostess, and she managed both to look up as we stepped inside, and to grasp the attention of the couple she was speaking to without offending, forming, in essence, a greeting committee as Giles and I brought the Hannigans over.

"Mr. Dane and Mr. Martin!" she exclaimed, rising, holding out well-adorned hands, her interest in the twins sparkling as she took them in. "How good to see you both! And who is this you've brought?"

After introducing them, I added, "Hannigan is the most talented artist I've seen in a good while."

"Is he?" She grasped Joseph Hannigan's hands. She could hardly take her gaze from his face. "Well, I should dearly like to see. Where do you keep your studio, Mr. Hannigan?"

"Just now, in the open air of the Campo della Carita," he said with a smile. "Although Dane has shown me the beauties of the Riva, and I may move my studies there."

"Quite the wrong side, you know," she laughed. "Though our dear Mr. Whistler and Mr. Duveneck will persist in renting there. The sunsets are sublime."

"So I've heard, though I've yet to see one," Hannigan said.

"But we've rented nowhere yet. My sister and I are staying at the Danieli until we can find other lodgings."

"You mean to stay a time, then?"

"Until the spring, at least," he told her.

Katharine Bronson looked—finally—at me. "Well, Mr. Dane, I do hope you've given them some guidance. Surely we must be able to find something for them? Really, there is so much available, though one does have to watch the expense. They see 'American,' and somehow think we've all vaults of gold to spend."

"That's quite the way of it," Miss Hannigan agreed. "I did think I'd found a place, but it turned out not to suit after all."

How perfectly she did it—not a pause, nothing awkward, turning the conversation to what must surely follow—and the thing Katharine Bronson would be most keenly interested in.

I saw Katharine put it all together—the rumors she'd no doubt heard, Sophie Hannigan's name. She clasped the arm of the little Mrs. Peabody. "Oh my dear! You can't possibly be the same Miss Hannigan who found poor Mr. Stafford?"

"I'm afraid I am."

"Was it as bad as we heard?" Mrs. Peabody asked breathlessly. "It must have been dreadful. I'm quite certain I couldn't have borne it."

"Did you know him well?" Miss Hannigan asked.

Mrs. Bronson nodded. "He was a fixture here for a time. But then, recently, I'm afraid, he fell in love and fell away. We all missed him."

"The landlady said he hadn't been eating," Miss Hannigan told them. "She said he told her he could live on love. So romantic, don't you think? And yet, so sad."

I was impressed with that too—the pretty story she made of it in only a few words. It reminded me fiercely of the Gardens and her tale of Mestre.

Mrs. Bronson tsked. "Miss Hannigan, you must tell us everything. If it's not too disturbing of course. And Mr. Dane, perhaps you could find our dear Whistler. I heard he arrived nearly ten minutes ago. I know he'd be delighted to meet Mr. Hannigan."

She took Miss Hannigan's hand and drew her to the settee. Sophie Hannigan gave her brother a quick, assured glance.

Hannigan turned to me. "Lead on."

I felt a bit smug as I took him out of the drawing room and into another. Katharine had offered to help them, which meant she liked them both—and that I had gained more cachet. "Your sister's well positioned to make a success. As will you be, if you can cultivate Whistler. If he takes a liking to you, you'll be in with Duveneck and the rest of them."

"You're very kind to take such an interest," Hannigan said.

"Well, if you make a success of it, I'll be the one who discovered you," I told him with a smile. "They won't soon forget it."

"That matters to you?" Hannigan's gaze was piercing; I felt he saw something in me I wasn't certain I wanted him to see.

"How can it not? Not all of us are lucky enough to be creative geniuses. Some of us must make our mark in different ways."

"But . . . your poetry—"

"I haven't written a word in years. My vision is gone, I'm sorry to say."

Hannigan looked puzzled. "How?"

It was taken. Leeched away by a demon I used to love. Well, how could I tell him any of that?

Hannigan watched me intently, as if my answer mattered greatly to him. It was flattering; it made me want to say something true. But all I had was, "It just left me."

"I would be lost," he said simply, in a tone that said he understood my sorrow and my bitterness, and I felt known in a way I never had before, steeped in his regard as if we were compatriots, brothers in art. I had to remind myself that we'd met only two days ago.

"Well, I doubt it will happen to you," I said. "Your inspiration seems little inclined to leave you."

He raised a brow.

"Your sister," I explained.

"Yes." The word was quiet, reverent. It spoke of something that beckoned and repelled at the same time. "She might inspire you too, Dane, given the chance."

They were just words, a casual statement. Meaningless. But suddenly I was thinking of all the ways Sophie Hannigan might inspire me as if he'd deliberately planted such erotic visions in my head.

It was my own desire, of course, my jealousy over the obvious strength of the bond between them. My own muse had been so fickle and inconstant. How nice it must be to have one tethered by blood and love.

We had come into the dining room, and Whistler sat at the table, wearing his distinctive, wide-brimmed brown hat, the white streak in his otherwise curly and nearly black hair falling over one eye. He had a piece of paper before him, and he was sketching, quick, forceful lines that reminded me of that confidence I'd noticed when I'd first seen Hannigan.

I leaned close to say, "Ah, there he is now, the venerable lion. You'll have to kowtow just a bit. If he likes you, he'll try to take you for a few francs here and there . . . it's best just to give in and think of it as a gift. He's a character, there's no doubt, and he's not above taking advantage of his eccentricity."

"Well, he has the right, doesn't he? He's a genius."

"And bankrupt after that lawsuit against Ruskin," I said. "Charm him, Hannigan, and this whole society will be eating out of your hands."

"I'll do my best."

"Come, let me introduce you." I led him across the room. Whistler looked up at our approach. When we reached the table, he took up the monocle falling below his narrow black ribbon tie, and held it to one eye. "Dane!" he called out. "I've been to the Rio Mendicanti twice. I've yet to see that colored water you've told me about."

"Perhaps the dyer is out of town," I said easily. "I'd like to introduce you to a friend of mine. Joseph Hannigan."

Whistler peered at him. "Hannigan? Any relation to the Boston Hannigans?"

Hannigan said with a smile, "I'm a great admirer of yours, sir. And very pleased to know you."

"What are you? A poet like Dane here?"

"Words aren't my strong suit, no."

"He's an artist. And a great talent," I put in. "I met him at the Accademia."

"Drawing the Salute like the other hacks?" Whistler asked.

Hannigan laughed. "I'm more interested in other views." He pulled out a chair and sat down at the table as if we'd been invited, a bit of hubris that both startled and impressed me.

Whistler frowned, though I thought he was impressed, too. "You don't want the views of the lagoon or the sunset off the Riva?"

"Well, they're beautiful, aren't they? But there's something more here." Hannigan looked as if he were searching for the right words. "Some . . . I don't know . . . sadness, I suppose."

"Sadness? Why yes, yes." Whistler said. "The melancholy is like nothing I've ever seen. The natives themselves—such want coupled with such beauty."

"Yes, I know exactly what you mean," Hannigan said. "The other day I saw a courtyard off San Bartolomeo more splendid even than a Venetian sunset."

Whistler raised a brow. "San Bartolomeo? Flowers and such?"

Hannigan shook his head. "Cracked paving with weeds between the stones. A simple wellhead. Stairs pitted by the weather, and a statue black with mildew in all the right places. I saw a woman there, one of those beadworkers. She had that reddish hair that Titian did so beautifully. And she wore one of those"—here, he gestured to his shoulders—"those old black shawls. The light was sublime. Everything decaying so prettily. Melancholy, as you said. Beautiful."

He'd been in Venice for two days, and I'd been with him for most of that. When had he had time to search out a courtyard off San Bartolomeo's campo?

Then I saw how he'd snared Whistler. Hannigan had said he had no skill with words, but, like his sister, he'd painted a picture as vivid as the one I'd seen in his sketchbook. Just as he'd done with me, I realized. That understanding, that perception . . . he had known exactly what would make Whistler pay attention.

Whistler shoved the piece of paper he'd been drawing over toward Hannigan. "Show me."

It was a test, of course, but when Hannigan reached into his pocket and took out a stick of charcoal, I saw Whistler's faint smile and knew Hannigan had passed at least one part of it. No real artist went anywhere without something to draw with, I supposed. Hannigan pulled the paper toward him, and in a few strokes he had the outline of the girl, the courtyard, the ruined paving stones. Whistler lifted a bushy eyebrow, obviously dazzled, as was I, all over again. I felt a warm pride and satisfaction that reminded me of why I'd brought him here. If Whistler was any indication—and he was—they were all going to love Joseph Hannigan, and that meant he would be a child of the salon, and kept busy enough that he would have no chance to happen upon Odilé.

Whistler put his hand on Hannigan's, stopping him mid-scrawl. Hannigan looked up.

"What was your name again?" Whistler asked sharply.

"Joseph Hannigan."

"Tell me where you come from," Whistler said. "Where did you get your training?"

Hannigan's smile was quick and blinding. As I watched him wrap James Whistler around his finger, I wondered suddenly if he'd done the same to me, if I'd unwittingly fallen into some trap. Then I pushed the feeling away. I was too cynical by nature, as Giles often told me. And as I watched Hannigan bind Whistler ever more tightly with his charm—as alluring in his way as his sister was in hers—my curiosity about them grew stronger than ever.

FOURTEEN

SOPHIE

The Bronson salon was the reason we'd chosen Venice. When New York City became impossible, the Bronsons—and their influence and patronage—became our lodestone. They, more than anyone in New York, had the power to make something of Joseph's talent. Now, to have everything we'd always wanted within our grasp, and so much more easily than I'd expected . . . it was somehow unreal. I hadn't quite believed it when Joseph and I had stepped into the Alvisi.

But when I saw the way people turned to look at my brother, the way his beauty and his charisma drew them to him, it no longer felt illusory, but instead all too familiar. It had been so long since I'd been at a salon or supper or any gathering of society that I'd forgotten the way Joseph attracted attention. The gazes of women and men alike slipped past me to look at him. And while I understood better than anyone his irresistible appeal, I sometimes wished that just once someone would look at me first. That I was not always in his shadow, that there was something in the world that could belong just to me. To truly be as special on my own terms as Joseph said I was—sometimes my yearning for it was so strong it took me by surprise.

But then again, I knew that everything we wanted depended on Joseph and always had. His talent and beauty would make our fortune. We were special, bound together for a reason. We had survived for a reason. All I had to do was remind myself of that, and I could put such selfish wishes away.

Just as I put them away now, as Mrs. Bronson smiled at me. I banished my nervousness and became the Sophie Hannigan we needed me to be. I told Mrs. Bronson and Mrs. Peabody the story of Mr. Stafford, embellishing, painting it as I liked, with romance and tragedy, along with just enough lurid detail to fascinate. Then I shuddered dramatically and told them how dreamlike it was, the discovery of the body and indeed of Venice itself.

Mrs. Bronson looked enthralled. She touched my arm. "Oh, we all feel so, my dear. And it will get stronger the longer you stay, I promise. There are some who cannot tolerate it at all. I'm afraid despondency runs rampant among our countrymen if they stay too long."

It was what Mr. Dane had said as well. "But you've managed to escape it, I think."

"I adore the city," she said. "I find such things interesting rather than enervating, though God save us all from the wretched scirocco. Come summer, it can sap your very will."

"And the mosquitos," put in Mrs. Peabody.

"Indeed." Mrs. Bronson nodded emphatically. "But the place is simply too hard to resist. The stories alone . . ."

"Not everyone finds them as you do, my dear," said Mrs. Peabody. "Most of us find the legends quite appalling."

"Legends?" I asked.

Mrs. Bronson said eagerly, "Ghost stories, myths . . . most of them quite awful, actually. Tales of devils walking bridges and terrible bargains. There isn't a gondolier in Venice who doesn't know each one, and they wouldn't hesitate to tell you if you asked. The Venetians are the most superstitious people in the world. 'It's bad luck to walk between the columns in the Piazzetta; a guest who crumples his napkin will never return to your table; if you see a humpback, you'll have good fortune . . .' There are a hundred other things. They don't actually *believe* in anything, you understand, so much as they have the *habit* of believing."

"Except for ghosts. They *do* believe in ghosts," added Mrs. Peabody.

"Ghosts, yes." Mrs. Bronson sighed. "And to be honest, I'm not certain they're wrong. I would never have taken those rooms, my dear, and the tragedy for the *padrona* is that no one else will either."

"Unless they don't know about poor Mr. Stafford," Mrs. Peabody said.

"How will they not? The Venetians are terrible gossips."

"That is true, I'm afraid."

Mrs. Bronson patted my hand reassuringly. "Never worry, my dear. We'll find the perfect place for you and your brother. In fact, I could have sworn I'd seen rooms for rent near one of the *traghettos*—"

"Oh no, you don't want that! The gondoliers camp out there, and the noise will keep you up all night." Mrs. Peabody shuddered expressively.

"I would appreciate hearing of anything," I told her with relief. "There was another lovely place off the Campo San Bartolomeo, but the landlady and I couldn't reach an agreement on the price."

"You should take someone with you," Mrs. Peabody suggested. "Someone who knows the city. Perhaps Mr. Dane—he knows his way about better than anyone."

"I hate to impose upon him more than I already have."

"Oh, but I'm certain he would be disappointed if you did not. He's the most helpful man I know—don't you think so, Anna?"

Mrs. Peabody nodded so hard it looked as if her neck might snap. "So very helpful. Indispensable, I would say. And entertaining too. We all love him."

"He found Giacomo for the Loneghans, remember? Their gondolier," she said to me. "Henry and Edith adore Mr. Dane. I believe their families are old friends. Do you know of the Loneghans, Miss Hannigan? Henry is quite the art collector. Mr. Dane is always looking for artists to present to him."

I tried very hard not to look as interested as I was. "Mr. Dane seems to know everyone in Venice."

"I don't know how he does it, to be honest, but if you need anything at all, the first person to ask is Nicholas Dane. If he doesn't know himself how to find it, he knows someone who does."

"He's been here that long?"

"Oh no, but I think he must make knowing everything his business—how else would he do it?" said Mrs. Peabody. "When did we first meet him, Katharine? Oh . . . it was at the theater, wasn't it? That night at the Malibran."

"Oh yes," said Mrs. Bronson, her expression mellowing in memory. "I remember a great deal of wine."

Mrs. Peabody's eyes were shining as she told me, "Mr. Dane knew Giovanni Lotti, who'd played the lead that night. Such a sublime performance! The crowd was quite large, but once Mr. Dane discovered who we hoped to meet, he got us backstage. We spent the entire evening with them."

"It's not the only debt we owe him. Especially after tonight, because he brought you into our midst, my dear." Mrs. Bronson smiled at me. "He always seems to know just who will best suit."

Had I needed more evidence that Joseph was right—and that I should keep to our plan regarding Nicholas Dane—her comment provided it. "I hope my brother and I don't disappoint you."

"Oh, never imagine so!" She glanced past me, then said in a low voice, "Here's someone else who will be anxious to hear your news of Mr. Stafford. Mr. Curtis—have you met him, Miss Hannigan? He and his wife and son are particular favorites of mine. They've been in Venice some time. Let me introduce you."

The next hour or so went on like that, with new arrivals coming in, and Mrs. Bronson drawing me into conversation, until I'd told the story of finding Mr. Stafford a half-dozen times, and the whole room knew of my search for lodgings. But Katharine Bronson listened raptly every time, and asked new questions with every listener. I wondered how she did it, and whether such charm was something one could learn.

Finally my throat was so dry I excused myself to get a glass of sherry. It was very good sherry, and I savored it as I looked toward the open balcony doors and beyond, to the impossible beauty of the Santa Maria della Salute across the Canal, the whole of it— golden angels with spears and horns and translucent white domes—struck pink and gold and blinding in the sunset. Again, it seemed impossible that I should be here, that we were so close. It only needed Henry Loneghan to make everything complete.

I turned from the view and moved through the crowd, past the laughter and talk and out of the *sala*, through the smaller rooms filled with smoke and people, searching for my brother. At last, I saw him—sitting at the dining room table, laughing with a black-haired man in a hat and one other, neither of whom I recognized, and Nicholas Dane. My brother held a sketchbook—not his own—and he was drawing something as Mr. Dane leaned over his shoulder.

Joseph looked happy. In his element. It reminded me of the time after our aunt had died, when Joseph had left school and taken up with the bohemians in New York City. *You'll love them, Soph. They're our kind of people.* And they were. The first time I'd seen him among them, I'd known it was where he belonged. I had never seen him laugh so easily except with me. Now I looked from my brother to Nicholas Dane, and was more resolved than ever to capture him for Joseph—and with him, Henry Loneghan.

My brother glanced at me. He gave me a quick nod, and then turned to say something to Mr. Dane, who looked in my direction. Then Mr. Dane was pushing through the crowd toward me, saying, "Your brother's sent me to fetch you. He's made friends of Whistler and Frank Duveneck. Come and meet them."

As he turned to lead me back, I caught his arm. "I don't want to intrude."

"You won't be intruding. In fact, you'll only increase Whistler's liking for your brother. He has an eye for attractive women."

"Does he?" I asked, and then, quietly, "Do you?"

He stopped short, looking surprised. "Pardon?"

I felt the heat rush into my face, but I pushed on. "I asked if you had an eye for attractive women. Or, I suppose . . . for women in general."

His expression became careful, wary. "Why do you wish to know?"

"Perhaps because I'm interested."

"You're interested in whether I have unnatural desires?"

"That wasn't really my question, but I suppose—"

"What about you, Miss Hannigan? Do you like men in general? Or perhaps . . . you have a special liking for one in particular?"

He glanced toward the table as he said it, to Joseph, and I went cold, thinking of gossip, of Edward, but then I thought, *no, there is nothing in it.* He had only casually glanced that way. He was merely asking if my feelings were otherwise engaged, and I supposed that was a good thing. My hand was still on his arm. I tightened my fingers and lowered my voice and said, "I am quite unattached, Mr. Dane. But I must admit I find you interesting. I suppose I'd hoped . . . you might find me interesting too."

I held my breath, wondering how he might answer, if I'd read him correctly. Some men did not like such directness, but he had not responded to subtlety at the Gardens.

He glanced down at the glass I held in my other hand. "You look as if you could use another drink."

Too direct, then. I'd read him wrong, as I'd read him wrong nearly from the beginning. Nicholas Dane was not going to be so easy as Joseph had thought. He obviously wasn't attracted to me. Perhaps it would be best just to leave him to my brother.

I sighed, disappointed, frustrated, and released Mr. Dane's arm, trying to smile. I held out my glass to him. "Yes, please. Sherry."

He took my glass and gestured to Joseph. "I'll meet you there." Then he pushed into the crowd.

I watched him go, and then I went over to where my brother sat laughing with the others.

It was after midnight when Joseph and I finally returned to the Danieli. My brother fell onto the bed, throwing an arm over his eyes. "I've had too much to drink."

"No one would know it." I lay on my stomach next to him. "You were brilliant."

"As were you, I think." He pulled at one of my hairpins until a coil of hair tumbled to my shoulder. "I saw you with Dane earlier. He looked entranced."

"He's not," I told him miserably. "Do you know what he asked me tonight? He asked me if I had special feelings for any particular man."

Joseph pulled loose another pin. I shook my head a little, letting my hair fall. "He's only asking if you're taken. That means he's interested."

"I thought he looked at you when he said it. I wondered if . . . if he'd heard—"

"No one we know is in Venice, Soph," he reassured me quietly. "And it was only rumors anyway. I have the sketches. No one saw them."

"Yes, I know, but—"

"Did he admit to liking you?"

"No. No, in fact, he quite pointedly ignored the question. I don't think I'm going to get very far with him, Joseph. I think it might be better if you handle him. He wants to be your friend. He already likes you so much."

He curled a strand of my hair around his finger. "He's fighting his desires. I don't know why."

"He's hard for me to read."

"But not hard for me." He looked up at me with the full force of his dark blue gaze. "Trust me. He wants you. Keep trying. We'll think of something he can't ignore."

I tried to hide my dismay. Joseph was not usually wrong when it came to people, but in this case, I thought he was. I saw only futility in my pursuit of Nicholas Dane. He was handsome enough to have his choice of women—why should he look twice at me?

But I only sighed and nodded, changing the subject. "Did you like Whistler? I couldn't tell."

Joseph shrugged. "He's brilliant, there's no doubt. I can learn from him, and I will. And he fits in well there. He's eccentric and he says what he thinks. He's everything they want to believe about artists."

"And he doesn't speak of money."

"He doesn't, though he thinks of it." Joseph laughed. "He thinks of it a great deal. He and I are alike that way. He knows what I do: those people like to pretend money means nothing. They'll run from anyone who finds it important."

"Well, they have plenty of it, don't they?"

He went quiet again, twisting a strand of my hair into a paintbrush of sorts, running the soft ends over his mouth. "These people make stars, Soph. Never doubt it."

I didn't. I'd seen it in the way Mrs. Bronson turned me into the guest *du jour*. "Well, you were shining tonight. The brightest in the heavens. They love you already."

"We've been given carte blanche," he said. "Welcome any-time. You heard her say it, didn't you?"

I nodded. He smiled, and then he frowned again just as quickly. "God, I nearly forgot." He let go of my hair and reached for his sketchbook on the bedside table, along with a stub of charcoal. He drew something quickly, and then handed it to me.

"Is that it?" he demanded. "That courtyard you told me of, the one with the bead girl?"

"The one off San Bartolomeo?" I looked down at the sketch. He'd captured it almost perfectly, from only the words I'd told him. "Yes, that's it, but the stairs were on the other side."

His forehead furrowed. "I wonder if that matters. Perhaps he'll just think I misremembered it."

"Who?"

"Whistler." His frown became a satisfied smile. "It was how I caught his attention today. Drawing it for him. I could tell by

116

speaking to him that he had no interest in the usual views. He's looking for something more sublime. I agreed with him and showed him this."

His cleverness astonished me, as it always did. "Oh, Joseph, this *is* going to work!"

I nestled into his side, laying my head on his chest. "You'll be the most famous artist in Venice before next year."

"You mean in the world," he said, his voice rumbling against my ear, his long fingers pressing into my shoulder.

I put my arm around his waist, holding him tight. "In the world," I agreed.

FIFTEEN

NICHOLAS

I was impatient and irritable all day. I disliked waiting. Idleness annoyed me—I was too easily bored, too restless—and I was troubled by the way my mind leaped to things I did not want to be thinking about.

Twilight softened the usual blur of Venice, melting edges, holding them in wavering suspension. The chill of fall was in the air now, and as I pulled my suit coat closer, I tried not to think of Joseph and Sophie Hannigan and the desires her words had raised. *I'd hoped you might find me interesting too.*

I cursed beneath my breath, banishing them both to some far part of my mind, ordering myself to concentrate as I came upon the cafe where the organist had agreed to meet me again tonight. I had told him what I'd told all the others, trying my best to persuade him, but as much as I wanted to win him, I was not sanguine about my chances. How often had I done so, after all? Once or twice perhaps, out of dozens.

I went inside and ordered a bottle of wine, poured a glass, and drank it slowly, waiting. The time came and went; still I waited. An hour passed, and then two. I'd half expected him not to show. He was no better than Nelson Stafford, than any of the others—still enraptured with her, even as she was draining him to nothing.

But then the door opened, and I saw with surprise that it was him. He came over to the table, giving me a guilty look, which told me better than words what he'd decided. "I wasn't going to come. But then I thought you should know. I don't want to leave her. I love her."

Well, that wasn't news, was it?

Still, I smiled. "Then perhaps you'll prove me wrong about her. I hope you do. Come and have a drink with me."

"I'm to meet her—"

"Not until later, I think," I said. "Am I right? I won't keep you from her, I promise. But we're friends now, and surely a friend can spare the time for a glass of wine."

He said, "Very well. But this time you must let me pay."

I cannot remember what we talked of—perhaps he told me his life story; they often did. We ordered more wine, emptying three bottles. He drank most of it.

It was late when he finally staggered to his feet, saying, "I must go. She's expecting me."

"Let me walk you there," I said, though I intended to do no such thing. He was drunk enough that I thought I could get him to his own rooms without a struggle. Even a night away from her would help him.

He wavered, catching himself on the edge of the table. "I can do it."

"Oh, I don't think you can, my friend." I rose and put a hand on his arm. "But I'll see that you get there without falling into a canal."

"Oh yes." He frowned. "I can't swim. Perhaps . . . a gondola—"

"So late, you'll never find one. It's only a short walk to the *traghetto* station."

We stumbled out of the cafe. He fell into me at the door, and then again in the street, bouncing from the wall to my shoulder until I grabbed him to keep him from plunging into the canal that the *calle* opened into. He gave me a grateful smile. "You're a good friend, Dane," he slurred. "Have I told you that? A very good friend."

We turned onto a narrow *fondamenta*. A flickering candle from one of the hundreds of corner shrines reflected across the dark silk of the canal running alongside. He stopped, reaching out to finger the petals of a rose that had been left for the saint. A glazed porcelain statue of the Virgin was set within the alcove, the candle casting a soft shine over her—someone had cared for her recently, as there was no sign of mildew or dirt. She looked polished and only a little worn. Bouquets of dead flowers lay about, little plates of half-eaten food, no doubt nibbled at by the huge river rats, all left for her consideration, gifts for prayers granted or hoped for.

Murphy took up the rose. It was pink and tied with black grosgrain. He swayed as he put it to his nose and frowned. "There's no smell. She wouldn't like it. She likes the smell."

"So she does," I said softly. "And it's bad luck to take anything from the shrines."

He dropped the rose back at the Virgin's feet.

"Has she told you her stories?" I asked.

The candlelight lit him oddly, sending one half of his face into shadow while the other half looked yellow and jaundiced, his eye watery and glittering. He put his hand to the wall near the altar as if the world were spinning. "Stories? Something 'bout . . . Schumann."

"Schumann?"

"He saw angels."

"Has she told you of John Keats? The tale of his Lamia?"

"What's that?"

"His poem," I said impatiently. "Have you never read it?"

He shook his head. The motion seemed to dizzy him. He staggered, catching the wall hard with a shoulder. "I'm not much for poetry."

"'Lamia' was about her. About Odilé. She was John Keats's inspiration."

"His inspiration? But . . . wait—isn't he dead?"

"Some fifty years or so ago. One of the disadvantages of her patronage, I'm afraid."

"Fifty years? But then how—" He put his hand to his head. "I've had too much wine."

I pressed, "How could she have been his Lamia, you mean? If he's fifty years dead? She could not be so old, could she? Look at her—such a beauty. Why, you'd think her not above thirty-five. But that's all a lie. She's very old, my friend. Older than you or I can fathom. Two hundred years or more, I think, though I'm not completely certain. She's never told me, you see. I've had to guess."

He looked at me blearily. "Two hundred years? What're you saying? I don't understand."

"No, of course not." I stepped close. "She *is* Lamia, don't you see? The serpent who turned into a woman, who seduced Lycius with her beauty. It was Odilé that Keats described. He saw the horror of her, but he died before he could tell the world. But I'm here now to do it for him. I know what she is."

"A serpent?"

121

"She's draining the talent from you. She inspires you now, but in a few days, you won't be able to compose—her hunger will take everything from you."

He stepped away from the wall, frowning, wavering. "You're not making sense. How could she do that? How could anyone?"

I let out my breath in frustration. "My God, must I put it in words an imbecile could understand?"

He blinked. "Why are you telling me all this? What has it to do with anything?"

It was useless, as pointless as it ever was. "She's a succubus, you fool."

He started, jerking away from me, too fast, losing his balance. I reached for him just as he flailed again for the wall, this time missing it. His head cracked hard against the brick. His eyes rolled back, and he crumpled, unconscious, onto the edge of the narrow *fondamenta*, rolling into the canal with a soft but heavy splash—all before I could do a thing to help him.

I fell to my knees to grab for him, but he was already out of reach, sinking below the surface, slipping away so that my fingers only brushed him but there was nothing I could grasp. I could not swim, and so I could do nothing but watch him disappear beneath the murky black. He bobbed and then he was gone, leaving nothing but bubbles, sinking to a shallow and watery grave, food for the crabs and the rats that haunted the canals.

I kneeled on the *fondamenta*, watching the surface of the canal. He did not rise again, and the water returned to its quiet lap as if nothing had disturbed it. I stayed there, staring, for a very long time, feeling failure and sorrow and a terrible dismay. I closed my eyes and said a quick prayer for his soul. I told myself it was a better fate than what had awaited him. A mercy, in fact. Then I climbed to my feet and walked away.

SIXTEEN

NICHOLAS

"A*h! Vanitas Vanitatum! Which of us is happy in this world? Which of us has his desire? or, having it, is satisfied?*"

Thackeray could have been talking about me when he wrote those words. There were times when I felt that my inability to be satisfied was the defining element of my character. Add to that impetuousness and impatience, and you will understand why, when I was twenty-two, my father asked me to leave home.

He didn't put it quite that way, of course. What he really said was, "It's time to put these scribblings behind you, my boy, and find something that will pay you a good wage. I can't support you forever, you know."

My father was a barrister with political aspirations, and he raised his children to be examples of his intelligence, charm, and reliability. My older brother, Jonathan, took up the banner and ran with it, deciding early to follow in our father's footsteps and study law. My younger sister, Amelie, married very well, bringing a fortune to help support my father's—and my brother's—ambition. I was the only failure, leaning as I did toward study and poetry—what could a scholar ever be but a teacher?

I felt I was better than that. I knew, somehow, deep in my soul, that I had the talent to be something special, to be the kind of poet who influenced and inspired others. But when I told my mother this, she only smiled and patted my cheek and said, "You needn't try so hard, Nicholas. Jonathan will make a splash for all of us. He's quite brilliant. You know, I wonder sometimes how you can belong to us. No one else in the family has such an interest in books."

"Perhaps I was a changeling," I told her, and the truth was I felt it. If there was a family in the world to which I did not belong, it was my own.

But I felt no real impetus to leave it either. I had no great love for suffering, and I was as aware as my father of the difficulties of making a living as a poet, and so I stayed until people began asking questions about my prospects, until my father began to look toward an arranged marriage with whatever heiress he could find who might not think an idle scribbler too great a burden. When he found one, a Miss Isabelle Blakely, who it seemed liked the look of me, if nothing else—"It's a blessing that you're at least graced with good looks," Father said—I knew I no longer had any choice but to go. Isabelle Blakely was long nosed and weasel faced, and pretending I was enthusiastic about bedding her, not to mention spending the rest of my life with her, was more than I could do.

So I left. I had no plans and little money—only what my mother pressed into my hand and what my sister, out of sentiment, provided, a small stipend that my father knew nothing of. She kissed me as I left and said, "Don't get lost, Nick. Promise me to keep in touch."

"Well I shall have to, won't I? If I'm to receive your contribution to my great escape."

She laughed. "Yes. So you see, I've my hooks in you yet. And I shall keep them there, my dear, until you find your way home again."

Which I planned rarely to do. But the money was little enough, and I knew Amelie would not miss it, and that she liked the idea of having me in her debt, so I didn't feel guilty over it either.

I had one or two successes, nothing stellar, but enough to make me believe—wrongly, as it turned out—that I was well on my way to finding the recognition I craved. I published a small book of poems. When I sent a copy to my father, it occasioned not even a reply. The book garnered decent reviews, one critic going so far as to say, "Dane is a talent, if a lesser one." That stung, but I held the words *a talent* close and tried to ignore the rest. It became a motivation to prove the second part of the review wrong. All I needed was some new scenery, some inspiration. The publication brought me funds enough to travel for a few months, so I set off for Paris. Twenty-three years old, and with a burning ambition of my own, to become the poet everyone said I could not be.

I had an ease with people born of years of being paraded before the most well-connected and influential in London, better-than-decent looks, and a faith that doors would open for me wherever I went, which, for the most part, they did. Paris was the city of my dreams; I had rooms overlooking a picturesque market, and I made friends of other expatriates, like-minded artists and writers. If there existed a place on earth where I might find the success I longed for, I thought Paris must be it.

Instead, it was where I found her.

She had the kind of beauty to strike a man dumb. Dark hair heavily threaded with red. Gray eyes, slightly slanted, as if there'd been some Eastern stain in her ancestry, that made one think of Circassian women and harem girls and unbridled, exotic sex. Her unblemished skin held those dusky Eastern undertones as well. And her body . . . large, full breasts, shapely hips. She was older than I by probably ten years, but that only added to her appeal. She had a ready laugh, and there was a frankness to her that startled, a will to take what she wanted that younger women didn't possess. Experience, I suppose, but it was more than that. It was as if she held innumerable secrets, and she held them like a temptation and a challenge—*discover what I know, and I can show you the world.* I could not imagine anyone walking away from her. God knew I couldn't.

I stumbled into her as I stepped from a bookstore, and she invited me for a glass of wine. It wasn't until much later that I thought to wonder why a woman like that would want me—though I'd had my share of pretty women, and I was not ignorant of my own attributes, she seemed well beyond my reach. But when she proffered the invitation, I was thinking with a different part of my anatomy, and impetuously—my flaw again—I accepted. As the evening wore on, and she cajoled my stories from me, I didn't realize how few of her own she revealed. When, after hours of my half-drunken revelations, she put her hand on my thigh and purred that she wanted to take me home, I nearly spilled my wine in my impatience to go wherever she might take me.

I barely noticed the rooms or what part of the city they were in. I could not have found my way there again if she'd chosen to abandon me that night. All I knew was a peeling green door, unlit narrow stone stairs, the smell of damp and her. She gave off a scent I cannot describe: musk and almond, subtle and pervasive—it made me mad with desire. It seemed I'd been hard for hours by that time; she no sooner unlocked the door than I pushed her through it. Before I knew it, I was naked and her hands were all over me, drawing me down to the floor, the glow of streetlamps through the window casting shadows on her perfect skin. I felt I could pump her for hours, for nights, for days. I felt unstoppable, invulnerable. The energy that coursed through my veins, the smell of her, the taste of her . . . I understand it now, but at the time it was so foreign to me I couldn't begin to comprehend it. Had I died in that moment, I would have felt complete.

I don't know how long I was in those rooms with her. Days, I suppose. Weeks. She told me a story of John Keats I'd never heard. That he had despaired of ever having fame, that he knew he was destined for an early death and expected his poems to fall into obscurity. "Here lies a name that was writ in water," was what he'd wanted on his tombstone.

"But there was a woman," she said in her strangely accented voice—French, but faint, corrupted by something else, something obscure.

"A woman?" I asked. "You mean his fiancée—what was her name? Fanny something?"

"No." She shook her head so her hair trailed across my chest where she lay in my arms. "A different woman. His greatest inspiration, it was said. The woman he wrote 'Lamia' for."

I quoted it, because I was vain enough to want to impress her. "'She seem'd, at once, some penanced lady elf, Some demon's mistress, or the demon's self . . .'"

She turned her head into my chest so I felt her smile. I felt her lips move against my skin, felt, rather than heard, her say, "Yes. That one."

"She truly must have been his inspiration then. It's a beautiful poem."

"I have always thought so," she said. "Though like all poets, he exaggerates."

"Like all poets?" I teased.

She ran her hand down my chest to my navel, slowly, steadily. "No one knows about the woman. They believe he was inspired by a dream or a vision. No one sees that it was really about her." Her hand crept lower. I felt myself stir, aroused again so quickly. "And, like every woman, she did not receive her due."

It was all I could do to say, "Yes she did. She was immortalized in 'Lamia.'"

"Spoken like a man," she whispered into my ear. "Will you forget me that way, I wonder? When the poems you've written for me are published, will you tell no one my name?"

I had written so many in these days with her. My best work, I knew. She fired me like nothing else ever had. I could not write quickly enough. "I'll tell the whole world," I said, rolling her onto her back and plunging into her so she stiffened and gasped in pleasure. "I'll let no one forget what you are to me."

She told me of Byron, of how many women he'd had in Venice, and the one among them who had been the most important of all, the one who inspired *Don Juan*, but who had gone unrecognized. "He wrote a hundred lines or more a night," she told me as she stood against the window, silhouetted in the early morning light. "He was insatiable—both for her and for words. It was as if he found them in the very air."

I was impressed that any man had the strength to write a hundred lines in a night.

"The story," she went on, "is that she made him an offer. She promised fame and fortune. She vowed to be his greatest inspiration."

"And what did he say?" I asked.

"He disdained fame—or so he said. He wanted everyone to think he hated it. He wanted to pluck fame out." She made a sharp, fast motion with her fingers to illustrate. "He said he did not want to be beholden to a woman. They had already caused him such problems."

"His wife, you mean. It's said he hated her."

"He hated what he'd done to her," she corrected softly. "She alone knew his cruelty—how could he forgive her for that? But no, it was his sister's betrayal that burned most painfully."

I frowned. "His sister?"

"They were lovers, you know," she said, turning fully from the window. "It was why he left England. It wasn't the scandal of his marriage, but his affair with his sister. Ah, no . . . that's right . . . she was only his half-sister. Does that make a difference?"

"Not in England."

"Well, in the end, even she was no match for his new muse. He was . . . overcome. Or so the story goes. And while he needed no more fame, he wanted immortality. He wanted to guarantee his genius would live on. And he could not deny the inspiration she brought him. Once he'd felt it, none other could compare. So he accepted her offer. But he grew arrogant and left her before *Don Juan* was finished, and so . . . it never was. A pity, isn't it?"

"Is this true? How do you know it?"

She came to the bed, which was covered with my papers, covered with words, and kneeled on the edge. "Why, everyone knows it, my love. If you go to Venice, you'll hear whispers of it still."

But I was confused. "Her offer, you said. What offer was it he accepted?"

"I told you. She inspired him to immortal genius."

"And in return?"

"His very soul, of course."

She pushed aside the papers and pulled up her chemise to straddle my hips. "Would you have taken such a bargain, if she had offered it to you?"

"Why not? Isn't that what inspiration is? Losing your soul to something more sublime?"

She pushed away the sheet between us, wriggled so she was against me, burning hot. Her hands were on me, and I let the notebook and the pencil I held fall away. She kissed me softly. "Oh how well you understand it, my love."

But the truth was that I didn't understand at all, not until much later.

When did things begin to change? It's hard to remember now, but it couldn't have been more than a month. For days before that, words had been jumbling in my head. The simplest things eluded me. *Angel* became *goddess* because suddenly I could not remember how to spell the former, and the rhyme never came right after. I could not find the words to describe her mouth. I reached back through my memory, trying to find inspiration from others. Songs of Solomon. Keats. Byron and Browning and Coleridge and Shelley. I could not retain more than fragments of what I'd always known. Then one day I woke before she did. I sat up, noting the way the morning shadows fell across her face, feeling the beginnings of a poem stirring in my head, and grabbed my notebook and my pencil. But the moment I touched the lead to the page, the whole thing fell away, leaving me only with one word. Love.

It was all I knew. Love. *Love love love love love.*

When she opened her eyes, I was in despair, and I saw some fleeting emotion cross her face, something I couldn't read, soon gone.

Everything unraveled. The inspiration she'd brought me that had me sitting up all night, making love to her and writing down the words that flooded me after, was gone. Melting away so swiftly I doubted it had ever been. I was insatiable, unsatisfied and aching even after I came. The only thing to do to start over again, one endless round of lovemaking, as I searched desperately for what she'd brought me so easily before. But the gnawing dissatisfaction that had disappeared for such a short time always returned, worse than ever, and nothing she did could appease it.

She was as compelling as ever, it was only that she no longer quenched my raging thirst. She never complained of it, no matter how I used her. She became for me every whore I'd ever bought, every woman I'd seduced, every one who had seduced me. I was angry, unmoored, wanting to punish. "What happened to it?" I demanded, time after time, pounding against her, aching with frustration. "Why don't I still feel it?"

She said nothing, but I began to see myself in her eyes, an image that sickened me, a man weak and desperate, spent, a failure. I began to hear my father's voice in my head. *You'll never be important, Nicholas. You haven't the talent.* Desire fled; when before all it had taken was the scent of her to arouse me, now nothing did, no matter how she or I tried. I became nothing, impotent and empty, no words, no will, no sex.

I began to hate her.

And still, I could not leave her. The memory of what she'd been for me was too strong. I could retrieve it, I knew. I could not have lost it forever. I stared down at the papers I'd written, lines upon lines of my handwriting, though they were words I no longer recognized as mine. How had they come to me? I felt weak as a worm. My lungs would not work; my limbs would not carry me. It went on like this for days, weeks. Perhaps longer—even now, I'm not certain how long I was with her. Even now, that time is like a dream.

It was some time before I realized she had left me, that she was not coming back. I didn't believe it when she told me she was going, you see, because I no longer trusted what I saw in her eyes, or who I was speaking to: her, or my father. It was weeks before my strength returned to me, before I woke one morning to see the sun streaming through curtains I hadn't had the will to close, before I smelled the rotting oranges on the table, before I saw mold growing like a skin on a cup of half-drunk coffee.

She left me nothing but a small leather sack full of coins, as if I were a whore to be paid. The note she left with it was written on a scrap of paper torn from the corner of a poem I'd written. Five words: *Take this and take care.* I pitched the note in the fireplace, into dead coals. I took the money and the sheaf of poems I'd written. I left the apartment, but I didn't leave Paris. I should have left. I should have forgotten about her.

But I could not rid myself of the scent of her. I could not just let it go. She had turned me inside out, and I was looking to find myself again, to find the words that eluded me. I was convinced she was the key. If I could find her, I would write again. I had never been so inspired as I was with her, and I wanted that again. With her help, I knew I could be the man I was meant to be.

I went through the motions of my life as it had been before she came into it. I spent time with my friends, I got drunk. But other women left me cold. I wanted only her. And then a group of us went to the exhibition at the Salon. We stumbled into a room where people were gathered reverently around one work. It was large, probably four feet by six, in a gilded frame. I waited my turn to see it, growing impatient at how silently people looked at it, how struck they seemed, the way they tore themselves away as if they'd been under a spell. And then, finally, a group left and my friends and I surged toward it to take their place. When I saw it, I understood what had kept everyone so spellbound, why they stared in unabashed adoration.

It was a portrait of her.

The artist had captured her perfectly, playful and sensuous, captivating, and he'd done it in a way I'd never seen, with brushstrokes and a technique so new and vibrant I knew she'd inspired him as she inspired me in the beginning.

I knew the painting would be famous. I knew it would still be spoken of in a hundred years, two hundred. She had given him what she hadn't given me: fame, immortality, and I knew—though of course it made no sense at all, it wasn't the least bit rational—that she'd withheld such things from me deliberately.

I discovered the artist's name and left the exhibition in a fury. I searched him out, knowing that where he was, she would be too. But when I arrived at his studio, it was only to find him distraught and disheveled. He looked as if he hadn't slept in days.

"She has left me," he said to my query. He pointed to the canvases scattered about the room, all of them half finished, all of them bearing her likeness. "Three days ago, God save me! If you find her, please . . . bring her back to me. I need her. I will die without her."

"You don't know where she's gone?"

He shook his head. "She promised to be my inspiration forever. She promised it, if I would give myself to her."

I had been turning to go, but something about his words caught me; something I remembered. I frowned, searching for the echo. "She said that?" I asked slowly. "She promised to stay?"

The artist dragged his hand through his hair, leaving streaks of paint. In despair, he said, "She told me she could bring me fame. She said my work would be known forever. What else should I have done? I loved her. She was my muse! Should I not have taken the bargain?"

Now I remembered her stories of Keats, of Byron, of the woman who had inspired them, the offer she had made. "What bargain? What bargain did you make with her?"

He pointed again to the canvases. Tears filled his eyes. "How beautiful she is! How could I say no?"

I left him there with his unfinished canvases and his dreams of her, the stories she'd told me ringing in my ears. Byron's story. The woman in Venice. *She inspired him to immortal genius. And in return? Why, his soul, of course.*

It was impossible. It couldn't be. Byron had died more than forty years ago, Keats before that. She wasn't old enough to have known either of them. She could not be the woman in the story. It defied all logic.

But the idea plagued me. I haunted the streets of Paris, mulling over every word she'd ever said to me, certain there was something there to find, something to help me make sense of this puzzle. The artist exhibited nothing else; I began to hear stories of his despair, and I thought of his unfinished canvases. I thought of Byron not finishing *Don Juan*. God, what nonsense! Such bargains were only fiction, Faustian tales; there could be nothing real in it.

I lost track of her. It seemed she had simply disappeared, but I was obsessed. I did not forget her. It was two years before I heard of her again. Everyone was talking of Vienna, of a composer there and his new opera that had astounded all who'd heard it. The fever to see it moved through Paris like a storm. It was about a woman of great mystical power, a muse like no other muse. It was said to be based on truth, that there was such a woman, the composer's inspiration.

I knew who it must be. Who else?

By then, I'd published my second book of poetry, the poems I'd written under her spell. The reviews, again, were good. Better than for my first, though some spoke of a certain weakness in the rhymes. But I had written nothing new since she'd left me, and the months had brought me only frustration. It was her fault, I knew, that the poems I'd written weren't good enough, that I could not collect my thoughts enough to write again. My anger with her grew. I wanted back the talent she'd taken from me. I wanted answers. But more than that, I wanted her. The publication brought me a little more money, and so I set off for Vienna to hunt down the opera's composer, to find her.

When I went to his rooms, he was bent over a pianoforte, sheaves of paper strewn across it, the polished wood dotted with ink. His eyes were bleary; as sleepless as the painter's had been, as mine. He said to me with a despairing hope, "You know her? Ah, then, you know why I must have her back. To bury myself within her again—she did not tell me she would go! It wasn't part of the bargain! I didn't know!"

The bargain, again.

"Where did she go?" I asked.

He could not tell me. I left him with his despair.

I stayed in Vienna, waiting to hear of someone else, some new sensation, rumors of another sublime work that would change the way we looked at everything. My obsession with her invaded every hour, my resentment grew like a disease within me. What had she seen in them that she hadn't seen in me? She had given the painter and the composer a fame that would out-live them; their names would be spoken with reverence throughout time. It was what I'd wanted for myself, what I had always wanted. But she had not offered it to me. I needed to know why.

That such thoughts were absurd escaped me; I was no longer rational. I had no idea then what she truly was, but she began to take on an otherworldly power. I was by then so certain she had been Keats's and Byron's muse that I no longer even asked myself how it could be possible for a woman to inspire a poet who'd died before she was born.

Then I began to hear of Florence. Everyone wanted to go there suddenly; they spoke of dreams and visions. It was the sign

I had been looking for. I had no doubt she was there. The only question was whether I would once again be too late.

I found myself in Florence in the middle of the summer. As always, I ingratiated myself into a new crowd, and I began to hear the rumors of a beautiful woman who was cutting a swath through the city's artistic crowd. I met a mediocre musician who'd had her—*you would not believe this one, my friend. I could not stay . . . she exhausted me*—and an immature sculptor—*What breasts! To capture such a thing in marble . . . oh, but her beauty was too much for me.* In the beginning, I was jealous; I could not believe these hacks had touched her. But then I realized that she had made none of them the offer she'd made the artist in Paris or the Viennese composer. They were like me.

I did not want to think about what we had in common. I kept looking for her, and then, one night, in a crowded saloon, I found her. Her beauty stunned, as always. Despite my obsession with tracking her down, I had not thought what I would do if I saw her again, what I would say. I suppose there was a part of me that believed I never would. When she caught sight of me, she turned to leave. I dropped my drink in my haste to get through the crowd and out the door.

I grabbed her arm; her scent came to me in a cloud that knocked me back. My desire for her rose as heedlessly as it ever had. I pulled her into the alley, pressed her to the wall. I was rough and unthinking. I wanted to hurt her. But her expression was unyielding—she gave me nothing, even when I kissed her. The aphrodisiac of her surged through me, but with it came the vision of my impotence when she'd left me. My weakness, my humiliation. My desire withered; I pulled away only to see contempt in her eyes.

"Why?" I heard myself asking, demanding. "Why them? Why not me?"

And she said in words made even more brutal by her gentleness and compassion, "You haven't enough talent to change the world, *cheri*."

The words resonated, I heard within them every review I'd ever received, my father's criticisms. She told a truth I did not want to hear. When she pulled away and left me, I let her go.

I went back to the artists gathered at the table I'd just left, the musician and the sculptor, the club of cast-offs I'd somehow joined without knowing it. Hacks, I'd called them—and here I was, one of them. I drank until the world swam before me. I listened to them talk about her latest conquest—a writer—though I remember little else about that night, or the next two. I only know that when I woke three days later to a just-risen sun, the effects of the drink lingering in a blistering headache and nausea, I was in a courtyard I didn't know, collapsed near a well. I crawled to it on my knees, ragingly thirsty, and dragged on the rope for the bucket. The rope caught, and I cursed and went to the edge to drag loose whatever held it. I looked down into the dank, dark depths only to see a face looking back at me, pale and wide-eyed and bloated. I thought at first it was my reflection, but then realized with a shock that it was not, that it was a drowned body, and one I thought I knew.

Bits and pieces of the nights before came to me then, but I pushed them away; I didn't want to see. I staggered to my feet and left that cursed place, stumbling back to my rooms, falling upon the bed and into sleep, into a nightmare where I watched her through a window, listening to her cries of pleasure, seeing her shapely legs grasping the hips of the man driving into her, a vision that melted into dark stairs and a courtyard, a man with his head in his hands, a despair I could not lighten.

I woke sweating and sick. When I heard, later that day, that the man in the well had been found, and that he had been her latest lover—the writer—I was not surprised to realize I already knew.

It had been a suicide. That one, and yes, the sculptor too, who cried into his beer as we talked of her and then jumped from the balcony. I began to haunt the galleries of Florence, searching for something I did not even know. It was there I saw the painting that cast all my gnawing suspicions into illumination. It was by Canaletto, one of his iconic views, this one simpler than the others, a Venetian garden, and a woman sitting on a marble bench. Her gray eyes seemed to leap off the canvas, to follow me wherever I went. Her face was as familiar to me as my own. It was Odilé, unmistakably.

The painting was more than one hundred and fifty years old.

I returned to my rooms and dug through the books I carried with me always, among which was a small volume of Keats that included "Lamia." I searched feverishly through it for the poem, and when I found it I pounced upon the lines I'd quoted to her, the ones about Lamia being a demon's mistress, or a demon herself. I read what Keats had written of her *gordian shape of dazzling hue*, her serpent's coils before she'd transformed herself into a woman, her startling beauty. *For so delicious were the words she'd sung, it seem'd he had lov'd them a whole summer long.* I read the code within those words now. I knew what Keats spoke of was what I knew about her myself, her beauty and her lies.

When news reached us of the Parisian artist's suicide, I was in a tavern drinking, of course. My friend, the musician who unknowingly shared my history with her, burst through the door in a blaze of sunlight and dust. He threw himself down at my table and told me the news. "He left a note saying that he had lost his vision. Can you imagine what a hell that would be? He said he had nothing more to live for. How well I understand!"

I thought of Byron. *Once he'd felt the inspiration she could bring him, none other could compare.* I thought of Keats, and "Lamia." *Though he exaggerates. No one sees that it was really about her.*

When I began to hear the rumors of the Viennese composer's madness, I understood the bargain at last. She gave them inspiration; she made their work immortal. But it came with a terrible price: *His soul, of course.*

It never occurred to me to wonder how I had come to believe in the reality of an immortal muse. All I knew was that I was the only one who had made the connection, and because of that, I was something very special indeed. I might not have enough talent as a writer to suit her, but I had something much more important. I knew the truth of her.

I was up two nights mulling over it. I began to believe that if I could stop her, if I could destroy her, I could restore the talent she'd stolen from me. I would be able to write again, and not only that, I would save others from a similar fate. Who knew what more Byron could have accomplished had he not known her kind of inspiration? Perhaps his greatest masterpieces were still ahead of him. How could we ever know what the Parisian painter might have done, or the Viennese composer? Who was she to decide when an artist's best work was behind him? How could she know what was so unknowable? She had given knowledge and beauty to the world, yes, but how much more had she taken from it?

My task became clear. I had been given a sacred duty, one no other man could share. She had already left Florence, and I followed her. St. Petersburg, Constantinople, too many others, arriving in each only after she'd already gone, stumbling over the revelation and despair she left behind, always lagging by a single step. But then, finally . . . Barcelona. I knew her well by then; I knew how she moved and what she looked for. I discovered who she'd recently brought to her bed—a talented violinist—and when I found him, he was waiting at her door, sitting on the edge of a stone planter.

"She will destroy you," I told him. "She will make you a bargain. Inspiration and fame for your creative soul."

I talked to him for more than an hour, trying to convince him to leave her. The next morning, when I went to the cafe where we had promised to meet, he wasn't there. In frustration, I went back to Odilé's, hoping to waylay him as he left.

He was there. Slumped over the planter, a pool of blood gathering beneath him from a self-inflicted wound.

I was dismayed. But I'll also admit I felt a kind of satisfaction. I had failed to keep him alive, but I *had* saved him. I had seen the misery and despair that awaited him, and I knew: Far better to be dead.

After that, what can I tell you? I knew she was on the hunt for the one to replace him and I did my best to dissuade each one. I didn't realize how well I'd interfered with her plans, nor how advanced her hunger had become. Not until I realized men were disappearing, every one of them an artist of some kind. The talk of foul play was everywhere; the cafes were filled with tension and suspicion. I knew it must have something to do with her, though in the past she'd kept only one at a time. I also knew that I must do something about it, because who else could? Who else knew what she was?

I went to her rooms and knocked, but there was no answer. When I tried the door, it was locked tight. I tried to peer in the window, but the drapes were drawn, and there seemed to be nothing but darkness beyond. And yet, I knew she had not gone. I watched her too closely; I would have known.

I went around to the back and climbed over the wall into the courtyard. It was hot, the sun blinding on the pale stone paving. Flies buzzed around the fallen fruit of an orange tree, and the smell of rotted oranges was heavy on the air, reminding me a bit too well of Paris, and my own misery.

I tried the door. It was locked, but I heard a sound from within, a cry, quickly stifled, and that was enough to force me to action. I took my knife from my coat pocket and forced the lock. Then I pushed the door open slowly and stepped into darkness.

The smell was horrible. Something dead. Rotting flesh. The darkness was heavy and sweltering. I broke into a sweat not just from the heat but from sudden fear. Carefully, I walked through the house. It looked abandoned, not a soul about. Unwashed crockery in the kitchen, food set upon by flies. As silently as I could, I made my way through the empty rooms.

When I got to the door at the end of the hall, the final room, I took a deep breath and twisted the knob. The door swung open—

And what met me was a horror that haunts me still.

There were bodies everywhere. Men, all naked, pale bodies in the darkness, some already bloating in the heat. I stared in shock, and then I heard a noise. I saw a shadow writhing among the dead, and I realized it was her. Odilé, but not Odilé. She was naked as well, her hair loose and tangled like a madwoman's. But it was her eyes that were the most terrible of all. Glowing eyes, dark as obsidian, reflecting a hunger so deep it was like falling into a void. She raised her head and smiled, and in that smile was evil and madness.

It was then that I truly understood what she was, what Keats, in his dying visions, had seen. It wasn't only that she'd inspired "Lamia." She *was* Lamia. She was a succubus. The word was not just a word—a myth—it was real.

"Come to me," she said, in a voice that was not her voice, but a monster's. I heard something new in it this time: desperation. "I will choose you, as you wish." She laughed then, a sound like a nightmare.

It took all my will to run. I heard her calling after me as I fell over my feet in my haste to leave that hell. I burst out into the sunshine of the day and fell onto the stones of the courtyard, gasping. And I felt something in me turn and twist, my life tuning to hers, the task I'd been given by God or fate slipping into place. I knew I had brought her to this. These last months, as I had driven her lovers away, meaning to save them, her hunger had grown and grown, impossible to sate. My efforts to keep her from making her wretched bargain had made her a monster.

After that, I spent months reading everything I could find on monsters and demons. I read every poet who spoke of strange women and beautiful muses and opiate dreams of inspiration. There, in the legends, I discovered the key. Three years. Every three years, she must choose *the one,* she must make the bargain: inspiration and fame—one great immortal work of genius—in return for their creative force. And if the bargain wasn't made, she would become the monster I'd made her in Barcelona.

And once I knew that, I knew how to destroy her. When I next saw her, in Paris a year and a half later, she was as beautiful as ever; there was no sign of the monster she'd been. But I knew it was there. I knew it lived inside her, and that it was waiting. The men she'd drained in that dark room in Barcelona had given her the strength to lock it away, to become human again. But I wondered what would happen if there were no men, no life force for the demon to draw upon. What if I could keep her from making the bargain once more, and then, when she turned, lock her in a room alone? What if there was nothing for her hunger to devour but its host?

I knew it must work. And when she was gone at last, I could once again be the man—the poet—I was meant to be. I would never be thought lesser again.

SEVENTEEN

ODILÉ

For two nights, I sat beside the window and watched the wavering, twinkling gondola lanterns moving to and fro against the pitch dark of the Canal, the shadows of the huge rats scampering about the *fondamenta*. I waited for the sound of a bell that never rang. It was nearly dawn when I knew he wasn't coming, but still I sat there watching the fog roll in across the Grand Canal so the barges and the fishermen were only faint shadows within it, and every clank and splash and call was strangely muffled and echoing at the same time—the fog played with Venice's natural tendency to confuse sounds, creating a labyrinthine puzzle of them, close and far, winding and whispered, the eerie yowling of a cat a block away sounding as if it stood at my elbow, the clang of Antonio pounding something in the courtyard seeming to come from across the city.

I knew my musician was dead then, but still I waited through the second night, hoping for his return until I could wait no longer, until my hunger gnawed as if it might chew its way out. With it came weariness. Only a few weeks left. I had thought perhaps the musician would do—his compositions had a fatal sweetness I thought could be inspired to greatness. And what a story to tell—wrested from an obscure church in Venice, a mysterious woman driving him to ever greater efforts. He was sweet as his music, fervent enough to cast intensity into his work, and perhaps he might have been the one to give me the recognition I longed for: "It was she. It was Odilé. Without her, I am nothing. . . ."

But he was gone, and I knew I must start again. I closed my eyes against exhaustion, desperation and the press of time.

Two nights with nothing had left my hunger pitched and sharp. Not for much longer would I be able to hunt without consequences, but there was no help for it now. I could not stand to be still; I must find the one.

I wished for a salon, an exhibition, something certain. But the only salon in the city was closed to me, and the Rialto was still the easiest place to find artists of all kinds. If nothing else, the market always held the quick relief of street performers. For a few more days, feeding on lesser talents could ease the pain. But only a few more days. Soon, they would not be enough even for that.

By the time the gondola was ready, the fog was starting to lift, the sun casting hazy beams through it that warmed the chill morning. Even the short trip to the Rialto felt too long. When we were finally there, and I stepped onto the *fondamenta* near the Rialto bridge, I heard music coming from beyond the vegetable stalls with their pyramids of green-striped melons and cabbages, squashes and carrots and deep red tomatoes. A violinist, playing with some wistful beauty. Not enough, I knew, for anything more than a respite, but it would have to do.

I made my way through the crowds haggling at the stalls, hurrying toward the music, ignoring the men who looked up when they caught sight of me, their quick and intense interest. My appetite had grown so ravenous now that they must feel it, though they didn't realize what left them gaping and breathless, what filled them with a lust that had them hurrying off to their wives or lovers.

I pushed through the crowd at the edge of the fish market and was disappointed. The violinist was an old man, and I yearned for youth, for innocence, for things I could never have again, things that made me feel alive. He gasped when I came near—I felt the surge of his talent as he gripped his chest, and I quickly moved away.

I went past the fishing boats moored along the *fondamenta*, with their stinking nets drying in the sun, tawny sails with their decorations of crosses and saint's symbols limp and half furled, toward a cafe I knew, where performers often entertained at the outdoor tables. And there, yes, was a man with light-brown hair and a winning smile, singing Verdi. A pile of centimes lay in the soft hat at his feet, winking in the sun. He was young and pretty. He had enough talent to ease that empty, churning ache for a day or two perhaps. When he finished I caught his eye and crooked my finger at him. He stepped over to me, curious, a bit disbelieving, and I whispered what I wanted of him.

He swallowed. "Where?" he asked hoarsely. "When?"

I meant to tell him to come with me to the gondola. But the crowd watching him had been slowly wandering away while we spoke, and suddenly I saw what they'd hidden from my view. The words I'd been about to say died on my tongue.

The glint of the sun on blond hair. A pale face and pale blue eyes. He was sitting at one of the tables, alone. He raised a cup to me, smiling that mocking smile I knew so well.

I said to the singer quickly, in a low voice, "This afternoon. In two hours—can you meet me then? At the Ca' Dana Rosti?"

"Two hours, yes," he said. He gave me a little bow and smiled. I watched him go, and then I turned back to the cafe.

I went slowly up to the table. He watched me, that smile never leaving his handsome face. He glanced in the direction the singer had gone and raised a brow. "Coming down a bit in the world, aren't we, Odilé?"

I ignored that. "Nicholas. How strange to find you here in the sunlight. I'd begun to wonder if you were a vampire. You spend so much time lurking about in the shadows."

"I go where you go," he said lightly. "I lurk where you lurk."

"Such clever words. Have you written much poetry lately?" I goaded. "I do keep an eye out for you, but the landscape seems so barren lately—nothing at all from my favorite poet. But perhaps you've published something that managed to escape my attention?"

He took a careful sip of his coffee and said, "Unfortunately not. Some foul succubus left me without words."

"You should stay away from such creatures. They can be deadly."

"No more so than I."

I played idly with the many loops of Venetian chain on my wrist. "You're like a sheep on a rail track, Nicholas. A momentary obstruction only."

"In your whole history, there has never been anyone like me. Be honest"—he leaned forward, his eyes gleaming—"You're afraid of me."

It was true, but I would never let him know it. I was afraid of him, not because he could destroy what I truly was, but because he could destroy Odilé. I could not forget Barcelona, or my fear of the monster inside me, my fear that it was all I was destined to be.

I forced the memory away and gave Nicholas a quelling look. "You've such a high opinion of yourself. It was always tiresome."

"Eventually, I'll stop you. I've *been* stopping you."

I raised my eyes to his. "Do you think so? Do you think those men meant anything to me? I didn't want either one. I wouldn't have chosen either one. They were weak, Nicholas. Like you."

"Is that so? Which of us was the weaker in Barcelona?"

"You cannot beat me, Nicholas. Why must you try?"

"I think you underestimate me."

"Oh, I hardly think so."

He rose. "Really? How do you feel lately, my love? Are you starving yet? Are you killing canaries as you pass?"

I met his gaze. "Why don't you come home with me and see if you can satisfy? Or no . . . ah wait . . . is there anything left of you to feed upon? Or are your journal pages only"—I ran my fingers down his shirtfront and felt him freeze, the hold of his breath—"blank?"

He stepped back abruptly. "Perhaps I am not what you think I am."

"No?" I smiled again. "We shall see."

His pale eyes glittered. "Yes, we shall," he said, and then he was off before I could say another word. As he walked away, I remembered with unease the look in his eyes in Barcelona. Despite my posturing, the truth was that Nicholas did know how to hurt me—he was the only one on earth who did.

EIGHTEEN

SOPHIE

My efforts to find a place to lease were unsuccessful. Katharine Bronson had been right. The moment that most discovered I was American, the price for lodgings went up, taking each palazzo firmly out of our grasp.

I was despairing when I returned to the Danieli late that afternoon, but Joseph was in a good mood. He was wearing only a sheet tied about his waist, dragging to the floor, and his hair was wet, sending rivulets over his shoulders and his bare chest. His white trousers, striped green with what looked like algae, hung over a chair, steadily dripping into a chamber pot he'd set below.

"I went swimming," he told me at my question. "With Frank Duveneck over at the Palazzo Rezzonico."

"You were swimming at the Rezzonico?"

"In the Canal," he said. "The tide was coming in. I thought you might like to try it too, but Duveneck tells me ladies bathe only at the Lido."

I felt a momentary resentment, a little jealousy that he'd been splashing about in the cool of the Canal while I'd sweated and climbed innumerable stairs to look at innumerable rooms too rich for our purse.

"Will you help me take this off? I'm about to perish." I took off my boots and my stockings while Joseph came over to unfasten my gown, helping me out of it, and then loosening the laces of my corset so I could unhook it and let it go too.

"Did you find anything?" he asked.

I shook my head. "There's nothing to be had. Or I mean, there are a hundred places, but they're all too dear. I hardly know what to do. I don't want to return to New York yet—"

"We won't be returning to New York before the spring," he told me calmly as he went to the dresser. When he turned around again, he was holding a little basket. "I bought you some figs. Sit down for a moment and eat one. They're very good."

I smiled with gratitude. My brother's thoughtfulness was the one good thing in a discouraging day. He sat on the edge of the bed, holding the basket out to me, and I came and sat beside him, taking a fig and biting into it. "I think this might be the most delicious thing I've ever eaten."

Joseph laughed. "So tell me what you looked at today."

I gave him the litany, but he seemed unfazed. "I imagine someone at the salon will help before the week is out. But I'll go looking with you tomorrow, if you want."

I knew he would be able to help—he could make anyone do anything just by smiling. But I shook my head and rose to go the washbasin. "You've work to do."

"Wait," he said.

When I looked over my shoulder, he was staring at me with that expression I knew very well, dazed and intent at the same time.

"You look . . . you're pearly."

"It's sweat," I said, grimacing. "I'll wash and—"

"Not yet." He rose and stood back, rubbing his chin as he looked at me. "Take it off."

I felt a familiar shiver of excitement and longing as I obeyed him. I pulled down the sleeves of my chemise, letting the whole thing fall to my feet, slipping out of my drawers until I stood naked before him. Joseph surveyed me critically, but I was used to that. I waited until he gestured to the bed. "Lie down."

When I did, he directed, "On your side," and then he leaned over, positioning me, running his hand over my hip, placing my arm just so. He handed me a fig. "Press it to your lips—as if you're just getting ready to take a bite. Yes, that's it." His sketchbook was on the floor by the bed, and he grabbed it, hooking the leg of a chair with his foot and pulling it over, reaching into a pocket for a piece of charcoal before he realized all he wore was a sheet. He took a piece from the pile on the bedside table, and began to draw, quickly, efficiently, giving me curt orders. "Open your mouth more—I want to see your teeth. Look at me. Yes, that's it. Pull your shoulder back a bit."

This was second nature and always had been. I could not remember a time when Joseph had not drawn me—he'd done so from the time he'd first known what paper and pencil were. There had been dozens of sketches about our house in New York. Portfolios full of them. They were pinned to the walls in the nursery, in his bedroom, in mine—a hundred different aspects of me, illustrating nearly every moment of my life, from childhood to adolescence, into adulthood—captured forever. Most of them, the ones Joseph and I did alone, were lovely, but some— the ones posed for Miss Coring, the ones she'd insisted on, had been . . . I had no words for them. Even now, thinking of her, thinking of those terrible times—

"Soph." Joseph's voice broke through my thoughts. I looked

up to see he'd gone still, the same shadows in his eyes that I knew were in mine. His voice was deep, whispered. "Don't. Don't think it. It's past. It's done. It can't hurt us now."

It wasn't true—I felt the past at my back always, ready to destroy the fragile world we'd made, but I blinked and tried to smile. Though I knew it didn't fool him, I said, "Yes, I know. I'm sorry. Did you want me to actually bite into the fig?"

He sighed and put the sketchbook aside. He came onto the bed, stretching himself out beside me. He took the fig from my fingers. My heart felt full and heavy.

"I know a story," he said. "About a prince and a princess. She was very beautiful, but he had a big nose—"

"It wasn't that big," I protested.

"—and they lived in a room that was dark and full of terrors, but even though they were prisoners, the two of them liked it because it belonged just to them. They knew there was a world beyond it, and there were beautiful things in it, but nothing seemed as beautiful as what they had together. They needed no one else. They wanted no one else. Then one day, the demon-queen who kept them prisoner threatened to take the prince away forever. The princess was desperate to save her brother— what would she do without him?"

The story was old as time, one of the first I'd ever invented for him, for us both, and I knew what he was telling me. To put this memory away, to put it into a box with all the little boxes we kept locked and hidden away in a place where light rarely escaped. This was second nature too. Stories to hide truths that didn't bear looking at. Stories that clothed ugliness in bright costumes and golden crowns, where Joseph and I escaped on pretty white horses, riding into a brilliant Venetian sunset, leaving demons and dragons and sieges behind.

I continued with the words we both knew so well. "Then the

princess discovered that a golden crystal owned by a terrible wizard could defeat the demon-queen. If she could win it, she could save the prince."

"Though the way was hard, and the only way to reach this wizard's stronghold was to take a bridge over a chasm—"

"—and there was no rail, only a narrow bit of twisting, flexible gold that wound and dipped and swayed with every footstep—"

"But she could not fall, or the chasm would swallow her alive."

My heart seemed to swell with gratitude and yearning and sorrow. I ran my fingers down his cheek, needing the feel of him. He grabbed my hand, keeping it there.

"She was a very brave princess," he whispered.

"Who could not live without her brother," I whispered back. "She would have done anything for him."

He brought my fingers to his mouth and kissed them, and I felt the moment flare to life between us, the way he struggled to control it, to resist. "If that's so, she should do what her brother wants now, and not think of the past. It's only the future that matters. All right?"

I felt sorrow, relief—too many things. "Yes. All right. But only if you promise too."

He said nothing, but pressed the fig he held to my lips, feeding it to me as if I were some ancient Roman queen and he was my servant. Then he sighed. "I suppose we'd best get dressed. I've promised Duveneck we'll be at the salon tonight."

I climbed off the bed. "I wish I had another gown to wear. They'll know we have nothing when I show up in the same one every night."

"You'll have another gown." Joseph's voice was low and fervent. "I promise it. We'll have everything we want, Soph. Everything we deserve. As soon as we convince Dane to recommend me to Loneghan."

NINETEEN

NICHOLAS

My meeting with Odilé had sharpened my senses. It seemed I felt everything too strongly as I came into the salon of the Alvisi and saw the Hannigans. Sophie Hannigan was laughing, revealing that slight overbite, and I felt the quick and brutal sting of desire. She had her hand on her brother's shoulder, and I noted that same strange magic between them that held the eye. I felt oddly as if I were falling into something I was not quite prepared for, though there was nothing overt, nothing I could point to and say, *yes, there it is, that's it.* They were in a group with Duveneck and Giles, and I made my way over, snagging a glass of sherry on the way. Giles looked up from his sketchbook, and pushed his glasses back into place. "Nick, there you are! Where the hell have you been?"

"About." I smiled at Sophie Hannigan, who met my gaze with a steady one of her own.

Joseph Hannigan said, "We thought perhaps you'd fallen into a canal."

"Like that unfortunate organist," said Duveneck. "Did you hear about him, Dane? That one at San Maurizio? Found dead just last night. He'd been floating in a canal near San Anzolo. Knocked himself in the head, apparently. You'll have to be careful of that when you're walking to your new place, Hannigan. Those *calli* are as dangerous as canals."

I frowned. "Your new place? You're leaving the Danieli?"

"Mrs. Peabody found us a place to live at last," said Sophie Hannigan.

I felt a quick dread. I had not thought of this, and it seemed a gross lapse. Please, God, that the lodgings Mrs. Peabody had found were far from the Dana Rosti. As casually as I could, I asked, "Close by, I hope?"

"Yes, indeed. The Palazzo Moretta."

"Do you know it?" asked Hannigan.

I nodded in relief. Close, yes. On this side of the Canal, near St. Mark's. Nowhere near Odilé. "I think everyone knows it. It's a good choice. I'm certain you'll like it. When do you take it up?"

"We're to make arrangements tomorrow," Miss Hannigan said. Truly, she was glowing, as if finding a place to live had eased some great burden, and I cursed myself for not seeing before how important it was to her. I could have found them someplace easily enough, had I applied myself to it. It was only a sign of how distracted I was in their presence that I hadn't already seen to it. It was only pure luck that my momentary lack of attention hadn't been fatal.

I forced myself back to my purpose. They would be moving tomorrow, and no doubt Odilé would still have her street singer. But the next day . . .

"Ah, well, I'd hoped tomorrow to show you both the Lido. The weather won't hold long, and the two of you should see it. But perhaps the day after? Once you've moved in?"

Hannigan said, "Duveneck and I planned to go to Torcello."

"Well, that's pretty enough, if you like empty campos full of weeds," I persisted. "But the Lido is something altogether fine. Do you know Byron used to gallop his horses there?" I ignored the usual uneasiness I felt at the thought of him. "Not to mention sandy beaches and a Jewish graveyard."

"A Jewish graveyard?" Hannigan asked with interest.

Duveneck put in, "You'd like it, Hannigan. Desolate and falling apart. Mostly abandoned. Dane is right. We should go there instead while the weather's good."

"We could make a party of it," said Miss Hannigan.

"It sounds the perfect way to spend the day," Giles agreed.

Two mornings later, the five of us took the omnibus to the Lido. The steamer had a loud and annoying whistle it blew at every fishing boat that wandered into its path, and its cloud of trailing gray smoke was often blown by the breeze into our faces, both obscuring the view and choking us as we crossed the lagoon to the long and narrow island of sand that protected Venice from the Adriatic.

But for the steamer smoke, the weather happened to be good. The early morning fog had dissipated by the time we left, and though there was a definite edge in the air, the skies were blue and clear.

"How do you and your brother like the Moretta?" I asked Miss Hannigan.

She favored me with a bright smile. "It could not suit us better. There are fantastic murals in the salon. Neptune and his mermaids. And painted pillars and balconies . . . it's beautiful.

Or it was once. Now it's rather decrepit, though still lovely. Mrs. Bronson helped us win acceptable rent, so I'm quite satisfied."

"I'm glad to hear it. I should like to see those murals sometime."

Her smile grew, and I thought I saw a singular warmth in her eyes when she said, "Oh, I quite mean for you to."

Again, her directness was disconcerting. Before I could respond, Giles said, "It's a good thing we came today. It's starting to be cold." He shivered as we leaned over the rail, watching the passing islands, one of which held the male lunatic asylum, and the other the monastery of San Lazzaro.

"Oh, I think it perfect," said Miss Hannigan, lifting her face to the breeze coming off the bow. "It was too hot for me."

"It's all those clothes you wear," her brother teased.

She made a face at him and then turned to me. "San Lazzaro—that's the monastery where Byron studied, isn't it?"

"The same," I said. "There's a plaque there commemorating his stay, if you want to see it."

"Hmmm. Not today," she said, closing her eyes. "Today I want to lie in the sand."

The image that brought to mind was too provoking; I couldn't look away. I had recovered myself by the time the omnibus brought us, along with quite a few others, to Santa Maria Elisabetta, where there was a restaurant and a bathing establishment. At the height of the season, the sandy beaches were crowded with bathing tents and Germans, but today it seemed relatively quiet. The cold fog had frightened everyone away. There were no bathers bobbing in the shallow, shoaled waters, which were an astonishing blue.

The Lido had changed from Byron's time; the fields dotted with poppies were mostly gone, and the unpaved walk leading from Santa Elisabetta to the Adriatic had been improved. Now, the walkways were paved and gaslit; there was a slew of lodging houses and a salon with an orchestra and shops. The restaurant's food was no better than it had been then, perhaps, but the wooden platform that reached out over the water made up for a multitude of sins.

It was the first place we went, and Joseph and Sophie Hannigan took in everything with a pleasure that seemed to put a bloom on their already impossibly captivating sensuality. Once again, I felt irresistibly drawn to them, and I knew the others were no better. Duveneck laughed longer and harder than I'd seen in a long time, and Giles did whatever he could to please them both. The twins were like some strange, addictive drug, a spell I had to work to resist, and I was not doing a very good job of it. We lingered over a meal of olives and cheese, watery crab soup and crisply fried minnows, washed down with a considerable amount of wine, all set to the tune of talk and laughter.

When we were finished, we took off our boots and walked along the beach, trailing our toes in the foam of the slight waves. Mist wisped from the water, curling about us and then dissipating again. We settled at a spot a short way down the beach, stretching out in the warm sand. Giles and Duveneck opened the sketchbooks they'd carried with them and began busily capturing the view. Hannigan laid himself out, crooking his arms beneath his head, closing his eyes and looking for all the world as if he meant to spend these hours asleep.

"You don't mean to draw?" Giles asked him in disbelief.

Hannigan slitted open an eye. "When Sophie decides she wants to dance in the surf, I will. Until then, I'll leave the view to Turner. He's done it best."

"What an extraordinary thing to say." Duveneck stared at him in dumb surprise, his hand paused over his paper. "Do you really mean that Turner's had the last word on it, so the rest of us should not even try?"

Hannigan had closed his eyes again. He didn't bother to open them. "Not at all. I only mean that the view I want to draw is Sophie in the waves."

"Well I'm not bathing," Miss Hannigan said. "I haven't even got the costume, and I can't spoil my dress."

"You could take it off and still be fully clothed," her brother pointed out. "You've six hundred petticoats on. But I wasn't talking about that anyway. It would be pretty to see you walk along the shore as if you were surveying your kingdom."

"With Venice like a fairy city in the background," I heard myself say.

She looked at me in obviously delighted surprise. "Why, Mr. Dane, did I just hear a poetical observation?"

I smiled at her. "Hardly. One can't help but see it. I'm not the only one who's made the comparison."

Hannigan leveled himself onto his elbows, squinting into the distance. "It looks not quite real," he agreed. "Look at the way the mist gathers off the water."

"It makes it look as if the city's floating," Giles said.

"Or emerging from the clouds," Duveneck put in.

"Or just waking from a spell," Miss Hannigan said, her voice soft and reverent. "The eyes of the Doge's Palace are blinking open after a century asleep—do you see them? How fine they are. All the ghosts in the city have fled beneath their gaze. That's what the mist is, you know. The spirits racing away."

And as with her story of Mestre, it wasn't the words so much as the way she spoke them. That storyteller's voice, that compelling timbre. She raised a vision of the Palace—the center of spies and duplicity, executions and betrayal—as a benign and benevolent guardian of the city. The ugliness in it she'd swept away. We were all staring at her, and her brother whispered, "Go into the waves, Soph. Dance for us."

She turned to look at him, and what passed between them raised in me such a yearning to touch her that I dug my hands fiercely into the sand. And strangely, too, I had the sense that it was what Hannigan wanted of me—that he had somehow, and quite deliberately, used his own allure to feed hers. Foolish to think it, of course. How was such a thing even possible?

Miss Hannigan rose. "Very well, I'll do it. And you can all draw me. We'll have a contest."

"What's the prize?" Hannigan asked.

"A kiss," she said, ruffling his hair.

"Well, that's hardly fair," I protested. "I can't draw."

"Then you must write a poem," she said, turning to me, her hands on her hips. "In fact, I charge you with this commission, Mr. Dane. Write me a poem, and I'll give you a kiss whether you win the contest or not."

The thought of it was impossible. I could not be kissing her. Feeling this desire could only be dangerous. I did not want or need a lover. My task required all my attention. Still, my mouth went dry. "No matter that it would be a very bad poem?"

"I can't imagine it could possibly be."

"I've told you, Venice has taken my words."

"Then I will endeavor to be your inspiration," she said.

She reached up, took out a long pin and then lifted off her hat. She flung it to the sand, where it landed neatly beside her boots and limp stockings. Then she reached up again, and I realized she meant to take down her hair. The thought of Sophie Hannigan like that, hair down, barefoot in the waves. . . .

Her brother said, "Leave your hair up."

She frowned and lowered her arms. "Up? Are you certain?"

I thought all of us would have protested—I didn't think there was a man on that beach who wouldn't have liked to see Sophie Hannigan's hair falling—but there was some unspoken command between the two of them that kept me silent, and I was certain the others felt it too.

Hannigan nodded, and his sister said, "Very well. Are you all ready?" and sashayed down to the water's edge.

She paused there, her purple skirt gleaming in the sunlight, the stripes of her bodice blending from this distance to look like gold. She looked for a moment at the haze of the city beyond, and then she turned to us, and lifted her skirts. Slowly. Revealing pale ankles and slender calves. Teasing so deliberately and well I could not imagine that she hadn't done it before. I could not take my eyes from her. The skirt came higher, just above her knees, the start of her thighs, before she stopped. She laughed— a sound that rang over the beach and echoed in the water. I was stunned to silence; she was nearly the most sensual thing I'd ever seen. I wanted to tumble her into that water.

She skipped through the light surf, splashing it into filmy rainbows about her legs, changing before my eyes into the very essence of abandon. She was a naiad, a mermaid, otherworldly and beguiling and enchanting. I felt she'd been invented just for us, with no other purpose than to twist and turn as her brother directed—*Dance for us. Leave your hair up.*

It was disquietingly erotic, a surrender such as I'd never before seen. She had become what he'd told her to be, but she was in her own story too, not just the princess surveying her kingdom, but one who danced among the fleeing ghosts as if she delighted in the brush of their spirits against her skin.

The others were drawing furiously; I heard the scratch of charcoal on paper, but when I glanced at Joseph Hannigan, I saw he wasn't drawing at all. He was motionless, staring at her with a raptness that seemed to match her surrender. As if he felt my gaze, he turned. For a moment, his emotions were starkly visible: a tormented fascination, painful longing.

I felt as if his gaze held the answer to a mystery I'd only just glimpsed, one that, before that instant, I'd hardly known was there. It was the most unsettling feeling I'd ever had.

Giles said, "You aren't writing, Nick," and Hannigan blinked; the moment was gone so suddenly I wondered if I'd truly seen it. He picked up his sketchbook and began to draw, and the spell was broken.

"I haven't got any paper," I said. "Nor a pencil."

"You won't win your kiss then," Giles said.

"Take this." Duveneck tore a sheet from his book, and handed it across to me, along with a charcoal pencil. I took them, and the moment I did, a thought came to me, vague and unformed, that made me forget what I'd just seen in Hannigan's eyes. It was an idea more than words, an image of the light that was Sophie Hannigan twisting in the mist—and then it was gone. Still, it surprised me. I told myself I'd imagined it. My words had been stolen from me long ago, wrested by a gray-eyed demon who had swallowed me whole and spit me out again, and I had no hope of finding them again.

I did end up scribbling something, but only because the more I watched her in the sun and the water, the more I wanted that kiss, even knowing I shouldn't. Ah, but it was only a kiss. What could it hurt?

Miss Hannigan's face was flushed when she finally returned, cheekbones pinked. Her eyes were sparkling. "I hope that was long enough," she said, sinking down between her brother and me, careless of the sand clinging to her wet skirt.

"Dear God, that was enchanting," said Giles, too fervent as always.

Frank Duveneck said with a smile, "You were inspiring, Miss Hannigan."

"Well, I hope to be," she said. "Now you must all let me judge."

Giles handed her his sketchbook. It was, in his usual way, mediocre. He had not quite got her limbs right, though Venice behind her was beautifully rendered—his style finding the fanciful in it, of course. "Very pretty," said Hannigan, looking over her shoulder. "Have you tried allegory, Martin?"

"He does allegory well," I offered. "I've told him so a dozen times."

Duveneck was next. I had little liking for his style; it was too German, too much an impression, but Hannigan looked it over with obvious admiration. "Look how he's captured the motion, Soph," he said, and I saw Duveneck's pride in the compliment.

She handed the sketchbook back to Duveneck and took her brother's. That he had done her better than the others was no surprise. He'd drawn her not in the gown she wore but in a shift, the sleeves of which had slipped to reveal her rounded shoulders, and petticoats that she'd bunched in her hands, so festoons of ruffles and lace fell over her fingers. The light played all over her, a masterpiece of chiaroscuro—how he'd managed it with only charcoal at his command I did not know, but she looked not quite real, like the naiad I'd imagined her to be, and he'd seen the ghosts too—their fingers reached from the mist about her feet, clinging to her as if they loved her. It was her story brought to shimmering, breathless life.

"Christ, that's lovely." Giles's voice was hushed.

"It is indeed," said Duveneck.

"Oh! You all did wonderfully, but I'm afraid Joseph has won." Sophie Hannigan looked at her brother as if she saw no one else. She lurched into his arms so hard he fell back onto the sand, laughing as he grasped her, and she kissed him lingeringly and too long for a brother and sister.

The thought I'd only half-formed sprang fully realized, unwelcome and disturbing—that the twinned charisma I'd seen in them might be something else altogether. Something not so magical but . . . unwholesome. The display was strange and titillating at the same time. The others, too, were staring. She was laughing when she drew away and looked at us—I think she saw nothing the least bit wrong.

Hannigan sat up and reached for his sketchbook, seemingly as oblivious as she. Duveneck glanced away as if he were embarrassed; Giles fumbled to retrieve his pencil, which had fallen into the sand. Sophie Hannigan turned to me. "What about you, Mr. Dane? Do you have a poem to show me? Do you wish to collect your prize?"

She smiled; I saw a challenge in her eyes. I tried to forget what I'd seen. I handed her the piece of paper I'd scrawled upon. "I warn you, it's not very good."

Her smile grew. "You shouldn't be so modest." She glanced down at the words, mouthing them as she read. *There once was a girl on the Lido . . .* Her mouthing stopped halfway through, as the limerick turned. I saw the flush move into her cheeks, and then, at the end, she laughed—a short, sweet explosion of sound.

She was still laughing when she looked up. "Why, Mr. Dane, this is a very bad poem."

I smiled back at her. "You didn't say it had to be good. Only that there had to be one."

Hannigan reached for it. "Let me see."

She snatched it away from him, crumpling it in her fist. "It's for my eyes only."

"Why, is it indecent?" Giles asked.

"Horribly so." She looked at me, chastising. "I don't think you truly entered into the spirit of things."

"They drew what they saw," I told her. "I only did the same."

"You're very clever, Mr. Dane."

"My mother always said so."

"I'm not certain I should reward you."

I met her gaze. In a low voice, I said, "A pity. And I'd so looked forward to it."

She did not look away. "I suppose I did promise."

"Yes, you did."

She leaned forward. She pressed her lips to mine, a quick, hard brush of her mouth. I'd no sooner started to reach for her than she pulled away again. The kiss she'd favored me with lasted less than a quarter as long as the one she'd given her brother. Even so, it was disconcerting how completely that nothing kiss aroused.

Hannigan closed his sketchbook. "So where's this Jewish cemetery? I'd like to see it."

The rest of the day was spent exploring the moss-covered ancient tombs of the abandoned, brick-walled Jewish cemetery, half buried as they were in sand and tangled about with weeds, sparsely shaded with stunted trees. Four men with Sophie Hannigan darting among us like an elusive, sensual nymph. I was tense with longing, and exhausted with the effort of ignoring it.

It was almost a relief when the day was over. I wanted only to get back to my darkened room and drown my desire and confusion in a bottle of wine. But halfway there, while we were all staring silently at the enchantment of the setting sun—the point of the

Dogana and the cupolas of the Salute and the majesty of Giorgio Maggiore only shadows against the vibrancy of aquamarine and lavender and violet skies above a horizon striated with gold and topaz and ruby, and all of it mirrored on the still waters of the lagoon—Duveneck said with a sigh, "It's a pity the day has to end."

"It doesn't," Giles said with alacrity. "Let's all go to Nick's and my rooms. We've plenty of wine."

"Our rooms are scarcely big enough for us," I protested.

"We'll go to the roof. You can see the whole city from the garden."

And so it was decided; once the omnibus landed us at the Piazzetta, we set off for our rooms, and wine. We went into the little courtyard, up the stairs, and when the others started to the roof, Sophie Hannigan held back, saying to me, "Shall I lend you a hand with the wine, Mr. Dane?"

Though I didn't trust myself with her alone, it seemed churlish to refuse her. I said, "Yes, of course," and she followed me inside and stood there, looking uncertainly about. I lit an oil lamp, which barely illuminated the litter of painting paraphernalia—Giles's easel, still with the unfinished painting from the gardens, paintbrushes soaking in jars of turpentine, jugs of linseed oil and crumpled metal tubes of paint—and beyond all that the furniture, none of it ours, and my books scattered about and not much more.

"It's . . . quite nice," she said.

"No, it's not. But it will do. It's only Giles and me, so no need for luxury. Come, the kitchen's back here."

I took up the lamp and she followed me to the small kitchen, used more for keeping wine than for any actual cooking. There was a bowl of shrunken figs on the counter—I could not remember where they'd come from or how long they'd been there—and a few dirty glasses with rings of dried red wine at their bottoms.

She came inside and touched the figs, smiling. "You're just letting them go to waste."

I heard myself say, as if in a spell, "You were beautiful today."

She smiled. "Ah, but that's not how you described me."

"I said you were beautiful in a different way."

"It was obscene," she said, but she was still smiling. "I thought it interesting, though."

"But not enough so to kiss me properly."

"Oh, Mr. Dane, but that *was* a proper kiss. I think it's an improper one that you want." I felt something in me give way as her voice softened to nearly a whisper. "Am I right?"

She didn't give me a chance to answer. Before I knew it, her mouth was on mine and every resolution I'd made fell to dust. She was right; an improper kiss was exactly what I'd wanted. I put my hand to the back of her neck. Her lips parted beneath mine so I could taste the sweetness of her, and she was as heady as I'd imagined, kissing me back with an experienced little flick of her tongue, pressing to me as if she knew exactly what she was doing. When she finally pulled away, I was breathless and out of control. I would have thrown her onto that table, but she put her hand against my chest, smiled at me and said, "They're waiting for us."

Which was true, I knew, though I was bewitched. I would have done anything she asked of me in that moment, and so I followed her as she took the wine, directing me like a child—*the glasses, Mr. Dane, the figs*—and the two of us went up to the rooftop garden, where the other three were laughing and talking, and she went to her brother and handed him a bottle of wine to open, and he put his arm around her shoulders—possessively, I thought in irritation, staking a claim—but only for a moment. He kissed the top of her head, and she moved away again, pouring wine and handing out glasses, giving me mine with a "Here you are, Mr. Dane," as if we were still strangers, when that kiss had been as erotic as any I'd known. Then she favored me with a knowing, seductive smile. I could not take my eyes from her the rest of the night. I thought of her brother's sketch of her on the bed, the way he'd drawn her in petticoats and chemise splashing about the waves, the way she'd been pressed against me and the play of her tongue with mine, and I was hopelessly lost in a single realization: *Dear God, I have felt this way before.*

TWENTY

ODILÉ

He was a peasant, unlearned and coarse. A child of the streets, with a voice good enough to win him a night's lodging and a meal, if not fame and glory. I waited for him impatiently after meeting Nicholas in the Rialto, and when he arrived, I was troubled and distracted enough that I wasn't careful. Though we spent only an hour together, I left the singer weak and groggy. I had drawn too much from him and yet it was not enough. I let him go, and he returned the next day, still weak, his desire mastering him. I should have shown him to the door, but at the sight of him, my appetite overwhelmed me. I felt a stab of pity for him, and fatigue too. I wished I did not need this so—I was tired of all of it. The sweating and the coupling, the endearments they all required, the pretense of affection or love or desire. It was all a lie, when what I wanted from them was not sex but their very essence. When all I wanted to do was to feed. And yet feeding required this contact, this tangle of limbs and the lock of mouths and caresses that meant nothing. There were times when I hated it, but to give it up, to admit I was exhausted of all of it, that there was no possibility of ever having what I wanted—that I could not yet do. While all those I had inspired had ultimately failed me, my hope remained that some day one would come who would give me what I longed for. One day, I would find him, and the name of Odilé León would be lauded forever.

But not yet, and for now, I was too out of control to look for him, and so I let the singer in and let him fall upon me. I took him to bed and worked my will upon him until I heard his heart pounding with effort, until his breath became ragged. His talent was too little to truly sate, and it was all I could do to hold back, to not take everything.

But I was too ravenous. The monster in me was too demanding. As I bucked and rocked upon the singer, I heard his gasping and was heedless. I drank and drank and leeched and drew, and the last bit of him roared within me, not enough, not enough, never enough, and then I heard him cry out—a scream, a gasp, and then a *snap* . . . and it was gone, so suddenly. Too suddenly.

The pain assailed me, my hunger grabbing, flailing, scrabbling in vain, because there was nothing there. Where he had been, there was nothing, and when I came to myself I saw him lifeless beneath me, staring up at the ceiling as I rocked upon him.

The horror of it stilled me. This was not what I wanted. Although I felt sorrow and regret, I felt terror most of all. The monster was gaining sway. It was growing too strong. I was falling into the trap Nicholas had laid for me. The writer's suicide, the organist's drowning—I knew he had pushed them to it. It was his fault I'd been brought to this. There were only a few weeks left, and I was beyond starving. I blamed Nicholas for all of it.

By the time I'd met Nicholas Dane, I'd known already the way a life could twist and turn with the most casual of choices. I knew it better than most, in fact. And like all casual choices, there was nothing in our meeting to tell me how significant he would be. Even if I had known it, I wonder what I could have done differently, or if I could have avoided it at all, if fate had set a certain scene it meant for me to play out. Or, as I'd once told him, not fate, but balance. The world craved symmetry.

It was early in the cycle when I'd met him. I had time to play, and so, though I was looking for the one, I was not looking very hard. I had been walking in the soft Paris night, on my way home from a cafe, when Nicholas stumbled into me. He'd been paying no attention, too busy writing as he walked.

I could have accepted his apology and gone on my way. The hunger was still containable. I should have walked away. But there was no sign, nothing to be wary of. How could I know?

I smiled and told him, "Perhaps you should not write and walk at the same time."

He looked abashed. He was also very handsome. Pale skinned, light eyed. His hair, a little too long, curling, gleamed golden in the lamplight. "Yes," he said. "Yes, of course you're right. But I had a thought I wanted to write down."

"A thought," I teased. "Do you have them so seldom that you must take note of them?"

He stared at me blankly. Then, when he realized I was teasing, he laughed. He had a good mouth, well shaped, full. "Unfortunately yes, at least lately. I've been trying to capture the beauty of Paris, but my mind's a sieve. I could probably hold rocks in it, but little else."

A sense of humor too, which I always enjoyed. "You've been trying to capture the beauty of Paris with words? Ah, I sympathize. Are you a writer then?"

"A poet. Or at least, an aspiring one."

A poet. Handsome. Young. Aspiring.

My whole body went tight. I took him out. I took him home. But as strong and vital as he was, I knew within weeks that he was not the one I was searching for. I stayed with him a bit too long even so. I enjoyed him; he was clever and handsome and he made me laugh. And so I played until I'd reduced him to everything I hated—pathetic weakness and gasping obsession.

My unwillingness to leave him turned out to be a bigger mistake than I could have imagined.

I never expected to see him again. But in a world where nothing ever surprised, he surprised me. And almost destroyed me. For me, those beautiful, sun-drenched courtyards of Barcelona were shadowed in a darkness I could not see through or past, and Nicholas Dane at the center of it, wearing an expression I had never forgotten. Terror and satisfaction together.

After Barcelona, I'd been forced to go into hiding. For months I'd skulked in cellars and sewers, waiting for the vitality of those I'd drained to work its magic upon me, to bring me back. I had rarely tested my limits, but now and again I had misjudged and brought myself to this. But this time was the worst. It seemed to take an eternity to return to my human form. I slithered through dank and darkness and stink and waited, the part of me that was Odilé held in thrall to the demon I'd become. I was terrified that I would be a prisoner forever, a *monster* forever. Madeleine's warnings wound an endless litany in my head.

It was a nightmare I had feared I would never wake from. And what was worse was the knowledge that no one could help me. No one could save me. I was alone in the world. It was a truth I had known but never fully realized, and now it was one I could not forget. Now, my singularity was a curse, wearying and desolate, an endless, unassailable loneliness.

Nicholas had taught me that. How could I ever forgive him?

TWENTY-ONE

SOPHIE

It was nearly dawn when we finally left the rooftop garden. We were all a little drunk from the wine, and the night had been as wonderful as the day, full of talk and laughter and stolen glances, a kiss that still lingered on my lips, a possibility I tried not to think about.

It was only a short distance to our palazzo, though neither Joseph nor I knew the way, so we all set out—Duveneck on his way home and Nicholas Dane offering to walk with us, and Mr. Martin protesting *why should Nick have you all to himself?*

I was glad for it; the truth was that had it just been the three of us, Joseph might have given me and Nicholas Dane the chance to be alone, and I was a little afraid of that, of how much I was growing to like him—and that kiss, which stirred feelings in me I knew were dangerous. I'd felt such things before, after all, and I must take care to be wise now. *There are no white knights, Soph. Not like in your stories. You have to see people for what they are, not what you want them to be.* Joseph's words, and I knew he was right. We were—finally—hobnobbing with people rich and influential enough to actually help us, and Nicholas Dane, while not the former, was certainly the latter. I sensed we were only steps away from Henry Loneghan, and I felt a dizzying satisfaction at the thought of it that made me laugh a little too easily, flirt a little too well. I had to step carefully. Joseph and I could not afford to disappoint Nicholas Dane or to make him angry.

We set off into the city, laughing and stumbling over one of Venice's rail-less bridges, the white stone slippery from the evening mists. "Careful," said Mr. Dane, taking my elbow as we crossed it. "The Venetians say there are four *p*'s to beware of. They translate to: white stone paving, whores, priests and jugglers."

"Jugglers?" I asked. "Why jugglers?"

He smiled; there was a pleasing wickedness in it that reminded me of his kiss. "Why, because they're all charlatans, didn't you know? Actually, the word is *Pantalone*. Do you know him?"

I shook my head.

"He's a character from Venetian comedy. A mountebank and a fool, but sinister too. No one you want to run into on a dark night."

"There's not much in Venice I'd want to run into on a dark night," said Mr. Duveneck, shuddering, drawing his coat close.

But Nicholas Dane's comments had intrigued me, and I found myself lingering at his side after we'd crossed the bridge and he released my arm. "You seem to know a great deal about Venice."

"Ah no," he said self-deprecatingly. "Let us say I know a very small amount about a great many places. A hazard of being so peripatetic, I'm afraid."

"Really? You've traveled a great deal?"

"I have."

"Where else have you been?"

He shrugged. "Everywhere, I suppose. I haven't lived in a single place longer than a few months since I left home seven years ago."

I couldn't tell whether there was regret in his tone or not—I guessed not. He had said he didn't care for his family, I remembered. "Why do you travel so much?"

"Looking for that elusive inspiration." Again I heard that bitterness I'd noted in the Gardens, that sense of something dark and unspoken.

But I knew a bit myself about dark, unspoken things, and so I said, "What happens when you find it?"

"I don't know." I felt him look at me. "I confess I'm curious to find out."

He'd said nothing really, and yet his voice was low and pregnant with something that made me shiver with sudden warmth. I thought of that kiss in the kitchen, the way my seduction had turned on me, how hard it had been to pull away. *Remember what happened before,* I reminded myself. *Be careful.*

I glanced away. "You must have some fascinating stories."

"Perhaps. But mine aren't pretty like yours. They have bite."

"Well, sometimes I think I should like a little bite."

He went quiet. His sudden tension made me wonder what I'd said. But when he spoke, his voice was wistful. "Don't be so quick to wish for it. I like your stories better. The world is an ugly enough place; a little beauty now and then restores a man's faith that there can be some meaning. I think you and your brother understand that. It's not a common thing. I'm grateful to find it in you."

I liked his compliment. I liked that he understood what Joseph and I both felt. I liked that it mattered to him.

We were quiet for a moment, and then he said softly, "You know, you are quite something, Miss Hannigan."

The words held an uncomfortable echo, and still I could not keep from going warm again. I was glad for the darkness that hid the flush I knew must be working its way over my cheeks. I could not help but feel that brush of possibility once more. Perhaps I might find something of my own in Venice after all.

Oh, but that was folly, wasn't it? I should not be feeling this. I did not want to feel it. I needed him for Joseph, for our plans. Nicholas Dane was a good man, but there was too much I could not tell him, too much he would never understand, because no one did. To think otherwise . . . I could not be so stupid again.

"Sophie, come on!" called my brother from ahead. "Don't linger or you'll get lost!"

I laughed a little nervously and said, "Oh, look how far ahead they are!" and hurried off after them, leaving Mr. Dane to catch up. I could not meet Joseph's gaze when I reached them. But when he touched my arm, I felt myself fall back into place, my brother providing, as he always did, the anchor I needed.

Still, I was very aware of Nicholas Dane as we walked through the twisting and turning *calli*, each of which seemed to take us ever deeper into some strange maze. It was easy to imagine getting so lost here one might wander aimlessly about for centuries. Our footsteps echoed and rebounded, seeming to come from all around us so I kept turning to see who followed. The shadows seemed deeper and more perilous at the street corners, where little shrines to the saints were lit by small and wavering flames of oil lamps that turned the shadows golden and then, at the edges, red. Everything around them seemed out of proportion, illusory and fantastical. Giles Martin swiped a piece of bread from one, munching on it as he walked, and Mr. Dane gave him a withering glance.

"Leave it for the rats," he said. "At least they're God's creatures."

Mr. Martin only grinned. "Now who's the superstitious one? I'm God's creature too, you know."

"A molding gone strangely awry," Mr. Dane said dryly.

I laughed, and so did Mr. Martin. Our voices braided together, echoing, twisting and transforming into something otherworldly. Every sound seemed funneled through the *calli*, footsteps echoing, the lapping sound of water though we were not near a canal, the muffled thud of a closing door, the screech of a window. Mr. Duveneck said, "You start to believe all those stories about Venice at this time of night."

"You're right," murmured my brother. "Ghosts in every shadow."

"And murderers around every corner." Mr. Duveneck lowered his voice, playing along. "I wouldn't be surprised to see a man in a domino and a stiletto lurch from a doorway."

"Oh, stop," I protested. "You'll give me nightmares."

Joseph laughed quietly. "Sophie has too good an imagination."

"And I don't want to be up all night thinking of ghosts."

Mr. Dane said, "Perhaps you could turn it into one of your pretty stories instead."

I glanced at him, and he smiled, and I could not help smiling back. Then we were there, turning a corner and suddenly at the courtyard entrance to the Moretta, a stone wall with a stout wooden door that bore a small opening crisscrossed with little iron bars. Joseph opened it.

We said our goodbyes. Joseph stepped inside, and as I followed, Mr. Dane grabbed my hand, sliding his fingers along my palm—a touch that sent a shiver through me—before he let me go.

Joseph closed the door, and we were in the quiet of the courtyard, its bordering pillars looming shadows, the ferns dripping down the walls like spreading fingers. The servants' quarters off the courtyard was silent, the elderly couple who rented it gone to bed. There was no light or sound from the Frenchwoman or her two young sons on the upper floor. The sky was moving into dawn, the deep black of night changing to slate as Joseph and I made our weary way up the stairs to the piano nobile. I was exhausted—the day had been so long that the time we'd spent on the Lido seemed a year ago. I was more than ready for bed.

"I have to go to the market today," I said. "We've nothing here to eat."

"I'll go with you," Joseph said. "We'll go to the Rialto. There's a pretty little corner by one of the fishmongers. I want to draw you there. We'll get you one of those shawls all the girls wear."

"All right," I agreed. I turned to go to the bedroom. "But later, please. So we can sleep—"

"Don't go to bed yet." Joseph took my hand. "Let's watch the sunrise."

I was too tired to protest. Joseph led me into the *sala*, which seemed huge and echoing and empty, the murals of Neptune and his mermaids shadowed. Joseph went to the balcony doors and opened them, and the cool, damp air rushed in. Then he led me to the middle of the room and pulled me down with him, so we were both lying on the cold, smooth floor, staring up at the ceiling with its painted sky, which was so far above our heads and so dark it might not have even been there.

"I thought you wanted to watch the sunrise," I said.

"I do." He pulled me close into his side.

I laid my head on his chest, listening to his heartbeat, along with the sounds coming from the city—the splash of oars, and a few voices. Someone laughing. I closed my eyes, breathing deeply of the early morning air, which smelled of algae and stone and salt, and my brother, who still had the scent of the Lido about him. Sand and sun and the tang of wine.

Joseph said quietly, "So much for him not being interested. Today he could hardly keep his hands off you. What happened?"

"I think it was the Lido."

"I knew he wouldn't be able to resist that. You were perfect."

"And . . . I kissed him tonight. In the kitchen."

Joseph stilled. Then he said softly, "You should bring him round to Loneghan quickly."

"I will."

My brother ran his hand down my arm, and then up again, a slow and steady caress. "Be careful, Soph."

His touch was mesmerizing. It raised a shiver that coursed through me and settled deep and low. "I will. I am. I *know*."

"I don't want you to do anything you don't want. You know that, don't you? I wouldn't ask it."

"I know," I assured him. "But I do like him. And he's easy to flirt with."

"Not like Stimpson or Davenport?"

I thought of the two men in our New York salon, who we'd both thought had an influence it turned out they didn't have. My seduction of them had been a waste of time. "I didn't mind flirting with them, either."

"But you didn't like sleeping with them."

I shrugged. "I thought they could help us."

He said, "What about Dane? Would you like to sleep with him?"

I thought of the way Nicholas Dane had looked at me. I felt again his mouth on mine, his tongue, the heat of him that made me respond in a way I hadn't expected. *You are quite something.* Yes, I was *something*. "I don't know. Perhaps."

"I like him too, Soph. But don't make him into another Roberts."

"No," I whispered. "Edward Roberts was a mistake."

My brother exhaled in a great sigh. "I just don't want you to make another one."

I heard his guilt and I said, "You weren't to blame."

"Wasn't I? Am I not always?"

The wry self-deprecation in his voice nearly broke my heart. "I was foolish. You told me and I didn't listen. I won't let that happen again. I promise."

I looked at him and our gazes locked and his was so full of *everything* that I nearly wept. Then he glanced at the ceiling.

"Look," he said reverently.

There it was, the thing he'd known to watch for, the reason we were lying on the floor beneath the sky-painted ceiling while the sun rose outside our window. Because it was rising for us in here, spreading over faux clouds and gilded plaster, gold and pink rippling, sparkling with the reflections of the canal below so the ceiling was aflame with light and motion, and it was as if the sun had chosen to present itself for us alone.

"Oh," I breathed, and Joseph laughed softly against my ear, and I lay there, awed and overwhelmed and no longer the least bit sleepy, watching the play of light across a painted ceiling, watching it come alive.

TWENTY-TWO

SOPHIE

I remember almost nothing of my life before our parents died, and I don't think Joseph remembers it any better. My only real memory of them was their funeral, and standing beside double coffins gleaming in an unbearably hot sun. We were seven, and it was the middle of summer, and the black wool I wore itched; I wanted nothing more than to be out of my stockings, playing with my brother in the park. I think I was sad. I must have been sad, though even that memory is as a dream—I cannot be certain it is quite real.

Our aunt, who was our guardian, swooped in and hired Miss Jessamine Coring to be our governess and then left again. My aunt did not like New York City; she kept the brownstone on Washington Square only because it was held in trust for Joseph, and because it suited her to keep us in it and away from her. Most of the furniture was sold to pay debts, and my aunt had replaced it with only the most necessary things, just enough to receive her when she flew into the city on her bi-yearly visits, when she would bring us into the alien land of downstairs to endure a long and wretched tea with her. She looked like a buzzard and had little patience for children, particularly for two she'd been told were so ill behaved.

Whether that was true or not I couldn't say. Surely Miss Coring thought so, which was why she never allowed us to leave the third floor. My world, which had never been broad to begin with, narrowed to the nursery, Miss Coring, and my brother, who was the center of it. Joseph and I had always been inseparable, and our isolation only brought us closer together. We saw no other children, nor did we think to miss them. We were too busy surviving Miss Coring and her mercurial moods. Joseph used to whisper to me, deep in the night, as we held each other against the darkness: *We're different, Soph. I know it. We're marked for something special.*

Well, I knew it was true about him, anyway. His talent was evident from the time he could hold a pencil. And, because he insisted on it, I tried to believe it about myself, though I never quite managed it. It was some time before I realized just how different we were.

I began to suspect it at sixteen, when Miss Coring died, leaving Joseph and me both rescued and abandoned at the same time, and Aunt Rebecca sent me to finishing school and Joseph to University. She tried to make us board, but neither of us would stay; we came back to the nursery each night, too fragile without each other, unable to make anything of ourselves apart, and so finally she gave up and left us to ourselves. But for the first time, I was exposed to girls my own age. I listened to their breathless talk, the things they cared about that all seemed so foreign and stupid to me. I pretended to care, to be one of them, because it was expected, but I felt every moment an imposter, as if I were living my life on the surface of a deeper and richer and more wondrous ocean I could not dive down deep enough to reach.

The feeling only grew worse when my aunt, hoping to arrange marriages for us both that would take us off her hands for good, insisted Joseph and I enter again into the society that was our birthright. My parents had never moved in the upper echelons of society—we were not rich enough to be Astors or Vanderbilts—but still, it was strange to come into that world of teas and suppers and balls, to come back into the life we'd had at seven as if we'd never left it. Old friends of our parents welcomed us as if we'd never been away.

Joseph, of course, was at home everywhere, so good-natured and lovely that everyone took to him immediately. But he was restless. At school, he'd made friends who introduced us to the circles we preferred, people more like us—different, *marked*— who did not spend their nights chattering about the latest fashions over too-sweet, warm lemonade. They talked of new worlds, of free love and women's suffrage, socialism and philosophy and art. Joseph flourished among them. *This is where we belong, Soph.*

I admit I took to it. It was heady talk, no matter how impractical. Joseph and I began to live double lives: evenings spent at society dinners, listening to the daughters of our hosts mangle the pianoforte, followed by late nights spent in rapt conversation about things that meant something, drinking and laughing until the early hours. Joseph believed—and I did too—that his talent would bring us everything we'd ever wanted, everything we'd dreamed of in those days when we'd invented imaginary worlds in the nursery together. He and I both believed that fame was our due—why else had we survived the hell of Miss Coring except for Joseph to be what he was? And too, our inheritance was so small that we desperately needed money. There were men—and women—in the salon who could help us get both things, and we set about using them to further Joseph's career. Joseph engaged the women, who seemed more than happy to be engaged. It was harder for me, though I managed one or two of the men. Joseph could lose himself in desire, though he never seemed to care much for any woman once he was out of her bed. I wished I could lose myself so readily, but my own desire was fleeting; no matter how often I longed for it to consume me, it never did. I began to wonder if I was destined to love only once, if the only desire I would ever feel was one that I could not express.

My brother and I had always shared everything, but I began to yearn for something special of my own, that belonged just to me, someone who could love me apart from Joseph. Perhaps it was too much to hope for, because such a thing seemed to elude me. Every boy seemed so *young*, so unlike my brother. If I could only find someone like Joseph. . . . When I complained to my brother he laughed and teased that my expectations were too high. *You're not likely to find a knight in shining armor in New York society.* But I saw too that he was glad.

And then I met Edward Roberts.

Edward had just returned from the Continent. His father had sent him to look into the prospects of a partnership with a Parisian art dealer. Of course, the moment I heard those words, I knew I must do my best to charm him. I used all the wiles that Joseph had taught me, the ways to keep a man interested, and I'd been glad when it seemed Edward was. At least, that was how it started. I'd meant all of it only to help Joseph.

In retrospect, I saw the things that should have told me what a disaster it would be, but to look at Edward, you would never have suspected him of being so devious. Joseph thought him stupid, in fact, which was odd, as my brother was rarely wrong when it came to people. But I knew why he thought it: Edward had that sort of perpetual puppy-dog look about him, large and winsome chocolate-brown eyes beneath a shock of golden-blond hair, an endearing willingness to please. At least, I thought it endearing. Joseph found it irritating, and I saw the measuring, half-angry way my brother looked at Edward when he thought I didn't see.

"He's after something," Joseph told me one morning as I posed for him in the sunlight coming through the nursery window.

"Not our inheritance, surely. It's barely enough to keep us for another two years. And he has money of his own."

Joseph rose and reached over to drape a lock of hair more artfully over my breast, then assessed it quietly before he sat and took up drawing again. "It's his father's money, not his, and I think his father doesn't quite approve of him. He'll need an heiress, which isn't you, so why is he wasting his time?"

"Because he likes me, perhaps? And he knows how talented you are. He says it all the time."

"Does he? To whom?"

"To everyone he sees. He admires you. You should try to like him. If you made half an effort, he'd fall over himself to introduce you to his father."

Joseph looked thoughtfully down at his sketchbook. He smudged something on the paper with his thumb, then wiped across his jaw, leaving a streak of charcoal before he went in to smudge again, distracted.

I came over to him and pushed away the tablet despite his protests. It fell to the ground and I plopped myself into his lap. I took his face between my hands, holding him still to meet my gaze. "You're not listening. We've been invited to Mrs. Ballast's for tea tomorrow. Please come with me."

"Mrs. Ballast can do nothing for us."

"No, but Edward will be there. And I want you to be kind to Edward."

He dropped his charcoal with a sigh and wrapped his arms around me, pulling me close. I felt his mouth against my bare skin as he murmured, "All right, Soph. You know I'll do whatever you want."

"You needn't sound so glum about it."

"I don't like him. But if you think he can help—"

I strung my fingers through his thick, dark hair, pulling his head back so he must look at me. "I *do* like him. Very much. And I know he can help. But you have to be nice to him too. And you can't be jealous. Please."

"What does my jealousy matter? It's not as if . . ." He let out his breath and jerked his head from my hold. "I'll be good, all right?"

"Thank you."

His wide and beautiful mouth quirked, though I saw how forced it was. "You sound half besotted. Don't tell me you're falling for him."

"What if I am?"

"He's not good enough for you. And he's not very smart."

"You would say that about anyone who showed an interest in me."

He planted a lingering kiss on my collarbone. His hold on me tightened, fingers clenching, and then he sighed and pushed me gently away. "On the contrary. The man who truly falls in love with you will be the most intelligent man in the world."

I got off his lap, taking my post at the window again, arranging my hair over my shoulder the way he'd had it. "You think Edward won't be that man?"

"No, I told you: I think he wants something from us. I just don't know what. Especially as we've almost nothing."

"But that will change, won't it? Once the world sees what you can do, it will all change."

"Yes, it will change." Joseph rose, reaching for my dressing gown and handing it to me.

"Are we done?" I asked in surprise.

"For now," he said. "I've got to go out."

"Out? Where? For what?"

"Just out," he said with a forced smile and that haunted look I knew too well. "I won't be late. Accept Mrs. Ballast's invitation for the both of us. Good enough?"

I nodded as I put on the dressing gown, fastening it as he left the nursery. I heard his footsteps down the hall, echoing in the emptiness. I knew where that haunted look came from, and where he was going to try to ease it, and I hated it, but there was nothing I could do. I would only make it worse if I tried. The will to resist felt sometimes held with only the flimsiest of strings.

I looked around the nursery, feeling the press of memories, both good and bad, though it was the room we spent most of our time in still, the world we knew. Joseph would not even go into his bedroom—he hadn't since he was old enough not to be forced—and now it was kept locked, opened once a week only for the maid to dust and air the bedding for one who never slept there. I understood that too. The room held too many memories of Miss Coring.

The name still made me shudder, nine years after her death. One would think it no longer had the power to wound, but still sometimes I tensed, thinking I heard her footstep, and I still dreamed of her bending over me, her dark eyes lit with that cruel excitement I'd grown to dread. *Come now, Sophie, dance for me and your brother. . . .*

I pushed the image away, replacing it instead with another, better one: Joseph on the floor, lying on his stomach while the summer sun gilded his dark hair, the voices of the street filtering in from a city we had never explored, a land that seemed foreign and removed, not anything to do with us. The only land we cared about was the one we invented, the one he drew while I described it for him, detail by painstaking detail. He'd put a hooked nose on my favorite prince, and I'd thrown myself at him in protest, wrestling the charcoal from his fingers while he laughed and laughed, then he'd held me so tightly I could hardly breathe, whispering in my ear, *Well, he can't be too handsome, can he? I don't want him replacing me.*

Joseph had been Miss Coring's target so much more than I. He had been too beautiful even as a boy, too talented. People noticed him. His beauty tormented her, as did our connection. The intimacy between us alienated her and made her angry—until we grew older and her hold on Joseph began to fade, and she figured out a way to use me to keep him close. We had been so isolated that I had not known the things she did to us to be different or to be wrong. Not until the night Joseph had come to my bed and stayed there, begging me to hold him tight, to keep him from answering a call he both dreaded and desired.

I could not forget the look on her face when she found us together the next morning, still wrapped in each other's arms, that expression that made me sick to my stomach even now. That morning, my love for my brother—the best thing in my life, the only thing that mattered—became tangled with shame and pain. It was the one thing I could never forgive her.

She died a year later. It seemed her heart was bad in more ways than one. I still remembered how I'd been sorting through things in the nursery when I'd heard these terrible, guttural animal sounds coming from the hallway. I'd gone out to see Joseph sitting at the top of the stairs, his head buried in his arms. It was a moment before I realized those terrible sounds were coming from him, before I realized he was sobbing. I'd sat beside him, wrapping myself around him, whispering, *It's all right, Joseph.*

It's all right. I'm here, and he'd said without lifting his head, *I hated her. I hated her. I hated her.* Over and over again, like a song, and I knew he had to say the words. I also knew they weren't the whole truth.

He'd laid his head in my lap while I ran my fingers through his hair where it curled against his collar. I told him, *Remember what you said? That we were marked for something special? Now we can be what we were meant to be, Joseph. Now that she's gone, we can do everything we've dreamed of.*

I had blinked the memory away that day, listening to the door close behind Joseph as he left. I had told myself it was better not to think of those things, to never remember, though the sting of what she'd done to us was still so sharp it was sometimes hard to do.

I'd left the nursery and waited for Joseph to come home, knowing that the yearning that had made him go would be allayed when he returned. He was so much luckier than I when it came to finding appeasement. But then again, he was a man, and such things were easy for them. When he came back—hours later, smelling of cheap perfume—he was himself again, and I had been relieved.

"I'm sorry," he said to me, smiling, playing. "I know you worry."

I knew he had no wish to talk about it. Neither of us did.

So I said, "Tea is at four o'clock tomorrow. Don't forget it and disappear."

I had no real hope that he would remember; he was never dependable. He'd be out walking and see a scene he liked, or a detail he'd missed before, and lose himself in sketching or painting. Hours would pass before he remembered the time. But he surprised me. At three thirty the next day, he was washed and shaved and presentable, though he never lost that slightly disheveled aesthetic that marked him as the artist he was.

When Joseph and I arrived at Mrs. Ballast's tea, Edward Roberts was waiting. His face lit when he saw us. He came forward to kiss my cheek and shook Joseph's hand perhaps a bit too long and enthusiastically. Joseph excused himself to speak to Mrs. Ballast's daughter, Angelica, and Edward drew me into the shade of a climbing rose. "Your brother doesn't like me," he complained.

I pressed my hand against his vested chest. "Don't be absurd. Of course he likes you. He's just . . . well, he's distracted. Something's always catching his eye."

Edward frowned. "A woman, you mean?"

I shook my head. "Something new to paint. My guess is that when he saw you he was already noticing the way the sun hit the yew, or something like that. He can't help himself. But I know he likes you, Edward. Why, he said something about it just this morning."

"He did?"

"He said"—I struggled to think of something—"he said you had a way with words."

Edward looked pleased. "My father says the same thing."

"You see?" I smiled. "I think you have a way with other things too."

His gaze darkened. He brought his hands around my waist, pulled me close, and kissed me. And it was no chaste kiss, either. For the first time, he kissed me until I was breathless, until I felt the stirrings of desire, until I thought *maybe*.

He drew away. His pale face was flushed. He said, "I've been thinking it's time I introduced you to my father. Your brother too. I think he would like you both," and I felt a flush of victory that made me kiss him again.

Joseph said to me later, "Now that we're to meet his father, you don't need to take this any further."

I didn't know how to explain to him that I wanted to. That I felt the kind of desire for Edward Roberts that I'd despaired of feeling, that I thought I might be in love at last. What had started as a way to help Joseph had turned into something else, something just for me. The way Edward looked at me, that gaze that reminded me of my brother's, made me begin to believe that perhaps Edward was not like the others, that he saw something special in me apart from Joseph. The day Joseph and I arrived at Edward's father's house for dinner, and my brother impressed the old man into offering him a commission—a portrait of his wife—I knew I had fallen in love.

Joseph's excitement and triumph only made me want Edward more. I could hardly sleep that night, tossing and turning restlessly until Joseph woke and said, "What ails you, Soph?" and I got up to wander about the house.

The next morning Edward and I had scheduled a carriage ride; when he arrived I drew him inside and up the stairs. I was trembling when I kissed him. We went into my bedroom, but I didn't want to stay—it felt odd and uncomfortable to have him there—and the nursery was worse. So I took him down the hall, to my brother's room, unlocked it, and pulled him inside. The room still held some of Joseph's things, old boots and shoes, books, sketches he'd pinned to the wallpaper. Edward pulled away, frowning, saying, "This isn't your room." When I told him it was my brother's, Edward seemed in a frenzy. He wrenched at my buttons as if he wanted to tear the gown from my body, and I fell into the familiar darkness of surrender without thought or resistance.

Afterward he looked at me with this expression I couldn't read and said, "You aren't like most women." I thought it meant he loved me. I thought I had what I longed for at last.

When Joseph came home that afternoon, his face was hard. Though Edward had left hours before, I knew Joseph understood what had happened between us. "You'd best watch yourself," he'd warned. "You don't want to get with child and have to marry him."

I'd flushed. "I think I love him."

Joseph sat down beside me. He took my hand and pressed it to his mouth. "Don't make the mistake of thinking it, Soph."

"He wants me," I said angrily. "He *sees* me."

My brother gave me a tormented look and released my hand. He rose, turning to leave, and I felt suddenly guilty and afraid.

I said, a little desperately, wanting to call him back, "I'm sorry. I'll be more careful, I promise. Shall I pose?"

He didn't turn around or pause or look over his shoulder. "Not like this. He's all over you."

And that made me angry enough to forget my guilt. Joseph was only jealous. He wanted to keep me too close. He didn't want me to find something of my own. I brought Edward home again and again, always to Joseph's bedroom, because he seemed to like it, and one day, when I lay sleepily in his arms as he gazed about the room, he said, "These sketches are beautiful."

"They aren't even his best. Most of these he drew when he was young. He's much better now."

"It's hard to believe he hasn't had any training. That one of you over there, with your chin upon your hand. How old were you when he did that?"

I glanced at the sketch he spoke of. It was one of so many; I hardly remembered the day Joseph had drawn it. My hair was tied up with a pink ribbon; his pastels pinked my cheeks and made my eyes bluer than they were as the girl I'd been stared dreamily into space. "About twelve, I think. Perhaps thirteen."

"He does you so well. That one over there too—it's beautiful. He's captured you entirely."

"He's had enough practice," I said with a smile. "There must be hundreds of sketches of me."

"Where are they? I'd love to see them."

"Oh, everywhere," I said, wanting to please, taking his interest in my world as evidence of his love. "But I know there's one portfolio in here."

I went to my brother's desk, never used now, and pulled out the case I knew was behind it. I took it to the bed, laying it on the crumpled blankets, and Edward scooted out of the way so I could open it. This portfolio held only a small fraction of the work Joseph had done—there were similar folders everywhere—but when I opened it, hundreds of drawings threatened to pour out. I eased out several, sifting charcoal dust over the coverlet, graying my fingers. Some of them I put surreptitiously aside—the ones Miss Coring had made me pose for. Joseph had never been able to bring himself to throw away anything he'd drawn, even these, and I was not surprised to find them shoved away here, but I could not bear for anyone else to see them. I could not bear to remember. The others I drew out one after another to show Edward, sketches of me dancing in a thin shift, my hair flying, another where I peeled a peach while juice dripped down my fingers, a third where I sat on a chair, wearing one of Joseph's shirts, my knees pulled to my breasts.

Edward took in a hard breath, and I knew he found them beautiful too. I wanted him to love my brother's talent as I did, and so I took out more, some of my favorites now: an odalisque of me on a settee, arching in a stretch, my hair falling over the side, nearly to the floor; another where I looked over my shoulder, my eyes dark and haunting; another sprawled in bed, looking ravished and sated, hair tangled, sheets crumpled between my legs.

I handed Edward one I particularly loved, where I lay on the floor in a pool of sunlight that dappled my skin, saying, "This was always one of my favorites."

He didn't take it. He was clutching the one of me on the bed almost convulsively. When I looked at him in surprise, he said, "You're posing . . . from life. In almost every one."

"Yes, of course."

"But—"

"But what?" I frowned, confused.

Edward only gave me a long, slow look, very contemplative, an expression that made me nervous for no reason I could say.

"What is it?" I asked. "Why do you look at me that way?"

He shook his head and handed me back the drawing. "You're right. They're all very beautiful."

I put the drawings away. I thought no more about it. I was naive, I suppose—no, more than that, stupid. It never occurred to me to think the sketches were anything but sublime. I loved how Joseph captured yearning and desire and love with every stroke. I was not quite me in them, but at the same time I was more me than anyone could know. I believed Edward had seen that as well.

It wasn't until two days later that I realized what Edward had really seen.

He had arrived in the afternoon, which was odd—he usually visited me in the morning, after Joseph had gone off on one of his excursions. I hadn't been expecting him, but I was glad, as always, to see him. As he drew me upstairs to Joseph's room, he seemed possessed by some strange fever. He undressed me with such slow care I didn't understand it—he'd never been anything but hurried before, impatient. And though he was slow and thorough, he seemed oddly anxious, as if he were waiting for something. As he unlaced my chemise, he said, "Let's take our time, darling, shall we? We've all afternoon."

But we didn't, I knew. We were coming to the time when Joseph would be home, and I knew he would not like to come upon Edward and me like this. And then, just as I had the thought, I heard the front door open and close; I heard my brother call, "Soph? I'm home. Where are you?"

I panicked. I started for the door. Edward held me tightly in place. "You don't understand," I told him desperately. "He'll hate this—"

"Will he?" Edward asked, and there was a blandness in his tone that made me stop to look at him.

"Sophie!" Joseph was coming up the stairs.

I said again, "You don't understand."

"What don't I understand?" Edward asked, and there was an excitement in his eyes that startled me, a vibration that told me he'd been waiting just for this, that he'd come at this time deliberately, meaning to confront my brother. But I had no idea why. I didn't understand at all.

And then I heard Joseph reach the top floor. I heard his step stall as he noticed the cracked door of the bedroom that was always kept closed. "Sophie?"

I heard the strain in his voice, and just as I wondered how I would explain this to him, what I could possibly say, he pushed open the door. He paused, taking in me with my hair down, clad only in a chemise falling from my bared shoulders, and Edward without a shirt.

Joseph said, "What the hell are you doing in *here*?"

I tried to push away from Edward's hold, but his hands

squeezed almost painfully tight, holding me in place. I said, "It's not what it looks like."

"Oh, no—it's exactly what it looks like," Edward said to my horror, a satisfied look in his eyes. "It's not as if he doesn't know what's been going on, darling. You do know, don't you, Hannigan, that I've been fucking your sister?"

"Edward," I breathed.

My brother didn't even blink. He only stood there like a statue, pale and chiseled and beautiful, with a look in his eyes that made me want to be sick. "I know," he said softly.

Edward said, "We were just getting ready to commence. So why don't you—"

"Edward, please," I managed.

"—join us?" Edward proposed.

I gasped, turning to him in surprise.

Edward looked at me almost contemptuously. "Come now, don't act so shocked. Don't tell me you haven't played this game before."

Joseph said in a strained voice, "I think you should go."

Edward released me. His muscles were clenched; he leaned toward Joseph as if he were pulled. "Join us." His voice fell to a whisper, a plea. "Please God, join us." The urgency in it alarmed me. He crossed the room in two steps, moving before I knew he'd done so. He was not taller nor bigger than Joseph, but he pushed my brother up against the wall easily, pressing himself to him the way he'd once pressed himself to me. He grabbed Joseph by the back of the head, thrusting his fingers into my brother's hair, and Joseph let him, doing nothing as Edward Roberts jerked him down to kiss, hard and thoroughly, as if he might swallow him whole. I could only watch in shock as Joseph surrendered to it. It was as if Miss Coring were in the room again.

There was no point in resistance—how well she'd taught us that. How well I understood.

Edward pulled feverishly at Joseph's shirt, pulling it from his trousers, his hands beneath it, running up my brother's bare chest. "Christ, I want you," he was whispering—I think he had forgotten I was even in the room. "I have wanted you since I first laid eyes on you."

And then I knew. I knew what it was Edward Roberts meant to have from us, and it wasn't me. It had never been me. I had never been special to him. It was Joseph, always, and suddenly every strangeness I'd noted about Edward's desire, every little thing I'd found odd and dismissed, the way Joseph's presence excited Edward even in his absence, made sense. I cried out, putting my hand to my mouth almost immediately to stop it, too late, and it was that sound that seemed to galvanize my brother. He looked at me—I saw the misery in his eyes, that haunted look again—and then he pushed Edward hard, so hard that Edward stumbled back. Before Edward gained his feet, Joseph hit him. The cracking thud of the blow resounded. Edward went flying, sprawling on the floor at my feet, hitting his head on the bed-post. A bruise was already forming on his eye.

"Get the hell out," Joseph said steadily. "Don't trouble my sister or me again."

Edward scrambled to his feet. He grabbed his shirt from the bed. His eyes were blazing even as the one swelled shut. "You'll regret this. Both of you," he snarled. "There's a word for the two of you. You've fooled everyone, but don't think I'll let you get away with it."

He stumbled from the room. Joseph and I both stood numbly, listening to him clatter down the stairs. The front door slammed shut so loudly I felt the shudder of it up to the third floor.

It wasn't until then that my heart broke and the horror of it hit me. It wasn't until then that I began to cry.

Joseph took me in his arms. He lifted my chin and kissed away my tears. "Sophie. Sophie. It will be all right, I promise. I promise." He brought me down on the bed with him, the bed he never slept in, the one he hated, and held me close. We stayed there until dawn as if it were a badge of courage, as if we could somehow banish the old demons that lingered and the ones that had just appeared.

The next afternoon a message came from Edward's father saying that he was canceling the commission he'd given Joseph, and, for his wife's trouble, he would keep the sketch Joseph had already made—a thing of beauty in itself. He hadn't paid us a cent. By the following day, three invitations to teas and suppers had been rescinded on some pretext or another. The day after that, two women I knew turned away when I stepped into a shop, and hurried off as if they hadn't seen me.

"I don't know what he's told them," I said to Joseph in dismay. "What could he have said that wouldn't hurt him as well?"

"You do know," my brother said grimly. "You know very well."

That night, at the cafe, as we drank beer and laughed and talked with the artists I thought were our friends, I caught some of them whispering, though they quieted when we came near, and I saw one or two of them staring at me when they thought I wasn't looking. I knew Joseph saw it too. When we got home that night, he went out again right away, saying only that there was someone he needed to talk to, no matter that it was one in the morning.

He didn't return, not until I was at breakfast, when he came through the door of the nursery looking so thunderous I dropped my spoon into my tea.

"What is it? What's wrong?"

"Roberts has some of the sketches," he said, sinking into a schoolboy's chair that was far too small for him. It creaked beneath his weight. He leaned forward, elbows on his knees, and buried his face in his hands.

"The sketches?" I asked stupidly.

"How would he have found them?" he asked. "Why would he have them?"

"I . . . I showed them to him. I didn't let him take one."

"But he knew where they were, didn't he?"

"Yes," I admitted. "Yes, he did. I didn't know they were secret."

He looked up at me bleakly. "They aren't secret, Sophie. But why did you need to show him?"

"What do you mean?" I began to feel uneasy. "They're beautiful. I wanted him to see how talented you are. And you've shown them to others."

He let out his breath and looked away. "The salons . . . people there appreciate them. They've helped us."

"Yes. But I don't understand what you mean about Edward."

Joseph met my gaze steadily. "You already *had* him, Sophie. There was no point. And now he has two of the ones she made me draw."

"I didn't show him those," I whispered. "They're obscene."

"Well, he has them. He's been telling people about them, but thankfully he hasn't shown them yet."

"It wasn't our fault," I said weakly. "She made us—"

Joseph gave me a look. The truth in his eyes silenced me.

"No one understands," I managed.

"No, they don't. But it doesn't matter, does it?" He didn't elucidate, and I didn't need him to. I knew what it would mean, what people would see. I'd seen it before, hadn't I? That long-ago morning when Miss Coring had come upon us. Horror and jealousy, arousal and disgust. And while the other sketches had shown the love I felt for my brother, and that he felt for me, Edward had found the ones that showed the ugliness, that made our love into something else. They could destroy us.

"What does he want?" I asked.

"Money," Joseph said frankly. "Money to keep him quiet and buy them back. But it will take almost everything we have. And . . . and we'll have to leave the city for a time, Sophie. The rumors . . . it would be best if we left."

"We could tell everyone the truth. We could tell how he . . . how he attacked you and—"

"And what? It would only make things worse. He'll show the sketches in reply and then . . . then it doesn't matter what's true. No, it's best to go away for a while and let the talk die down."

"Where would we go?"

Joseph hesitated. Then he said, quickly, as if he'd been thinking about it for some time, "Everyone's talking of Venice. And there are people there—people who have money. People who would make good patrons."

I remembered the talk I'd heard. "The Bronsons are in Venice, aren't they? And the Loneghans."

"Yes. We won't have much left when this is over. Maybe not even enough to get us there. But you could figure it out, couldn't you? You're good at managing. Perhaps you could find enough to tide us over for a few months. Until the spring at least."

"And if you found a patron, it wouldn't matter how little we start with."

He nodded. "I'll make it all right, Soph. I promise. I'll make it work. You know I can."

"Yes," I said. "I know it."

He smiled, and in that lovely smile, everything fell away, Edward and the ugliness he'd brought, my own hurt and anger over the way I'd been worked, my foolishness. I forgot it all when Joseph crooked his finger at me, when I went to him, into his arms, the plan and his will already easing, mending, healing. We would go to Venice. We would leave all this behind. We would make my brother as famous as he was meant to be.

The two of us are marked for something special.

I felt his kiss on my hair as I clutched him, as I pressed my face into his chest and breathed deep of him, the other part of me, rolling the promise around and around in my head until I was reassured and safe again in the world we had made for each other.

TWENTY-THREE

ODILÉ

The singer's body had been taken away. Antonio's silent efficiency asked no questions, and I'd said only that the man had suffered from a heart condition, which was true—my leeching of his creative vitality had stopped his heart. I regretted it—such a loss of control was not ever what I liked, and it was only further evidence that I could no longer delay. And now two days had passed. I told Antonio to ready the gondola, and pressed my hands to my stomach as if I could press away the pain, and with it, my fear. The monster churned, struggling to emerge. There was no more time.

"*Padrona,* there is a man here to see you. Signor Balbi."

I jerked around, startled at my maid, Maria's, voice. Impatiently I said, "Balbi? I don't know who that is. Get his card and send him away."

"He is the police."

"The police?"

She nodded vigorously. I was surprised, and then annoyed and then curious enough that my pain eased. I could not think what the police would want with me, though I was not the least bit trepidatious. What reason had I to fear mortal police? "I see. Very well. Show him in."

Mr. Balbi was a tall man with graying hair and an equally gray Vandyke beard. I had the impression of robust fastidiousness, discerning perception, and not a little vanity. His hair was well oiled, his beard immaculately trimmed. He wore black, which reminded me of the old days in Venice, when the nobility had worn only that color, and I had the sense that he'd deliberately dressed to suggest it. His watch chain—only one and unadorned with any kind of charm—was his only decoration.

"Madame León," he said as he strode toward me—he spoke immaculate French, though with that Venetian accent, that mangling of consonants. "Please allow me to introduce myself. I am Inspector Alberto Balbi, of the police department. Thank you for seeing me."

I took the card he offered, barely glancing at it before I put it on the table. "How can I help you, Inspector?"

"A trifling matter, really," he said with a very pleasant smile. "Last night, we found a body floating in the Rio Orseolo. A man by the name of Giovanni Santo."

He looked at me as if he expected a reaction. I had none to give him. The name was unknown to me. "And?"

The inspector frowned. "Giovanni Santo was last seen with you, madame."

My hunger roiled. I could not help the catch of my breath. The Inspector heard it too, I realized. And took it for some admission.

"It is true, then?"

I tried to smile. "True? I'm afraid I don't recognize his name, so I could not tell you."

"No? He was a peasant. A street singer."

This time, I had to sit down. "Pardon me, Inspector, but I am not at my best this morning."

"Ah. I hope you are not ill."

"No. A . . . chronic condition, I'm afraid."

"A chronic condition?" His dark eyes narrowed. "No other reason? You were not hurt? Not beaten?"

I realized suddenly what he was truly asking, and I gave him a cold look. "Would you care to check me for bruises, Inspector?"

"Oh no, I don't think that will be necessary."

"Why are you here, Inspector? Do you mean to ask me if I killed Giovanni—what was his last name again?"

"Santo."

"I haven't seen him for two days."

"But I think you were the last to see him alive, madame. He had been in the water that long."

"Do I look as if I could overpower a man like that?"

He shrugged. "What could not happen in a moment of surprise? An easy push into a *rio* . . ."

I regarded him wryly. "You should have been a storyteller, Inspector."

"He was your lover, was he not?"

"He was," I said wearily. "For all of two nights."

Balbi raised a dark brow. "How sad for you."

"I didn't know him well enough to be sad," I told him frankly. "I saw him on the street, and I brought him home. I never asked his name, and I didn't care to have it. Does that shock you?"

"Nothing in Venice surprises, madame. We have heard you had an . . . attachment to Nelson Stafford and Jonathan Murphy too."

"Yes. What about them? Are you accusing me of killing them as well? Nelson Stafford was a suicide. Jonathan an accident. They had nothing to do with me."

"Ah, then it is only that you're unlucky?"

"Yes," I said. "Very unlucky. But I do not believe that is a crime."

"No, no crime," Balbi said, shaking his head, a thin smile. "When did you last see Giovanni Santo? Was he alive?"

"Very much so. He was exhausted. We'd been up all night." I did not take my gaze from the Inspector's as I lied. I had no worry for the servants, as both Antonio and Maria were devoted—and overpaid. "I kissed him goodbye. He went off into the morning. I've not seen him since."

"You didn't follow him?"

"No."

"You didn't have him followed?"

"Why would I care to?"

"To see that he did not go back to his fiancée, perhaps? You were not jealous? Not enraged that there was another?"

I laughed. "I had no idea that there was. But even so . . . my dear inspector, do I look to you like a woman afraid of competition?"

His gaze swept me. "No indeed. I should say the opposite in fact, that other women are afraid of you."

It was a compliment, but I did not acknowledge it. "I wanted Giovanni Santo for nothing more than his skill as a lover. Which he provided. Gladly. What other women he had, or what else he did, I have no idea. Nor do I care."

I waited for him to do what was polite and take his leave, but he only stood there for a moment, looking at me as if he expected some answer to come to him. The only answer there was I couldn't give him. Nothing about the truth would satisfy. There was nothing he would believe.

"Thank you for your time, madame. Those are all the questions I have for now, but you have my card, if anything should occur to you that you think I should know."

"I can't imagine what that might be."

"Even so." He smiled. "And . . . might I make a suggestion?"

"I suppose I cannot stop you."

"Perhaps you might take a break from love. So the city can recover."

He turned and left the *sala*. I heard his footsteps on the hard floor, echoing down the *portego* until he was gone.

It was only then that I allowed myself to be angry. At myself for draining the singer. At the writer and the organist for being weak and stupid. Venice was proving to be unlucky indeed. And now the police would be watching me. It wasn't that I was afraid of them—laws had no relevance for me. But I was afraid of being hindered even more, especially now, when there was so little time.

I felt as if I were unraveling, the terror within me pushing, insistent. Police or no, I had to find the one. I had to find him now.

I summoned Antonio, and set off for the Rialto.

TWENTY-FOUR

ODILÉ

The day was beautiful, and the market was crowded. There were performers everywhere who faltered as I drew near. A magician by the fish market seemed to have more talent than most, and I paused to watch for a moment. His breathing ratcheted; he fumbled in whisking a coin from his palm, dropping it so that it rolled, flashing and glinting, across the stones. A flurry of peasant children rushed to snatch it. The world was changing color before my eyes, leaping from sepia to vibrance and back again; my edges shivering. I needed *something*, and quickly.

I stepped forward, meaning to touch the magician's arm, to smile, to drag him away, when something made me glance at a nearby fishmonger's. There, tucked like a jewel among stones, was a dark-haired girl wearing a black shawl, and an astonishingly attractive man. I don't know why they caught my interest—perhaps it was the way he touched her, the way they seemed to have eyes for no one else. But then I realized he was posing

208

her, and when he stepped back it was to pick up a sketchbook from where it lay on a nearby coil of rope. An artist.

My hunger surged sharply; I had to clench my teeth to keep from crying out. I moved toward them, slipping through the crowd, easing up behind him. He was so focused on his drawing he didn't seem to sense me. I glanced over his shoulder at the sketchbook, wondering with an almost painful anticipation what I would see.

The drawing there nearly made me weak with relief.

The way he'd captured her, the bold strokes, the chiaroscuro . . . what he had made of her was not just beautiful, but sublime.

Smells were suddenly too sharp—the algae in the sun and the grease from the fritterers', acrid oil and smoke from the omnibus—and my skin felt stretched tight, my fingers flexing with need. I felt I might swoon. My waiting was over. Here he was at last.

It was all I could do to say, "That's lovely."

He started, nearly dropping the charcoal. He looked over his shoulder—he was more splendid even than I'd thought—and I saw surprise come into his deep blue eyes, and then the look I had grown used to, the expression I craved. Appreciation. Desire. He went still, obviously speechless. My hunger working on him already.

I gestured to the sketchbook, to his hand poised over it as if it had frozen in place. "You're exquisite."

"Thank you so much." The voice came from just beyond. His lover had stepped over to us. I'd already forgotten about her, but his gaze riveted to her as if she held it captive. She gave me a warily apologetic smile. She touched his arm, and he leaned toward her movement, and his allure seemed to intensify, nearly unbearably so. The monster in me lashed out. A man carrying a cage with a cockatoo was passing. The bird was bright, glowing white with a blue plume, one moment singing merrily, the next struck silent, a victim of my hunger. I saw the girl look toward it as the man raised the cage. I saw her frown with him as the bird toppled from its perch.

She was still frowning when she turned back to the artist and said, "Joseph, we should be going."

I was confounded when I realized he was going to obey her, and, desperate to keep him from leaving, I said quickly to her, "Look at how well he's captured you, and only in a sketch. How passionately he must love you."

She seemed taken aback, slightly mollified, but still wary. There had never been a woman I couldn't best. I looked at him. "Have you done her in oils?"

He licked his lips. "A few times."

"But you've sketched her often before. I can see that you have. There's a familiarity there." I smiled at him. "She is your muse."

Again, he swallowed. "My . . . twin. Sister."

His sister. I was surprised again. There was an intensity between them that spoke of greater intimacy than siblings, twins or no. But it was also welcome news. She was even less competition than I'd expected.

She held out her hand. "I'm Sophie Hannigan. And this is Joseph."

"Odilé León." I took her hand, the coils of Venetian chain slipping nearly to my fingers. Though it was him I cared about, I meant to charm them both. "You're American, yes? Have you been in Venice long?"

Joseph Hannigan cleared his throat. "A few weeks."

"Where are you staying? The Danieli?"

"The Palazzo Moretta," she said.

"Ah. The mute courtesan's palace."

She gave me a puzzled look.

"Do you not know the story?" I asked.

"I didn't know there was a story."

"It is named for the Carnivale mask, one of the ones the patrician women wore. It was held in place with a button between the lips." I spoke to her, but I felt him listening; I worked to seduce him with every syllable.

"Really?" she asked. "But then . . . how did they speak?"

"They did not. That is why the palazzo is named for it."

"I don't understand."

I stepped closer to them both, confiding. "The gondoliers say that the man who built the Moretta was in love with a courtesan. He bought her jewels and silks, anything she wanted. But no matter how he begged, she never said a single word of love to him. It was the only thing he wanted. In despair, he threw himself from the balcony into the canal below."

"Oh . . . how sad."

"Do you think so?" I gave her a reassuring smile. "But love always ends badly, does it not? Do you hear his ghost at the Moretta?"

Her brow furrowed. "His ghost? Oh, I don't think there is a ghost."

I looked at her brother, who seemed spellbound. My demon raged now that it had recognized his talent. I laid a finger upon his wrist, the pulse of him coursing through me like ambrosia. "What of you, monsieur? Do you hear him?"

"No." It was a whisper.

I had him. But I saw too the way he glanced at her. Although he wanted to follow me, he would not leave her. I felt a prick of irritation, but in a way I respected him for it. Venice was no place for a woman alone. And what did a night matter now that I had found him? I would send him an invitation when I got back to the palazzo; he would be at my door tomorrow night, and then he would be mine forever.

So I withdrew my finger and smiled. "A pity. Well, it was lovely to meet you both. I hope to see you again, yes?"

"Perhaps so," she said.

I barely looked at her, but I gave him a lingering glance, and I felt his gaze on me as I left them. He would think about me the rest of the day and into the night. His dreams would be full of me. By the time he came to me, his devotion would be a foregone conclusion.

My hunger snapped and coiled at the thought, pain sweetened by anticipation. Soon, the rapture would be mine. All that was left now was to convince him to make the bargain—and when had I ever failed to do that? I was jubilant as I gathered up the magician and used him to ease the hunger Joseph Hannigan had roused to a frenzy, and then I prepared to receive the one.

TWENTY-FIVE

SOPHIE

When she turned away from us, the gold on her wrists—both wrists covered in Venetian gold like shackles—caught the sun, flaring into a halo so bright that the rest of the world seemed to dim about her. I watched her until she disappeared, feeling as if I had been touched by something strange and unpleasant, a shadow over the sun.

I turned to my brother, wondering if he'd felt it too, and the look on his face startled me. He was staring after her as if he were enchanted.

"Joseph," I said, hearing a hint of despair in my voice and wondering where it had come from, why I suddenly felt it.

He turned to look at me as if he were dragged to it. His gaze sharpened—suddenly he was himself again, the brother I knew. He dropped the charcoal into his pocket and began to shut the sketchbook, but I stopped him. "Let me see."

He held out the book obligingly. The drawing was as wonderful as she'd said, as I'd known it would be. Again, me but not me. A pretty girl with yearning stark in her expression, eyes closed, face lifted into a breeze. And all around her life going on, so vibrant I felt again what I'd been feeling as he'd drawn, that longing, a wanting so ephemeral I couldn't hold on to it long enough to look at it. *Look at how well he's captured you,* she'd said, but her gaze focused on Joseph. She had not even seen me until she'd looked at the sketch, until she'd been led by my brother's vision. She was like everyone else. She could only see me through him.

The thought filled me with a bitterness that surprised me. Uneasily I looked at Joseph.

He closed the book. His smile was soft and comforting. "It was nothing, Soph," he said, answering a question I had not asked, and I realized that he felt as undone as I did.

Uncertainly, I said, "She was beautiful, wasn't she?"

"Yes she was." Joseph tucked the book beneath his arm. He tilted my chin and kissed me gently, lingering to whisper once again, "It was nothing."

But his words didn't reassure me, and that night at the salon, I sought out Katharine Bronson and said, "Joseph and I ran into the most interesting woman in the Rialto today. Her name was Odilé León. Do you know of her?"

Mrs. Bronson's gaze clouded. It was such an odd expression for her that I was puzzled. "Oh dear. Odilé León, did you say?" When I nodded, she laid her hand gently upon my arm. "I should stay away from her if I were you."

"Why do you say that?"

Mrs. Bronson sighed. "You remember poor Mr. Stafford?"

"I'm not likely to forget him."

"No, of course not." She gave me a commiserating look. "You remember that I told you he'd taken up with a woman and stopped coming to the salon?"

I felt a twinge of dread. "I remember. And the landlady said he'd told her he could live on love."

Mrs. Bronson nodded. "Well, it was Madame León he took up with. She's quite irresistible, I understand." Her voice turned cold. "She and I had rather a . . . falling out."

"A falling out?" How odd to think of Katharine Bronson arguing with anyone.

"Over a good friend of mine. A sculptor. He was very taken with her. He was never the same after, I'm afraid." Her gaze went distant; she called herself back with obvious effort and made the attempt at a smile. "It was quite some time ago, but I cannot bring myself to welcome her back. I should keep an eye on your brother, if I were you. And speaking of irresistible, my dear, I've noticed that Mr. Dane seems to have a particular eye for you these days."

"He's very charming." I was uncertain what else to say.

"And not here this evening, I noticed," she said, glancing about. "Do you know, did he intend to come tonight?"

"He didn't tell me," I said—which was true, although I'd expected to see him.

"I wonder if he knows the Loneghans are back in the city."

"I didn't realize they were gone."

"They've been in Egypt these last few weeks," she said. "Looking after one of Henry's archaeological sites. They returned yesterday."

"Oh. Will they be here tonight?"

"They rarely attend," she said. "Henry isn't inclined, you know, and Edith does as Henry likes. I do hope you have the opportunity to meet them, Miss Hannigan. Edith would so enjoy you and your brother."

"I hope to meet them as well," I said, trying not to sound eager. Her words distracted me completely from Odilé León. I had a task to accomplish, though I had to admit there was more to it now. I'd thought often of Nicholas Dane in recent days, the way he'd looked at me, the things he'd said. Despite everything I'd told myself, I was looking forward to seeing him again. I warned myself to be careful as I went in search of him, but it turned out I hardly needed to. Mr. Dane was annoyingly elusive tonight. When I ran into Mr. Martin, he said fawningly, "I haven't seen him since this afternoon, but I've no doubt he'll appear."

He didn't, which dismayed me. After the kiss we'd shared . . . *Well, what did you expect? Nothing,* I told myself. I wanted nothing. I *should* want nothing. It was better this way. But still . . . I could not help my disappointment.

"Martin didn't know where he was?" Joseph asked when we returned home that night.

"No. I've told you." The cast-iron rail was cold beneath my hands as we went up the stairs to the piano nobile.

"Perhaps something came up," Joseph said.

"Do you think I offended him again?"

"I don't know. Did you say something offensive?"

"No, of course not!"

"Don't snap at me—it was your suggestion. What was the last thing he said to you?"

"'Good night, Miss Hannigan.' You were standing right there."

"I mean before that." We were at the landing. He stepped back to let me go into the *portego* first. "When you kissed him, did—"

"Mr. Hannigan?"

216

The voice came from the courtyard below. Both Joseph and I paused and glanced over the railing. There stood the plump shadow of Mrs. Bedemann, faintly illuminated by the gaslight coming from the open door of the rooms downstairs, which she leased with her husband. She advanced to the foot of the stairs, waving something in her hand.

"I have a message for you. No one was home, so the man left it with me."

Joseph said in a low voice, "There's word from Dane now," and hurried down to fetch it.

My heart raced as my brother hurried back up again, taking the stairs two at a time. I followed him into the *portego* and through the darkness to my bedroom, where he lit a lamp.

"Is it from him?" I asked, trying to take it.

He snatched it away. "I don't know yet." He glanced down at it. "Oh. No. It's for me."

"For you? Only you? From whom?"

Joseph slid his finger beneath the seal, breaking it. He unfolded the paper. "It's an invitation to dinner," he said slowly, reading it. "From Odilé León. At the Casa Dana Rosti."

I was dumbfounded.

Joseph said, "For tomorrow night. Eight o'clock."

"But . . . we don't even know her."

Joseph threw the invitation to the top of my dresser. "This is how you get to know people, isn't it?"

"Yes, but . . . why would she want to invite you to dinner?"

"I don't know."

But I did. *She is irresistible to men.* I remembered the way Joseph had looked at her, and my uneasiness returned. I looked at my brother, who had taken off his suit coat and was unbuttoning his shirt, and I said, "I spoke to Mrs. Bronson about her tonight. Do you know that she was the woman Mr. Stafford died of love for? She was the one he killed himself over."

Joseph took off his shirt and laid it over the back of a chair. "She can hardly be blamed for that."

"How do you know? Perhaps she was cruel or . . . or vicious."

My brother laughed. He sat on the edge of the bed. "Vicious?"

I took a deep breath and knelt on the bed behind him, putting my hand on his shoulder. I could not keep myself from saying, again, "She's very beautiful, isn't she?"

"Is that what troubles you?" He tilted his head to look at me. "That she's beautiful?"

"I worry, that's all. Mrs. Bronson said she was irresistible to men, and—"

He laughed again. "Afraid she means to ravish me? Shall we call her out? Pistols at dawn?"

His exaggeration made me smile. "That's so old-fashioned. Poison would be better, I think."

"I'm glad to see how well you guard my virtue."

"Your virtue was lost long ago. It's your mortal soul I'm trying to protect."

"Another lost cause, I fear." He sobered suddenly, all teasing gone, replaced by that quick and fatal darkness, that unappeased longing. It reminded me that Odilé León was just another beautiful woman, and there had been many of those. I had nothing to fear from her.

Joseph took my hand from his shoulder, kissing my palm, then closing my fingers around the kiss as if he meant for me to keep it tight. "I think I'll get a breath of air. It's muggy in here tonight."

It wasn't the least bit, but I knew it wasn't mugginess he was trying to escape. "Joseph . . ."

He went to the door, then paused, turning to look at me again. "Come with me to her dinner."

"She didn't invite me."

"But I am. Come with me. We'll tackle her together. I'll just tell her I mistook the invitation."

"What can she do for us, Joseph?"

"I don't know. I suppose that's what I want to find out. How can it hurt?"

He was right. I could not dispute that, though I didn't really like it. "Very well. I'll come."

He gave me a soft smile, whispering, "Good. Now go to sleep. I won't be far. Just in the courtyard." Then he left me. I felt strangely abandoned as I watched him disappear.

TWENTY-SIX

SOPHIE

The evening was chilly as we made our way to the Casa Dana Rosti the next evening. Marco had put the *felze* on the gondola, and the black cabin was dark and silent, muffling the sounds even though the window blinds on each side were open. As I glanced out the window, I thought of Mrs. Bronson's words and the uneasiness I'd felt from the moment I'd seen Odilé León, and I wished we had not come. But it was too late now. The gondola stopped; we were here. Joseph was already pulling the bell cord as I disembarked. I heard its chime beyond, and the door was opened almost immediately by a woman who eyed us warily in the moment before she cast her gaze down and said, "Welcome to the Dana Rosti, monsieur, mademoiselle."

The receiving court was cold and dim, with gaslights along the walls that colored the white marble a dim yellow. It felt very like a tomb, I thought, shivering, and not only because of the damp chill. I would not have been surprised to see crypts along the walls. The servant led us to the stairs at the side, marble as well, which disappeared upward into a darkened archway. Joseph took my hand as if he felt my discomfort, tightening his fingers around mine reassuringly.

At the piano nobile, the servant turned abruptly to another door, opened it, and ushered us into the *portego*, which blazed with light. Three great chandeliers with tiers of candles sent a glare on the dark shine of terrazzo floors. The *portego* was lined with doors, each topped with bronze angels above gilded, sculptured shells, surrounded by equally gilded plaster festoons. The walls were pink and crumbling, that sort of lovely decay that marked all of Venice, set off by panels of marbled wallpaper in pale green. Candlelight seemed to dance on every surface. The place was beautiful and decadent, made to charm.

Our footsteps were loud on the floor, and there was no other sound as the servant led us down the hall to a doorway on the right. Double doors opened onto the *sala*, which was as elaborate as the *portego* had been, frescos—seascapes—lining the walls, heavy bronze drapes hiding what I assumed were balcony doors. There was not much furniture—a few settees, a chair or two, a pianoforte, but all were elegant and well placed. There were sculptures here and there and paintings hanging from rosetted cords. The room, as large as it was, felt cozy and close. Several candelabra bore flickering candles; the gas sconces were unlit. The ceiling loomed darkly above. After the blaze of the *portego*, the room seemed both dark and romantic.

I did not see her at first. Not until the servant announced us, and she rose from the shadows and came forward. I found myself silenced once again by her beauty. She wore a gown of deep burgundy that glowed vibrantly, as if it were fed by some other, unseen light, and it struck her dark hair with copper. She wore a necklace of gold and rubies that seemed to pulse against her skin, and that fine Venetian chain wound around both wrists dangled and looped, falling over her hands.

I caught the quick flash of surprise in her eyes when she saw me. I had the impression that Odilé León was not often surprised—and that it was not something she enjoyed.

"Miss Hannigan," she said smoothly. "How lovely."

She spoke in English, that faint French accent warming her words. Joseph took her hand and bowed over it. She seemed to shudder; it was almost imperceptible, but it troubled me, as did my brother's voice when he spoke. It was deeper than usual, almost hoarse as he said, "I hope you don't mind that I brought Sophie. I did not like to leave her alone."

"No, of course not." She smiled, but I saw a strain in it, a glitter in her eyes, which were very dark in the candlelight, though I'd thought yesterday they were gray.

"Come, will you have some wine? Or something stronger?" she asked as she moved into the soft light, her gown shimmering. A small table held decanters of Murano glass, beautifully wrought. She paused there, turning slightly, and I thought she knew just what impression she made standing that way, that she had done it deliberately. I felt a stab of jealousy when I realized how Joseph was staring.

It didn't matter, I told myself again. She was just another woman, though more beautiful than most. I had lived this before, a hundred times.

"Wine would be perfect," Joseph said. "For the both of us."

As she poured, the decanter clinked against the glass once, and then twice, as if she were nervous, though I saw no evidence of that. She brought two glasses to us. The crystal was cut and beveled, the wine, when I drank, of a quality I recognized. Like Mrs. Bronson's sherry, I'd never had finer. Everything in this room, in fact, spoke of riches.

I had never felt so out of place. I wished I had not come, but then again, neither did I want Joseph to be alone with her. I said, "I spoke to a friend about you. She told me you were once connected to Nelson Stafford."

She frowned as if she did not know the name, and then her expression cleared. "Ah, the writer. The one who took his own life."

I nodded. "I found his body."

"*You* did?"

"I was looking for places to lease and came upon him. The landlady said he had died of love for you."

Her expression went soft and a little wistful. "I see. You found him, and so perhaps you feel for him. Perhaps you feel a responsibility. Perhaps you have come to chastise me."

Joseph opened his mouth to say something. I touched his arm to stop him, and said, "I would not presume. It's none of my concern. But I cannot forget him."

She took a sip of her wine, keeping the swallow in her mouth for a moment, pressing the rim of her glass hard against her full lower lip—hard enough that I thought it must have hurt. It went momentarily white before she released it again. She glanced at my brother, a sideways look; I felt something leap between them, and I was glad when she looked away again, when she said lightly, "Perhaps it will reassure you to know that I realized too late how . . . delicate . . . Mr. Stafford was. In mind, if not in constitution. My only fault is that I chose wrongly. The weight of another's despair can be hard to predict. But Venice is to blame as well, you know. You feel it too, mademoiselle. Your brother's portrait of you reveals as much. You feel the things that breathe in the air here. Venice yearns. Its beauty is a monster. It raises foolish, unattainable desires. It makes one want what one can never have. Or what one should never want."

I thought of the way I'd looked in my brother's portrait, those things I'd felt as he'd drawn, the things I yearned for. I was afraid of what she was saying and how she seemed to see what I felt. *Foolish, unattainable desires.* The things I wanted that I should never have wanted, that I should not want now. I felt my brother's quick glance, and I went hot.

She smiled slightly, as if she knew how she'd disconcerted me, and said, "I am glad you have come tonight. I'll endeavor to make it worth your time. The Venetians would say: *venga a mangian quattro risi con me*, which means, come and eat four grains of rice with me. They are known for their economy. But have no fear, I don't mean to starve you like a Venetian. You must be hungry. Come to dinner and I'll tell your brother why I invited him here tonight." She put a slight emphasis on the word *him*.

We followed her from the salon into the dining room—smaller, but still elegant, with a gleaming table of mahogany and a candelabra set at one end. It was already set for three—how efficient were her servants.

"Please, sit," she said, putting her hand on my brother's arm to direct him to a chair, breathing deeply as she did so, as if she gained satisfaction from the touch. It was odd, and again I felt a hovering shadow of discomfort. But I sat in the other chair. The gilded embellishments on the ceiling winked now and again out of the darkness, the candlelight wavered, sending highlights of red into her hair, glancing off the rubies at her throat, shimmering on her gown.

The first course was a luxurious crab soup, rich with cream and flavor. When it came, she inhaled deeply of it. "I love the smells of Venice. They are different from any other city. Do you not think so?"

I managed, "I can't really say. We've been to so few. But certainly it's different."

She took a spoonful of soup. "You will find no other place like it, I promise you. No other city has legends and ghosts like Venice. Have you yet seen the one at the Moretta I told you of?"

"No. Are you certain there is a ghost?"

She nodded. "It is why the owner does not often rent to Americans. They complain of it too much. Strange noises and such. Odd smells. I think the Germans enjoy it—but then, they have a sense of the macabre, don't they?"

"Odd smells?" my brother asked. "Like what?"

"A strange perfume, I hear," she said, and he smiled at her in a way that tightened my stomach. "Musk and sandalwood. And shadows."

"Shadows?" I asked. "I had not thought shadows had a smell."

Joseph said, "Oh, you know they do, Soph. You describe it when you tell your stories."

She asked, "Your stories? Are you a writer then, mademoiselle?"

"Sophie doesn't write them down," Joseph said.

"Ah. I so enjoy stories. Perhaps you would tell me one someday. Perhaps about the Dana Rosti. It has its own ghosts. Sometimes I think I can hear the sounds of past Carnivales in its walls." Her spoon clattered violently and suddenly against her bowl. She bit her lip hard, pushing the bowl away, and gestured abruptly to the servant standing in the shadows. I noticed that she gripped the table as the servant took the dishes.

"Is something wrong?" I asked her.

Her fingers relaxed, and she raised her hands, sending the Venetian chain gently undulating. "I have been ill, and I'm afraid I'm still a bit weak. But I'm growing better. There is no need for concern."

The next course came, a steaming platter of saffron-scented rice, plump pink shrimp and gleaming black mussels, shining clams, and glistening sausage, along with round, crusty loaves of bread. She tore off chunks of it, handing it to us, along with a small bottle of olive oil, saying, "You must dip it in oil. It isn't like the bread in Paris—nothing is—but it has its own charm." She put a chunk of it to her nose, closed her eyes, inhaled. "It's from the baker down the street. I think I can smell his children in it. Dirt and sunshine."

My brother laughed. She opened her eyes, smiling back at him as she put aside the bread and gestured to the dish of rice and seafood. "I first tasted this dish in Valencia, and it has become one of my favorites."

She served us herself. When I took my first bite I nearly swooned.

"You see?" she said. "You like it?"

"Oh my. Valencia, you said?"

"A beautiful city. Have you ever been?"

"No. I'm afraid this is our first trip abroad."

"Your first? Well, how much you have to look forward to, then. Where do you go next?"

I glanced at my brother, who was toying silently with a shrimp. "I suppose back to New York."

"Venice only?" she raised a finely shaped brow. "Then this is no grand tour. You've come for a reason."

Joseph's eyes were so dark in the candlelight they looked black. "For study."

"There is no place more suited for the study of art. But you must be careful, monsieur. The salons and entertainments will distract you from your purpose. I've seen it happen more than once. If you mean to learn in Venice, you should paint every day, whatever inspires you. No salon can teach you what the city itself can."

I protested, "James Whistler is at Mrs. Bronson's every night. And Frank Duveneck. Joseph can learn from them too."

Her gaze turned slowly to me. "Yes. But true greatness means a singular vision. To learn technique is necessary, yes? But the rest . . . to put it to the test, to press the boundaries of genius . . . that needs a faith in oneself."

"Which I have," said Joseph, leaning forward. "I know what I'm capable of. I know I can make people see something they've never seen before."

She looked at him, her eyes glittering. The world went suddenly muted, muffled and silent as if a scrim had fallen to dim it, and she was the only thing at its center. I felt her separateness, a darkness I could not interpret. It was oddly familiar—she reminded me of something I knew, though I could not quite think what.

She said softly to him, "Ah yes. But what good is such vision if no one knows you exist?"

"You understand," said my brother in surprise.

I was surprised too—not just that she'd said it, but that he'd admitted it. I didn't like it. Joseph had never talked of his ambition with anyone but me.

She said slowly, "You want fame, of course you do. But the question is, as always, what are you willing to sacrifice for it?"

Her voice had gone low and mesmerizing. Joseph's hand was clenched on the table, the planes of his face had gone stark, fiercely beautiful, his high cheekbones and the blade of his nose, his strong jaw and the slight cleft of his chin. I felt a terrible yearning in him, something dangerously fierce.

She said, "I can tell you that Vivaldi risked everything."

I felt drawn back to her, almost against my will. She pushed her barely touched plate away, put her elbows on the table, and rested her chin in her hands. The Venetian chain slipped and dangled, catching on the ends of her sleeves. Her expression went dreamy and far away.

"Venice holds him as one of her own," she went on, almost whispering, as if she were speaking to an intimate, a lover, looking only at my brother. "They say his ghost still walks the *calli*, that you can hear him play on the nights when storm clouds chase the seawater into the canals, that on those nights, the cries of the gulls are the notes of his music.

"But before he was a ghost he taught at the Pio Ospedale della Pieta, where he composed works for the orphan girls there to sing. Such beautiful songs. Such beautiful voices. They were famous the world over. Ah, but Vivaldi was dissatisfied. He wanted his music to be known not for the voices that sang it, but for his own genius. He wanted something separate, for himself. His own."

Again, I felt that twinge of discomfort, as if she saw something I didn't want her to see, a sense that she spoke to me even as she did not turn her gaze from Joseph.

"And so one night, he called for the devil, which is easy to do in this city, you know. Perhaps too easy. He waits outside St. Mark's for those who are despairing, who cannot find God inside and so come to him."

The candlelight wavered; her voice was like a spell.

"And the devil knows just what you want. He heard Vivaldi's call, and so that night, he played in the *calle* beneath Vivaldi's window. The sweetest, most enticing music. He wooed Vivaldi with what he loved, and Vivaldi opened his window to the devil. He welcomed him inside. He—"

She stopped short, drawing in her breath sharply, pressing her hand to her stomach, bowing her head. I was still wrapped in the spell, but Joseph was on his feet, taking the few steps to her side, his fingers caressing her bare shoulder. "What is it?"

She straightened at his touch. Her obvious relief was so strong it struck me as peculiar. She reached for his hand, squeezing it, and looked up into my brother's face. He went rapt with an expression so erotically stark it made my heart stop. No different than the other women, I told myself, but it was growing harder to believe.

She tried to smile, "No, I'm fine. A momentary pain. What remains of my illness. It is nothing. Truly."

Joseph frowned. "Should I call for a servant?"

"No." Again, the smile, a shake of her head that sent her earrings dancing against her jaw. "Please, sit down."

My brother's hand was still on her shoulder, his long fingers reaching to the swell of her breast above burgundy satin the color of blood. He withdrew as if awakened from an enchantment and returned to his seat. Her hand went to where his had been as if he'd left it cold. She turned to me. "Stories of artists who sell their soul to the devil are all the same, are they not? The rise. The fall. The cost. What is your story, mademoiselle? Tell me how you came to be here in Venice. Where you have come from. What you want. That is a story I would like to hear."

I took a sip of wine, trying to control the sudden trembling of my fingers. "I'm afraid it's a very boring story. Our parents died when we were young, and our aunt raised us. We've come to Venice so Joseph can study."

The way she looked at me made me cold, as if she saw the memories I kept locked away, and I did not doubt that she could—had someone asked me in that moment, I would have told them Odilé León knew all my secrets.

She said, "There are no boring stories. Only a failure to truly listen."

"I think you would have to listen hard to find interest in ours."

"Ah, but dead parents . . . that is a tale for tears, an unhappiness that endures. I have known many who are defined by it. I would hope the two of you have transcended it."

Joseph said, "It was a long time ago."

"But no less tragic for being so." Her eyes were a strange color, that pale gray I'd first seen, but dark too, and at the same moment, as if the color shifted with the light. "I have learned that the world likes balance, yes? One cannot have sadness without happiness. Does Venice make up for your sadness in some small measure?"

Her words, her eyes, called images to my mind—my first starlit night in Venice in the gondola with Joseph, the day on the Lido, my brother laughing, and Nicholas Dane in a darkened kitchen, candlelight shining on his golden hair. I heard myself say, "Oh yes."

"Oh yes?" she turned in obvious delight to my brother. "Do you hear that, monsieur? Your sister is in love with Venice, I can tell. And perhaps"—she turned back to me, her eyes shining, teasing—"there is a reason for it other than the city's own charm? A new lover, perhaps?"

How could I be surprised she knew it when she seemed to know so much? I felt myself flush. "Oh no. No, nothing like that."

"But there is a man. Come, come, there is no use hiding it. I can see it in your eyes."

My brother frowned at me. "We've made a friend who's been very helpful. He's taken a liking to Sophie, that's all."

She lifted a delicate brow. She looked at Joseph and then at me as if she'd seen something between us that intrigued her. "Ah, is that all it is? A friend?"

"Yes," I said, taking a quick sip of wine. Joseph gave me a reassuring smile, but I saw how carefully Odilé watched us, as if she were determined to decipher something that puzzled her. Again, I felt it as something familiar.

She said, "Monsieur, now I think perhaps it is time to tell you why I've invited you tonight. What proposition I have to offer."

Joseph's gaze jerked to her. "A proposition?"

Just then, the servant returned, bearing a silver tray. On it were many little mahogany-colored fluted cakes. She set the tray on the table, and then next to it a small cloth bag. I heard the clanking of coins.

Odilé León took up a little silver fork, speared one of the cakes, and set it before my brother, easing it off the tines with her fingers. "*Canelés*," she said. "A specialty of Bordeaux. I've heard they were first made by nuns. Strange, don't you think, that nuns and monks make the most sensual food and drink? Do you suppose it's their closeness to God that gives them such secrets?"

She speared another and gave it to me. I took a bite. It was crispy on the outside, and chewy, custardy on the inside, tasting of vanilla and burnt sugar.

Joseph said, "Or perhaps it's their yearning that lends such flavor."

"Yearning," she repeated. "Yes, you may be right." She reached for the little cloth purse, hefting it in her hand. "I would like to commission you, monsieur."

"Commission me?" Joseph looked at her in blank surprise. "But why? Why me? You've seen nothing of my work—"

"I saw the sketch you did of your sister in the Rialto."

"And you would commission me on the basis of one sketch?"

She leaned forward, handing my brother the purse. "It was enough to show me that you are exactly what I am looking for. What I have been looking for for some time. This is half of what I will pay, with the rest to be paid upon completion."

The bag weighted Joseph's hand. I wondered how much was in it. Joseph asked, "Completion of what? Who is the subject? Yourself?"

Odilé León smiled. "I think you know something of desire, don't you? Of the kind of yearning that gives life flavor, as you say, the thing that makes us feel immortal. That is what I want. A portrait to show me that. I want to look at it on those days I have forgotten there is such a thing to feel." She took up another *canelé*, the golden chains of her bracelets sparking in the candle-light, twisting as if they were alive. She took a bite of the pastry, closing her eyes, savoring.

I heard Joseph's quick inhalation. I saw once again the bewitchment in my brother's eyes, her dark magic, familiar again, and so palpable it prickled my skin. The night seemed to close in on me, that heavy Venetian sea air, weighted with the things she'd spoken of, devil's bargains and desire, a yearning that beckoned, that knew me by name, that laid my secrets bare.

TWENTY-SEVEN

NICHOLAS

I watched the Dana Rosti, as I'd been watching for hours, feeling a grim satisfaction at the presence of the police gondola. So they'd caught on to her involvement at last—I could not have asked for a better way to slow her. Odilé must be suffering. Perhaps the loss of the singer and the two days without sustenance had weakened her into paralysis. It was a pleasant thought, no matter how unlikely. I had an image of Odilé naked and writhing, her own coils strangling her tight.

She would have a new victim soon, but the thought of spending another night waiting for the appearance of her latest lover held no appeal, and I had other interests now too. I hurried back to the rooms I shared with Giles. He was dressing to go to the Alvisi, and when he saw me come in, he paused, frowning as he knotted a broad swath of bronze silk about his throat.

"Where the hell have you been, Nick?"

"I had some business," I told him, going to the kitchen, where the dirty glasses from two nights ago still littered the counter. "Is there anything here to eat?"

"Not a thing," he said, following me. "You look like death."

"Yes, well, I'm cold and hungry. And tired." I grabbed a very hard roll that I didn't remember either of us buying. My stomach growled as I gnawed at it without much success.

Giles finished knotting his tie and scrutinized me. "You'd best go to bed. You look done in."

"And give you the chance at Sophie Hannigan without any competition?" I teased, making my way to my room. "I should say not. Just give me a moment to dress."

"You missed her last night. She and her brother were both at the salon. Asking for you."

I paused and looked over my shoulder at him. "Both of them were asking?"

"Well, she was." Giles frowned as if he didn't like the thought of it. "In fact, she seemed quite distressed that you weren't there."

I couldn't help but smile. "Was she?"

Giles sighed. "You've done it, haven't you? Won her before I've even got a chance? You weren't in the kitchen five minutes!"

"Long enough for a kiss."

He made a face.

I clapped him on the shoulder. "I am sorry, my friend. But I couldn't quite help myself."

"She is astonishing," Giles agreed. "And so is he, you know. The two of them are . . . well. . . ."

"They did well enough on their own last night, I take it?"

"As if they were born to it."

His words brought back that little consternation; I remembered how I'd felt seeing Hannigan with Whistler. How little he'd

234

needed me. I pushed the thought away. "I'm going to get dressed. Wait for me?"

Giles sank onto the settee and crossed his arms, letting his head fall against the wall with a helpless thud. "I suppose there's no hope I could take her from you?"

"Not if I have anything to say about it."

I left him to dress, and we were on our way within the hour. That evening fog was gathering again, the damp chill of Venice easing into my bones. When we arrived on the doorstep of the Alvisi, I barely said two words to the servant. I raced up the stairs, Giles following breathlessly behind, calling irritably, "Slow down, Nick! What's the hurry?"

I stepped into the *portego* and scanned the crowd, but I saw no sign of them. Not there, and not on the balcony. In the main salon, Katharine Bronson was holding court with three others. She raised her eyes to me as I entered, beckoning me over.

"Mr. Dane, how we did miss you last night!" She turned to the three. "You've met the Paulsons, haven't you? And Mr. Sweeten?"

I had, and I nodded a hello to each of them, barely able to contain my impatience long enough to ask, "Have the Hannigans arrived?"

"Oh, I'm afraid not yet," she said. "But bring them over when they do, will you, please?" She turned to the others. "Mr. Dane has brought us the most marvelous artist and his sister. You really must meet them. They're twins, and quite extraordinary. . . ."

I wandered away as soon as it was prudent. I went to the *portego*, positioning myself with an eye to the door, and involved myself in several absurdly boring conversations while I waited for a glimpse of them. But the hours passed, and they did not arrive. I began to feel anxious. After eleven o'clock came and went, and then midnight, I cornered Giles and said, "Did they say anything to you about not coming tonight?"

"I would have told you if they had," he said with exasperation.

When the clock struck one thirty, I told Giles I was going home and left the Alvisi. I did not go home, however. Instead, I made my way to the Moretta. Had there been a single light on, I would have rung the bell, but the place was dark. They had obviously already gone to bed.

I told the gondolier to take me to the Dana Rosti. There was only a single light on at Odilé's, and no flickering shadows. No one was about, no visiting gondola. I realized then that I'd been afraid Odilé had found them—though I knew it was impossible. I'd been watching. I would have known. It was very late now, nearly three, and abjectly still; even the mist hovering about the water did not seem to shift as my gondola moved through it to the *fondamenta*. The night felt strange, as if the world were on watch, but it was only that I was, I knew, and I let my unease fade into relief. They were not here—of course not. Why should they be? I paid the gondolier and disembarked, parking myself again beside the rotting boat. And then I turned up my collar and prepared to spend another watchful night among the ghosts of Venice.

TWENTY-EIGHT

ODILÉ

They were gone by midnight, and when they left, the room seemed eerily quiet, hushed, the candle flames flickering as if people still moved about. I blew out all the candles but for a single hand and sat for a moment in the dim light, trying to catch my breath, which was unsteady and painful.

The evening had been a trial. I was used to desire, to wanting—it was the reason for my existence, after all—but I could not remember ever feeling any such as this. The power of it was a ravishment, twisting me about until I felt myself dissolve in its fury, until I was nothing but yearning. I wanted him as badly as I'd ever wanted a man. He had raised my hunger to a fever—it had been all I could do to control it—and yet, my appetite seemed not to affect him. I'd felt nothing from her, which told me she had no talent at all despite what he'd said about her storytelling. But his . . . it must be more prodigious even than I'd suspected. Perhaps more so than any I'd ever before had. I felt a frisson of excitement through my pain.

What do you most desire, Odilé?

I closed my eyes against the rushing currents of remembrance. The one memory I wished to forget, so stubbornly and starkly clear. The night so blackly dark, the storm raging outside, wind screeching down the narrow, twisting streets, rain driven across the stones. The knock upon my door so very late. The alarm I'd felt when I opened the door to see Madeleine standing there, alone, not a servant in sight.

"What is it?" I'd asked her. "What has happened?"

She pushed her way inside. Her blond hair straggled loose over her shoulders, and she looked drawn and pale, her eyes like shining bits of coal in contrast. I closed the door and pulled my wrap more closely about me. She went to the fireplace, which was barely warm, the fire banked for the night, and held her hands out to it, revealing the bracelets about her wrists—she was still dressed for a party, though it was nearly morning. She rarely left her entertainments early, and I knew something must have happened to bring her here.

My alarm grew. I hurried to the hearth and stirred up the embers, building the fire again. "Shall I get you some tea? Or wine?"

She was shivering as she shook her head, but I went to the kitchen and warmed some wine for her. When I brought it, she drank it gratefully. Still, she said nothing, and I let her sit in silence until I could no longer bear it. "I don't understand. Why are you here now?"

She turned to me, and there was something in her face—I cannot describe it, but it terrified me. She held out her shaking hand to me—pale, thin fingers. She whispered. "Look at what I am."

I had no idea what she meant for me to see. "You look as if you've had a fright. And you're freezing."

She shook her head again, almost violently. "You've allowed yourself to be blind, Odilé. *Look* at me. Tell me what you see."

I was puzzled and feeling more uneasy by the moment. "I see my friend, Madeleine Dumas, who has inspired great men, and who will inspire a great many more."

She laughed, but it had a brittle edge. "You said you wish to be like me. Is that still true?"

"Yes, of course," I said. "Why would it not be?"

"Will you still, I wonder, when you know the truth?"

"What truth is that?"

She leaned across the space between us to grip my arm. She was very strong; I felt it would be a struggle to break free, and was amazed that I even thought to do so. This was Madeleine, my friend and mentor and yet . . . in those moments she seemed not that, but something else. Something that did not belong here, before my hearth.

"Madeleine, you're frightening me."

At those words, her grip loosened. Her eyes dimmed, returning to their usual luminosity. Her face seemed not so grave or gaunt—there was the pink in her cheeks, the smooth brow, the fine down at her temples. She drew back.

"How old am I?" she demanded of me.

The question confused me further. "I don't know. As old as I am, I think. No more than forty."

Her lips twitched in a smile. She looked to the fire, which was now burning hotly, casting her face in an orange-and-yellow glow. "I have lived five hundred and thirty-two years."

I thought she had a fever. Or that she'd gone mad. The insanity of the poet she'd abandoned had been somehow contagious. I did not know what to say.

"I am tired," she said. "I have been tired for some time. And

I have looked for someone to take my place. But I have never found her. Until now."

"You need sleep. Come, and I'll—"

She jerked from my proffered hand. "Do you not understand, Odilé? I am telling you the secrets you have been begging to know. Did you truly want to know them? Or was it only talk?"

Her eyes were burning again. I remembered the conversation we'd had only days ago, the talk of demons, my sense that there had been something in it I was not seeing. Carefully, as if approaching a wild animal, I said, "I truly wish to know."

She smiled thinly. "You think I am mad. I can assure you I am not."

The air seemed to shiver about her. I found myself stepping back.

"I have lived for five hundred and thirty-two years," she said again, this time slowly, as if I were an idiot who could not grasp the words. I could not move nor look away. "I was given this gift when I was thirty-two. I wanted youth, you see. I wanted never to grow old. I did not understand the burden of it then."

"The gift," I said carefully. "What gift is that?"

"Can you not guess?" she asked.

"No."

Her smile grew—this time it was bitter. "We have been called many things. Demons and angels, daughters of Lilith and Naamah, sirens and banshees."

I felt I was in some strange and disturbing dream. "What?"

"Have you not heard of women who mated with fallen angels? Who became demons themselves?"

"You . . . you had a fallen angel?" I could not believe I'd even said such words.

She shook her head impatiently. "I just told you. The gift was passed to me. The fallen angels are only the story of how we began. But this is truly what I am, Odilé. A succubus. It is what I have been for five hundred years. It is what I wish no longer to be. I am tired, *cherie*. But I cannot just give it up. There must always be one of us. Do you understand? I cannot die until I pass it along. You must take the gift from me."

I *didn't* understand. Not a single thing she was telling me. *A succubus?* It was absurd; a fever dream, an illness.

She went on, "When you brought me that poet, I knew you would be so much better at this than I. You told me I could change the world if I chose better. Now, I'm offering that to you. *You* could change the world. You have the eye it needs. Think of what you've told me. You wish to leave a mark. You want your name to be remembered. I can give you that."

My mind was churning—to listen, to put her to bed, to call the apothecary. . . . But I felt paralyzed by her gaze, and gradually I became aware that I saw no madness in her eyes. But how could that be? Everything she was saying was impossible.

She said steadily, "You have known from the start that I was not like anyone else. What is in me speaks to you, *cherie,* you know it does. You are beautiful and skilled. I can make you more beautiful. I can give you the power you crave. I can take away the yearning that torments you. You know I can."

Truth has a way of speaking, of sneaking in beyond fear or dread. My instincts tingled. Everything I had always wondered about Madeleine made sense of those words: her irresistible beauty, the madness of those who fell under her spell, the power of her inspiration.

Still, I denied it. "What you speak of is impossible."

"Is it? Imagine it, Odilé. Imagine: men inspired by you. Men who will never forget you. A world that will not forget."

She knew what to say, what would most affect me.

"Those things can't just be *given*," I protested. "Such a talent—"

"You are wrong. It *can* be given. I can give it to you. Look at me, Odilé."

I saw the change in her gaze, the blackness within her eyes glittering, writhing. Supernatural. Occult. Demon eyes. I remembered the eyes in the portrait, her asking what I thought of the cost of immortality.

"No," I whispered in horror. "No. Impossible."

She rose, stepping so close I felt the warmth of her breath as she spoke. "It is a *gift*. And I can give it to you. Ask me, Odilé. *Ask me.* Be what I am."

I could not believe, even as her words wheedled into my heart, even as temptation roused. What she was offering me—it couldn't be, could it? But then . . . I *had* recognized her. I had seen the otherworldliness in her eyes, and I knew it was real. And the truth was that I *did* long to be like her—how could I resist the offer now? If such a thing could be—I had wanted this for so long, my whole life. To be known. To be remembered. To leave a mark . . .

I felt now as if my destiny, as if every step I'd ever taken, had brought me to this moment. My hunger for it bloomed irresistibly, as she must have known it would.

I heard my own voice, hoarse with longing, whisper, "Yes. *Yes.* What must I do?"

The satisfaction that came into her expression would have chilled me had I not wanted what she offered so badly. "There are things you must know first. Listen carefully. There are rules you cannot break. You will appear to every man as desire. But only those with talent can feed you, and if you resist your appetite for too long, it will draw from the world around you—a bird's song, a farmer whistling, a juggler's tricks—even such little talents you will leech away. To *truly* appease your hunger requires bedding." Her smile turned cunning. "You are a succubus, after all. Temptation incarnate."

"And then?" I asked.

"The energy you take from an artist leaves a poison in their blood—a kind of madness, if you will. For them, that madness becomes inspiration. You will be a muse, at least for a time, to every man you feed upon. Those with too little talent, you will drain to death, so you must be careful. But this is the most important thing of all, Odilé; this you must not forget: Every three years, you must choose *the one*."

"The one?"

"The artist you will make a bargain with. He must agree, Odilé. He must sell you his very soul: his talent in return for inspiration. Once the bargain is locked, you will feel a rapture such as you have never known. You will inspire him to the utmost of his ability. To him, you will be the muse of all muses."

"As you were to the poet," I said.

Her smile was sharp—I saw in it no sorrow over his fate. "Yes. Everything he is, he will pour into creating one final work. It will be the culmination of his brilliance. And then his talent will be gone, never to return. Some of them go mad after. Or take their own lives. They will never create again. But your hunger will be appeased. For a time it will hibernate. And then, the cycle will begin again. Your hunger will grow and grow, day by day, week by week, until you choose once more."

"It seems a hard bargain for them," I said, remembering her poet's despair.

Madeleine shrugged. "You told me you thought inspiring the world worth any cost. Have you changed your mind?"

I thought of the brilliance of the man's poetry, the reason I'd brought him before her. "No. And if I don't find the talent I want? If I don't choose?"

Madeleine's eyes darkened. Her face went sharp and still. "You do not want to do that, *cherie*."

"What will happen?" I demanded. "You must tell me. Tell me everything if I am to do this."

"In your worst nightmares, you could not imagine it." In that moment I saw truly the demon I had only glimpsed before. I saw the eyes that had followed her from a painted portrait, a terrible void that raised an answering horror in me. "The demon inside you will grow until you are nothing but your hunger. It will swallow everything, every bit of talent in its path. It will be too hungry to be discerning. You will drain everything of its creative force until the hunger is sated—for after all, everyone has *some* creativity, *some* imagination. You will *become* the monster, and it will take time to return to yourself. If you allow it to happen too often . . . at some point you will not be able to control the demon. Odilé will disappear forever, no matter how often you feed or what death you leave behind. You—Odilé— will be gone, but the demon will survive—you will *become* it, and you will be so until you can find someone to accept the gift. For the succubus monster cannot be killed; it cannot be destroyed. It can only be passed on."

Such terrors cannot be truly imagined without experience, and I could not imagine them then. I wanted what she offered so badly. Badly enough to believe that such a dark circumstance could never happen to me. How hard could it be to choose one every three years? I had been a courtesan for most of my life and had nothing but a bleak future. But this . . . to be the muse to inspire such brilliance, to be celebrated and adored. The world would be mine. How could I not want it?

"Very well," I said. "I understand. Give it to me. I will take it."

Madeleine stepped over to me and took my hand, gripping it tight, so the jewels of the bracelets at her wrists bit into my skin. She leaned close, whispering in my ear, an urgent command, "What do you most desire, Odilé?"

I felt the ritual in it. "To be remembered."

She pressed something into my hand—I looked down to see a knife. I had no idea where it had come from. When I looked at her in question, she said, "You must use it, *cherie*. There can only be one of us, and one must die for the next to live."

I stared at her in horror, realizing at once what she meant for me to do. I tried to jerk away, but she held me fast. "No," I said. "I can't do that! You're asking me to kill you. How can I? I love you. I would not trade you for this."

Her fingers tightened on my wrist. Those demon eyes gleamed. "You will not refuse me now."

"I can't do this. No, I won't do it."

"I am ready to die, Odilé. I am tired. I cannot pass on without your help. I *want* this. Be the friend you say you are. Take this burden from me. *Take it.* Do it. I am ready. Do not disappoint me."

I wish I could say I refused such an abomination, but I did not. In the end, I wanted what she offered so very much. Now that she'd provided such possibility, how could I go back to what I'd been?

She curled her fingers around my hand, forcing me to grip the handle, giving me strength when I had none, driving my hand hard when I hesitated. I plunged the knife into her. Her eyes widened; she caught her breath. I felt the warmth of her blood on my hand. I saw her relief and joy.

The last thing she said to me was, "Do not forget, Odilé. You can choose only *one*."

Then I felt a rush in my blood, a powerful force crashing through me, a blow that hurled me breathless to the floor, my fingers and toes burning, the very tips of my hair. I was on fire, I was consumed. I screamed out, and then, suddenly, there was a sucking that pulled at my skin as if it meant to turn me inside out, a shiver in the world that glowed before my eyes, and then it was still and gone, and I was lying beside Madeleine's body with blood on my hands. I felt her absence in a great, dark emptiness. She was gone, and I had done this. My only friend was gone, and I was alone—though I did not realize then how truly so.

I rose trembling, trying to clean my hands on my skirt. The blood would not be wiped away, as if it intended me to wear it forever, a reminder of the cost. As I stumbled to my feet, feeling sick, I caught sight of myself in the mirror above the fireplace. I froze in astonishment. The reflection that looked back at me was myself, but augmented, heightened. I had always been beautiful, but now there was something else in me too, something I recognized, because I had seen it in Madeleine. A glow in my gray eyes, a hollow darkness in their depths.

I was too beguiled by the change to be afraid. That came much, much later.

The memory faded. When I opened my eyes now, I was almost surprised to find myself in my Venetian *sala*. My eyes stung with tears—how I missed her still. How I regretted she was gone. And the worst of it was the joke—because I had not got what I'd wanted, had I? I was a muse, yes, but who knew that Odilé León had inspired Byron or Canaletto or Schumann? Who knew my name?

I went to my bedroom, and lit the gas. Near the wall was a heavily padlocked trunk bound with straps. I drew the key from my pocket and twisted it in the lock. I lifted the lid and stared down at wrapped parcels. I took them out one at time, portraits—all of me, miniatures, sketches—music and poems, sheaves of paper bound with ribbon growing stiff and faded, tattered books. I rifled through them. There, near the bottom, was what I wanted, a journal so yellowed with time that its pages flaked at the edges.

I took it up. The writing was fading, pages after pages of my own flowing script, listings of everything I'd discovered. Ah, so few pages truly! Madeleine had said so little of where we came from, why we existed, and while I had done my best to learn more, there was not much to find. Most of what had been written about succubi was of horror and resistance and immorality. Lilith, the mother, the wife, the first. Having refused to lie with Adam unless as an equal, she had exiled herself from Eden and taken up with the fallen angel Samael and become a succubus. When God sent three angels to capture her, they found her in bed with Samael, and when she refused to return to Adam, they threatened to kill her demon children. Still, she refused. The legend said that she took her revenge even now by injuring babies in their sleep. But if there existed a Lilith still, I didn't know, and it wasn't the babies that disturbed those who wrote of her, but her monstrous appeal, the irresistibility of the desire she raised. Lilith, the incarnation of lust, was identified with Asmodeus, the devil of fornication. *Subtle in wickedness, eager to do hurt, ever fertile in fresh deceptions . . . they stir up tempests, disguise themselves as angels, bear Hell always about them . . . through the wantonness of flesh, they have much power over men.* Proverbs 2:18: *Her house sinks down to death, and her course leads to the shades. All who go to her cannot return. . .*

I knew the names of succubi throughout the ages. Naamah, Agroth, Mahaleth. Lamashtû, the demon succubi of Mesopotamia. Qarinah of Arabia. Lilitû in Assyria. Lamia—only another name for Lilith. Circe. Leanan of the Scottish sidhe, a blood-sucking demon who was the muse of poets.

So many and yet . . . and yet I had only met Madeleine, and she had implied there were no others. *There can only be one of us,* she'd said. But the *Malleus Maleficarum* stated that "Incubus

247

and succubus devils have always existed." *Devils,* plural. If that was so, where were they? How was it possible that I was so alone?

Though I had written down every "fact" I'd read or discovered, I had no idea which were truth and which lies, which pure inventions. There had been times, horrors—Barcelona—when I'd thought the wickedness attributed to succubi was the truth. But in my more rational moments, I knew that what I'd told Madeleine was true, that the pleasures I could give changed the world, and that was the real reason we were feared. Desire made fools of us all, did it not? What was more controlling than unconsummated desire? What but *wanting* sent men on fatal quests or led them to begin senseless wars? What else led to thievery or murder? It wasn't desire that was the enemy, but the inability to assuage it. Desire was only an emotion. It was no more evil than love.

And if succubi were only evil, how did one explain the rest of the gift? How could it be said that art and beauty were unholy, whatever their inspiration?

There was a reason we existed—*I* existed. To give mankind a reason to strive. In a world that wanted balance, it made sense that something must exist to counter death and disease and suffering. Inspiration. Beauty. Love needed hate. Destruction was necessary for creation. A price must be paid for great and lasting beauty. Art required *sacrifice*, and that was where I came in.

Balance. Symmetry.

I no longer pondered philosophy; I had, like Madeleine, grown weary of the debate. There was nothing new in the world. It was why I hunted only youth, because they at least had not grown weary of living. Their joy in it, their innocence, invigorated me. But it was not really new. It was not mine. It was only a mirror image, a reflection. It was never something I could touch.

In Joseph Hannigan, I had been given something special, and I wondered: would he be the one to give me the credit I had spent four lifetimes waiting for? The reason I'd asked for the gift, the reward for *my* sacrifice at last?

I believed he was. But then . . . I'd thought that of Byron too, hadn't I? And Schumann. Canaletto. All these years, and still I was foolish enough to believe in generosity of spirit, no matter that I had been disabused of its possibility time and again. How foolish still to hope for it, to look in a man's eyes and believe that his gratitude would be lasting. To think that he would immortalize something more than his own talent and give his inspiration a name that generations would whisper with awe, to give me what I deserved.

But some foolish hopes never dissipated, and Joseph Hannigan was different enough to restore them. He had surprised me tonight, a rare enough thing. Not just with the depth of his talent, but with his comprehension of the world and his devotion to his sister. I didn't understand it, but in the end it didn't matter. I'd seen his expression when he looked at me, and I knew it would be no great challenge to get him here again. All I need do was persuade him to accept my offer, to make the bargain. I did not expect a struggle. It was never a difficult thing to tempt a talented man.

TWENTY-NINE

SOPHIE

I woke the next morning to the sense that I was somehow a ghost within the world, separate and unseen. My brother only made the feeling worse—he was, in fact, the cause of it. He sat on the settee, feverishly drawing, but he was distracted, so deep in thought it was as if I had ceased to exist for him. Every comment I made was met with either silence or a strange, unfocused stare, a blink, as if he were catching only glimpses of me, a spirit there one moment and then gone the next, and he shook his head in confusion and turned back to his drawing. I had never seen such a thing in him, not even during those early years with Miss Coring, when his infatuation trumped his anger and hatred.

It was Odilé León, I knew. The spell of her lingered, and if *I* felt that way . . . I stole a glance at my brother, at the charcoal dust marking his hands and the cuffs of his shirt, how his hair fell into his face and how he did not shake it away, too consumed by whatever it was he saw in his head, and I remembered the way he'd looked at her last night. The way he'd touched her.

Joseph had had many women—of course he had; one had only to look at him to know it. But I'd never felt in him this kind of restlessness, and it seemed to have sneaked beneath my own skin, to needle like a constant itch one could not find the center of. I felt that familiarity again without knowing where it came from. I only knew it was troubling, that it had to do with her and that strange commission—*You know something of desire.* I'd been as confused as my brother by her offer. How could one pay so much money on the basis of a single rough sketch? I felt it had more to do with her obvious attraction to Joseph than any wish to hire his talent. Everything in me said we should turn down her offer. But then . . . how could we? We needed the money so badly.

Unless . . . I thought of Nicholas Dane, the Loneghans, Joseph's and my plan. What if I could bring that to bear now? Loneghan's money and influence would easily trump Odilé León. And if I could bring him in, Joseph could give up Odilé León's commission. Neither of us would have to see her again. All I must do was convince Nicholas Dane . . .

The thought of him brought a tingling anticipation I refused to let myself feel. I could not afford to feel it, not now, when I needed him more than ever. *There are no white knights, Soph, not like in your stories.*

That night, as we climbed aboard the gondola to go to the salon, Joseph gave me a curious look. "What are you thinking? You're . . . I don't know what it is."

It was nearly the first full sentence he'd said to me all day. I said, "I'm hoping Mr. Dane will be there tonight."

Joseph hesitated. Then, "What do you mean to do?"

"If he's there, I will have Henry Loneghan for us by the end of the evening."

My brother gave me a considering look. "We have a little more time, you know. Now that Madame León has provided—"

"She can only give us money," I said firmly. "Henry Loneghan can give us everything. We won't need Odilé León or her commission then."

I saw the question in his eyes, but he didn't ask it. Instead, he seemed vaguely troubled. "All right. Just remember, Soph, don't say yes, but—"

"—don't say no either. I know what to do."

"You'll let me know if you need me."

I nodded, smiling. "Just be as charming as you always are."

When we arrived at the Alvisi, I left him with a kiss and went to look for Nicholas Dane. The crowd was not so great tonight, and I found Mr. Martin right away in the main *sala*.

"Miss Hannigan! You look radiant this evening," he said, bowing over my hand like some courtier.

"You're too kind. I don't suppose Mr. Dane managed to come with you this evening?"

"As a matter of fact, he did. He's here." Mr. Martin peered about nearsightedly. "Well, not *here*, but somewhere about."

I buried my excitement in determination and wandered through the crowd, craning for the sight of Mr. Dane. When I spotted him at last, on the far side of one of the smaller salons, talking to a bushy-mustachioed man, I felt again a surge of warmth, and I was possessed by the sudden wish that he might sense me, that he might turn to find me across the room as if he knew already I was there. What would it be like, I wondered, to have someone look for only *me*? And just as I had the thought, impossibly, as if he'd known, he did turn. His gaze landed on me as if I'd yanked it there. I caught my breath at the pleasure I saw in it and had to forcibly remind myself of my task. I put a command in my eyes—*come to me, follow me*—and then I turned and left the room, moving slowly, my heart racing, wondering if he would.

In moments, he was at my side, cupping my elbow in his hand, his low voice in my ear, "Miss Hannigan, how I have missed you these last days."

Careful, Sophie. I made myself remember everything at stake and I gave Nicholas Dane a flirtatious look. "Have you? Then why haven't I seen you?"

"My other business kept me away. But my thoughts have never left you. I was looking forward to seeing you last night— more than I can say. But alas, you weren't here."

I touched his arm. "Is there somewhere . . . private we may go?"

He glanced down at my fingers, and then up again, swallowing convulsively. "Of course," he said with alacrity, taking my arm again. He led me through the rooms, smiling and nodding at those he knew, brief hellos, as he took me to what looked like Arthur Bronson's study. It was unoccupied, but the scent of tobacco lingered. He did not close the door for propriety's sake— and I was relieved. I could not do anything too stupid with the door open.

I said, as we went to a settee against the far wall, "You know this house well."

"I've spent nearly every night here for some months," he said. "This is where Arthur retreats when the salon becomes too much for him. Tonight he's too busy talking to an old friend to leave."

The plan. Loneghan. Think. I said, "Did you really think of me these last days?"

"Yes," he said.

"It makes me feel better to know it. I'd thought perhaps you found me . . . lacking."

He looked bewildered. "Lacking?"

"What else was I to think? I kiss you and then you disappear without a word. I thought I'd displeased you. I understand, of course, if—" I lowered my eyes, raising them again, putting all the wiles I knew to work—"well, perhaps I'm not very good at kissing."

We were already sitting very close. Now, he moved closer, almost sitting on my skirts. It seemed to take him some effort to say, "Not at all. No, you're . . . you're very good at it, in fact."

"And of course, I've been quite distracted lately, so perhaps it wasn't my best effort—"

"Distracted?"

"I think I could do it much better if I had another opportunity, you see, if there weren't other things on my mind. And I do like you so much, you know. Well enough to try again, once I have things right—"

"What things?" he asked—so quick, so very eager. The way he looked at me . . . how heady it was. His gaze rested again and again on my lips as if it were all he could do to resist them. My own mouth went dry. "What isn't right?"

"Well, truthfully, I'm worried. We came to Venice so Joseph could study, but it's been more expensive than I'd planned. All that time in the Danieli when I could find no place to lease, and now . . . I'm afraid we may have to return to New York unless . . ."

"Unless?"

"I'm sorry. I should not burden you with this."

"No, no, it's quite all right." His hand came to my arm, his fingers pressing against the silk of my sleeve, a touch I found myself liking a bit too much.

"I'm afraid there's no help for it. I will miss you, Mr. Dane, but the truth is that Joseph and I haven't enough money to stay."

"I see. What if . . . what if there was a way, if I could . . . I know your brother is here to study, but would he be averse to taking a commission, do you think?"

My heart jumped. "A commission?"

"I could introduce him to Henry Loneghan. He's always looking for new artists. I could recommend your brother to him."

"You would do that for us?"

"Of course. Your brother's the most talented artist I've seen in years. Henry will love him. I'll do it tomorrow. Will it help, do you think?"

"Oh! Oh, yes, it will help. It will help tremendously!" How easy it had been after all.

"I can't promise anything, of course, but Henry respects my opinion. I can't remember the last time he refused me. In fact, I don't believe he ever has."

I did not try to restrain my smile. "You are the best of friends, Mr. Dane. Truly. Joseph will be so grateful."

"I'm glad for that, but it's *your* gratitude I'm most interested in." His hand moved to mine. He eased his thumb beneath my fingers, against my palm. Even with my glove between us, it felt intimate.

The desire I'd been fighting rushed through me. "I see. And do you have some idea of how I might thank you?"

He leaned forward. "Perhaps that kiss—"

He said the last of it, the hiss of the *s*, against my lips. I felt the warmth of his breath in the moment before his lips touched mine, before they were pressing, opening, and I sighed against him, letting him in, putting my arms around his neck, pulling him closer, kissing him back. For a moment, I forgot everything I was supposed to be doing, every plan. His hand came to my breast; I felt the heat of it even through the layers of silk and corset and chemise; I felt something in me dissolve, a growing swell of longing. I arched against him, hearing a whispered sound, a moan, and suddenly Joseph's words were in my head. *Don't say yes, but don't say no either,* and I knew I was in danger of doing everything he'd warned me not to do.

The past rose up before me. Everything I'd ruined because I'd so wanted to be special on my own that I'd been blind. I was supposed to fascinate Nicholas Dane and nothing more. I was only to use him to get to Loneghan. Not to like him. Not to want him. I could not do this. I could not risk it.

I harnessed my yearnings; I locked desire away, and in that moment I felt Nicholas Dane's kiss change, as if he felt my withdrawal and meant to fight it. But I pulled back. I was breathing hard, and so was he. "Not here," I managed, forcing a smile, trying to make him think that what he'd felt was only my fear of being discovered.

He looked as if he were stumbling from sleep. He murmured something beneath his breath, words I could not hear.

I rose, and he let me go. I smoothed my skirt, tucking a loosened hair back into my chignon. My fingers were trembling. "We should go back to the *sala*."

"Yes, we should," he said, rising as well, and I saw him struggle for composure. As if he could not help himself, he leaned close, brushing his lips over my skin, just below my ear, raising a little shiver. He whispered, half to himself, "No, it's not what I thought, after all, is it? It's violets. That perfume you wear?"

"Yes," I breathed.

He drew away, smiling, but it didn't quite reach his eyes. He was angry, I realized suddenly, and with dismay. Apparently Nicholas Dane did not take *no* well. Oh, I had already ruined everything.

"I'm sorry," I said quickly. "I had not meant to—"

"Arouse me beyond reason?" he asked lightly. "Torment me like some wicked sorceress?"

"No." My heart was pounding. "None of those things."

"You wouldn't be the first." His eyes clouded; I saw his effort to clear them. He smiled once more, but again, it seemed distracted. "Come, let's return to the hordes."

"Yes," I agreed, feeling a nervous relief. I was glad when we went back into the crowd, and there was Joseph, looking at me with a question in his eyes. I pulled Nicholas Dane over to him, and said, as a kind of guarantee—if Joseph knew it too, Nicholas could not take it back, no matter how angry he might be— "Joseph, Mr. Dane has promised the most wonderful thing!"

"Has he? What wonderful thing is that?"

"I mean to recommend you to Henry Loneghan," Nicholas said. "I believe he should see your work. I'm hoping to convince him to commission you."

Joseph did his best to look surprised. I think no one but me would have seen the pretense. "Why, I'm . . . well, I don't know what to say."

"Your sister seemed to think you wouldn't be averse to such a thing."

"Not at all." My brother smiled, his dimples breaking. "Thank you, Dane. It is . . . more than I should ask."

"You didn't ask it. I offered. I should have thought of it days ago, in fact, but I didn't realize your . . . situation. I'll speak to Henry as soon as I can. He'll want to meet you."

"I'll make myself available any day," Joseph said.

"Good." Nicholas smiled. "Now I'm afraid I must be off." He shook my brother's hand, and bent to me, a light kiss on my cheek, very friendly, nothing untoward in it. "I'll see you both soon."

He started off. My brother frowned and mouthed, *What happened?* and I hurried after Nicholas Dane, catching up with him halfway down the hall. I called softly, "Nicholas."

He stopped and turned.

"I . . . if I've made you angry I do apologize. Perhaps I was too forward . . . that is . . ." I let the words fall, not knowing what else to say.

His gaze softened. He glanced about, and then he took the two steps to close the distance between us. "What did you call me?"

I frowned—I had called him by his Christian name. "Oh, I—"

"Say it again," he demanded.

"Nicholas," I said.

"I like the way it sounds from your pretty mouth. In fact, I like everything about your mouth. Have I told you that?"

There were people all around. He spoke quietly enough that I thought they couldn't hear, but it lent enough of an impropriety to his words that I felt a little trill of arousal.

"No." I could barely force my voice. "I don't think you have."

"Well I do," he said. "Good night, Sophie." And then he turned on his heel and strode away.

THIRTY

NICHOLAS

The Citta di Firenze had good wine, and Henry Loneghan liked it. We'd spent many an evening relaxing at its tables, and he'd been the first to suggest we meet there when I told him of Joseph Hannigan.

"He's brilliant," I'd said. "He does people beautifully. Surely you need a new portrait done?"

Henry shook his head. "Of me? Good God, no. We've already an absurd number of them."

"Then Edith. Isn't it about time for another of her?"

He hesitated. "She hates to sit for them."

"Ah, but he's a handsome fellow. She'll like looking at him. And he has a charming sister who I'm certain would come along to entertain."

Henry stroked his voluminous white beard—he had more hair than any one man had a right to own, along with a high forehead that gave him a noble and well-bred air—of which he was both. He'd been a friend of my father's when they'd both been in the House of Commons, and he'd taken an interest in me over my brother Jonathan, which was one of the reasons I liked him. But Henry's passion was for art, and his disdain for politics had only grown as he'd aged, and so perhaps that explained why he'd chosen a ne'er-do-well poet over a barrister. He was also one of the only people I knew who'd actually bought my poetry.

"At least talk to him," I urged Henry now. "I thought of you immediately when I saw his work. You'll like him. I do."

"Well, thus far you've proved to have an unparalleled eye for such things," he said. "And perhaps . . . we were looking for a piece for the second salon."

So now here we were—Joseph Hannigan, Henry Loneghan and I—lingering over a third bottle of wine. Henry had been impressed with Hannigan the moment he'd walked into the res-taurant—and I was glad to see Hannigan had taken the meeting seriously; though he still wore no hat, he had dressed well. He had an ease and charm that put Henry immediately at his, and they were laughing together before dinner had been cleared.

It was a good thing, as I had little to contribute to the con-versation. I was tired; I'd had a few long and exhausting nights with almost no sleep, not all of which was due to my self-imposed sentry at Odilé's. At least some was the fault of Sophie Hannigan and her kisses—dear God, that kiss at the salon. . . . I didn't want to think of it just now, or the strangeness of what had happened, the strength of my arousal and then the smell of almonds that had paralyzed me, a perfume that had not been hers, but Odilé's. It had made me jerk away from Sophie precipi-tously—and I hoped she hadn't noticed. But the uneasiness that had come over me then hadn't gone away.

It was all I could do to devote myself to urging and directing Henry Loneghan tonight. When Henry finally gestured to Hannigan, saying, "Now then, let's see your work, young man," I knew I had succeeded. Henry liked Hannigan—there was virtually no chance he wouldn't like the work. My job was done. I poured another glass of wine and sat back in my chair, watching as Hannigan handed over his sketchbook and Henry began to leaf through it.

Henry paused at the first page. His eyes, still sharp for his age, narrowed; he perused every detail before he said, "Very good," and went on to the next. I could not help but notice it was a sketch of Mestre, but not Mestre as it was—Mestre as Sophie had described it in her story, shimmering and beautiful and not quite real. What a gift it was, to see the world that way.

Henry glanced up at Hannigan with an admiring expression. "Where did you get your training?"

"I haven't any," Hannigan confessed, sitting forward, eagerness in his bearing. In the dim gaslight of the restaurant, he was more striking than ever. "Not formally, anyway. I began copying when I was very young. My aunt wasn't interested in paying for lessons, so I did what I could."

"Extraordinary," Henry said. "I must admit I've rarely seen such raw talent. And what you've done with it—" He fell silent when he turned the page, freezing. I had some idea what he must be looking at, and I knew it for certain when he said, "Who is this?"

Hannigan leaned in to see. "My twin sister. Sophie."

It was not the sketch that had first captured me, nor the one at the Lido. This was one I hadn't seen, the fish market at the Rialto with the Grand Canal and the edge of the Fondaco dei Tedeschi in the background. She was staring into the distance, her chin lifted, her eyes closed, with yearning so starkly and seductively written on her features that I could not help but stare. Again I felt consternation that her brother should see such things in her, again the question of what it might mean.

I felt Hannigan's glance, and I looked over to see a thoughtfulness in his gaze that confused me before he looked away again. Henry closed the sketchbook with a definitive slap. "Well, there's no need to see more. You're hired, Mr. Hannigan. This spring, I would very much like a portrait of my wife done with your talented brush. And I think perhaps I shall want something else too, but we can talk about that then. If you're willing, of course."

This spring. I saw Hannigan's disappointment, which he hid the next moment.

"The spring?" I asked.

"Unfortunately I've been called to Rome," Henry said. "A pity, as we've just got here, but I trust I can reserve your services in advance, Mr. Hannigan?"

Hannigan smiled charmingly. "Yes, of course. I'd be honored. I am very grateful, sir."

"As am I, to Nicky, for bringing you to me. Your eye for talent has only grown more discerning, my boy. I expect Mr. Hannigan here will set Venice afire."

I felt justified and proud, half in love with Hannigan myself for how well he'd impressed Henry and how well it reflected on me. As Henry wrote a small cheque to Hannigan, I wondered if it was enough to keep him and his sister in the city—and what I could do if it were not.

After Henry took his leave, I said, "I had no idea Henry was leaving again so soon. I do hope his promise is enough to keep you here."

Hannigan took a sip of wine. He was nearly vibrating with excitement. "I would stay a year living on the streets for Henry

Loneghan," he said, and I found myself liking him even more, glad that I'd brought him, glad to help him—eager to do so.

"And to think I nearly didn't go to the campo with Giles that day we met," I told him.

He smiled, clasping my arm. "I'm very grateful you did."

The words were simple and heartfelt, and I was startled at how strongly I responded to them. It was that magic in him again—I felt it intensely in that moment, along with the desire to be his friend, to stay his friend. I'd somehow spent my life waiting to sit in this cafe with him, sharing a bottle of wine.

I was tired, and the wine had made me sentimental and maudlin, erasing my usual cynicism—I have no other way to explain why I felt so caught in his spell. I found myself saying, "You and your sister may be the best thing that has ever happened to me," and meaning it in a way I rarely meant anything.

"Sophie has that effect on people."

I felt a surge of jealousy at the thought that there might be others like me. "Does she? I suppose the two of you have left more than a few broken hearts in your wake."

Hannigan laughed humorlessly. "I don't know about that. But Sophie's very special."

"Yes, she is. And so are you. The two of you . . . well, I have to say that no one knows what to make of you. There's something . . . I think you confuse people." I wondered if he heard the accusation I was not quite making.

"Because we're twins, no doubt." It had the sound of having been said a hundred times before.

"I think it might be more than that."

His expression went carefully blank. "What do you mean?"

"Well, she's your muse, isn't she?" I said. "What you do with the stories she tells . . . it's unlike anything I've ever seen. Your sketch of Mestre—and the Lido too—you drew the world she gave us. The two of you made something so beautiful it changed the way I saw it. I'll never think of those places the same way again."

He looked surprised, and then thoughtful, as if there was something in me he hadn't expected and now needed to reassess. "No one else has ever seen that," he said softly. "Or if they have, they've never said it. It's Sophie's talent, though she thinks she has none. She doesn't know how important she is. But without her . . ."

"Without her, what?"

His gaze locked to mine. "I'm nothing."

I felt a needling discomfort, the sense that he was challenging me, that he *wanted* me to ask the question of what they truly were to each other. But I suddenly couldn't ask. As disturbing as my suspicions had been, I now wasn't certain I wanted to know whatever dark thing was between them—and it *was* dark. I saw it in his eyes.

Instead I was struck by the urge to show him I was different than everyone else, that I saw the sublimity in them that made the rest of it somehow not matter. I wanted him to think me more perceptive, worth keeping. "I think many men would give a great deal for such a muse. I would have given my soul for it." *I almost had.* "I understand why you keep her so close. Had I something like that, I would never let it go. You're destined to make a mark. I confess I'm envious."

"Are you?"

"It's only because I've had too much wine that I'm admitting it, you know. I'd prefer you keep my ambitions a secret, if you don't mind. It's less humiliating when everyone doesn't witness your failures."

"How have you failed?" he asked. "Was it fame you wanted?"

"Fame? Perhaps. But I think it's more that I want to believe that my time here on earth has some meaning, that I've made some difference."

He smiled. I saw in his dark blue eyes empathy and affection, and I felt appreciated and valued.

"You understand," I said.

"Perhaps more than you know," he answered. He picked up his glass, draining it. Then he said with sudden energy, "Let's go back to the Moretta and tell Sophie about Loneghan."

"Won't she be abed?" I asked.

"We'll wake her up," he said. "Come on."

Well, of course I was not going to say no. The prospect of rousing Sophie Hannigan from bed was impossible to resist. I forgot my exhaustion. By the time we stumbled up the courtyard steps to the rooms he shared with his sister, I was wide awake, and we were both laughing. We went inside, and he turned to me, putting his finger to his lips to signal quiet, and then took me to her bedroom. She wasn't there, and the bed looked unslept in.

Hannigan frowned. "Where the hell is she?"

"Did you really think not to wake me?" Her voice came from behind us, and we both whirled to see her standing there wearing a dressing gown, her hair in a long braid trailing over her shoulder. She was smiling. "You sounded like a herd of donkeys."

Hannigan laughed and swooped down on her, wrapping his arms around her in a hug so exuberant he lifted her from the ground. "Loneghan's hired me to do a portrait of his wife."

"He has?" Her eyes lit; she threw her arms around his neck and kissed him soundly—a kiss that held, as always, a bit too long, and suddenly my mind was full of darkened rooms and entwined limbs. Again, I felt as if he'd somehow heightened her already considerable appeal. She drew away from him, her eyes sparkling as she looked at me. "It's all because of you. We have so much to thank you for."

"We do," Hannigan said, releasing her at last. "I've brought him here to celebrate."

"I've a bottle of wine in the *sala*." She turned to lead the way, hips swaying beneath thin layers of muslin, and Hannigan and I followed like bucks after a doe—or at least I did, and I would have sworn he was not much different.

In the *sala*, she'd lit an oil lamp, which lent a dim and romantic glow. A book, *Don Juan*—Byron again—was open, face down on the settee, and on the table next to the settee was a glass half full of wine, and a bottle beside it.

"There's still some left," she said, lifting the bottle to show us. She had been drinking while she waited for her brother, and I realized she was affected—how much so I didn't know.

Hannigan took the bottle from her hand. "How much of this have you had?"

"Only a little." She leaned into him, putting her arm around his waist, smiling up at him. "I've been waiting all night to hear what happened. What did Mr. Loneghan say? What exactly?"

She'd mollified him just that quickly, I realized. A touch, a word, and he was back to excitement and satisfaction. "He liked the work. He asked where I'd had my training."

"What did you tell him?"

"That there had been none at all." He stepped from her hold, drinking from the bottle before he handed it to me. Then he sagged onto the settee, pulling the book from beneath his hip and setting it on the table.

She laughed, a pretty, bell-like sound. "Oh, you didn't!"

"It's the truth, isn't it? Copying from books and other men's sketches and art exhibits. I still haven't got Da Vinci's shadows exactly right."

I took a drink. "You don't need to know how to do Da Vinci's shadows, so long as you know how to do your own. Henry isn't looking for someone to copy Da Vinci. He's looking for someone with a new vision. That's you."

Hannigan looked at me. I thought I saw hesitation there—or uncertainty, which was strange coming from him.

In surprise, I said, "Don't tell me this is the first time you've been commissioned."

He said, "No. It's only . . . never one so important as Henry Loneghan. Well, there was one in New York, but it never worked out." His gaze went distant.

His sister was next to him before he'd even finished speaking, a swirl of concern and muslin. She put her arm around him, tangling her fingers in his hair. I felt bedeviled, seduced by the two of them. How in God's name did they do it? She smiled up at me until I nearly forgot what we were talking about.

I finished the last bit of wine and held out the bottle. "Well, this is done."

"We'll need another," she said, rising quickly. "There's one in the kitchen. I'll get it."

She hurried off, a blur of white in the darkness.

I asked quietly, "What happened with the commission in New York?"

"Nothing really." Hannigan laughed shortly, leaning forward, his elbows on his knees. "The man who hired me . . . his son took a liking to me. I didn't return the sentiment. The commission was canceled. But"—here a deep breath—"the son's dead now, more's the pity. A few weeks ago. Don't tell Sophie. She doesn't know. It would . . . distress her."

"Why would it distress her?" I asked.

He looked at me, his eyes looking almost black in the lamplight. Black and deep and oddly fathomless. I rarely felt sad, but in that moment, Joseph Hannigan's regret over his sister's grief filled me with sorrow.

"She liked him," he said simply.

"Even though he caused you to lose a commission?"

"It was hard for her, that's all. I'd rather not remind her of it."

"I see," I said, though I didn't, not really. I felt there was something more here, but I didn't know if it was important, or how to discover it—or frankly, if I cared enough to try.

Just then there was the sound of breaking glass from the kitchen. Hannigan jerked around, but I was halfway there before he could rouse from the settee. "I'll go see," I told him, and in moments I was in the kitchen, staring down at Sophie Hannigan, who was on her hands and knees, mopping up bits of broken glass littering the floor.

"I dropped the glass," she said unnecessarily as she looked up. Her braid fell over her shoulder. The open collar of her dressing gown revealed the beginning swell of her breasts. Her eyes were so blue—not so dark as her brother's, but the same shape, with the same intensity. Her hair shone in the light from the flickering oil lamp the way his had shined in the sun on the Campo della Carita. The urge to touch her was irresistible.

She frowned slightly and sat back on her heels, letting the cloth she'd been wiping with drop. It fluttered to the ground near her knee. "What is it?" she asked in a husky whisper that inflamed me.

I hardly knew what I was doing. I took two steps and pulled her to her feet, into my arms. I backed her up until she was against the table and could go no farther. I pressed into her until I felt those soft breasts against my chest, until I heard her little cry of pleasure—or perhaps it wasn't pleasure, perhaps it was dismay; the truth was I didn't care. I shoved my hand in her hair, tangling it about my fingers to keep her still, and then I kissed her, an open assault. She tasted of wine and sleep. I clutched her hip with my other hand, jerking her ever closer, settling myself in the indentation between her thighs, wanting her to feel how hard I was. I heard her gasp and bent my head to her jaw, her throat, the swell of her breasts.

The taste of her skin, after so long away, was its own torment, that familiar honey, that faint and delicious salt, that smooth tautness I had never been able to get enough of, that smell of musk and almonds—no . . . no wait, it wasn't almonds. It was violets. Violets. *Violets.*

The same confusion that had rocked me at the salon the other night returned. The memories—honey and salt and almonds—weren't of Sophie, but of Odilé.

I jerked away from her, my desire fading in fear and dismay, cursing beneath my breath.

"Oh, I'm sorry," she said—breathlessly.

It took me a moment to understand that she was apologizing. What transgression she could possibly think she'd committed I had no idea. I was ashamed that she should think it, afraid of what was happening to me, angry. I'd thought my desire for Sophie meant that Odilé's spell had faded at last. How wretched to discover it wasn't true, how bound I still was. Was I never to be rid of her?

It was all I could do to say to Sophie, "You've done nothing," and even then I felt how abrupt the words were, how clipped my voice. I tried to smooth it. "Truly, nothing. It wasn't you, Sophie. It's me. I'm the one who should be sorry. For"—I took a deep breath. When I looked back at her again, it was with at least some modicum of civility. "For . . . attacking you that way. It was unforgivable."

She clutched the edges of her dressing gown, drawing together what I'd loosened.

"I'm sorry," I said again. "Forgive me."

She looked at me as if she didn't quite believe me, a feral wariness—well, I couldn't blame her. I had just made a complete mess of a perfect opportunity, and all the pretty words in the world couldn't change it. Damn Odilé. Damn her for Paris, for every moment since, for what she'd done to me, for not expecting it. I hated her so much in that moment.

I said softly, "I am undone by you, Sophie. But this . . . this . . . you deserve better than this. I'm sorry for being such a savage. It was only . . . I seem to lose all sense when I'm with you."

They were the prettiest words I could think of just then— and it was a struggle to think of any, I promise you. But they were working, I saw. Her fingers loosened on the dressing gown; her eyes grew soft and luminous.

I whispered, "Come to my rooms one night—or one day, if you prefer. Whatever is easier. I'll arrange for Giles to be gone. We'll have the whole place to ourselves without interruption."

She licked her lips, which sent a little hitch snaking through me. "I don't know. I don't know if I could—"

I heard footsteps. Her brother. She heard him too. She dropped her hand from her dressing gown and straightened, hurrying back to the mess on the floor, picking up the rag again. I didn't move from my position against the wall. Respectably distant.

Then he was in the doorway. He frowned and ran a hand through his hair, looking at the glass she'd swept into a little pile before I'd interrupted her. "What did you break?"

"A glass," she said. "I saw a spider and it startled me into dropping it."

"I see." I thought I saw speculation in his gaze—perhaps he

felt the currents swirling in the room. I did not doubt for a moment that he did.

I pushed off from the wall. "It's late. I should be going, I think."

Sophie looked up. "Oh, but there was another bottle of wine."

"Save it for another time," I said.

"I'll walk you out," Hannigan said. I said good night to Sophie and let him herd me to the door. Once there, he paused and said, "I owe you a great debt, Dane. For Loneghan. Whatever I can do for you, you've only to say the word."

I knew exactly what he could do for me, but how was I to say, *Don't stop your sister from coming to my bed*? Instead I only smiled and said, "You owe me nothing. It was a pleasure to see how well Henry liked you. You'll do a fine job with the commission. I've every faith."

He took a deep breath. "Well, thank you. You've made a great deal possible."

I wasn't certain what that meant. It didn't matter. "It will be enough for me to see your success and know I had a small hand in it."

"Neither Sophie nor I will ever forget it," he said, and the way he said it was strange. The goodwill that had been between us seemed to evaporate. Suddenly I had the distinct impression that he had put me in the past already. The dim gaslight from the *portego* behind him cast him in half-light and shadow, and he looked for that moment like one of William Blake's dark angels, both beautiful and terrible.

It felt like a warning. For a moment I could only stand and stare. Finally I managed, "Well then, good night."

"Good night, Dane," he said, and closed the door.

THIRTY-ONE

SOPHIE

Joseph came back into the kitchen, where I stood staring down at the glass I'd swept into a pile, watching the reflections of the oil lamp upon the shards, my heart racing, uncertain what I felt: longing or fear or despair.

He said, "He's done what we needed him to do, Soph."

I looked up at him, knowing exactly what he meant: I could set Nicholas aside. And he was right. But I still felt the press of Nicholas's lips against mine, his hand on my breast. I still churned with wanting him even as I knew I must not. I had promised myself already to resist him now that he'd won us Loneghan. I would not have let myself kiss him at all tonight, truthfully. In fact, it was Joseph's fault I had. Joseph's fault that I'd dropped the glass, that I'd been so struck with confusion and sorrow that I hadn't been able to think anything but *Edward. Edward was dead.* I don't know why I felt sorrow. I was angry with Edward Roberts. I hated him, in fact, for what he'd done to us. But that he was dead startled me. It brought everything back so fiercely—the way I'd felt about him, the things I'd wanted—and it was in the midst of that confusion that Nicholas Dane had stepped into the kitchen and given me that look of yearning, that look that had been my downfall before, that I'd seen in Edward's eyes, no matter that it had been a lie. A look to make me feel special simply because I was me.

It had seemed so easy to step into Nicholas's arms, to let him comfort me. Edward was dead, and I would never have known it had I not overheard my brother's words. I could not believe Joseph had kept it from me, though I understood too why he had. He knew I would feel this way.

And in the end, it had been that which saved me. Joseph keeping it secret reminded me of what Edward had done to us, why we were here and what was at stake.

I said to Joseph now, "We don't have to accept Odilé León's commission. We have Henry Loneghan. He's the one we need. You'll have to focus on him. You can't afford to waste time with her."

My brother had braced his arm against the door, above his head, and I saw his muscles tense. "What about the money?"

"We'll have enough with Loneghan's commission." I pleaded. "We don't need her. Tell me you'll turn it down. Write to her tonight."

Joseph's expression was thoughtful. "It's not the waste of time that has you bothered, is it?"

Suddenly it all came together, the things I'd seen in Odilé, the things that had felt so familiar. "She reminds me of someone."

He raised a questioning brow.

"You don't see it?"

He said quietly, "She's not Jessie, Soph."

I winced. I hated it when he called her by her name. I preferred the distance of *Miss Coring*. I preferred anger and hatred in his eyes over that gentle sorrow.

I whispered, "Don't you remember the story, Joseph? How the

princess saw in the demon-queen something terrible from the start, no matter that she seemed so kind and good?"

"You never saw that in her," he said, a little brutally. "Not at the start. Neither of us did. And what bad have you seen in Odilé León? You seemed to like her at dinner."

Of course, I couldn't tell him why I felt as I did. How could I tell him the truth, that the world had become muted in her presence, subsumed by her fierce energy, her spell? How could I say the truth, which was that I saw in her the thing that could take him away from me? That had nearly taken him once before?

"She looks at you as if she means to swallow you whole."

"Why does that trouble you? There have been others—"

"Not like that," I said firmly. "She frightens me. You know what Mrs. Bronson said about her."

"I'm not Nelson Stafford, Soph," he said. "I'm not about to die of love for Odilé León. I want her, but that means nothing. You know that." His eyes were luminous in the dimness of the small lamp. In them, I saw a love and devotion that was mine alone. "You've nothing to be afraid of."

"I don't want to lose you."

"That will never happen."

"You say that, but—"

"She needs someone like you," he said. "I think she's very sad. There's something tragic about her. I think she would like your world. You should tell her one of your stories."

As always, I was struck by how much my brother saw. But I didn't like that he'd seen it in her. "I doubt she would find my stories interesting."

"She's like all of us. Just looking for her own happy ending. I want to know more about her. But I'm only painting her. Nothing else."

I knew him as well as he knew me, and I gave him a look

that made him glance uncomfortably away. I said again, "We don't need her, Joseph. Not now. We have what we came for. Tell her no, and I'll say the same to Nicholas."

I felt an ache in my chest even as I said it, but it was a bargain I knew would get Joseph's attention. It did. "Loneghan's hired me, yes, but I can't do the work until spring. He and his wife leave for Rome this week. They'll be gone for months. He gave me some coin in promise, but it isn't much. Not enough to keep us."

"Spring?" I could not hide my disappointment.

"So you see . . . there's no choice. I can't say no to her. But you can write to Dane, Soph. I wish you would. I know you like him, and I do too, but"—he took a deep breath—"Loneghan's ours. The Bronsons accept us. What else do we need him for?"

I glanced down again at the pile of glass, feeling suddenly sad. I didn't know how to tell him that for a few moments Nicholas had felt as if he belonged just to me. It was not true, of course—I knew Nicholas was as caught in my brother's spell as everyone was. It was only a matter of time before I would fade in importance, as I always did.

"You're only jealous," I said.

"Yes." Joseph's voice was a whisper. "Though that's not it. Not really. I want you to be happy, but . . . but you like him too much already. I can't watch you go through that again."

"I know." My brother was right. Better to end things with Nicholas Dane now, before he became just another Edward Roberts, another relationship ended in scandal and disaster and regret.

I felt Joseph move; I saw the shadow of him crossing the floor to me, and then his arms came around, drawing me back into his chest. "I'm just painting her," Joseph whispered again. "I promise." I felt his kiss upon my hair, and the spell of Odilé León was gone; he was there with me again, mine alone, and relief swept my sorrow and fear away.

THIRTY-TWO

ODILÉ

I sent an invitation for him to come to tea at six to discuss my commission, and when he accepted, I was more than relieved. I waited for him impatiently. When the sun began to set, I lit the lamps, covering them with rose-colored shades to make the light lovely and romantic. It was a struggle to be charming now, when I most needed to be. That morning, as I'd passed through a shaft of sunlight against the wall, I'd caught sight of my shadow and was horrified at the way it pulsed, the demon inside me impatient, clawing at the confines of my skin. With every passing moment, the monster grew stronger, and soon I would not be able to hold her back.

Desperation was not an emotion I liked, fear even less so, and yet I felt both. I could no longer afford for anything to get in the way. I went to the balcony, searching for any sign of Nicholas. I'd seen him often of late, lingering on the *fondamenta* of the abandoned, ruined palace next door. His distinctive blond hair always glinted, whether in sunlight, moonlight or gaslight. But he was not there now, thankfully. This was my last chance. Less than a week and a half left.

I turned back inside to wait for Joseph Hannigan, and I did not have to wait long. When the two of them—two, not one—came into the room, my disappointment was so sharp that for a moment I could not rise to greet them. He'd brought her—again. I was surprised and angry. I'd meant to have him in bed before the hour was out, and now I would have to find a way to get rid of her. It was all I could do to smile.

"Welcome. I'm so glad you could accept my invitation."

"How happy we are to see you again." Joseph Hannigan made no apology or excuse for bringing her. He set aside the sketchbook he carried and bowed low over my hand. When he raised his eyes, he captured mine, quite deliberately, and his smile was seductive and slow. I had seen such things a hundred times, a thousand, and still I lost my breath. He knew how to do this, as young as he was. It was not really surprising, not for one so attractive. I pressed my appetite into submission as best I could.

"Madame León," Sophie Hannigan greeted me in a low voice.

I felt a rush of resentment and barely managed to say, "Hello again, Miss Hannigan."

As they sat down—she on the settee beside me, and he on the chair opposite—I rang for tea. It was brought almost immediately. I had not planned for tea and conversation—rather, for wine and seduction—but I tempered my impatience as I poured them each a cup. To be done with her was all I could think . . . how to see her out the door and keep him behind? I took a deep breath. "Has my commission inspired you, monsieur?"

"I've been thinking about it," Joseph Hannigan admitted.

"Have you any ideas?"

He smiled. "A few."

"Such as?"

"I'd be better at showing you." He set aside his tea, and reached for his sketchbook, leafing to a blank page. "You said you wanted something about desire. I'd thought . . ." He reached into his pocket for a stick of charcoal.

And then, most surprisingly, his gaze went to his sister. He had been mine since he'd arrived, but once the charcoal was in his hand, it was as if he were transformed. He no longer saw me, no longer saw anything but the vision in his mind's eye. I saw hunger leap into his eyes. But his hunger wasn't for me.

Another surprise.

I glanced at Miss Hannigan, who sipped her tea. She looked like nothing so much as a well-brought-up woman, properly demure, hair swept up, the little straw hat with its bunch of wilting silk flowers that had once been jaunty, the high collar of her striped bodice, the smooth sweep of a corsetted bosom. She did not see it at all, not his hunger nor his need for her.

It disconcerted me. I had never seen attention turn from me if I was in the room. He said, "Put the tea down, Soph," in a soft, soft voice.

She did as he asked without question. He made a gesture, and she arranged herself on the settee as if she'd done so a hundred times, as if she knew just exactly what pose would please him. There was no hesitation, no rearranging of limbs, just a graceful acceptance that for the moment, her every movement belonged to him. She seemed, in fact, quite incapable of making one of her own. It was an abdication of her will that was startling in its conclusiveness.

I saw the itch in him when he began to draw, as if he couldn't help himself, as if the simple fact of her presence fed him. The air felt charged with pleasure and surrender, arousal and denial. I knew, of course, how much seduction there was in

the creation of art—it was a sexual act. But the intensity of this
. . . I had never seen anything like it. I could only watch and
wait as he drew.

After a time, he looked up, and I saw his interest come to
me again, a dimpled smile that blinded as he showed me what
he'd done.

It was his sister as she'd leaned against the settee, but not as
I'd witnessed her. Her shoulders were round and naked. Her
eyes were closed, her mouth slightly parted, her hair falling. She
looked sensuous, tempting. In full command of her power. It
was unsettlingly lovely and disturbingly intimate.

The demon in me whipped and bit. "That's beautiful," I said,
though it was much more than that. But now I needed his full
attention. "Yet . . . I would like to see more."

He frowned as if such a request was unfamiliar. I was certain it was. I was certain that no one had ever seen his work
without breathless admiration. But I . . . I had seen immortal
talents. I had watched them bloom before my eyes.

He asked, "More?"

Sophie Hannigan sat up, frowning—a matched set of frowns.
"Didn't you like it?"

"Oh, but of course I did." I smiled. "It's only that I should
like to see more than a face. A body, perhaps. And hands. Hands
are so difficult, are they not?"

Joseph Hannigan pulled the book back. "Yes, all right," he
said easily. "As you wish."

"And perhaps . . . something not so familiar," I said. "You
will sketch me, I think."

He glanced at his sister. I caught the sudden wariness between
them, the fleeting touch of longing, and of something else, something darker. I could not take my eyes away, and they seemed
oblivious to my scrutiny. I tried to grab him back to me.

"Perhaps I should let my hair down. Would you like that, monsieur?"

He looked at me. I could not read his expression. I felt her watching, her tension.

"How will you have me?" I went on. "Perhaps on the chaise over there? I could be reclining like some Arabian houri."

He glanced at the chaise, hesitating, then said, "Yes, that."

I took down my hair, slowly, seducing him, ignoring her. I heard her sharp breath as I let the tresses fall, as I lay upon the chaise, stretching like an odalisque. I saw the flare of her nostrils, the hard rise and fall of her breath. Her gaze slid away and I saw her frown in confusion and apprehension. I followed her glance to where my shadow reclined against the wall, pulsing, the heartbeat of the monster—though of course she could not know that.

"How much finer this would be in the sun," I murmured, looking to Joseph Hannigan. "Do you not think so, *cheri*? You must be here in the morning, when the reflections off the Canal are so lovely. I could pose as a mermaid. Like that mural in the Moretta. Neptune among his subjects. Is it still there? It was such a pretty thing."

"It's there." Sophie Hannigan's voice was brutally intrusive as it cut through the ambient sounds from the city beyond the window. "Though faded a great deal. It is not so beautiful as it first seems. If you touch it the gilding comes off on your finger."

Her brother glanced at her, but I twisted my arm sensuously, calling him back. "I fear I love the sun too well. I'm afraid I have freckles now. All over, more's the pity—or, perhaps not, I suppose. A man I knew once told me that freckles were a map for kissing. A path to pleasure."

Joseph Hannigan's gaze jerked back. He drew convulsively, reflexively, but inwardly he went still, coiling deep. I gained strength by the moment, every time he looked at me.

I said, "Do you not think so, monsieur? I think most men cannot help but imagine kissing the freckles on a woman."

He said hoarsely, "I don't know what most men think."

"No, of course you do not. You're quite singular, aren't you, Joseph Hannigan?" I purred his name. I saw his quick swallow, and I could not help my smile. "Is he not so, mademoiselle?"

"Oh yes. There's no one like Joseph." Miss Hannigan's answer was sharp edged. She met my gaze with a challenging one of her own. I was surprised again. My hunger clenched as if she'd somehow denied it. Everything took on hard lines. I was suddenly too aware that the evening had faded to twilight.

"It's done," Joseph Hannigan said.

I went to look over his shoulder, pressing to his back. "Oh, how wonderful! Why, what a mind reader you are, *cheri*, to see my yearning so well."

I touched his hair, winding a bit of it about my finger. I felt him tense; I heard his breathing quicken, a thudding echo in my own chest, his talent searching for the void in me. I let my finger fall from his hair to the edge of his collar, the warm skin at the nape of his neck. I expected to see him shudder. But although I knew he felt my touch, I had the strange impression that he didn't feel my hunger at all, and I was seized with an excitement of a kind I'd rarely known. So *much* talent. Oh, I could not wait—

Sophie Hannigan said, "Joseph always makes everyone look so much more lovely than they are."

I wanted to laugh at the ineffectiveness of the jab. Instead, I ignored her, leaning close to Joseph Hannigan to whisper, "You have drawn the secrets in my eyes. Don't you wish to discover what they are?" I saw the rapid beat of his pulse in his throat, and I wanted to put my mouth to it, to draw it in, to stop it. "I will show them to you, and then you must show me yours."

He licked his lips. "My secrets might frighten you."

"Frighten me? Ah, but how intriguing. Now you only make me want to know more."

"You say that now."

"You can't frighten me, monsieur, except by refusing what I have to offer you."

I heard Sophie Hannigan's sharp intake of breath, her whispered, "*Joseph*," but he did not look at her, and neither did I.

"And what is that?" he asked me.

"Everything you want. Everything."

His eyes darkened even more, and it wasn't just desire I saw now, but something else that burned, and I recognized that too. Ambition.

But at that moment she made a little sound of dismay, and his gaze slid to her. I felt a surge of anger, my hunger snapping, snarling. I put the command in my eyes that had bid a thousand men to do as I asked.

"Your brother is staying with me tonight," I said quietly. "And you must go to your lover."

She stilled. "My lover?"

"This friend you told me of. He has become more than that, has he not?"

"No."

Not quite true, I thought. "Or perhaps you are too afraid. Do you not know what to do? Would you like me to tell you how to win him?"

A flush moved over her pale skin; I saw her confusion. "Joseph?"

He said, "I'll stay. You'd best go home."

I was more relieved than I'd expected at his words, and that was new too. It had been a very long time since I'd had to worry about a man accepting my bed.

Sophie Hannigan looked startled. I saw the sudden shine of tears in her eyes. But she blinked them away and took a deep breath. "Very well then. Good evening, madame. Thank you for the tea."

"It was my pleasure," I said. She looked angry as she turned to go. But what did I care for her anger? I had him now, and I meant to keep him.

THIRTY-THREE

SOPHIE

I turned away, feeling off balance, both angry and near tears. I did not want to go, and yet I wanted more than anything to put these rooms behind me, to forget the look I'd seen in my brother's eyes when he'd told me to go without apology or pause. I was afraid of Odilé. She reminded me so much of Miss Coring in that moment that I could not think how I would open the door and leave Joseph behind.

And yet there I was, out of the *sala* and into the *portego*, to the door. My hand was on the lever when I heard the rapid footsteps behind me, my brother's voice calling urgently, "Soph. Sophie, wait."

I turned to see him hurrying toward me. In relief, I said, "You've changed your mind?"

He shook his head. "No. But it's all right."

My relief turned to a dull and aching dismay. "You said you were only going to paint her."

He let out his breath, raking his hand through his hair. "Look, you know how it is."

"This feels different," I whispered.

His hand dropped to his side. "You don't need to worry. It is *nothing*. Just pleasure. Nothing more. You understand."

I turned again to the door. "Well then, I'll see you in the morning."

"I'll be there before you wake," he assured me.

As I opened the door, his hand came to mine, closing over my fingers, stopping me. "I want you to go home, Soph. Home. Not to the salon. Not to him. Promise me you won't."

His eyes were burning, fervent; I felt his fear for me. But I was angry. "I promise," I said, but even then I don't think I meant it. I felt miserable and alone and stupid, a mix of emotions I hardly understood. I felt secondary again, and while all the world might see me that way, my brother had never before been the one to make me feel it. I was suddenly possessed by the need to be something different, something separate. Myself, alone, though how to do that, how to *be* that when I was so afraid . . . when I could not bear to let Joseph step away. . . .

Joseph broke into a relieved smile that brought out his dimples. He leaned down, kissing me gently. "Good. I'll be back before dawn."

He drew away, and let me go, and when the door shut behind me I heard the thud of it like an echo in my heart. I felt myself again in a muted world, colorless and bleak.

Marco had waited, and he didn't even raise a brow when he saw I was alone, or when I told him to take me home. The journey seemed long and cold; we passed the Alvisi on the way, and I saw the gondolas moored out front.

I wondered if Nicholas was there, if he was waiting for me. I thought of last night, and the way he'd pressed himself to me, the way he'd said *I'm undone by you, Sophie,* in that wonderful voice. I thought of how much I liked him, how that voice had made me think, once again, of possibility. And then I thought of another voice, equally hoarse with desire, spoken in a New York City bedroom while I stood helplessly watching. *Please God . . . join us.* That too made me think of Odilé, as if everyone who had ever hurt Joseph and me, or might, had coalesced in her.

I was glad to be home when we arrived at the Moretta. How nice it would be to be alone for a change. A bath, and some wine, and perhaps I would go back to *Don Juan.* Byron's romantic cynicism seemed perfect for tonight.

I went up the stairs and inside, telling myself everything was all right, just as Joseph had said it was. He would return with the dawn, crawling into bed as he always did after nights away, pulling me against him and whispering groggily in my ear, "I'm so tired, Soph," in the moments before he fell deeply asleep. Everything would be the same.

But as I stepped into the *sala,* the emptiness of the palazzo seemed to mock me. I glanced up at the ceiling, the gilded painted sunset, and I remembered the way Joseph had brought me down beside him to watch it come alive with morning, how he'd known that would happen. I felt the loss of him like a disease; suddenly I was so alone and lonely I could not bear it, and I called Marco to take me to Nicholas Dane's.

THIRTY-FOUR

NICHOLAS

I was asleep on the settee when the bell rang, my sleepless nights caught up with me at last. I blinked awake, disoriented and confused. Giles came out from his bedroom, knotting his tie. "Were you expecting someone?"

He went to the window and opened it, looking out and then saying in surprise, "Oh! I'll be right down." He turned to me and said, "It's Miss Hannigan."

"Just Sophie?" For a moment I was certain I was dreaming.

"I'll bring her up." Giles went out the door.

I sat up, wondering what the hell Sophie Hannigan was doing alone at my door, and whether I should be worried or dismissive or thankful.

I still hadn't decided when Giles returned with her. He was smiling like an idiot. She was not.

"Look who's here, Nick!" Giles announced as if I didn't already know quite well.

She said, "I hope you don't mind that I've come without an invitation."

I saw the rise and fall of her breasts beneath her cloak as she took a deep breath. She glanced rather meaningfully at Giles, who frowned, obviously not understanding.

I said bluntly, "Go on to the Bronsons', Giles. Give them my regrets."

He said, "Oh," in a discouraged way that I was sorry for. "Yes, of course. I'll leave the two of you to yourselves." He waited half a moment, as if she might call him back, and then he grabbed his coat from the hook beside the door and went out.

She hadn't moved from where she stood.

"Is something wrong?" I asked.

She shook her head. I realized she was trembling with the force of some barely contained emotion. She reached for the buttons on her cloak. I watched as she undid them, as she slipped it from her shoulders, as she laid it over the chair.

I realized then why she was here, why she *must* be here, and I was paralyzed by the power of my yearning. And afraid too that I must be wrong.

She removed the pin from her hat and took it off, laying it aside. She came toward me, coming to a stop in lamplight that cast her in soft gold, highlighting her hair, her skin, the stripes of her bodice. "Why don't you take me to your room?"

I was already hard. It was absurd how thoroughly she managed it. But still I tried to temper my desire, to be gentle when I'd never been so with her before. I led her into the bedroom, shut the door, and turned to her. I reached for the pins in her hair, bending to kiss her. No sooner was my mouth on hers than she was pawing fiercely at me, pulling my shirt from my trousers, undoing the fastenings as if she could not wait another moment. The fragile rein I had on my control snapped. I plunged my hand into her hair and jerked her to me, kissing her crudely, half swallowing her, and she answered me just as brutally. I drew away from her long enough for her to drag my shirt over my head and toss it to the floor. Her eyes burned like jewels, so deep and dark and hungry it hurt to look at them.

Her hands ran over my chest, scraping me with her nails. Then she made a little sound of frustration, grappling with the buttons of her bodice. When they were undone, she said, "Help me, please," and a quick memory assailed me of Odilé doing the same thing, Odilé smiling, crooking her finger at me while I followed her like a puppet on a string.

I forced the memory away, blinking until I saw Sophie before me again. I grasped the silk of the bodice—so damn tightly fitting I had to peel it off, feeling her warmth against my knuckles as I revealed her smooth shoulders, lace-trimmed chemise, corset. I tossed the bodice aside. She turned her back to me so I could undo the fastening of the skirt, which I did quickly, pushing it down, impatient, over her hips until it fell to the floor. She stepped from it, her back still to me, and I saw Odilé stepping from a gown just that way, deep red pooling on the floor, but Odilé had not been so well underclothed. She'd worn pink satin, I remembered, decorated with lace so delicate and fine I could see the color of her skin beneath it.

I swallowed convulsively. *No*, I told myself. *Not Odilé. Sophie.* The two of them played hide and seek in my head. *Not Odilé*, I told myself desperately. Sophie. *Sophie.* I pushed her up against the wall. Her little gasp of pleasure mixed with Odilé in my head, laughing at me, mocking me, and I nearly cried with frustration as I trapped Sophie. I dragged up the fabric of her petticoats and chemise; she was wearing drawers, and I bit off a curse—too much, too slow. She fumbled with the ties as if she understood; the muslin fell to her ankles, and I felt the cold and relentless draw of that void in her, the need to fill it, to let it suck and swallow, and I was terrified. My arousal began to fade in fear; before it could, desperate to keep it, I undid my trousers, releasing myself, taking her from behind, shoving into her without finesse, sheathing myself deep within her, and again I heard her small cry.

I grabbed her hips, fabric and lace spilling over my hands— not satin, but muslin and lawn, not pink but white; I held those details firm. I said them over and over again in my head. Not pink. Not satin. I buried my face in her neck, her shoulder, breathing her in. Violets, not almonds. Sophie, not Odilé. Not Odilé. Not Odilé.

"Sophie," I whispered. "Sophie. Sophie," like some spell to cast over myself, an amulet against possession. But now it was no longer about pleasure, it was about not letting Odilé defeat me, and so I worked the woman pressing back into me until I gained sway over my own mind, until I came with a cry that did not sound like me, helpless and frustrated, joyless and unsatisfying. It was the worst I'd ever had, even worse than those days when everything was fading, when there had been no satiation even in the one I'd thought I loved, when desire had been only a torment.

I collapsed against her until the throbbing ceased, until I realized I still had her pinned against the wall, that my fingers gripped her hips so tightly they cramped, until I heard her breathing like little sobs. I was horrified and dismayed, hating myself, shamed at how I'd used her.

"I'm sorry," I whispered to her. "I didn't mean for this."

Her breathing quieted. She said nothing.

I withdrew from her, loosening my hold on her hips, seeing the red marks I'd left behind, crossing over other marks, ones I hadn't seen until that moment, too caught up in my own tortured desire. White marks crossing her buttocks, one wider at the end, narrowing to what looked like a scratch, the other above, near her hip and streaking in a single line across the dimples there. Scars. The sight of them distracted me from what had just happened between us.

I said, "What are these?"

"What?" she asked quietly. I don't know what I expected. Tears, perhaps. Anger. I deserved both. But she seemed . . . accepting. Which was perhaps worse. It made me feel wretched.

I backed away from her, letting her chemise and petticoats fall to cover her again. "Sophie. Dear God, I cannot apologize enough. This is not who I am, you must believe me." I wanted it to be true. I told myself it was true.

She frowned, turning fully to me. "I don't know what you're talking about."

I was relieved. Then flabbergasted. I had never had such a violent encounter with a woman, at least, not with a woman who hadn't wanted it. I could not believe she was dismissing it so lightly. "Sophie, I—"

"You're sorry you invited me," she stated calmly. She stepped away from the wall. "I should not have come, but I was . . . well"—she took a deep breath—"it doesn't matter. You needn't worry. I understand. I'll go."

"No!" The word erupted with such force I startled both of us. "I don't want you to go."

She looked at me in obvious confusion. "You don't?"

"No. No, not at all, but I can't believe you want to stay. Not after. . . ." I let my words trail off when I saw the way she was looking at me, as if she'd seen nothing wrong or unusual in what had happened.

"You don't wish me to go?" she asked. "Do you mean it?"

"Yes. More than anything."

She hesitated as if to test the truth of my words. Then she bent to take off her boots, to roll down her stockings. She reached up behind and pulled the laces of her corset, loosening it, and then she unhooked it and let it fall, kicking it away. She unfastened her petticoats and pushed down the sleeves of her chemise, past her breasts, which jiggled enticingly at the movement, to her waist and then lower, slithering out of layers of fabric like a snake discarding its skin, a slight wiggle of her hips. Then she stood gloriously naked in front of me, hair falling like a curtain down her back, over her shoulders.

She turned again to face the wall, pressing herself against it, looking over her shoulder and saying, as if she meant to reward me, as if this was what I deserved, "Is this what you like? Do you want me this way again?"

The memory of the Lido came racing back, unbidden, her surrender to her brother's request, her acceptance that she was made to be whatever he desired. This was so reminiscent of it I found myself looking over my shoulder, half expecting to see Joseph there, sketchbook in hand. She gave herself to me now that same way, and it was so odd, so seductively innocent, and so unlike Odilé that it released the image of her at last. I managed to say, "No. I want you in bed. Please."

She stepped past me, lying down, though she didn't cover herself as most women would have, and I thought how comfortable she was with her nudity and wondered at that too. I took off my trousers quickly—the world felt balanced again when I was as naked as she was. She was so pale she looked like a swath of moonlight slanting over the coverlet. I sat down beside her on the mattress and urged her onto her stomach. I ran my finger down her back—she had a mole on her shoulder blade that affected me strongly. I couldn't keep from touching it, and then I traced down her spine, to the worst of the scars. "Tell me first how you got these."

"Ignore them," she said, shaking her hair so it fell in a waterfall across her back. "Joseph does. He's never even drawn them—except for the one time. I hardly remember they're there."

Her words raised so many questions I hardly knew where to begin. I started with what seemed easy. "What do you mean, he only drew them the one time?"

"He drew them when they were made," she said matter-of-factly. "It was his punishment. She made him draw them bleeding, before he could salve or wrap them."

I was horrified and confused. "*She?*"

"Our governess. Oh, don't look so shocked. Were you never beaten with a birch rod?"

"Yes, of course I was beaten. But my father used a strap or his hand. And I think he never plied his full strength."

"Oh. Well, Miss Coring was not so kind."

"What in God's name did you do to deserve this?"

She looked away quickly, and that small denial unsettled me even more, though I could not have said why. "It was a long time ago. I was fifteen. She was sorry after. She brought me cherry tarts to make up for it, and Joseph got iced cakes. Our favorites."

"Cherry tarts are your favorite?" I stroked the scar delicately. "I'll remember that."

She shuddered. "Oh, please don't. I can't abide them now. I don't know when that changed, exactly."

"Perhaps the day she beat you with a birch rod."

She smiled almost wistfully. "My brother and I were uncontrollable. Or so she said."

"I see. Did she beat your brother this hard too?"

"She had other ways of punishing him."

"Like making him watch you bleed?" I asked.

The look she gave me was darkly miserable and knowing, accepting and tormented. I had never encountered such an expression before. "Yes," she said, but it wasn't an answer. It was a whole, a wealth of truth, a mockery and a secret and an open door, and I realized that there were depths to Sophie Hannigan that I had not seen before, that I could not guess at.

I felt a consuming need to protect her. I leaned down, kissing the scars, running my tongue along them, along taut, smooth skin. I felt her shiver, and then she twisted beneath my mouth, turning onto her back, opening her arms and spreading her legs, saying almost desperately, as if she were afraid I would refuse, "Please."

And there she was, the woman in her brother's sketch, a yearning and desire and vulnerability in her eyes to make one weak, and I felt her burrow into me and stick, a thorn easing ever closer to my heart, and I made love to her as she asked, as I wanted, forgetting Odilé in the arms of the woman who most reminded me of her.

THIRTY-FIVE

ODILÉ

The twilight had gone dark and quiet beyond the balcony, the glow of other Venetian windows and lanterns flickering through the shifting fog, there and gone again, leaving us alone in the world, nothing existing beyond this room. My appetite quivered, anticipating satisfaction with barely reined impatience.

I poured wine, drawing things out now that I was certain of him, craving the pleasure-pain of consummation long denied, breathless with triumph. I tried to temper it—this was only the prelude, after all. What mattered was the bargain I meant to make with him. I would make of him something so grand, and what he could do for me—the thought of it gripped me hard, a pain so fierce I dug my nails into my palm to distract me from it.

He wandered about the *sala*, looking at the paintings upon the walls. He stopped before one, tilting his head as if he wanted to see it better in the candlelight, and I came over, handing him the wine.

"Do you know the artist?" I asked him.

"Canaletto, isn't it?"

I smiled. "Yes indeed. You see how well he paints Venice? How wonderfully he paints the sky? He has the colors right, don't you think?"

"It's beautiful," he said.

"No one sees Venice quite as Canaletto did."

"They say Venice was his muse."

"Of course they do. But there was a woman too, you know."

He took a sip of wine and turned to look at me. His eyes were very dark in the candlelight, nearly black. "Was there?"

"They say he met her on Ascension Day—do you know of it? It is a great festival here in Venice. The Doge would ride out into the lagoon on a ship, the *Bucintoro*, and throw a wedding ring into the water to symbolize the marriage of the city to the sea. Canaletto used to say it was his favorite work, because it was the day he met her." I remembered the way he had come ashore, laughing, stumbling, a servant carrying his easel and box of paints behind.

"Who was she?"

"He refused to reveal her name. They say she was a great courtesan, but that is only supposition."

"What happened to her?"

"She inspired him, and then she disappeared." I took another sip of wine, closing my eyes, remembering.

The thought of it brought yearning, raising an answering ache, a demand.

"Are you in pain?" Joseph Hannigan asked quietly. "Shall I call someone?"

"A momentary weakness. It will pass."

"Is there something I can do?"

"Not quite yet," I told him, savoring the play, the way neither of us spoke of why he was here. I reached for the painting, twisting it on its golden cord, turning it to the wall so he could see the writing on the back. "She made him famous. This was his only acknowledgment."

Joseph Hannigan read it aloud. "'Without you, my love, I am nothing.'"

"But he left her nameless and faceless to the world." I turned the painting back again. "Do you think she minded it?"

"I would mind it."

"Ah, but you're a man, and men are used to having their names shouted. Would it trouble your sister, do you think? Does she mind serving as your muse?"

He looked as if it were a question he had never considered. "She doesn't seem to."

"What reward does she have from you?" I stepped closer. "Or do you simply assume it is enough for her to know what she is to you?"

He stepped back, obviously uncomfortable, uncertain.

"I see you have never thought of it." I reached out, pressing my finger to the buttons of his vest, each in turn, bottom to top. "Perhaps you should. Else one day you might wake up to find her gone to pursue her own desires. Disappeared, as Canaletto woke to find his own muse had fled."

"Sophie wouldn't leave me," he said hoarsely.

"Are you so certain? I think you take too much for granted, *cheri*. Does she want only the life you give her? Have you ever wondered what she yearns for? What she would give anything to have?"

He looked troubled. I let my fingers climb to the silk about his throat.

I went on, "Few men ever wonder such things. They are the center of the world, after all. But women are not so different in what they want. They are used to hiding their desires and dissembling, that is all. No woman is ever quite as she appears."

He grabbed my hand, stilling it. "I know that's true. Women have many secrets. But I think I know yours."

I wanted to laugh at his presumption. "Do you? What are they?"

"I see sadness. Regret. Yearning."

My urge to laugh disappeared. His perception astounded me. I had no idea what to say.

"Am I right?" he whispered.

I could take him now. This moment. Oh, how I wanted him. All my senses heightened, his presence—the smell of him, the anticipated taste and feel—became more painful. But not quite enough. The dark monster in me stirred and whimpered but I wanted to see him sweat. I wanted to know I was inside this man, that he belonged to me entirely, that he would die to have me.

I slipped my hand from his hold, stepping away and sauntering to the balcony doors, looking out. "See how beautiful the night is, even in the fog."

I heard him pause, and then the sound of paper rustling, and I looked over my shoulder to see him with the open sketchbook. "Stay just that way," he said softly, and my entire body cramped—already now, I felt my gift working upon him. I let him draw for a time, listening to the scratch of charcoal on paper.

"The sunsets here in Venice are more intensely colored than they have ever been. Do you know why?"

"Why?" His voice was very quiet.

"Because of the smoke from the mirror and glass factories. There were only craftsmen before, not such manufacture. There was never such smoke. It's strange, don't you think, that something that so befouls the air can be so beautiful?"

"Beauty from ugliness," he mused wistfully. "No. I don't think it strange at all."

I turned to look at him, compelled by that wistfulness, and saw the secrets that were suddenly in his eyes. He had paused, his hand poised and still. I went to him and said, "Let me see."

"It's only a sketch," he said, but he gave it to me.

Certain things registered first: the beauty of his lines, his skill with chiaroscuro, his ease with the human body that one did not always see, even in the most sublime of artists. But it was his technique that set him apart—the uniqueness of his shading, his *way* of seeing, beauty heightened and enriched but still with edges, with danger, with darkness. I saw myself as no one else had ever portrayed me; not just beauty but terror and awe too, as if he had seen within me the monster and found it not just deadly but fascinating.

Beauty from ugliness.

So much talent. It was what I'd waited for. But I felt a little trickle of fear too. He had seen so much more than I expected. The world seemed to tilt; it was strange and discomfiting. I looked up at him in confusion, but the way he watched me so intently—paused, waiting—reassured me and banished my fear. I could not contain my hunger. The world shimmered before me, melting and blending, wavering like Venetian light.

"Odilé?" he asked me, bewildered. His voice was only a murmur through my pain, but it called me back. He stared at me as if he saw my rapaciousness and very nearly welcomed it. There was only curiosity and a strange acceptance, as if this were familiar to him, and that too unsettled me. But now it was time.

I let the sketchbook fall, and then I led him to my bedroom, to pillows and perfumed sheets. I pushed his coat from his shoulders.

He shrugged out of it, heedless as it fell to the floor, as his vest followed, and his tie and shirt. Then he was barechested and hot against my hands. He reached for me, and I pushed him away, saying lightly, "Let me look at you," and he went still. I let my gaze travel over him—lean, muscled chest and arms, broad shoulders, a sprinkling of dark hair over his sternum. His clothes hid no weakness. He was more beautiful without them.

I said, "Take off your boots."

He bent to do as I asked, and when that was done I stepped close to him again, tsking when he tried to touch me. "Not yet," I whispered, and then I undid his trousers, pushing them and his underwear over his lean hips, revealing him completely. He was ready for me, and oh, he was something to savor, but I was starving, everything in me saying *now, now*, an exquisitely brutal anguish.

I stepped back, unbuttoning my gown, dozens of little pearl buttons slipping through their loops. He watched me with his own hunger. I let the gown fall, and this time when he came to me, I let him touch. His voice was as reverent as his expression when he said, "I never knew they made things such as this." He eased his finger beneath the silken strap of the camisole, bringing it over my shoulder, letting it fall to reveal my breast.

"Then you've spent no time with courtesans," I teased him.

"Is that what you are?"

"Perhaps. In another life."

He moved like one in a spell as he undressed me. When I stood naked before him, he skimmed his hands over my body, my breasts, my hips. His fingers slipped to the bracelets on my wrists, tangling through the many loops of fine chain as if he meant to remove them, and I said, "Leave them."

He raised a brow, but he didn't protest. His eyes darkened. He made a sound deep in his throat and jerked me against him, whispering in my ear, "How do you like it? Tell me what you like."

The question was strange—shocking even. I could not remember ever being asked it before, and suddenly I was quivering. I wanted nothing but gluttony. It was all I could do to say, "Whatever you want."

"Oh, but I want everything."

"Do you?" I reached for him, stroking him with a feather-light touch. "What about this?"

"Yes," he breathed.

"Or this?" I unsheathed my nails, biting into him. His breath was quick and hard, indrawn, but he did not flinch.

"Yes," he gasped, a breath that seemed to rack him, but he didn't move. It was as if he were waiting for instruction, but his desire was coiled so tightly I felt it, I knew it must spring. I wondered how far I could push him before it did. I teased him with it. "This?" I asked as I stroked him. I raked my nails down his chest, leaving marks, whispering, "This?"

His answers became harder wrought, assents in the licking of lips, in caught breaths. I waited for him to lose control, to toss me to the bed, to devour me with brutality, but he only closed his eyes and threw back his head and let me torment him. It became a game, one I'd played before, but never with a man who lasted so well. I saw the muscles in his throat work, the tense flexing of his shoulders. I put my mouth to his skin, tasting the salt of him, and his breath came harder and faster. I kissed him, his sternum, his navel, lower, and he only flexed his hands and swallowed.

Then, finally, my hunger became too much, something I could no longer resist. I pressed my body to his; I whispered against his mouth, "I would like you to take me now," and it was as if I'd released a caught and panicked animal. We were on the bed before I knew it. I was a prisoner to my craving, which wrapped around us like tentacles, sinking its teeth into him, gorging so relentlessly that I knew he could not last long, and found myself regretting that already.

But he was like no other man I'd known. He was willing to do anything, to give anything. He surrendered himself to pleasure without holding back. He was as responsive to gentleness as pain. He had no boundaries; nothing made him recoil or hesitate. *Yes,* he said, and *yes* again, an endless and inexhaustible string of *yeses* that drove me to greater efforts. It was its own kind of aphrodisiac.

I took him until I'd absorbed all I could, until I was swollen and consumed. And even then, even in satiation, I was . . . fascinated, enthralled by him—how impossible this was! He lost himself so completely it was as if he were nothing but desire, an entity that lived for pleasure, bound only by the limits of his own body. I did not understand it, though I would have said I understood all there was to know about pleasure.

I gripped him tight; I heard him groan, and I said urgently, "Look at me," not knowing what it was I wanted to see, what I thought might be there, only curious to know what made him what he was, what secrets I might discover in his gaze. He obeyed me. He opened his eyes and looked into mine, and I saw elation there, and freedom and relief.

But I did not see Joseph Hannigan. It was as if he became someone else, *something* else, and suddenly the image of his sister was in my head, her own surrender to his drawing, the acceptance that seemed almost a release, as if she were not herself but something else entirely.

The image was there, and then gone, gone just as he came with a hoarse, guttural cry, collapsing upon me, burying his face in the hollow of my shoulder, his heart hammering. And after a few moments, he raised his eyes to look at me, and he was there again, the Joseph Hannigan I recognized, with a door in his eyes that I realized suddenly had always been there, though I had not noticed until I'd seen its absence. Closed tight. A prison door, I thought, and felt suddenly uneasy and off-kilter again.

He kissed me softly and then rolled off, limp and drained, his breath heaving in a sigh. The marks of my possession were all over him. I should have felt sated, but that uneasiness lingered. He had given so much of himself, and I wondered how such surrender could withstand the destruction of my hunger, as avid as it had grown. How long had I to bring him to the bargain before I drained him completely? Such weakness was part of the process; eventually it ravaged them all. My only task was to convince them to take the bargain before it ruined them. Even Byron had lost his strength. I had relished such debility in him; it had given him humility. I did not think I would relish weakness in Joseph Hannigan, and that surprised me too.

The bells of San Silvestro began to chime. Beside me, he stirred. "Is it so late?"

That he could even speak was a miracle, given how well he'd fed me. I turned onto my side, pressing myself against him, saying, "Go to sleep. You deserve it."

But he rolled away from me. He sat on the edge of the bed and buried his face in his hands, rubbing as if he meant to wake himself up. In the candlelight, I saw the moles scattered over the pale skin of his back, stretching from his shoulder down his spine. They looked like a constellation, I mused, and one I knew, the Serpent's Head constellation in the late spring sky, missing only one star—on his shoulder blade—to make it complete.

I felt the urge to touch each one, but he did not give me a chance. He said, "I must go. Sophie will be worried."

I was annoyed that he'd mentioned her, at the evidence that she was never far from his mind, though I'd thought of her too, only a short time before. "She knows where you are. Stay. You must be exhausted."

"I have to. I'm sorry." He twisted, smiling at me, placating, leaning in to kiss me quickly. "You understand, don't you? She'll be waiting for me. She won't expect me to stay."

"She won't? Why not?"

He stood, walking quickly to where his clothes lay abandoned on the floor, picking up his underwear, his trousers, pulling them on.

I could only gape at him. Not only because he was leaving me, but because he didn't stagger or lose his balance. He seemed just as he had when he'd taken me to bed. Strong and vital, not the least bit changed. I sat up, searching for weakness in the dim flickering of the candlelight. I saw none.

He fastened his trousers, pulled on his shirt. I said, "You'll come tomorrow? Shall I pose for you again? For studies?"

His smile was quick and blinding. "I won't need studies. I have you in my head."

"Still . . . you will come?"

He shoved his feet into his boots. "If I can. It will depend on what Sophie has planned. I'll send a message saying when you can expect me."

I did not quite believe he would go. I watched him pick up his vest, his coat, his tie. I thought he would pause before he reached the door. I thought he would do what they all did, throw everything to the ground and come back to bed. I thought he would say, "I can't bear to leave you." I wanted to see his surrender again, that release that banished the prison in his eyes, that was as alluring as anything I'd ever seen. I wanted to make him the offer and have him say *yes, yes. It's all I've ever wanted.* I wanted the rapture of him, and the possibility that he could make of me something at last.

But he did not turn. He did not rush back to my arms, and I realized that I had been wrong about how well I held him. She was there still—his sister, his muse—and I was struck with an almost impossible fear. I'd misjudged how connected they were. I realized that without her assent, he would leave me now, and he would not come back because she would keep him away. I sat up in bed in a panic. Desperately, I called, "Joseph—"

He paused at the door, turning with a smile—was that impatience?

"Does your sister like the theater?"

His brow furrowed. "She does."

"Then I will treat you both. Will she like that, do you think? Tomorrow night? Will it please you?"

"Sophie would like it," he said.

"Then it will be done. I'll call for you both at eight. Don't forget."

"How portentous you make it sound," he teased back.

I did not tell him how very much it was, and he threw me a last smile and was gone.

THIRTY-SIX

SOPHIE

I woke in a panic, uncertain what time it was. Nicholas was quiet beside me, his chiseled face soft and easy in sleep, and I remembered last night, the way he'd touched my scars, his tender dismay when I'd told him their origin. He had such gentle eyes; for such a pale color, there was no coldness in them at all. It was that gentleness that had led me to tell him what I'd never before told a soul, and when he had not turned from me, I had felt as Vivaldi in Odilé León's story, wooed by a devil's temptation, by the hope and fear that I might have what I'd yearned for, that someone had at last seen me without Joseph's brush to guide them.

Those possibilities again. Such heady things. I could not keep myself from wanting to believe in them. And yet . . . how could I explain such an ephemeral thing to Joseph? My chest was tight at the thought of it. I did not want to make things worse by having my brother come home to find me gone, to know without my telling him how I'd broken my promise. The morning was slipping into being and I must be away.

I crept from the bed, dressing and going as quietly as I could. The skies were beginning to lighten with impending dawn as I roused a sleeping Marco. I had thought there was a chance I could make it home before Joseph, but the moment I stepped inside the *portego*, I felt him there, the way I always felt him. He was on the settee in the *sala*, waiting for me, the color of him washed blue-gray by the burgeoning light of not-quite morning. I stopped just inside, both relieved at the sight of him—he was here, he was unchanged—and dreading his reaction.

His gaze swept me. "You went to him. Even after you promised you wouldn't. You *promised*."

He was hurt; I saw it in his eyes. And angry too. I went to sit beside him. "You were with her and you didn't care how I felt about it. You've no right to be upset over this."

"You never meant to deny him, did you? Despite what you said?"

"I don't know," I said helplessly. "Yes and no."

"Sophie—"

"What makes you so certain he'll hurt me?"

"Because I'm never wrong about that, am I? You think every man's a savior, but there are no saviors, Soph—there's only me. He'll just get in the way and we don't need him. We have Odilé."

The sound of her name on his lips startled me. It was so horribly intimate. "She doesn't know the right people. She can't bring you fame, not the way Nicholas can—"

"We don't know that's true."

"We *do*." I struggled for the words to tell him how I felt, but I could not find them, and so instead I said the ones I knew he would understand. "Think, Joseph. You must see that I can't just throw him aside. Nicholas knows the people who can introduce you to the world. Who does she know? What will she do with the painting she's commissioned? Hang it in her parlor, where no one ever comes? She can't help us, but Nicholas can. And he'll do it for you. For me."

"I've heard those words before. You said the same thing about Roberts and look how that turned out."

"Why didn't you tell me he was dead?"

He didn't seem surprised that I knew. "I couldn't bear to see that you might still care."

"I don't care, Joseph. I'm . . . I'm glad, actually. He caused us so much trouble. I'm *glad*."

He looked at me as if he didn't quite believe me, as if he were searching for reassurance and forgiveness, and suddenly I *knew*. "How did it happen? What did you do to him?"

"I wrote his father a letter. Anonymous, but with enough detail that it was hard to deny. I think he already suspected the truth of his son." He paused and then said, an edge in his voice, "I'd known what would happen before I even sent it. Roberts was weak. I couldn't risk doing such a thing when we were there, but once we were gone, once we had the sketches back . . . well . . ."

"Well?"

"He committed suicide. He jumped off the Staten Island ferry. They didn't find his body for three days."

I felt a little leap of—what? Triumph, vindication? Or was it regret and sorrow? Perhaps it was all of those things.

Joseph took my hands. "So you see? Say goodbye to Dane. We don't need him."

The way he was looking at me—how very well he knew me. Still, I could not quite make the promise he wanted. "I can't. Why do you have to go back to her? Wasn't last night enough? What is it about her that intrigues you so?"

"I don't know," he said. "I suppose . . . I want to know her secrets."

I felt cold. That curiosity was new too. "What if she discovers yours?"

"I don't think she'd care. I think she'd understand."

"The way Edward understood?"

"She's not like that."

"Joseph, I don't trust her."

"Why not? She's saved us already. We need the money, and she has a great deal of it. And she likes you, whatever you think. She wants to take us both to the theater tonight—"

"So she can seduce you after?"

He made a short laugh. "Believe me, she doesn't need to make an effort."

I felt sick. "Please don't say such things to me."

He swallowed hard—there was a misery in his eyes that matched what I knew was in mine. "It's no different for me than for you. There's no room for anyone else, Soph, don't you see it? Not Odilé, not Edward. Not Dane."

The truth of his words was a balm, a wish, a poison. I felt the fullness of him as I always had, and yet . . . and yet something felt wrong. Though I could not put my finger on it, I knew it had something to do with her.

Joseph said, "So you'll come to the theater?"

"Yes." In that moment nothing could have kept me away. I *didn't* trust Odilé, and Joseph was in peril—I knew that, if not how. And I would do what I could to keep him from her. "Yes, of course I'll come."

He squeezed my hand. "You'll see I'm right."

I didn't say anything to that—there was no point. I was too tired to keep fighting with him, and I hated to be at odds with him anyway. I pulled away, but gently, and rose. "Well, I'm to bed. I'm exhausted."

Joseph said, "You won't see Dane again?"

I hesitated. Perhaps Joseph was right to be afraid. I could not control my feelings as he could. Perhaps what I had with Nicholas would only be a reprise of what had happened with Edward. But it did not feel the same, and I realized it wasn't just the way Nicholas had looked at me or the things I'd told him that made it so, but something more. Because now there was the danger I sensed in Odilé, and Nicholas felt somehow to be the counterbalance I needed, my own golden crystal to help me fight what I could not see. He would keep both Joseph and me safe—and the moment I thought it I was surprised. Joseph and I had always been our own bulwark against the world. We had never needed a champion.

But that was before Odilé León.

I argued, "I'll have to see him again, won't I? He knows everyone in the salon. I can't just ignore him. And I don't want him to be angry."

Joseph gave me a measured look. "Yes. All right."

I started across the *sala*. I was halfway to the door when my brother stopped me with a quiet, "Sophie."

I paused and looked over my shoulder. The light of sunrise came through the window, casting him in pink, making him so beautiful my heart ached. "What is it?"

"Do you . . . do you mind being my muse?"

The question was odd, but not as odd as the uncertainty in his voice, in his bearing. Joseph wore uncertainty poorly; it seemed to somehow misshape him. I heard in it everything he hid from the world, his own sense of worthlessness, the fear behind his ego. The things only I knew; things it hurt me now to see.

He went on as if he could not get the words out quickly enough. "Do you mind always being unacknowledged? Do you want acclaim? Should I thank you?"

"For what?" I asked, puzzled. "You're my Prince Resolute. You've saved me from monsters and demon-knights. I'm the one who should be thanking you."

His face sagged. "That's not what I mean."

"How can you not understand?" I whispered. "Don't you know? When you draw me, I'm alive. I have only ever existed because of you."

I would have said more; I would have told him I had hopes there was someone else who might see me as he did. I might have told him of the possibility I felt. I thought perhaps he was ready to listen. But then I saw how he was staring at me, as if I were suddenly a mystery to him, or rather, as if the world had fallen away and he stood on some great precipice with only the barest of inches between him and the fall. As if he did not know whether to jump or back away. Then he buried his head in his hands, his hair falling forward to hide them from view.

"Joseph?" I asked, bewildered now, and afraid.

He said, "I'm all right. Go to bed."

And I felt . . . separate from him. Apart. It was the thing I'd thought I wanted, but the feeling was terrible and frightening, and not what I'd wished for at all. He'd said there was no room for anything else between us, but I felt it now: a wedge where there had never been before, and I did not know what to do.

THIRTY-SEVEN

NICHOLAS

S he was gone when I woke up. I went to the rooftop gardens, hoping that perhaps she'd gone there to take in the dawn. She was romantic enough to do so, I thought, no matter that the air was cold and a roseate fog obscured most of the city. I found myself standing at the edge of the roof, imagining her beside me, her dark hair falling over her shoulders, the brightness of her smile as she watched with me the gray shadows of the city emerge from that strange pink fog, and I thought, *there's a poem in that*, which surprised me. I remembered the image that had come to me on the Lido, the words dancing just beyond my reach. I felt off balance and bemused.

It was not only the poetry sneaking into my head that made me feel so as I went back down the stairs to my darkened rooms. No other woman had left me in the middle of the night—well, none but Odilé—and I wasn't certain what it meant, or if I should take it to mean anything. I told myself it was better this way. I had things to do, after all, and now I could be at Odilé's before the morning expelled back into the streets her newest conquest. So I tried to put Sophie out of my mind and hired a gondola to take to my usual spot on the narrow *fondamenta* next door to the Dana Rosti.

The fog was even more chill than usual, and I shoved my hands into the pockets of my coat and wished for a hat—though I wanted Odilé to know I was there and watching, and I knew she never mistook my blond hair. The Dana Rosti was silent and still, and I found myself daydreaming about the soft heaviness of breasts in my hands, a lithe body twisting beneath mine, soft little pants in my ear. Words came into my head that had me reaching for a pencil and a notebook I had long since stopped carrying, and when I realized what I was doing, I was surprised at myself all over again.

Impossible. I hadn't written a poem in years. To feel its stirrings now was bewildering—how could it possibly be? For the first time in forever I was sitting outside Odilé's rooms and thinking of someone other than Odilé.

I struggled to keep my thoughts straight, to keep at bay the desire to rush to the Moretta. I must concentrate on the task at hand. It had been days since the street singer had met his fate, and I knew Odilé would need to feed. There was not much time left, only a little more than a week, and I felt certain she had not chosen. I felt a thrill at the thought—this time I'd been successful beyond my greatest hopes. Seven years, and it was almost over.

I heard a noise—the opening of the balcony door. I looked up to see her step out. She wore something silken and light, ivory-colored, trimmed in lace. Her hair fell in thick waves to her waist. She came out fully onto the balcony and rested her hands on the stone balustrade. The sun sparked off the gold she wore at her wrists, and I blinked away the glare. I waited for a man to follow her. But no one did, and she looked vibrant, not the least bit weakened. I knew she had fed, and that he must still be in those rooms behind her.

She looked down to where I stood, and came to the very corner of the balcony. She leaned over the balustrade, her dressing gown gaping so she looked ready to fall out of it. Her smile was flirtatious and taunting and it still had power.

"Hello, Nicholas," she called. "How boring for you to always stand there. Perhaps you should find your own pleasures, instead of hoping to watch mine."

I stepped to the edge of the *fondamenta* to see her better. "You look vibrant, my love. Who's feeding you so well these days?"

Odilé laughed. It caught in the air, flung about in that way Venice had of muting and distorting sound, lost before it reached my ears though I knew that three *rii* away someone was pausing in their garden, peering up at the sky, wondering if angels were laughing in the clouds above his head. Her hair fell over her shoulder, trailing over her hand. "Oh, I do miss you, Nicholas. In fact, why don't you come up? Let me drain you as I should have years ago."

"As tempting as the invitation is, I think I'll decline."

"You're so much more clever than you look. Go back to London. Venice in the winter is so disagreeable. And as pretty as you are, I confess I grow weary of seeing your face every day."

"You've only yourself to blame for that," I told her.

"Never say I did not warn you," she said. "But now . . . as lovely as it's been talking with you this morning, I am tired. I'm afraid I was up all night with another amusing man. Unfortunately, he fled before the dawn. How clumsy of you to be so late."

I didn't believe it. "Before the dawn? And you let him go? How clumsy of *you*, my love. But then again, you are looking a bit—oh, I don't know—*monstrous*? Perhaps he caught a whiff of your poison. I cannot be the only one to smell it."

I could not tell if I'd affected her or not. She only said coldly, "*Adieu*, Nicholas," and stepped back inside with a shake of her head that sent her hair rippling down her back.

I waited for a bit longer, trying to peer behind the windows, to see movement in the rooms beyond, but I saw nothing. It became clear that she was telling the truth—I was too late. There was no point in lingering.

I went to my room, impatient for time to pass, for the salon, where I knew I would see Sophie again. I pulled a book from the pile on the floor and lay on my bed, which still held the faint scent of her perfume, and suddenly I was thinking of violets in the sun and dark hair in candlelight, and I reached for a pencil, dismayed not to find one, nor paper either, confused by the force of the words spinning in my head, the intensity of their demand to be written down. How could it be? But still . . . the urge was irresistible, and finally I found Giles's sketchbook and tore a corner from the page, a bit of charcoal, and I was scrawling, words tumbling, a single line. When it was done, I stared at it in surprise. It was decent enough, but how could it be even that? How could it exist at all? Odilé was still alive, and she held my talent fast. I crumpled the paper in my hand, letting it fall heedless to the floor, my sense of being off balance returning with a vengeance.

I left for the salon the moment it was possible. The Canal was cloaked with a thin layer of fog that shifted in wisps, blowing away like smoke with every movement. Dark gray clouds gathered in the distance, an impending storm. My feeling of vulnerability grew—Sophie Hannigan had a power over me I could not define, that even frightened me now in a Venetian twilight. I understood—or thought I did—why her brother felt he could not be without her. I felt the faint prickle of warning. I told myself not to fall so hard. It had been my undoing once before.

Yet the spell of her remained, and the salon did nothing to break it, because she wasn't there, nor her brother. I had no idea why. I wondered if she were avoiding me, if I'd done something to offend her—well, of course I had—and that was why she'd left me this morning without a word. The very idea that it might be so made me nearly insane with apprehension and concern. I could not stay at the salon. I was too distracted to be anything but unsociable. I didn't know if I was coming or going, and I was angry at myself for feeling so. I couldn't keep the image of her from my head, the way I had pulled her into my side and urged her to lay her head upon my chest, how I'd threaded my fingers through her hair. She'd made a little sound, I remembered—a mewling, quiet sound, and then she had fallen into sleep, into soft, steady breathing, her hand curled near her face like a little child's, and I'd looked down at her and thought I had never been so content nor so satisfied.

Not even with Odilé.

The thought startled me now, as did the realization that it was true. In that moment, everything—Odilé, my task, every obligation I had—seemed to melt away. Suddenly I was thinking of a future I'd never before contemplated. A home somewhere. Children. Poetry in my head, wanting to be written. Poetry about dark-brown hair that caught the sunlight on the Lido, about skin pale as milk, a beguiling mole like a star on a shoulder blade, and a name to break the spell I'd been under for years.

And I knew: I was in love with Sophie Hannigan, and everything had changed.

THIRTY-EIGHT

NICHOLAS

How did one dismiss a seven-year obsession? I knew that I could not embark upon a future with Sophie until I'd put Odilé from my life forever. Only a little more than a week—it seemed both a small time to wait and forever.

The ominous clouds had spread over the city, covering the far-flung stars, bringing a spattering of rain that looked ready to turn into more. I hired a gondolier to take me from the Alvisi to the Ca' Dana Rosti. This time, I paid him to wait with me. From the levered window of the *felze*, I had a perfect view of her entry. I watched her windows, catching movement here and there, shadows across the lamps. And then, just as the wind began to pick up, bringing with it the rain, her door opened.

I straightened, watching as her gondolier came out. He stepped into the gondola, readying it—ah, so Odilé was going out tonight. No doubt to meet her new victim.

She wore a cloak, its dark hood raised to hide her face. But even so, she had that particular grace no other woman seemed to possess, that made her recognizable no matter the disguise. She murmured something to her gondolier and disappeared into the *felze*.

The gondola slipped into the Canal. I called softly to my own gondolier, "Follow them. But don't let them know it."

"*Si, padrone.*"

I felt the boat rock beneath me as we moved out into the water. I could see the gimbaled light of her gondola before us, cast in a red shade. She was heading toward St. Mark's and the Piazza. The rain smattered against the roof of the little cabin, spackling the water. A flash of lightning lit the sky, limning the shadow of her gondola, the hooded gondolier, so it looked eerie and foreboding, a funereal barge.

Well, it was, I thought grimly, as thunder crashed so loudly it seemed to shake the boat.

The water grew rough with the wind, splashing against the sides of the gondola, rocking enough that I wanted to be out of it. Another crash of thunder, and then a blast of such livid lightning it seemed to electrify the world—and as if in response, Odilé's gondola turned into the Rio de San Moise.

I felt a moment of disconnect—strange that she should come here, where I had interests of my own. Just as I leaned forward eagerly to see what lights were on in the Moretta, hoping for a glimpse of Sophie as we passed, Odilé's gondola stopped.

I thought it must be a mistake. Why would she stop here? I felt the sudden slowing of my own boat, and my heart dropped. I watched in disbelief as the palazzo door opened, and two figures came out.

Lightning struck, bleaching the narrow *rio*, flashing off the buildings, a bright and terrible illumination lasting only long enough for me to see one of the figures—hooded and cloaked—look up in wonder. I saw a pale face I recognized, dark hair, in that moment before it went dark again.

Sophie.

The other figure—obviously her brother—took her elbow and helped her into the gondola, following behind. Still, I could not believe it. Not when they'd boarded, and not when the gondola set off again.

God, no. Not Joseph Hannigan. *Please, don't let it be him.*

When her gondola reached the *fondamenta* of the Rialto, it stopped. Thunder cracked—so loud it seemed to rattle everything. I watched as the three of them disembarked; I heard male laughter and a little feminine shriek as the rain crashed down in earnest, and they were hurrying toward the shelter of an overhanging awning.

"*Padrone?*" asked my gondolier.

I lurched from the *felze*, saying tersely, "Let me off."

I hurried after them down the slick, paved *calle*. Hannigan was in the middle, a woman on each side holding on to his arm. They were running through the pounding rain, ducking into the well-lit entry of the Teatro Goldoni's square, marbled facade. I had no ticket for admission, but that was easily remedied. I bought entry to the pit, where I would hopefully be lost among the other patrons. But I didn't want Sophie or her brother to notice me, so I hung back at the edges of the crowd, looking up into the boxes, where I knew they must be.

The Teatro Goldoni was small and ornate; the boxes, which ran along the sides in the Italian fashion, were all gilded, and the ceiling hung with a great gas chandelier. The gaslamps along the periphery made the whole place sparkle and glitter, refracting light. It wasn't hard to see—or be seen—which was the rule in Venice. No one came to the theater to actually watch the plays. Most of the nobility leased boxes year round to entertain their friends—it was cheaper than paying for the gas and servants in their own homes, and now the theater was full of laughter and talk. Light glinted off raised opera glasses as the boxes began to fill.

She wouldn't be in the lower tier of boxes—too close to the pit. The second tier was the fashionable tier, but I didn't expect her there either. She was no part of society, and many of those boxes were already leased. So the third . . . I wished for opera glasses of my own as I strained to see. Some of the boxes had drawn rose-colored, velvet curtains for privacy—as I said, most weren't here to watch the play. I didn't think conversation was her purpose; though to be honest, I wasn't certain what her purpose was. If she'd found Joseph Hannigan, that was one thing. But why entertain Sophie? Women had never mattered to Odilé.

I was just beginning to wonder if perhaps they hadn't rented a box after all when I saw Odilé come into one. She put her hands on the rail as she had on the balcony of the Dana Rosti, and just as it had then, the light sparkled upon the golden bracelets sliding down her wrists. And then I saw Sophie come up beside her. I drew back farther into the shadows. There was no woman who could compare to Odilé—her beauty was astonishing—but Sophie looked fresh and vibrant, and my desire surged as fatally as ever.

Then Hannigan stepped up next to them. He and Odilé made a stunning pair, I had to admit. Mine could not be the only eyes watching them. Without thinking, I shoved forward, ignoring the men talking and gesturing about me, the smell of wet and sweat and the aniseed that was a favorite chew, the raucous laughter and smoke, unable to look away as Hannigan leaned to whisper something in Odilé's ear. She smiled up at him, caressing his jaw with an intimacy that clearly marked them as lovers.

I felt a sinking despair. How could she have found him? I'd been watching every moment, guarding him constantly, with no distraction—

Except that I *had* been distracted, I realized. Sophie had turned me all about. While I had been concentrating on winning her, Odilé had slipped, unnoticed, inside.

And now . . . *and now.* . . .

Christ, what was I to do now?

THIRTY-NINE

SOPHIE

It was a comedy—I could not understand Italian, but it was something about an innkeeper who was a flirt. "Many consider it Goldoni's masterpiece," she told me, explaining the plot as it went along, so I could follow it well enough even if I couldn't read its subtleties.

"Oh, my dear, there are no subtleties," she'd laughed.

Just watching the people was enthralling, and the Teatro Goldoni was so opulent it was like being inside a candle flame—flickering everywhere with gilt and gaslight. The production was well costumed and staged so there was always something to see, and she had candied fruit and wine sent up. But I could not really enjoy it. The conversation my brother and I'd had that morning sat like a stone on my heart.

When the play was over, she said, "Let me take you to dinner."

Just as I began to make our regrets, Joseph accepted for the both of us. It was close to midnight—the play had been preceded by a ballet and a shorter piece—and I'd been up most of the night before with Nicholas. I just wanted to go home, but instead I managed a dull smile and put on my cloak.

It was still raining hard when we left the theater, and the street before us was beneath at least an inch of water, the sky black as pitch, all color lost, the gaslamps a sickly dim yellow, their light absorbed by rain. It was like stepping into an underwater world, deep and mysterious—but for her. She managed somehow to look bright and shining in the middle of it.

The Little Horse restaurant was small and owned by Germans, she said, though it looked as Venetian as everyplace else. It was nearly full, the sound of talk loud, the musty smell of wet wool pervasive, along with those of polenta and oil and fish. She had wine brought, and a plate of the little fried crabs called *moleche*. My brother picked one up by its claw and ate it in a single bite. She laughed at him, and he smiled back as he chewed.

I understood his fascination with her. She was elegant and refined and beautiful, but I couldn't help wondering why she'd wanted me to come, why she worked so hard to charm me now.

She poured wine into my glass and fastened that strange gray gaze on me, leaning her chin upon her hand. "You enjoyed the play, Miss Hannigan?"

"Yes, very much so."

"Do you like opera? The La Fenice opens just after Christmas. And there is the Teatro Rossini too—though the operas there are second-rate, they are still entertaining. Would you like to go? Shall I get tickets?"

Again I wondered at her effort. "I do love the opera. But you mustn't go out of your way—"

"If not for you, then who should I go out of my way for?" she said. "I have taken a great interest in both you and your brother,

Sophie—might I call you that? It seems so formal to keep saying Miss Hannigan. Not at all as I wish to be."

For my brother's sake, for everything he'd said to me this morning, I tried to smile. It was all I could do to say, "Of course."

"And you must call me Odilé. Sophie, tell me what you most want to do while you are in Venice. Make a wish, and I shall make it come true."

"I want Joseph to be famous," I said without hesitation.

"Yes indeed, we all wish for that. But surely there must be something you want for yourself?"

I shook my head. "No. That's our dream. It's the one we've always had."

She raised a finely arched brow. "Ah, how lovely. Twins dreaming together. Inspiring each other. But . . . you do not have a dream that is just your own?"

I thought of all the stories I'd invented over the years, the things I'd wished for. Escape. Relief. Forgetfulness. But they were all too private to mention to anyone but Joseph, who shared them. And I would not tell her my only other dream, the one I hoped was coming true. It was not for her to know. "Not really. No."

Odilé frowned—so small, nearly imperceptible, as if she were puzzled. It was fleeting, but I saw it.

Joseph smiled and said, "It's not just for me. It's for Sophie too. We're together in this. In everything."

After this morning, his words were reassuring.

Odilé looked at me and said, " I think that is not quite true, is it? Perhaps it is what your brother wishes to believe, but I see something else in your eyes, my dear Sophie. Your friend has become your lover at last, and you think of him now."

I felt my brother tense. She sensed it too; I knew it by the way she said to him, "Come, *cheri*, you mustn't be so selfish. Your sister has given you everything, has she not? But the inspiration you require draws a great deal of strength. Perhaps it is time to release her to find happiness on her own."

I felt a quick panic. "Oh no. No, I don't mind it at all—"

"Of course you do not," she said thoughtfully. "But a man recognizes when he is not singular in one's affections. I cannot help thinking it is perhaps why you have never known the kind of love you yearn for. Your brother is in the way."

The truth of what she said took me aback. The past fluttered at the edges of my vision. The look on my brother's face reminded me of this morning, his head in his hands, his confusing reaction to my words, as if he saw something he had never before seen, an uncertainty and awareness that worried me.

Odilé went on, "Do you know there is a heart in the archway of the *sotoportego* of the dei Preti? Legend says that if two lovers touch it at the same time, they are destined to love forever. If a person alone touches it, he or she can make a wish to find true love. There is a story to go with it—about a pair of lovers, of course—but it hardly matters. The superstition is all that remains of them now. Perhaps you should go there, my dear. Or take your lover with you. Such a promise will reassure him."

Joseph stared at me and I felt a surrender in him I didn't understand. Outside the wind howled. The restaurant sign squeaked loudly back and forth. Odilé glanced toward the door, shuddering delicately. "This storm feels ready to break open the world." She reached for the wine as if it were a restorative. "Ah, there is no more. *Cheri*, will you get us another? And tell the waiter it must be a Bordeaux—an old one." She smiled at Joseph, who rose to do her bidding, and the moment he left the table, she looked at me, saying urgently, as if she meant to get the words out before he returned, "How much do you wish for his fame, Sophie? How much does he?"

Her voice had such power. My heart pounded as I heard myself say, "It is all we've worked for."

Her eyes seemed to glitter. "What would you sacrifice for it?"

"Anything. Everything." As soon as I said it, I wished I hadn't. I felt as if I'd confided some terrible secret. I felt as if I'd given her a way to imprison me.

"Ah." She smiled a little, reaching for a crab, dangling it for a moment over her plate before she dropped it and picked up her fork, breaking the tiny crab apart with the tines, making a fatal cut, splitting the crab's back. It was nothing now but scattered crumbs on her plate, crabmeat and bits of fried batter. She laid the fork aside and picked up a bit with graceful, slender fingers. Her bracelets slipped and gyrated about her wrists as she dropped it into her mouth. I felt the weight of her gaze. For a moment, I felt as if we were connected—fatally, perfectly.

And again I saw in her Miss Coring. The same gaze, the gleam of reflected lamplight. *Come, Sophie. Come and dance for me and your brother. Take off your nightgown and dance. . . .*

"I need you, Sophie," Odilé whispered, startling me from the memory. "More than you can know. If I were to ask you to . . . do something for me, would you promise to do it?"

"What is it?" I heard myself asking.

"Release your brother. Leave him to me."

"Leave . . . Joseph to you? What do you mean?"

Her gaze held me tight. "Put Joseph in my hands, and I will make him a king. I will have the whole world lauding him. I will make him more famous than he has ever dreamed."

I did not bother to ask how. I didn't need to. The promise in her eyes burned. I saw truth in it. I felt her yearning calling to mine, her promise steeped in the pulse of my blood. And that promise felt as binding as the stories I'd told myself, years and years of story—spinning in my head as I danced in a nursery room

326

for my governess and my brother as they lay entwined and writhing, the spell I cast as I held my brother's gaze, my every twirl and
dip embedding the charm deeper and more true. As long as neither of us looked away, we stayed in the world I made for us. Miss
Coring did not exist. He was mine and I was his, and nothing
could come between us. I was the princess rescuing both herself
and the prince from the demon-queen in the tower. A golden
bridge to salvation, crossing miles of river, of ocean, of canals that
snaked through a city built of Faustian bargains and nightmares
that did not frighten me because I'd put them there. I had made
them. *I will save us. I will save us. I will. Save us.*

The urge to promise was overwhelming. I opened my mouth
to say the words, to say *Yes, yes*—

And then Joseph returned. He sat heavily, saying, "He's
looking for a Bordeaux, but he doesn't think he has one."

"Ah." Odilé made a delicately fatal shrug, very French, and
threw me a glance full of meaning. "Well, then, perhaps it is a
sign that the evening should end. How lovely it has been though,
has it not? I must thank you both for sharing it with me."

She paid the bill and we went out into the storm. The night
was wild, the wind rushing, the rain blowing in torrents. Above
our heads, the restaurant sign swung violently. Everything seemed
strange—skewed, weirdly shadowed, off perspective. I put my
hand to my eyes, feeling suddenly dizzy. "It all looks so odd."

Joseph took my arm, a reassuring warmth. "It's only the
storm."

But I wondered how he could not see it. How his artist's eyes,
which daily saw things I'd never noticed, could miss the sudden
strangeness of the world.

We hurried to the gondola. Once we were inside, Odilé
asked me, "Should we take you home, Sophie, or to your lover?"
and it was only then that I realized that of course Joseph would

go with her, that I'd felt his impatience to be with her all night and had not let myself acknowledge it. In this, I realized, she was not like Miss Coring. Joseph had never wanted another woman enough to leave me, but I felt that to be true now. Because Odilé *was* desire, more than any woman I'd ever known, and Joseph needed that. He needed to drown himself in it, to forget. But understanding why he wanted her didn't make it any less painful. I felt afraid and abandoned. As if she sensed it, she put her hand to my cheek, leaning close so I smelled her perfume of almonds and musk, swirling about my nose, into my head, dizzying and sweet and wonderful, and whispered, "I will make him a king," and I heard Joseph saying, as if from far away, "We'll take her home."

The journey was too quick; before I knew it the gondola stopped. I was unsteady enough as I disembarked that Joseph helped me while Odilé waited in the *felze*. He had my arm firmly in his grasp as we stepped to the door, and I turned to him, saying urgently, "Don't go with her, Joseph."

He gave me a chiding glance. "You know I have to. We need the money. There's the commission to think of."

"And you *want* to be with her."

He glanced away uncomfortably.

"Why don't you just admit it? You'd rather be with her tonight than me."

His gaze leaped back. I saw a terrible, aching sadness. "What of it? You're no better, are you? You'd rather be with Dane."

"No, I—"

"You're in love with him, Soph. D'you think I can't see it? You've gone and done it despite everything I've said."

He waited for me to deny it. I felt his hope, and I wanted to reassure him. But I couldn't. "Perhaps I am."

He froze. A long moment of silence passed between us. Then he said, "I don't know when I'll be back," and kissed me. His lips were cold, wet from the rain. He stepped away, back into the gondola, and I stood there watching as he disappeared into the *felze*, watching helplessly as her gondolier took him away.

I heard guttural cries from somewhere, the rush of the rain, the snakelike hiss of the wind through cracks in the walls. In that moment, I believed that Venice was full of ghosts and devils, that demons haunted its shadows, that I was one of them. A spirit left to haunt the *calli* and *rii* of a city that was to make our dreams come true. I could not shake myself of the sense that I was fading, that in my quest to be special in my own right, I was losing Joseph, that I had already lost him.

Our rooms felt empty—more than empty, deserted—and the house pressed against me as if to say that I didn't belong here. I went into the *sala* and lay down on the floor, staring up at the blackness that was the gilded-sunset ceiling, trying to remember how it had been to lie here with my brother, to watch the morning dance, but the memory would not come. I felt his absence as a hole in the world, something too big to feel, unfathomable. I closed my eyes, imagining an old, old story: a princess alone in a room, a prince returning from a battle, the demon-queen slain and her blood upon his sword, triumph in his eyes. *Do you see what I've done? I've killed her, my love. I've killed her for you, for the both of us—*

A scuffling broke into my imaginings. My eyes flew open. I jerked up, peering into the darkness, my heart racing. It was Joseph, returned. Joseph triumphant. But there was nothing there. Only silence, and just as my heart was settling, just as I felt the dullness of despair, I saw a movement, a shifting in the air, as if someone stood just beyond my vision, watching me in the darkness. I smelled cold and shadow. The hair rose on the back of my neck; I felt a quick terror, and then . . . calm. As if whatever stood there in the darkness meant to let me know it was not a danger.

I remembered what Odilé had told us about the ghost in the Moretta. The man who had thrown himself off the balcony out of despair and love. I whispered, "What do you want?"

My voice sounded too loud. The air shifted, only darkness again, whatever had been there gone, and I was shaken, my heart racing again. Impossible that I should have seen it. Impossible that the stories were true. And yet, I knew better than most that they were. I felt myself suddenly to be in the middle of one. The stories I told always ended happily, but the ghost's lingering presence, his sorrow and his pain, reminded me that sometimes tragedy was the rule.

I thought of Joseph turning away from me on the stair, the goodbye in his kiss, his words *I don't know when I'll be back*, and Odilé's: *I will make him a king. . . . Release him,* and with the ghost's absence, the spell of Odilé snapped, and I knew that I had made a terrible mistake tonight in letting my brother go.

FORTY

NICHOLAS

I could not have told you what play I'd seen at the Goldoni. I could not have given you a single character or scene had my life depended on it. I did not stay until the end; I could not bear to. Instead, I set out for home, sick and afraid, with visions of Odilé's lamia-serpent tightening her coils in my head. I hurried through the pouring rain, thunder and lightning crashing around me, a foul wind blowing, the rainwater that flooded the streets seeping into my boots.

I did not sleep, and by the time the storm gave way to dawn, my fear had turned to anger and desperation.

I went to the Dana Rosti, to my place on that wretched *fondamenta*, where I huddled, shivering, waiting for him to emerge. The curtains were drawn, blocking light and movement from the windows, and I watched in frustrated dread. I knew he was there, just as I knew he must come out at some point, unless her hunger was so great it destroyed him. But I didn't think that would happen—not yet. There was so little time now before she would turn, and she needed to choose. That she would choose him was inevitable. I had known it the moment I'd met him, hadn't I?

The thought of what she would reduce him to—all that talent, gone. Nothing left in those deep blue eyes but misery and despair and madness. And what that would do to Sophie . . . what would she be without him? To think of their magic stripped, the two of them less than extraordinary. . . .

I forgot what I'd lost in my own encounter with Odilé. I forgot what I thought I would win with her destruction. I thought only of Joseph and Sophie. I waited impatiently for him, running my various persuasions through my head, an endless circle of pleas. I thought he would listen to me. And if I could not persuade him on my own, I would go to Sophie. I had rarely convinced a man to leave Odilé, but I'd never had so much at stake before—not just the fate of the world, but my own, most personally.

And so I waited, shivering with cold, as the morning dawned gray and overcast, with a breeze that rippled the murky waters of the Canal and a dampness piercing to my bones. I had begun to wonder what I would do if he never emerged when I heard the balcony door open, and I glanced up to see Hannigan step out. He wore only a pair of trousers and his shirt, which was open and fluttering as he came to the balustrade. He braced his hands upon it and leaned over.

She did not come out behind him—a blessing I didn't think would last long. But I grabbed the opportunity and stepped from my hiding place, striding quickly to the center of the *fondamenta*, waving. I saw him see me and start.

"Dane?"

"Quiet," I said. "Can you come out for a moment? I want to talk to you."

Concern swept his expression. "Is Sophie—"

"Ssshhh. Come down. And tell no one. Hurry." I stepped away before he could say anything else, hurrying to the narrow *calle* that separated this ruined palazzo from the Dana Rosti, and waited. I half expected to see Odilé come instead of him, her thin and nasty smile, a smug *You're not so clever after all, are you, Nicholas?* and I was relieved when it was only Hannigan who stepped from the gate. His shirt was buttoned now, and he'd put on boots. Closer, I thought he looked tired, and I wondered how much Odilé was affecting him. I wondered if she'd chosen him yet. If she had, it was over and done; there was nothing left but to help him end his misery—which I realized I would do, should he ask. I would not abandon him to madness.

Hannigan frowned when he saw me and hurried over, saying urgently, "What is it? If it's Sophie—"

"She's fine, as far as I know," I told him. "It's not Sophie I've come about—or, not really, anyway. It's you."

He swept his hair back from his face, his frown deepening. "Me?"

"You're in grave peril, my friend. Greater than you can know."

"What peril is that?"

"I have some history with Odilé León. There are things you should know about her."

"You've history with her?" He sounded frankly disbelieving—almost insultingly so. "What kind of history?"

"Just what you'd expect," I answered, more sharply than I'd meant. "I met her in Paris about seven years ago. I spent some time with her."

"Some time."

I nodded. "Doing just what you're doing. Making love. Creating art. She is the devil's own inspiration."

He frowned again.

I went on, "She looks for young men with talent. And then she destroys them. Each of them, and always. She'll destroy you too."

Now his mouth quirked in a wary smile. "You were with her, you say, and yet you don't seem destroyed."

He was like all the others. Caught in her spell. Not wanting to believe. I took a deep breath. "Because I escaped her in time. By the very grace of God, I suppose. But I've been following this woman for seven years, Hannigan. Seven years I've been watching what she's done to other men. Believe me when I say you must stay away from her."

I saw the suspicion come into his eyes. "So you can step back in?"

"I've no intention of doing that."

"I see," he said dryly. "So you follow a woman for seven years for no other reason than curiosity?"

I laughed shortly. "Dear God, if it were only that! No. In fact, you could say it's a calling, of sorts."

"A calling."

I was failing. Desperately, I said, "I know what you're thinking. You think I've never fallen out of love with her. You think I've been following her hoping that one day she'll take me back. I can assure you there's nothing further from the truth. She's a demon, Hannigan. Literally. I've seen things . . . you can't even imagine. I've made it my business to see that no one else falls under her spell. Especially a man I hope to make my brother someday."

He went very still. His blue eyes darkened.

I wasn't certain what I saw there, jealousy or anger or relief, but I plunged on. "It's not Odilé I love, but your sister, and I think you know it, which is why I'm asking you to listen to me now."

I had his full attention at last. "All right."

"This is going to sound absurd—like a fairy tale."

He crossed his arms over his chest. "I'm used to fairy tales."

I told him all I knew of Odilé, ending breathlessly with, "Each of them made a bargain with her—they wanted fame and inspiration and were willing to sacrifice anything to have it. And they do live on forever through a work of genius. A *singular* work, Hannigan. Think: what did any of them do beyond it? Nothing. That was what they sold to her. Their talent and their skill. Their vision. And she gave them immortality in art. She's a succubus."

"How do you know this?"

I expected so many other questions. I expected protests and laughter, denials—it was so absurd after all, wasn't it? But I saw with shock that he understood. And this—his casual acceptance of an impossible truth—surprised me more than anything else about Joseph Hannigan. It had taken me months to come to it. Months to believe it, and even now, sometimes, I woke in the middle of the night in a cold sweat thinking *no, no. This cannot be true. This cannot be my life. . . .*

But he was looking at me as if the world suddenly made sense in a way it had not before, and I found myself saying softly, "That first year, I followed her because I couldn't believe she'd gone. I was mad for her even as she left me despairing and half dead. I told you I talked to the artist in Paris . . . well, I spoke to many others. I suspected it then, but I knew it for certain in Barcelona. I don't know where she comes from, or if there are others, but . . . I saw her in a . . . in a dark little room in Barcelona. She was *crawling* like a serpent or a . . . a demon about a score of naked men. And they were all dead. Every one of them. She'd sucked their energy from them until they were nothing. She's like a vampire, but it's not blood she's taking. It's vitality. Creativity. I've felt it myself—I know what she can do. You must have felt it too. The speeding of your heart, the lack of breath—"

Now he looked confused. "No. I've never felt that."

"Then you will. How long have you been with her? A few days? A week? She's feeding off you and you don't even know it. But one day you'll wake up and you won't be able to draw. Your fingers won't know how to hold a pencil. You'll see nothing to inspire you, nothing worth marking down. She will drain you before you know it—unless she decides to make you the offer. But if she does, that's the true hell."

"Why would it be?"

"If you take the offer, you'll paint your masterpiece, and you'll have the fame you've always hoped for, but you'll never do another thing, no matter that everyone in the world hopes for it. They'll watch you, waiting for it, and nothing will come. You won't be as you are now. Everything that makes you Joseph Hannigan will be gone. Your vision . . . gone. Imagine it. You said you could not bear to lose it, but you will. I know what it feels like. For seven years, I've felt it—"

"She made you the offer?" he asked. "But then . . . why have I not heard of you?"

The words were like a blow, and following them came a swift stab of anger, a resentment I forced myself to swallow. "No. She never did."

He gave me a look—how to describe it? Knowing, thoughtful, pitying all at once. *Pity.* It enraged me. My fingers itched to wipe that look from his face.

But then it softened. He said, "I'm sorry," and I heard his sadness and knew that once again he understood something I could not even admit to myself.

And I knew too that I would not convince him. He wanted too much—I saw it now. That shining, blistering ambition, the same things that had once been in myself, that deep emptiness, that terrible yearning. . . .

"You'll start talking to angels the way Schumann did. You'll drown yourself in a creek like Gros. Or worse, you'll be a shell of what you were, a joke for English tourists to laugh over, like Canaletto. Which of those futures is yours, Hannigan? Which do you want? And what of Sophie? What will this do to her? I'm begging you, if only for her sake: walk away from Odilé now. You've got a bright future. Henry Loneghan will make something of you, and that's a better bargain to take. It won't cost you everything in return."

He glanced away. "You can't promise that—or money either. I haven't the funds to struggle for years. And Sophie . . . Sophie shouldn't. . . ." He struggled to find the words; I saw a strange bleakness in his eyes. "Sophie's sacrificed for me too long. It's not fair for me to keep her. Her gift . . . you understand how special she is. You're the only one who ever has. You know what she can do."

I frowned in confusion.

"I trust you, Dane. I would not be able to leave her to anyone else."

"What are you saying?"

There was a sound—the opening of the balcony door. He glanced over his shoulder. We were out of sight of the balcony, but I felt her there just as he must have—I saw him go taut, as if he were listening to something only he could hear, some song whispered in the air.

I grabbed his arm hard, calling him back to me as I said softly, urgently, "I'm thinking of Sophie too. What will happen to her if you're destroyed? Think of your sister, for God's sake. Your *twin*. Think of everything you have before you. Walk away."

He pulled away, gently but firmly. "I should be getting back before Odilé misses me."

"Don't go back. Come with me. We'll go to the Moretta. Sophie's waiting."

His smile was small, his eyes distant. "You go to her. Keep her safe. Love her. Promise me—promise me you will."

"Hannigan, for God's sake, don't do this."

He leaned close, whispering, "You don't understand. This will make up for everything," and then, before I could truly grasp what he'd said, he was stepping back to the door, opening it.

"Hannigan—"

He went through it. It closed behind him with a thud, the clink of the metal latch falling into place.

For a moment I stood there, disbelieving, though why I should have been I wasn't certain. I'd so rarely persuaded anyone, but I'd thought to have a chance with him. I'd thought, because he was my friend, because of Sophie . . . I still didn't quite believe I hadn't done it.

You don't understand. This will make up for everything. And with despair I realized that for him, more than anyone I'd ever known, Odilé was the answer to a prayer.

FORTY-ONE

ODILÉ

I had lived long enough to see that the world was slow in its weaving. Time had no weight and no purpose, the passing of days only a blink. Fate, or karma, or whatever one called the intentions of the universe, stretched through centuries, wounds not healed in a lifetime later mended by those without the history or knowledge to understand what part they played. Symmetry. And because I understood that, I understood that a single painting or composition or poem might change the future. Where its influence might end—if it ever did—was a mystery.

I had spent lifetimes watching the effects of my choices, and so I knew that Joseph Hannigan was meant to be the very best of them. The world had put him into my hands; I could only guess at its design. But I knew he would be known and lauded for a very long time, and I could hardly wait to put him to work. My appetite was gathering, preparing, both appeased by his talent and waiting for him. Joseph would lose vision and vitality gradually until the bargain was made and I restored him. The sooner he accepted my offer, the sooner he could begin his dance with fame. I did not think it would be difficult to convince him, not after last night. I already felt victorious after my conversation with Sophie. I had seen Joseph's face when he returned to the gondola, and though I had no idea what had passed between them, I knew I had won. His sister would no longer interfere. When I'd brought him home, he painted with a single-minded concentration as I posed for him, and then he made love to me until I was breathless. I was well-satisfied, and I expected him to be too weak to move.

But when I woke late the next morning, Joseph was not in bed, nor anywhere in the bedroom. For a moment I thought I had been wrong, that I had failed. He had gone back to her after all. I felt a rush of annoyance . . . and then despair. But when I stepped from the bedroom, there he was, at the easel. He was painting like a madman, not the least bit weakened. His strength was astonishing, bewildering.

He glanced up as I came out. I could not read his expression—thoughtful, anxious, agitated . . . He was in a curious mood, and I was wary as I said, "How does it go?"

He swept a piece of muslin over the canvas before I could come close. "Not yet. I don't want you to see it until it's done."

I was used to the caprices of artists, and so I let it go. He put down the palette and brush and came to me, running his hands down my arms, tangling his fingers in the bracelets. He leaned to kiss me, murmuring, "Do you wear these always?"

"They're my latest fancy," I said, lifting my arm, twisting my wrist so the chains slid against each other, glimmering in the morning light. "I like them. Don't you?"

"Yes." He caught my hand, and slid his fingers through the gold. I knew when he felt the scars marking my wrist. I felt his pause. I knew he recognized what had made them. He was too perceptive not to see. It would be polite to ignore them, to pretend he'd discovered nothing, and I expected him to do just that. But he never failed to surprise me. "How old are these?" he whispered, and again I saw that strange glitter in his eyes. I felt a suppressed excitement—or was it fear?

It distracted me enough that I answered him honestly. "A year or so."

"What happened a year or so ago?"

I pulled my hand gently from his hold. "It doesn't matter now."

"It does," he said. "I can't bear to think you felt such unhappiness."

"It was not unhappiness. It was despair. I think you understand something of that yourself."

I saw the darkness come into his eyes again, displacing what I'd seen before.

I spoke quickly, meaning to lead into the bargain I must make. "I want you to tell me something about yourself."

His expression veiled. "What do you wish to know?"

"What kind of child were you?"

"I don't know that I was ever a child."

I understood that too. I began to wonder if Joseph Hannigan and I might be kindred spirits. But then I asked, "Who was your first lover?" and the veil thickened. I could not read him at all.

He hesitated; I thought he would not tell me, and I wondered why. But then he said, rather bitterly, "Do you want to know the truth? Or the story I tell myself?"

I had asked this question a hundred times or more. The answers differed only in their frequency, never in their aspect. A whore. My cousin. A neighbor girl. A pretty grisette. But Joseph Hannigan's answer was one I'd never heard before. How could I ignore it? "The story you tell yourself."

The strange mood I'd felt in him shivered. He glanced at the covered painting. "I was fifteen and deeply in love. She was a princess."

His answer had his sister all over it. One of her stories, perhaps—or was it not a story after all? Had she been his lover? The thought was intriguing and distressing too. I felt a little twist of jealousy. Ridiculous. I no longer had anything to fear from her. But I could not keep the snap from my voice when I asked, "And the truth?"

"The truth?" His face was hard. "The truth is that it was my governess. And I was eleven."

It was a relief. This answer I understood. I'd even heard it before. Byron had stood in this very room, with the Venetian sunrise streaming through the window to cast him in a soft, watery glow, in loveliness, and told his own story with a harsh self-deprecation that Joseph Hannigan's blunt declaration did not hold. "I see."

"You don't sound shocked."

"No. I've heard such a story once before. But the man who told it had been younger than eleven. And perhaps more precocious."

"I was younger when it started," Joseph said thoughtfully. "She would touch me in the bath. I didn't think it was strange. I just thought . . . I don't know what I thought. Then she began playing with me at bedtime. By the time I was ten, she was suckling me."

"Was she very pretty at least?"

He didn't look surprised at my question. "Pretty? Not pretty. Not ugly. Nothing to distinguish. She was . . . ordinary. And older. Past child-bearing."

"Did you love her?"

"Loved and hated in equal measure," he said honestly. "She was kind sometimes. And other times . . . truthfully, Sophie bore the worst of it."

I tried not to wince at the sound of her name, at the fact that she was again in this room with us, and had been since I'd asked the question. "She did? How so?"

He went deeply, powerfully quiet. "That's Sophie's story to tell, not mine."

I felt his implacability, his protectiveness. I thought of the glances that passed between them, an intimacy that bound them, that had compelled me to look at them in the Rialto. The way they complemented each other. Again, I felt that disconcerting little twist.

There was a part of himself he kept separate—and that too was not like any of the others. After so many hours together, he should be telling me everything, spilling his secrets. He should be speaking of inspiration, of sublime visions, of how he would immortalize me in paint. I was used to adulation, superlatives, passionate avowals. I could not bear his distance or the fact that she was still—impossibly—between us.

I struggled to hide my dismay and my jealousy and said as lightly as I could, "You are such a mystery to me, Joseph Hannigan."

"I think you must be in need of a little mystery. Life must be so boring for you otherwise."

There was an edge to his voice. I wished I had not asked the questions, because whatever else they'd done, they put distance between us. I wanted to bring him back to me. I touched his chest, feeling his warm skin through his shirt. Time to lead him where I wished him to go. Time to talk of bargains. "I will tell you the mystery I'd like to know the answer to. I would like to know what makes you see the world as you do."

"Does it matter what makes me see that way, or only that I do?"

"I have spent a lifetime with artists of all kinds," I told him. "And that is the question that eludes them all. Where such talent comes from is a mystery. Is it a convolution in the brain that causes it? Or is it in the eyes? The heart? What makes the prism through which you see the world? What would you be without it?"

I wasn't certain why I'd asked the last question—I never had before. Nor did I know what it was about Joseph Hannigan that made me wonder it. I thought of the darkness I'd seen within him, the vastness of it, the way it seemed to form him, and wondered if it was his talent I'd seen, and what would happen if it were simply gone.

And I wondered if I would feel sorrow when it was taken from him.

The thought startled me, no less than the way Joseph was looking, again with the strange, edgy thoughtfulness, as if he saw in me something he had never expected to find.

"Those stories you tell me," he said quietly. "The ones about Byron and Canaletto, all the others. Did you ask them those questions too?"

I was so startled I wondered if I'd heard him correctly. *You*, he'd said, hadn't he? *Did* you *ask them?*

"It was you, wasn't it?" He seemed driven by some deep feeling, a kind of fatal courage. "In all of those tales. You're the woman. You're the one who made them the offer."

I could not answer. How could he know? And yet, that he did was obvious. My hunger slithered and whispered.

Carefully, I said, testing, "How could I be?"

"Don't pretend. I know already, don't you see it? I *know* what you are. I know what you do."

I was shaken. "But—"

"I know a friend of yours. My sister's . . . lover." The word was bitten off. I wondered if it was jealousy I heard. Or misery. "Nicholas Dane."

"*What?*"

"You know him, don't you? The things he told me aren't a lie? He's begged me not to take your offer. He's told me what you are, what will happen. But I already knew the truth, didn't I? You've told me. In every one of your stories, you've said it. Demon inspiration."

Nicholas was Sophie's lover. How had I not seen this? How had I not known? He would ruin everything. Only days left, and the monster would emerge. In panic, I said, "You mustn't listen to him—"

"I don't care what he says." Joseph's gaze was hotly blue, demanding. "I want you to do it. Make me the offer. Please."

It was what I wanted, what I had intended. My panic eased and my hunger deepened, whispering, *Do what he asks. Choose him.* But he seemed so . . . not angry, no not that. Despairing.

I hesitated. This was all strange. What had Nicholas said? What had he done? I had to think. There were consequences always, and Nicholas's involvement with the Hannigans was something I hadn't expected. I should not rush into this. Ah, but there was no more time. My hunger wheedled, *He belongs to you. Take him.* And I had waited far too long to deny it or to further delay. But I had to ask. "Why?"

Joseph's gaze delved deeply into mine, and those prison doors opened wide, revealing the ghosts behind them.

"I want to release her," he said, and there was a raw, brutal pain in his voice. "I have to let her go. It's time. She's in love with him, but she won't leave me, and I don't . . . I don't have the strength to fight her. Not unless you give me this. Give me your inspiration, Odilé. Take Sophie out of my head. Make it all worth *something.*"

I saw the otherworldliness shining from him, shimmering on his skin. I saw his desire and his need and his fear.

"Do it," he whispered.

Make him the offer. Choose him. My hunger reared, snapping, starving, that emptiness inside me reaching, my own darkness tangling with his. The pain of it had me crying out—only his hands on my arms saved me from collapsing. He was pale and glittering and beautiful, and I saw him through my own prism and wanted him as I had never wanted anyone.

I looked up at him, gasping, "What is it you most desire?"

He answered as if it were a script we performed, the perfect words, the ones I'd taught him with every story I'd told. "I want fame."

My hunger erupted, and he drew back, his intensity fading in sudden confusion and fear. I knew he saw my craving and had not suspected the monstrousness of it. But I put my hands to his face and forced him to look at me, and his distress melted away in a fierce desire. The walls about us seemed to waver and undulate; I saw myself as he saw me, glowing like some angel, a light that pulsed, and he pressed me to the wall. I undid his trousers and wrapped my legs about him and his vibrance flowed into me, still so strong, never ending—how did he do it? How was he never tired, never spent, never drawn?

My appetite was so painful now, so deep and unending that I felt myself falling into it, sinking deep as I made the choice. I felt the bargain lock into me like teeth, piercing deep, a spasm of pain and elation, exploding into pure light, into nothing but sensation. It was a rapture like none I'd ever known, intense, doubled. It made me scream, and through it I heard his racked gasp, his cry as he arched at the force of it, his hands slipping where they gripped my thighs, and then catching again, and the walls were wavering, dissolving, the world spinning away, so we were nothing but breath expelled into the universe, dissipating, wisping away. My breath, and his, and hers. *And hers. . . .*

I blinked, roused from bliss, startled back into the world—the *portego* and the strange light, gray and overcast, the terrazzo floor gleaming even so, the watery reflections cast about the walls no longer there—ah, but they had never been. They had only been in his vision, only me seeing through his eyes in those moments before I'd chosen him. Not real.

I felt his genius in my blood, coursing through me, stronger than I'd anticipated—so strong and full I could not hold it all. I felt it spilling onto the floor, spreading, a light around the both of us. I captured what I could—it would stay, ebbing back and forth between us as he needed inspiration, until he had what I'd promised, and then it would lock deep within me, feeding me for months, a year, while my appetite hibernated, until it woke again. I felt the gentle throb of him deep within me. His chest heaved where it pressed to mine as he tried to catch his breath. His face was buried in my shoulder, his hair soft against my cheek. His fingers dug into my thighs, holding me in place. He was trembling, and—surprise of all surprises—so was I.

"It's done," he whispered—I was uncertain whether it was a question or a statement. He sounded exultant and astonished. The words were a psalm sung in his deep voice, and in my ears they distorted as light distorts on water, rippling and changing until they echoed, changing into a voice that was no longer his, and one that felt dangerous. Her voice. *It's done.*

FORTY-TWO

SOPHIE

I jackknifed up in bed, gasping as if I were drowning, voices in my head—my brother's, Odilé's—my heart racing and my blood pounding as if I'd been running in a nightmare, but I had no recollection of any dream at all.

Overcast light streamed into my room; it was late morning, and I felt as if I'd been wrenched and torn apart and hastily put together again, and still the whispers of those voices tumbled about inside my head.

I pushed back the covers to get out of bed, feeling weak. It seemed to take all my strength to reach the pitcher on the washstand. My hand shook as I poured the water, and I grabbed the edge of the stand to anchor myself as I drank. I put on my dressing gown and made my way slowly to the kitchen. There wasn't much there—a bottle of wine that Joseph and I had half drunk, the heel from a loaf of bread. I took that, and after the first bite I was so ravenous I stuffed nearly the whole thing into my mouth—it was dry and chewy and far too big a piece for a single bite, and I felt like an animal as I ate it.

It restored me somewhat, but still the whispers whirled in my ears; I touched my temple and felt a strange, buzzing sensation, as if I'd shocked myself. Then the voices faded, and in their place came a pounding. Incessant and fierce. I wanted to put my head beneath a pillow to muffle it. But then I realized it wasn't coming from inside my head at all, but from the door.

I wanted to ignore it and go back to bed, but it wouldn't stop. I thought it might be Joseph. I remembered too late that Joseph would not be knocking this way—he would just come in—but by then I was nearly to the door, and I heard a voice now, low and urgent, on the other side.

"Sophie, for God's sake, let me in."

Nicholas.

Nicholas. I wrenched open the door, and he nearly fell inside, catching himself on the door frame. His hair was tousled; he had that look one got sometimes after a sleepless night—not tired but invigorated, tense, every movement too blunt and quick.

"Thank God you're here," he said.

But I didn't feel warm at his words, because there was something desperate about the way he said them. Something wrong.

"What is it?"

He had stepped fully inside and was already striding toward the *sala.* He looked over his shoulder, motioning for me to follow, saying, "There's something I must tell you."

I closed the door and stumbled after him. I said again, "What's wrong?"

He took a deep breath and closed his eyes. When he opened them again, his expression had softened. "I think you'd best sit down. It's not the easiest of things to hear, and . . . and you look rather . . . frail."

"I don't feel very well," I confessed, moving gratefully to the settee and sinking down upon it. "I woke with the strangest feeling. But then, I hardly slept."

"That makes two of us. Joseph isn't here."

It was not a question. "No. He didn't come home last night. He's with a friend—"

"Odilé León," he said.

That startled me. "Yes. How did you know?"

He looked suddenly exhausted. "Because I've been following her. I've known her a long time. She is, in fact, the reason I came to Venice."

My uneasiness grew. "The reason?"

"I've a story to tell you, Sophie, and I hope you will believe it."

I lifted my chin, thinking I already knew the story, feeling disconsolate and hopeless now on top of tired. There was only one reason for him to have followed Odilé to Venice. "You don't need to say anything more. In fact, I wish you wouldn't. You're in love with Odilé, and—"

"That's not it," Nicholas said abruptly, almost angrily. "I'm not in love with Odilé León."

"You're not?"

"How could I be, when I'm in love with you?"

No one had ever made such a declaration to me, and I wasn't prepared for my relief or joy. "Oh, Nicholas—" At the sight of his expression, I stopped. So somber. Worried. My joy curled back, chastened.

He came to the settee and sat beside me, but he didn't touch me or take me into his arms. "I want to protect you, Sophie. I would never involve you in this except . . . I spoke to your brother this morning. He won't listen to me, and that's why I've come to you. You'll need to be the one to convince him."

"Convince him of what?"

He took my hand, stroking my palm with his finger, closing it tightly in his palm. "I met Odilé León seven years ago. In Paris. We were lovers." He paused as if waiting for my response, watching for it.

I didn't know what to say. Of course. Anyone would have taken the opportunity to be with her. "I understand."

"No you don't. Of that I'm certain." His hand tightened on mine. "I was with her only for a short time, but it was the most productive period of my life. I wrote enough poems to fill an entire volume. And when she left me, I fell into despair."

"That was how you lost your words," I said.

"Words, inspiration, love . . . all of it," he said frankly. "But that isn't what matters." He went on, telling me an impossible tale of love and desire and inspiration. A horror story, with a beautiful demon at its center.

He was flushed; a strange energy vibrated from him. For a moment I thought he must be mad—*of course, how perfect. The man who loves me is mad.*

"I know it seems implausible, Sophie. I know it's impossible. But I'm telling you the truth. She has wrought both the greatest revelations and the most terrible destruction."

"Oh, Nicholas."

"You think I'm mad," he said. "I thought I was too, when I realized what she was. I didn't want to believe it. But it's all true."

I pulled my hand hard from his. "I'm sorry; I really do feel unwell. I don't think I'm hearing you correctly."

He grabbed my hand again, saying urgently, "I'm telling you the truth. She'll destroy Joseph too. I warned him this morning, but he wants what she can offer, Sophie. He'll take the bargain if she makes it. And if she chooses him, there's nothing we can do.

She'll take everything from him. Is that what you want? Joseph to be famous for one work—one single work—and then fallen to despair or madness after?"

I said wearily, "Is this what you spoke with Joseph about this morning?"

"Yes. And he told me he didn't care."

"You mean he believed you?"

Nicholas met my gaze. "He knows what she is, yes. He knows what she can do for him. I believe he means to ask her for it. He said . . . he said he didn't want you to sacrifice for him anymore. He asked me to take care of you."

His last words caught my attention. My dream from last night came back. Her whispers and his. My fears that Odilé was what my brother was looking for, a place to drown.

Nicholas said, "Sophie, listen to me. You discovered Nelson Stafford's body in that courtyard. He'd been Odilé's lover. And that musician they found in the canal—do you remember? He was with Odilé as well. Since she's been in Venice, she's left a string of bodies in her wake—all talented men. Three of them, Sophie. Three men who succumbed to her and were destroyed. The police have been watching her. Ask them if you don't believe me. They'll tell you what they suspect."

I remembered what Katharine Bronson had told me about Nelson Stafford. *He fell in love and fell away. . . . She's quite irresistible.* I thought of my brother's face in the rain.

"No," I whispered. "Oh no. Please."

"I've watched her do this in every city she's been in," Nicholas said. "But it was in Barcelona that I learned the truth of her. Her hunger is an entity of its own. If she doesn't choose within three years, if she doesn't convince someone to take the bargain she offers, she can no longer control it. She *becomes* the demon that lives inside her. That was what I saw in Barcelona. A lamia crawling over the bodies of the men she'd drained. A score of them. Perhaps more. But their deaths fed her and remade her. The demon retreated. She was herself again when I saw her next in Paris."

I went cold, cold to the bone. Cold so I could no longer feel his touch on my fingers. No, none of this could be true. *A succubus.* Such things were only myths. Creatures from stories. Fairy tales. And yet . . . I knew how such things lurked at the edges of the real world. I knew what it felt like to be held by demons. I knew what it meant to fight them.

And the truth was that now everything made sense. *Put Joseph in my hands, and I will make him a king. I will make him more famous than he ever dreamed.*

"What did Joseph say to you?" I demanded. "What did he say *exactly*?"

Nicholas whispered, "That it wasn't fair of him to keep you. He asked me to love you. He said he could not leave you to any-one else. He said this would make it all worth something."

My vision blurred. "No. No, he can't make the bargain. I won't let him. He can't have done it. He wouldn't leave me."

But even I no longer believed that, and Nicholas only gave me a grim look. "Then you must speak with him. Now."

He let go of my hands, and I rose, the room wavering.

He took my arm, anchoring me. "We can't afford to wait. We must go now."

The ground tilted beneath me as I went to my bedroom, as I dressed with shaking fingers. To get to Joseph, to stop him, was all I could think about. I knew I looked disheveled as I hurried out again, my hair still braided because I could not take the time to dress it. *Joseph, don't. Don't leave me. I will never survive it.*

Marco was waiting, and Nicholas and I were soon on our way to the Dana Rosti. My stomach twisted and turned as Nicholas told me what he wanted to do, what Odilé's end must be.

"I mean to destroy her, Sophie. I'd thought . . . if I could keep her from making the choice, if I could drive her to three years without it—"

"But the demon would be released, you said."

"Yes. But what happens if there's no one for her to feed upon? What if she's locked in a room with no escape? I think—I hope— that if that happens, she'll destroy herself."

I felt the intensity of his belief, the sheer *will* of his intention. The horror of it.

"It's been three years, Sophie," he said, now in a whisper. "I'm so close. Her destruction is only days away. But now . . . now there's Joseph, and who knows what he's done?"

When we arrived, Nicholas said, "It would be best if she didn't know I was here. She won't let me in, that's a certainty, and she might refuse you too if she sees me. You'll have to do this on your own, Sophie. Talk to Joseph—bring him out if you can."

I nodded. He helped me from the *felze* while still staying in the shadows of the cabin. Oddly, nearly the moment I set foot on the cracked, algae-strewn stairs, I felt steadier. I was infused with a sudden strength and determination as I stepped to the door.

I yanked the bell pull. There was only silence after, for what seemed a long time, and I looked over my shoulder for reassurance, but Nicholas was hidden in the *felze*. I reached for the bell pull again.

Before I could ring it, I heard footsteps on the stones on the other side of the door, and it cracked open to reveal Maria, who was frowning fiercely.

I tried to smile. "I've come to see Madame León. And my brother. Will you tell her please that Sophie Hannigan has come to pay a call?"

Maria's frown grew more ferocious. "The *padrona* is not see-ing visitors today, signorina."

My smile faltered. "Oh, but I'm not really a visitor. My brother is here, you know. Joseph, and—"

"They are both indisposed." She began to shut the door.

I put my hand to the door to stop it from closing. "I don't think you understand. Please tell Madame León I'm here. I'm certain she will wish to know—"

"She said no visitors, signorina," said Maria, her dark eyes seeming to glow strangely. "And not you most of all. She says to remember your promise. She says to go away."

The door closed so hard that I stepped back. I heard the slide of the lock, the footsteps fading. I felt the air shudder against my skin; the world faded and went dim, nothing in it but me, the only light at the center of shadows. I felt so profoundly alone that I gasped, reaching a hand to steady myself against the door. I blinked, and then the feeling was gone, but it left me greatly uneasy. *Joseph.*

I grabbed the bell pull angrily, nearly shaking it. The sound echoed, distant and faraway. I pulled it again. Then once more. Nothing. No one was coming.

In dismay, I stepped back, craning to look at the balcony above. "Joseph!" I called. "Joseph, it's Sophie! Come to the door!"

My voice seemed too loud, and then it vanished as if I'd shouted into a void. There was no answer. In disbelief, I shouted again. If Joseph heard me, he would come. He must come.

"Joseph! Joseph, please!"

Nothing.

From the gondola, Nicholas called in a low, hard voice, "Sophie, come away."

"I can't," I said in panic. "He'll come to me. He will. He always does."

"Not this time. I told you."

She says to remember your promise. Again I heard Odilé's voice. *Release your brother . . . Put Joseph in my hands and I will make him a king.* And the answer I'd meant to make. *Yes.* But I had never said it, had I?

"I never promised, Odilé!" I shouted. "I never promised!"

My answer was profound silence, my own voice echoing.

In horror, I stumbled from the step, onto the next, which was half submerged in the Canal, water to my ankle, my hem dipping. Marco grabbed my elbow, and helped me back into the boat, and then I was in Nicholas's arms.

"I must go to the police," I said.

He swept my hair gently from my cheek. "Why?"

"They can help. I know they can."

He gave me a sad look, but he didn't protest.

I felt nauseated and panicked. The boat moved off; I lay back with Nicholas against the pillows, taking comfort from the way he stroked my hair, thinking of when Joseph and I had lain upon the floor of the Moretta watching the sunrise, and I'd seen in his eyes a whole world that belonged just to us. . . .

When we reached the police station, Nicholas released me with a soft kiss against my hair. "Sophie—"

I turned back to look at him. "Yes?"

"Tell them only of your fears because of the others. Stafford, I mean. And the rest. Don't tell them the truth of her. They'll never believe it."

I laughed shortly, despair and panic and horror lodged tight in my breast. "No," I said. "Who would?"

FORTY-THREE

SOPHIE

I fought my nausea as I went into the police station, but my trembling was worse than ever. I had stopped just inside, uncertain where to go or what to do, when a man in a shabby coat came up to me, speaking that impossible to understand Venetian dialect, frowning at me in concern.

The way he looked at me made me think I looked as ready to swoon as I felt, but I managed to stammer, in the small bit of Italian I knew, "I need to speak to a . . . a . . ." I gave up, shrugging, saying in English, "An officer. An Inspector."

Understanding dawned in the man's eyes. He nodded and took me to a set of narrow stairs, pointing for me to go up them. At the second landing was a door; I stepped through it into a room fronted with windows. Even in the gray light, reflections from the water below spun over the ceiling, gray and white riffles. The room was filled with desks and men, all of whom looked up at me as curiously as if I'd materialized like a spirit before them.

I said, because I could not think of what else to say, "Odilé León."

I had not realized how much I had hoped Nicholas was wrong until I saw how her name galvanized them. One of them rose quickly and strode toward me officiously, spewing Italian until I held up my hand and said, "Does anyone speak French? Or English?"

He stopped, frowned, and said, "I speak both, mademoiselle. Which would you prefer?"

I looked at him in relief. "English, please. I've come to speak to a . . . an inspector, I think? About her. Madame León."

He nodded, and gestured for me to follow him, which I did, trying to keep up with him as he maneuvered through the labyrinth of desks. He stopped at a door at the far end of the room and rapped sharply upon it. At a grunt from the other side, he launched into Italian, got a reply, and then turned to me, saying, "Inspector Balbi will see you." He opened the door, and when I stepped inside, he closed it behind me.

The office was small and cluttered; a single, narrow window, paned and filmy with dust and smoke, looked blurrily out on the Canal below. The room stank of stale tobacco, and on the corner of a large desk littered with papers was a pipe and a bowl of emptied ashes. Seated behind it was a tall man with dark, darting eyes and a graying Vandyke beard.

He rose. "You have some information regarding Odilé León?" he asked me, very politely, in heavily accented French.

I nodded, and he made a motion—there was a chair behind me, and I sank gratefully into it.

"My name is Sophie Hannigan."

He frowned. "Sophie Hannigan? Why is that name familiar to me?"

It was one more thing that settled the truth more firmly. "I found Nelson Stafford's body."

"Ah." He sat down, leaning back in his chair. "Yes. You were looking into leasing. Quite unfortunate, mademoiselle. I am sorry for it. All I can say is that such things are not common in Venice these days."

"But more common than you'd like, I think."

His dark eyes glinted. He gave a short nod. "It has been an eventful summer. Why are you here, Mademoiselle Hannigan? Have you more to add to your testimony on Mr. Stafford? My man says you wish to speak of Odilé León."

I nodded. "I understand Mr. Stafford was connected to her?"

The inspector regarded me steadily. "And if he was?"

"I've been told that she was the one he committed suicide for. That he was in love with her."

"Who told you this?"

"Katharine Bronson."

"Ah. The Ca' Alvisi?"

I nodded. "She was only repeating gossip."

Balbi steepled his fingers before him. "In Venice, gossip is everywhere, but no one comes to the police to report it. I suspect this talk about Mr. Stafford is not the reason you are here. Perhaps he is not your only connection to Madame León?"

"My brother and I met Odilé León some days ago," I told him frankly. "And . . . and he has become her lover and he hasn't come home and I'm worried for him."

Inspector Balbi sighed heavily. He dropped his hands to the surface of his desk and leaned forward. "You should be worried, mademoiselle. I would venture to say that it is a hazardous duty to be Odilé León's paramour."

My chest tightened in dread. "I've heard she's connected not just to Mr. Stafford's death, but to others."

"Two others," said the Inspector. "Three altogether."

"Three." My voice was a whisper. "Then . . . then you must help me."

"How am I to do that?"

"You must rescue my brother. Go there and bring him out. At least long enough for me to speak with him."

"He is a grown man, is he not, mademoiselle?"

"Yes. Yes, but—"

"Then there is nothing I can do. We have no evidence against her. Each of those men was her lover in the days before he died, and I suspect she either had something to do with their deaths, or knows something. But she says she does not, and so—" he shrugged eloquently. "But if it were my brother in her bed, I would advise him very strongly to leave it."

"But I told you, he hasn't come home. I haven't been able to speak to him. She won't let me in."

Balbi's gaze was sympathetic. "Then I sincerely hope it is not his body we next fish from a canal."

I felt another wave of nausea; my heart pounded so loudly I could hear nothing else.

"Mademoiselle," he said, snapping to his feet, reaching across his desk as if he meant to save me from something, and I realized that I was rising, swaying. The world seemed to have lost its color, and I longed to peel back a corner to see if I could find beneath it dragons or princes or any of the things I knew how to conquer, because there was nothing here to grasp, nothing to fight.

Oh, what fools we'd been! How could I save him now?

I said goodbye to Inspector Balbi and left the police station blindly. When I finally reached the gondola, Nicholas gave me an anxious look and said, "What happened? What did they tell you?"

"We must save him," I said. "Promise me you'll help me. You know what to do. You know how to fight her."

"I haven't been all that successful, as I've said."

"But you know the truth of her, which is more than anyone else does."

He frowned. "If she's chosen Joseph, my love, there is little we can do."

"Please, Nicholas. I'll die if something happens to him. I can't be without him."

He gave me a strange look, but I couldn't read it, and I was trembling again. His arms came around me tightly.

I whispered, "He would not want to live that way, no matter what he thinks now. I can't let him. We must stop him before he makes the promise."

I felt the warmth of Nicholas's breath against my temple, his fingers in my hair, stroking again, and the worn softness of his coat against my cheek.

"You care for him as I do, don't you?" I asked him. "If you love me, you must love him too, because we're the same. You must be a true friend to him now, Nicholas, to the both of us. Can you be that?"

His fingers stilled upon my hair. I heard his voice through the beating of his heart in my ear, though it was soft as a whisper. "Yes," he said. "I can be that."

FORTY-FOUR

ODILÉ

I watched Joseph uneasily as he worked, not realizing I was frowning until he glanced up and said, "Have I made you angry?"

"No, of course not. Why would you say it?"

"You look . . . I don't know . . . annoyed. No—frayed." Before I could answer, he turned back to the canvas, already distracted, sighing, scraping at something he didn't like with the palette knife, muttering, "Something's wrong. I can't see what."

His words mirrored my own thoughts so exactly I was startled until I realized he was speaking of the painting. "Perhaps another eye would help. Should I take a look?"

He shook his head. "I'm not ready for you to see it."

It was odd—by now he should be painting feverishly, flooded with inspiration, but since the choice had been made, he'd been desultory, slow, dissatisfied with every stroke. It was exactly the opposite of what I'd experienced with my other choices, who had been tireless once the bargain was set. I told myself not to worry; his genius was in my blood now, where the succubus in me changed and strengthened it, feeding the magic again to him whenever we made love, and I knew he would find in it what he needed, no matter that it might take a few days.

I turned away, going to the window. I did not see Nicholas anywhere. I hoped Sophie Hannigan had him well wrapped about her finger—not that it mattered now. I had beaten my hunger; time was as nothing again. The choice was made and there was no going back.

Still I heard her voice in my head, like a song one couldn't forget. *It's done it's done it's done.*

I heard a sound behind me, and I turned to see Joseph. He came up to me, putting his arms around me, drawing me back against his chest, kissing my ear.

I shivered, suddenly cold, and twisted to look at him. "You're not finished for today?"

"I need some inspiration," he murmured. "Inspire me. Isn't that what you're supposed to do?"

I was relieved for the distraction, and so I obliged, but when we were finished, he only stared off into space, running his hand through my hair, but unseeingly, obviously thinking of something else. I was afraid to ask what it was. She was there in the room like a ghost.

He fell asleep. When he woke an hour or so later, he seemed listless. When I suggested he paint, he turned tired eyes to me and said, "Tell me a story instead."

"I've told you all my stories," I said quietly.

"That can't be true," he insisted. "I want to understand. How old are you? What made you this? Or were you born this way?"

I laughed. "Born? Oh no. I was not born to it. I was made, as all other things are made."

"All other things?"

"We do not stay as we were born, none of us." I poured a glass of wine. "We are *all* made. And this—what I am—was nothing but one more choice in a sea of choices."

"Have you ever regretted it?"

"To be a muse for the ages? To see adoration in every eye? How could one regret such a thing? What woman could regret it?"

I said it lightly, but he did not take it so. "I don't think adoration is all you hoped for, is it? It seems such a small thing to ask. Especially for someone like you."

"Someone like me?"

"There's a passion that burns in you. One that has nothing to do with the carnal. There are things you want. Tell me what they are."

Again, I was unsettled by his perception.

"What I want? I have everything I need or desire. I have you." I took up the glass and came over to him, kissing him lightly.

He did not respond. When I stepped away, I saw a bewildering thoughtfulness in his eyes. He said, "When you told me that Sophie might want something more than being my muse . . . you were right; I'd never thought about that before. And now I cannot help but wonder the same thing about you."

"There is no need to wonder. I am made to be a muse. It is my calling and my destiny."

"Yes, perhaps." He lifted my chin, forcing me to look into his eyes. "But that is not all there is to you. I can feel it."

I yearned to tell him everything. To have him truly know Odilé León—not the monster Nicholas knew, but the woman Madeleine had seen. The woman I'd been. I moved gently away. "I was nothing. And I wanted more than that. But what woman in this world ever gets exactly what she desires? We do not change the world with our gifts, *cheri*. We are only women. Born to inspire men to greatness, but never of our own accord."

"I don't think you believe that. Why should women not make something of their gifts, if they've been given them? Sophie's stories—"

Must every conversation turn somehow to her? "Her stories? And what does she do with those beyond amuse you on a lonely night?"

I had meant to belittle her. But his thoughtfulness grew. "She makes the world bearable."

"Ah, but the world only sees her through you, and you do not celebrate her, do you? How well she fades in the brightness of your star. The world does not remember the names of women. The world sees only men and not those who stand behind them." I spoke with all the pent-up frustration of centuries, all my sorrow and despair. He had brought out the emotions I usually controlled so well. But then again, I did not expect him to hear them. What man ever heard the real desires of women?

But he did hear. There, in his eyes, was compassion. Bewildering, again.

"I have never known anyone quite like you, Joseph Hannigan."

His arms came around me, and my wine ended up undrunk. He was as passionate as ever, as heedlessly lost in lovemaking as he had been before, and yet . . . he did not go back to painting that evening, instead lounging on the settee, his sketchbook open on his lap as he turned the pages. When I inquired, he said only, again, "It's nothing. I'm tired."

The next day was the same. After playing at the canvas for a few hours, frowning a great deal, exhaling in frustration, he stepped away, covering it, saying irritably, "When am I supposed to feel something?"

I had no answer for him—what could I say? *You have already been feeling it? I don't understand why it isn't marking you the way it should? I don't understand* you? I lit a candle and looked down at him as he slept. He was so beautiful, and he belonged to me now, and I should have been triumphant.

But I felt distress, because he should be wanting nothing more than to paint through the night or to make love. I should be posing for him, despite the fact that he claimed he needed no studies, that he saw things in his head as perfectly as he wanted them to be. Canaletto had insisted I stand near him as he worked. Byron had wanted me in the room so he could look at me whenever his strength lagged. Robert Schumann had asked that I remain near enough to touch. And Keats . . . lovely Keats . . . he had penned "Lamia" as he lay with his head in my lap.

But Joseph Hannigan did not want me hovering. He needed only to see me in his head.

I was struck by a sudden suspicion, an urge I could not deny. I got out of bed, pulling on my dressing gown, taking up the candle. He slept on soundly, not the least bit restless. I wondered if he even dreamed, or if he had fallen into that vast, dark oblivion inside himself. Another thing that troubled me.

I hurried from the bedroom, soundlessly, the candlelight wavering on the highly polished floor, my shadow flickering and shuddering as I padded out into the *portego*, to the easel there, the large canvas with its cloth covering.

I hesitated, suddenly uncertain and afraid. I didn't know what I expected to see. I didn't know what I wanted to see.

Carefully, I lifted the cloth, bit by bit, slowly at first, revealing the painted shine of a terrazzo floor so beautifully rendered that it seemed to be only a continuation of that beneath my feet, then the delicate arch of a foot, calves, knees, up and up and up. Finally I grew impatient with my own reticence and pulled the muslin off all the way, letting it fall in a *shush* to the floor.

That it was beautiful there was no denying. The marble walls danced with reflections; Venice's strange, wavering light cast everywhere—not only on the walls, but on the skin of the nude who stood there, her back to the viewer as she reached up to take down her hair. Strands were already falling, curling to the back of her neck, between her shoulder blades. She looked over her shoulder, and the look in her eyes was alluring, compelling—one wanted to follow her wherever she would go, even when following her meant going into the room beyond, which was dark with shadows, horrors leaping from each one, barely seen, barely articulated, but the mind saw them. The mind understood and recoiled.

I want to see something of desire, I'd told him. *I want to see your secrets.*

And here they were. Joseph Hannigan laid bare. Demons in the darkened room beyond, a spirit in a thin chemise wisping even as it spun, losing pieces of itself like smoke fading into the darkness, the shadow of a bed, shadow upon shadow, a woman with glowing eyes that seemed both malevolent and tempting, an outstretched hand, and another woman in the far corner—an angel with a face so terrible and yet so beautiful it was impossible to stop looking at her, to stop searching her face, which changed and shifted with each movement of the viewer. And all these things emerging from such vast and solid darkness that it seemed to have no end.

The woman in the doorway was the light in the center of that darkness, so softly spun in brilliance I did not know how he had accomplished it. The light seemed to emanate from her skin, an illumination that both revealed the figures in the room beyond and cast them more firmly into shadow. She was salvation—and she was stunning. Rounded hips, dimpled buttocks, her back arched just so. The hair glinting with reddish highlights that he was carefully darkening. Eyes whose slight slant had been rounded. Gray, yes, but opalescent too, a step to the right and they were not gray, but blue. The full upper lip had been smudged, made thinner to barely cover a slight overbite, the hip shadowed to make narrower what had once been full.

And there . . . on her shoulder blade, a mole like a star. A missing star meant to match other stars, to fill in another constellation, to make it whole.

Before I could fully grasp the meaning, I heard a shuffling behind me. I turned slowly, half afraid I would see her there, but no, it was him, come from bed, naked and frowning.

"What are you doing?" he asked.

"I couldn't sleep."

He came up beside me. "I asked you to wait. It's not finished."

"No, I can see that." I pointed to the mole on the shoulder blade. "I don't have a mole like that."

"It's Sophie's," he said softly. "I've always found it—"

"It's the missing star in the constellation."

"What?"

"The moles on your back form a constellation. They're missing only one star to be complete. This one, where it is, on her."

He looked surprised. "Really? A constellation? Which one?"

"The Serpent Bearer," I told him, looking back at the painting, feeling something in me tighten. "Ophiuchus. Who was Aesculapius—the healer. Or no, not the Serpent Bearer exactly. Your stars don't make the healer. They make the serpent he holds. The Serpent's Head."

"Sophie used to say they were a map." He was looking at the painting, his expression wistful.

"A map to where?"

"Somewhere only we knew." Wistfulness in his voice too.

I felt cold again, a bitter chill that made me wrap my arms around myself. "Snakes have many forms, you know. They have not always been evil or poisonous—or at least, not only so. Just as desire has not always been evil. In ancient times, snakes were a symbol of healing. Of wisdom. They can be very beautiful."

"Like the snake in Keats's poem," he said softly. "The lamia."

"Yes," I said, though the reminder was not comforting. I thought of Byron, who had called me a witch, a devil, but one he could not live without. And Robert Schumann, who had, in his madness, called me a demon as often as he had called me angel. And suddenly I realized that the angel/demon in Joseph's painting, the one whose face could not quite be grasped, was me.

The fear I'd been holding at bay pushed back hard. Joseph was staring at the painting as if it tormented him, as if it held what he most wanted—but just out of reach. I whispered, "Who are you, really? You and your sister—what are you?"

He looked at me. There was no puzzlement on his face, no surprise at the question, as if he'd heard it before, or expected it. "Nothing special."

But I saw the burning in his eyes when he said it, and I knew it wasn't what he believed. I knew too that I wanted him to tell me that she was nothing to him, that this painting did not hold the whole of their history, though I knew it did. I knew with a searing, painful certainty that she could not be fought or overcome, and I was jealous of her as I had never been of any woman.

I was to be his inspiration. I was to be the one who made his art and his life complete. I was to be everything, not this niggling little part he gave me. But how could that be? I'd made the bargain. I'd felt the rapture. I'd felt it bite and lock.

He said, "Are you all right? You look in pain."

"No," I said. "No, I'm perfectly fine."

But I looked into his face and felt the world tilt and distort—not what I expected at all. And I was deeply afraid.

FORTY-FIVE

NICHOLAS

Sophie was so heartbroken and weak that when we arrived back at the palazzo, I put her to bed. I stayed with her as she fell into sleep. Just before she did, she grabbed my hand and said, "Bring him back to me."

I wonder if I can adequately describe how devastating were those words? Here was the woman I loved to distraction, a pale ghost of herself, calling for her brother after having just told me she could not live without him. *We must save him. Be a friend to him.*

I wanted to save Joseph Hannigan of my own accord; I wanted to do whatever she asked of me, but as I watched her sleeping, her hair spread over her pillow, that soft exhalation of her breath, the need to have her entirely to myself was overwhelming. To be without him . . . for a moment, the vision was so tempting it was all I could do not to give in to it. But that was only my impetuous nature talking, and what had that ever brought me but trouble? I made myself think of the soft promise in her eyes, the way she'd thrown herself in my arms as if I were her salvation. I made myself think of the promise I'd made to him. *Keep her safe. Love her.*

I wanted to be what each of them needed. The truth was that I could not imagine them apart. I suppose it was the *twinness* of them, the magic I'd felt that had me half in love with both of them the moment we'd met. The loss of him would destroy her, I knew. I would do whatever I must to prevent that. I had no real hope that I could. But for them both, I would try.

Sophie could not get to Joseph or Odilé, and that would not change. Odilé must know as well as I the bond between the twins. She would allow nothing to weaken the hold she had on him. She would do her best to keep Joseph away from Sophie. But me . . . I thought Odilé would see me. She had no idea of my own connection to them.

So I went to confront her. When I arrived at the Dana Rosti, I did not bother to hide or dodge but went to the door and rang the bell. There was no answer, and I had not expected one. She would want no one to encroach upon the enchantment she wove. I crossed to the *fondamenta* of the palazzo next door, settled myself on the overturned boat there and waited for her to catch a glimpse of me.

The breeze coming off the Canal was brisk and wet; it was too chilly to stay there long, and fortunately, I did not have to. It was only a quarter hour before I heard the sound of the balcony door open, before she came out to the balustrade, her long hair blown from her face, her dressing gown gaping, her shadowed cleavage trailing to a darkness that even now raised my own hunger—but it was a faint monster now, a temptation but not a lure.

"Ah, Nicholas," she called down. "I have been watching for you."

"I've been otherwise engaged."

Her smile was piercing and oddly desperate. It struck a wrong note within me, but I could not understand why. "With your new little love? Miss Hannigan, is it? Dare I hope that she has snared you deeply?"

So she knew. I did not bother to deny it. "Return her brother to her, Odilé."

"Does she miss him?" Odilé's eyes glittered strangely in the overcast light. A serpent's eyes. "Does she dream of him?"

"I imagine as often as he dreams of her."

Her mouth tightened. Her face seemed to waver before me—for a moment I saw the demon, its terrible pale coils, and my mouth went dry.

"Ah, but this one is so different." Her voice held strange echoes, deep and terrible, a rasp like a raging wind. "He is nothing like the others, and so I think I shall keep him. Tell her he belongs to me now. The bargain is set." She laughed, and it too was terrible.

My last bit of hope evaporated.

"He will not be returning. He has given her up." Again, her face seemed to ripple. She clutched her dressing gown as if she felt a spasm of pain or distress.

This wasn't right. I felt as if I'd glimpsed a fissure in the world that closed again before I could view it. The *fondamenta* seemed to lurch beneath my feet.

When Odilé turned to go back inside, I said urgently, "Odilé, wait—" But she disappeared into the darkness. The door was still open; I took the last of my opportunities, shouting, "Joseph! Joseph Hannigan! Your sister asks for—"

The door slammed shut.

I had no idea if he'd heard me. I struggled to make sense of what had just happened, and why I felt so strongly that something was not as it should be. I raced back to the Moretta, relieved when I arrived to find Sophie in the *sala*. But she looked drawn; her skin so pale I saw the blue of her veins beneath her skin. She wore only her dressing gown, and she was sprawled on the settee.

When I came inside, she took one look at me and froze. "What is it? Oh . . . no . . . no, please, tell me he hasn't!"

I felt the world closing in on me, a realization hovering at the edge of my consciousness that I could not quite grasp. I hurried to her side, falling to my knees beside her, grabbing her hand. As Sophie stared at me with uncertain eyes, all the words I'd lost rushed back to me—a flurry of poetry. I wanted to stare into her eyes for a lifetime. I took a deep breath. "Odilé has chosen Joseph. He's agreed. It was what I was afraid of."

"But there's still something that can be done. You said you could help him—"

"If he hadn't made the bargain, yes," I corrected wearily. "But he has."

"No. You promised. You promised to save him." Her eyes glowed fiercely in the pale of her face.

"Sophie, I—"

She gripped my arm so hard her nails bit through my coat. "This will destroy him. Do as you promised. It's all I ask of you. If you love me, you will do this. I'll never forgive you if you don't."

She did not know what she was asking. She could not possibly mean what I thought she did.

Save him. He would not want to live that way.

He would not want to live. . . .

He is everything to me. I could not live without him.

The life I'd only just begun to imagine faded, the man I might have been had I not stumbled into Odilé in a Paris street.

A man with poetry flowing from my pen once more. A house and children. A life instead of the ceaseless burden of chasing a myth, so much energy focused on destruction.

And all I could say was, "It will be all right, Sophie. It will be all right." When I desperately feared it would never be so again.

FORTY-SIX

SOPHIE

I heard Nicholas's words, *It will be all right,* and I heard too the fatal despair within them, and I knew he believed Joseph was gone. I knew he felt there was nothing that could be done, and of all of us, he knew Odilé best. I could not blame him for his hopelessness.

But he did not know Joseph as I did. And he didn't know how well I had saved my brother before, or how he'd saved me. And perhaps I was naive, but I believed I could redeem him this time too. If I could get to him, if I could talk to Odilé, I could save him.

I knew Nicholas would not let me go near her now—at least not without him. And even through my grief, I understood that he could not help. This was between me and my brother. I remembered the way Joseph had said, *You're in love with him,* and I knew he'd meant to put me in Nicholas's hands. I knew it was

375

why he'd taken Odilé's offer. He'd meant to save us both from bonds we both feared—and hoped—could never be broken.

I would not let him do it, and I knew that if Nicholas was there, it would only strengthen Joseph's resolve to release me. This was something I must do alone.

But Nicholas was so protective and concerned that it wasn't until late the next night that I finally managed to make him go home, to at least tell Giles he wasn't dead and to get a change of clothes. He went—very reluctantly—which warmed me, I must admit.

"I'll stay in bed until you return, so don't hurry," I told him. "I'll just sleep."

He smiled and leaned to kiss me and said, his pale eyes bleak with worry. "An hour only. Sleep well, my love. We can talk about what to do about your brother when I return."

When Nicholas left, I crawled from bed. I was shivering. Too hot. Too cold.

I dressed—too slowly. It was so hard to get the buttons right when I was shaking this way. Finally I gave up, leaving some of them undone, leaving my boots unfastened because I could not manage them. I wrote Nicholas a note and left it on the bed, and then I stumbled down the stairs to find Marco half asleep in the *felze* of the gondola.

"Take me to the Dana Rosti," I said, rousing him. "And quickly."

Once I was in the *felze* and the gondola began to move down the narrow *rio*, out toward the Grand Canal, I closed my eyes, bringing my stories to life as I always did when I was afraid. Instead of dark and creepy Venetian canals and algae, peeling plaster and ominous shadows, I saw turrets and pennants, a moat gurgling with a monster's breath, a golden bridge swinging over a chasm filled with demons. I imagined a princess bearing a glowing crystal, her love for her brother her shield as she went to beard the demon-queen in her tower.

I tightened my hand on the strap as the boat tilted on a wave, and with that motion, my strength came to me. It felt right somehow, that we should come at last to this strangeness, that everything we'd done and been should lead us here, where there was no ambivalence, no disguising grays. Where the demons wore their real faces, and the horrors—for once—were those everyone understood.

FORTY-SEVEN

ODILÉ

He was failing.

"When will I feel it?" he asked me again, his dark-blue eyes filled with frustration and anger. He threw a paintbrush so it skittered across the floor, leaving streaks of yellow in its wake. "Where is the inspiration you promised me?"

"Soon," I assured him, though the truth was I no longer felt such assurance. How could I? Everything about him now was foreign to what I'd known. He left me disoriented, feeling as if parts of me were folding in on myself and then smoothing back again.

He stepped over to the paintbrush he'd thrown and picked it up, mopping up the swash of color with his bare fingers and then wiping it on his white trousers, which were now so marked with paint they seemed a strangely compelling work of art in themselves. He plopped the brush into a jar to soak and stalked away. I felt his anger and exasperation lingering as I covered the painting, and then I went to him, meaning to make him forget, to ease his despair, to feed him again, but he was already curled in bed, asleep, searching for the inspiration he found only in dreams. Not in me.

Had he ever found it in me?

Sophie, he said in his sleep. *Sophie*. When it should have been my name he was calling.

I sat beside him as he slept, twining his dark, thick hair through my fingers, my desire for him flaring at the slightest touch, a look. I was not sated as I usually was. I could not go, not until the painting was done and my work finished, but I wanted to. I was increasingly afraid of my desire for him and the still-growing vortex of my hunger. I wanted to leave the mess I'd made of him, but I told myself not to be impatient. He would be the best of them. It *must* work the way it always had. In time, he would find his inspiration in me. He would finish his painting. I would give him what I'd vowed to give him.

I heard the ringing of the bell from the far part of the house. It was very late—nearly midnight—a strange time for anyone to come calling. I ignored it, as I had ignored all the others. I touched his cheekbone. He stirred, raising a hand, brushing me away in his sleep as if I were an irritating mosquito. I felt that quiver inside me again, that folding in, a growl. I pressed my hand into my stomach to calm it. Strange. It shouldn't—

"*Padrona?*"

I sighed and rose, noting with dismay that he seemed insensible of my leaving. Maria stood in the doorway, looking nervous.

"What is it?" I asked.

"It is his sister," she said, lowering her voice as she said it, glancing past me to see if Joseph were there to hear.

"His sister? So late?"

Maria said reluctantly, "She seems . . . she looks very bad. Should I send her away again?"

I glanced over my shoulder to see Joseph, enervated, listless, and felt a surge of anger. Time to get rid of her once and for all.

"No. I'll see her in the courtyard. Do not wake him." I swooped past, out the door and down the courtyard steps just as the bell rang again. How long would she ring it, I wondered? What had Nicholas told her? Everything, I assumed, and felt a grim satisfaction in the knowledge that she must know the power I had.

I went into the cold, crypt-like courtyard, into the dim yellow glow of gaslight. I heard a soft sob on the other side of the door, a quiet, "Please."

I opened the door. She had been sagging against it. How pale she looked. Her hair was in a loose braid falling over her shoulder. She wore no hat, and a coat that looked to be a man's; it seemed to swallow her.

I saw the moment it registered that it wasn't Maria who had opened the door, but me. She put out her hand as if to stop me from disappearing. She pushed past me into the courtyard. "Please, Odilé. Please. I must speak with you. Where's Joseph?"

"He belongs to me now," I said coldly. "Why have you come?"

"Because I want my brother back. I know what you are and I want you to release him."

"You know what I am," I repeated.

"Nicholas told me."

"What? You believe him? No rational denial? No 'It cannot be true; such things are just horror stories?'"

"Stories are not always only stories," she said.

I laughed lightly, a little bitterly, remembering the princess lover, the map to a land only they knew. "Ah yes. You are no stranger to worlds that should not exist, are you, Sophie?"

"Is Nicholas right—did you make my brother the offer of fame? Did he sell his soul to you?"

"You know as well as I that he did."

"Then you must give it back."

"Would he want that, do you think?"

"He cannot live without it."

"He knew what he was giving up. Still, he asked for it. He begged for it. Even now, he paints away, asking me when fame will come to him. *When*? he asks—every day. *When*?" A true thing, though not precisely as I told her. "Do you think he wants to take it back?"

"He did it for me," she said sharply. "And so I want you to undo it. I know there must be a cost. I'm willing to pay it."

"Ah, I see you know the rules."

She regarded me steadily. "I know this: if you can beat a demon without sacrifice, then what you've won is not worth having. Can it be undone?"

I felt as if I looked at him when I stared into her eyes. That terrible, bizarre twinness. "No. But he will have the fame he desires. And the painting is a masterpiece already, even unfinished."

She let out her breath, sagging against the wall.

"He will be the greatest of all of my choices, if it comforts you to know it. Greater than Canaletto or Keats. Even surpassing Byron."

"But after that he'll never paint again."

I shrugged. "He may, but it will be nothing. Pictures for children. Uninspired landscapes. Canaletto painted until he died."

"They made a mockery of him."

"But he inspired so many before that. Is it not enough?"

"Joseph paints to save himself," she said. "And me. We only wanted to prove we were special. That we endured for a reason. That it wasn't all just . . . meaningless."

"You endured what? What wasn't meaningless?"

She looked away.

I thought of the horrors in Joseph's painting. Secrets laid bare, things better not faced, better locked away. I thought of the shadows in his eyes, in hers. The image of a small dark room in Barcelona swept, unasked for, into my head, the terror of a hunger that could not be appeased, a nightmare that led to such a desolation of spirit I would have done anything to feel again, no matter what that feeling was, so long as it was *something*. Enough to take a pointless razor to my wrist in a tattered Parisian room. And I thought: *she is like me.*

I turned away from her, staring at the wall beyond, the cracked, glowing marble. And I heard myself saying to her as if she were demanding it, though she'd said not a word, "I felt once as you feel. That suffering must *mean* something, that it holds at the end some reward, some justification. But now I think . . . it is just suffering. I have searched for meaning, just as you do now. I am no philosopher, but what I have seen these nearly three hundred years is that the world moves as it always has. There is no meaning. Only balance. Only symmetry."

She was quiet for a long moment. Then she said, "You'll be destroying something beautiful if you ruin him. Joseph and I . . . I can't live without him."

"Oh, but surely you can. Do you know what I think? I think you and your brother cripple one another. You hold him back, as he holds you. You will never truly be free of the past until you free yourselves. I think you have made yourselves like those twins—you know the ones I mean? Who share a heart or a liver and so cannot live without the other? How full are such lives, do you think? It seems but half of one to me."

She said quietly, "Or perhaps it's the other way around. Have you thought of that? Perhaps it's not half a life at all, but two instead. Two joined as one. Doubled instead of halved."

Doubled. I remembered the locking of the bargain, the magic that was more than his alone. Twinned desire—she and Joseph *were* like those conjoined twins, one needing the other to live. She was only half alive now, without him. Just as he was half alive without her.

And suddenly I understood the reason the rapture had been so intense, the reason I'd heard her voice, the reason everything was wrong. I was not his muse because he already had one, and she could not be replaced. She could not release him because she was buried so deep within him she could not be separated. The world he saw was hers. She was the very essence of him, his genius and his desire, and vice versa.

Madeleine's voice reached from a deep past, something I'd forgotten, words that held a new meaning. *Do not forget, Odilé. We can choose only one.* One. Not two.

This was why Joseph was failing and why my hunger still burned so fervently. The bargain had not been sealed because I could not get through the barrier the two of them formed against it. Two, not one.

The choice has not been made.

My body had told me this, had I the will to listen. The cold, the unceasing hunger, the sense of unfolding . . . it all made sense now. My pride had kept me from admitting the truth, and now it was too late. I had misjudged everything. I felt the monster rouse.

I heard a quick shuffling on the stairs, and Joseph appeared, his hair tousled from sleep, his shirt thrown on, unbuttoned, his white trousers spattered with paint.

He stopped short the moment he saw her. I felt the pull she had for him in a sudden stopping of my breath, a yearning so strong it seemed almost to wrench my heart from my chest. I saw the pain and the longing in his eyes, and with some part of me I felt her rise. I felt the sudden strength of her, a pulse of power that startled me.

He'd taken two steps toward her when the clock struck midnight. The church bells rang, la Marangona from San Marco. The tone held in the air. Midnight. The end of three years.

I felt the darkness within me stir. I felt the hand of the world and knew a quick and fatal despair as the demon inside me spread its wings.

FORTY-EIGHT

NICHOLAS

The night was cold, a lowering frost already in the air, the canals still and spreading a miasmic damp. I flipped up the collar of my coat and pulled it more firmly about me, grateful for the warmth of the stew and the fritters I'd brought for her warming my hands, and anxious to get back before she woke. And all the time my mind was spinning as I tried to decide what to do, how to save her brother, how to keep him from the despair and madness that would descend once his masterpiece was done. Now that the bargain was made, and pain could not be prevented, all I could hope to do was ease it.

I went up the stairs and in through the door of the *portego*, pausing to take off my coat, though the palazzo was as cold as any other damn room in Venice, and I should probably do better to keep it on. I huddled in my suit coat instead and picked up the food again, making my way to her bedroom. The place was dead quiet—*like a tomb*, I thought. When I reached her bedroom, I realized why. The Moretta *was* empty. Sophie was gone.

I stood in the doorway, the fritters leaking oil onto my hand through their crumpled wrapper, and stared disbelievingly at the mussed bed. The lamp was burning, turned very low, and I thought I must be wrong. She was here somewhere. Perhaps the *sala*. I set the fritters and the stew down and called, "Sophie!" As my voice echoed into darkness, I saw the note she'd left behind.

Nicholas, I've gone to save Joseph. I love you.

The leaping joy I felt at those last words was eclipsed by the first.

I've gone to save Joseph.

I cursed beneath my breath. What could she possibly hope to accomplish, even assuming Odilé let her in? The bargain was set; there was no undoing it. Odilé would offer no mercy.

I shoved the note into my pocket and grabbed my coat, stepping out again into the dark, freezing fog.

I wove through the narrow *calli*, dodging cats and the occasional rat as I made my way past the flickering oil lamps of the corner shrines and the shadows. I wished she had waited for me, but I knew she wasn't thinking clearly. The news about Odilé had shaken her badly, her brother's fate worse so, and I knew he had been right when he told me Sophie didn't realize her importance, that she thought she was nothing. It would be my task to convince her otherwise, to show her what a singular talent she had. There was magic in her, just as in her brother. I remembered the Lido, watching her spin her tale, watching the way she beguiled him, the strength and inspiration he took from her. The way he drew her as if she were his sole purpose for being alive. I still could not accustom myself to the bewitchment they cast when they were together. As if they'd been forged together in some brutal crucible, and had emerged strong and shining, fatally joined.

Fatally.

I cannot live without him, she'd said.

I stopped short. No. Impossible.

I thought of Odilé on the balcony, the way she'd seemed to shift before me, as if I'd been viewing her underwater. The serpent I'd seen behind her eyes. The desperation in her voice. *Ah, but this one is so different. He is not like the others. . . .* At the time I'd thought she'd simply been telling me what I already knew. He *was* like no one I'd ever met. Blake's dark angel. But now, suddenly, I wondered if it was perhaps something else.

Was Joseph Hannigan different because of his talent? Or was he different because of his sister? Was it because Sophie and Joseph were inexplicably connected, not just twins at birth, but twins in living?

I tried to make sense of my thoughts. Odilé's despair, the shifting . . . I had seen those things before, hadn't I? I had seen them in Barcelona, in the days before she'd withdrawn to that dark little room with a score of hapless, ill-fated men. I had seen the emergence of the demon when the choice had not been made. I had seen those men die.

The choice has not been made.

Odilé had misjudged the connection between Sophie and Joseph. The world they made required both of them. They were joined. No one could get in unless they agreed. Odilé could not take Joseph, because Sophie was in the way. To love one, you must love both.

I stared unseeingly at the shadows before me, my heart beginning to pound in my chest. None of this was possible. But I'd spent years now chasing the impossible, and I knew the truth of impossible things. Just as I knew now, deep in my heart, that I was right. The bargain had not been sealed. Whatever was in Joseph and Sophie had prevented it. Odilé had failed. Desperately, I tried to remember the date. October fourteenth, wasn't it? Nearly three years to the date of Barcelona. Lacking only a single day.

Tomorrow, the three years would be over.

The resounding *bong* of la Marangona shattered my thoughts. I started, looking up at the sky, while the great bell of San Marco tolled the midnight chime.

There was no more tomorrow, I realized with sudden panic. The time was up now, today. Joseph was with Odilé. And Sophie . . . Sophie was there as well.

I broke into a run.

FORTY-NINE

SOPHIE

Sophie," Joseph said, and his voice seemed to shiver in the air, across my skin, as did the lingering chimes of the bell.

My heart leaped to him; I felt a surge of strength and stumbled toward him.

She stepped between us before I could reach him. Her eyes were black in the dim light. How strange they were. "He belongs to me now," she said, and her voice too was strange, nearly hissing. It prickled the hair on the back of my neck.

"I won't let you have him," I said desperately, looking to my brother, and the sorrow in his face told me what I'd already known, what I hadn't wanted to believe.

"I'm sorry, Soph," he said softly. "I had to do it, don't you see?"

"You didn't have to," I protested. He and Odilé wavered before me. "Henry Loneghan is returning. There would have been others too. All we had to do was wait."

"But that's why. I don't want you to keep waiting. Not for me. You've sacrificed so much already. You're brilliant, you know, in your own right. The world you see . . . it's beautiful. It shouldn't be just me who knows it. Others should know it too."

My heart hurt so I could hardly breathe. "But I can't see it without you."

"Yes you can." I heard the tears in his voice. "Dane will help you. He's promised to. And he loves you too."

"Joseph, no—"

"It's too late for any of this," Odilé whispered. "Too late."

I glanced at her—those terrible eyes. Odilé's face seemed to ripple when I looked at her. I could not keep her features straight. I turned back to my brother. "Joseph, come with me. Please. You mustn't do this. You know what she is. You know what will happen. It will kill you."

I wiped my tears from my eyes, but still she undulated before me. It was as if her edges were fraying. Shadows—were they shadows?—drifted across her face, blurring her features. It was disorienting, nauseating—and then her features went so sharp they looked unreal. "There is no bargain." The words reverberated as if they came from the world about us and not herself. "I cannot get past your walls."

My desperation fled in sudden apprehension. Something was wrong with her, something terrible. "What do you mean, there is no bargain?"

"Did you not feel it? In dreams, did you not feel his despair? Your conjoined souls—" She laughed bitterly. "What were you when he was gone?"

The darkness in her seemed to spread, her shadow a concussion against the marble wall behind. I thought I saw wings. I could not take my eyes from her.

She said, "Do the two of you feel one another's every pain and joy?"

Her words raised an echo, a memory. Miss Coring spitting as she beat me, her eyes burning, and Joseph across the room with clenched fists, tears running down his face as she forced him to watch, and then after, to draw. Her furious satisfaction. *He feels everything you feel, doesn't he? Doesn't he? Well then, let him feel this.*

I forced the image away and tried to focus on exactly what Odilé was saying. "But . . . if there is no bargain, it means he isn't bound to you. He's free to go—with his talent intact?"

She stared at me—a long, tense moment. Then she laughed again, and it was a horrible sound, gurgling and chortling. "That is half true. You belong to each other, just as before. But now you will *both* belong to me."

"What do you mean?"

She ignored me. She went to Joseph, her dressing gown shifting about her bare feet like mist. He didn't move, but watched her warily. When she touched his arm, I saw his yearning, still there, still strong, and my heart sank.

She slid her fingers almost lazily to his wrist, and then she grazed his jaw with her lips. "You are so beautiful. So much talent. You could have been the best of them. Would you have sung my praises, my darling boy? How sad I will be when you are gone." She spoke in a whisper. I should not have been able to hear it, but it was as if she stood next to me, as if it were into my ear she was murmuring.

Joseph jerked his head at me. "Sophie, go home."

"Oh, but she cannot," said Odilé, stepping away from him, and her eyes grew so large they seemed to encompass her skull— I saw the demon Nicholas had promised was there, the black and fathomless eyes, the wretched, avaricious hunger that must consume everything. "Did you not hear me? It is too late for that. I have you both. There's no escape now."

Everything Nicholas had said about her was true, and in that moment I understood what was happening. The bargain hadn't worked. No one had been chosen, and her time was up. Three years, he'd said. Three years, and if the choice wasn't made, the demon would emerge and destroy everything in its path. She would kill everyone around her. Joseph. Me.

She stepped toward me. I had spent a lifetime imagining demons and monsters, but my imagination had not been nearly ambitious enough for what I saw now. Such pure voraciousness. I could only stand and stare as she came toward me, and she was still so beautiful, despite the menace in her eyes—

Joseph lurched between us. "Don't touch her, Odilé. Let her go. You have me. I'll do whatever you want. Just let Sophie go."

"No," I whispered. "She's right. It's too late."

Joseph threw me a glance and said through clenched teeth. "Run. Get out of here. Leave her to me."

"No. I won't lose you."

"You don't understand, do you?" asked Odilé, her voice singsong now, gentle and sad, as if she spoke to children. "You are already lost."

"We are indeed," said a voice from behind me.

I looked over my shoulder. The courtyard door was open, and there stood Nicholas. I felt a relief and joy that buckled my knees—and then horror that he should be here too, in danger. Joseph's hand tightened on my arm, keeping me upright.

Nicholas stepped fully into the courtyard. He was breathing hard, as if he'd run a distance.

"Nicholas," she said, and there was a wealth in that word, years of history, if only I could understand it. I heard affection and resignation, anger and resentment, love and hate. "Oh my darling, how sad that you have come just at this moment. This time, I fear it will truly mean your death."

He did not look at me, or Joseph. His pale eyes fastened on her. "Make an end of it, Odilé. Aren't you tired? Don't you wish for eternal sleep? After so many years, so many masterpieces—when does one call it good?"

Her eyes narrowed, her nostrils flared. But I thought I saw something else there too—something he'd said had resonated.

Nicholas went on, "Surely you have left legacy enough."

"Legacy?" Her body seemed to pulsate; the wings in the shadow on the wall fluttered. "I have no *legacy*. Who knows who I am? Who has ever heard of me?"

"You have provided inspiration for ages. Byron. Keats. Schumann." He spoke softly, urging. "What more is there? How much more can you want? It's time, Odilé. Lock yourself in a room. Devour yourself and leave us. Make an end of it."

I felt a lurch within me, a lightheadedness that had me gasping as if someone drew upon my soul. When I looked at my brother, I saw he felt the same.

Nicholas staggered; I realized he felt what Joseph and I did, as if breath and bone were being slowly leeched away. "You don't want to do this, Odilé. You don't want to kill us. Lock yourself away."

"And you think that will end it?" she asked, her voice hard, rumbling all around me, pounding against my ears so I had to restrain the urge to cover them. "Have you spent all this time believing that I can destroy myself?" Her laughter was like a clap of thunder. "If you lock me away, it will only be the beginning, you foolish man. The monster cannot be contained *in a room*. It cannot be destroyed. There is no space that can hold it."

She grew as if to emphasize her words, darkness covering the courtyard as if it were a tide that seeped from her, the shadow on the wall behind gone black, gaslight disappearing into a darkness so profound I could not see through it, and the four of us eerily illuminated within it. Odilé began to change, coils upon coils lengthening her body, jewel-like, stunning scales, blinding with a hideous light—Keats's Lamia, a woman's head and torso on a serpent's body. Her eyes flashed, endlessly deep, endlessly terrible.

"All you have done is unleash *this* on the world," the not-quite-Odilé creature hissed. "I cannot go back. You cannot destroy me, Nicholas. No one can. You have only created a worse monster."

I clenched my fingers upon the marble to keep myself upright. My head spun, and my heart beat so rapidly I couldn't breathe. Joseph fell to his knees; Nicholas stumbled. "There must be some way to end it," he insisted. "Nothing is indestructible. Tell me how to release you and I will."

Her neck undulated, her dark hair falling over her shoulders, catching on luminescent scales. "There can never be release. There must always be one."

Nicholas looked confused. "One?"

"One to inspire. One muse. Mankind would destroy itself without the angel's gift." Those dark eyes gleamed; Odilé's lips moved with a voice that mesmerized with its horror. She laughed again. "Inspiration to keep men from giving in to despair. There must always be one."

Nicholas was on his knees before her now, obviously trying to cling to reason, to understand, though I saw how fierce her draw was upon him—I felt it too. My thoughts were disjointed, the world spun and swayed before me. All I could think was how Nicholas's hair gleamed in the darkness. How strange that it should glow so. "One to inspire," he repeated in a whisper. "You mean . . . you can pass it to another?"

Her eyes riveted to him, and yet I felt them on me too, drawing relentlessly. "You were always so clever, Nicholas."

"Let me understand," Nicholas gasped. "If you pass the demon to another, it will be satisfied? It will not require our deaths?"

"Yes. But why should I do that, *cheri*? Why should I cast aside Odilé forever?"

My heart raced like a mad thing. Joseph clutched his chest.

Nicholas said hoarsely, "Because you are tired. Because there is nothing more you can want, Odilé. You have inspired so many already. You know what a talent Hannigan is. Why would you destroy him? What more do you want?"

"What if I tell you I have no desire to disappear into the great nothingness?" she asked. "Obscurity does not suit me. I have not yet fulfilled my own wishes. Why should I die unsatisfied?"

"Don't we all?" Nicholas asked. "Don't we—"

"No." My brother lifted his head. His face was pale, his eyes dark as he looked at her. "What if I could satisfy you? What if I could give you what you most desire?"

I thought at first he was mocking her, throwing back the words of her stories, the words of the bargain.

She laughed. "How can you even know what that is, Joseph Hannigan?"

Joseph whispered, "I could make your name famous for an eternity. *Yours.* I can make people remember Odilé León forever. That's what you want, isn't it? It's what you've always wanted."

She had been drawing from us relentlessly, and suddenly she wasn't. My head cleared, my vision sharpened. And I saw she was looking at him, her focus intent, as if she did not quite believe what he was saying, as if he had come upon a great truth, and I realized he had. He had, as always, seen what others had never noticed, what others could not see.

"How would you do that?" she asked.

My brother said with confidence, "You said I could be the best of them. If you let us live, I promise you I will be. I will paint a portrait of you for the ages. I will give it your name."

She went very still—it was unnerving, to see a serpent body so unmoving, to see not even a pulse in the coils.

Nicholas added, "He can do it, Odilé. You know he can. He'll paint a masterpiece, and I'll make certain he's famous for it. I know the people who can help. Even without your inspiration, he has a destiny. I'll do my part to make certain he meets it."

I felt a surge of hope as I saw how she considered it. But when her answer came, it was not directed at my brother, or Nicholas. Instead, she looked at me.

Her fathomless eyes surveyed me dispassionately; I felt their poison in my heart. "How is it you can best me? What is your magic, Sophie Hannigan?"

I met that gaze, though it took all my will not to turn away. I felt Nicholas's eyes upon me, nervous, yet determined and hopeful. I felt his love for me. I felt Joseph's too, and with it I felt the strength of the world we had made together. "You said there was no meaning in life, but I think that cannot be true. I think I can give meaning to yours, if you will let me. Joseph will paint you, and Nicholas will help him find the fame he deserves, and I . . . I will tell the whole world the story of who you were. I will make it one of Venice's best and most enduring legends. I will tell it across continents. I will never stop telling it."

Odilé was silent. The night sounds of Venice intruded—the splashing of an oar, the faint strain of a gondolier's song from far away—such normal sounds that they seemed fantastical, unholy and fearful.

"Is it not enough, Odilé?" Nicholas asked softly. "Or would you prefer another two hundred years of disappointment?"

It seemed I saw several lifetimes pass through her eyes. Regrets and sorrows and joys, but most of all, I saw exhaustion and relief, and I knew what her answer would be before she said, "I accept your offer."

My brother sagged in gratitude. Nicholas smiled.

The jewels of her coils stung my eyes. I felt the lure of her as strongly as I ever had, the temptation and enchantment. Even in her horror, she was splendid.

Her voice was sibilant, hollow; it seemed to sink into me as if it were my own pulse. "And so . . . which one of you will take the gift? There must always be one."

FIFTY

NICHOLAS

I was so overcome with relief at Odilé's agreement that it was a moment before I understood what it really meant, that one of us must take her place. And then, as that horror dawned, another grew as I realized that Sophie was rising as if drawn by some bewitchment. Beside me, Hannigan cried out, "Sophie, no!"

There was a determination in her eyes—and something more than that. I saw once again that despair I'd seen in my bedroom as she'd told me the story of how her scars had been made.

"No," I said quietly, and when she looked at me I felt both pain and joy. "Not this, Sophie. This isn't for you."

"You don't understand," she said.

"She is tired of living in the shadows, is that not true, *cherie*?" Odilé whispered, and that voice, even touched with its serpent's hiss, was as seductive as ever. "What she wishes is to walk into a room and have people see her. She does not wish to fade next to her brother. She does not wish to be second best again.

This is what you want, is it not so? Tell them, Sophie, what it is you most desire. Tell them who you really are."

"Sophie," I said desperately. "You're not second best. Not for me and not for Joseph. You're *everything*, don't you see? You don't need this. Don't do it."

Sophie said tightly, "Someone must, and—"

"Then let it be me," Hannigan interrupted. He lurched toward Odilé, holding out his hand. "I'll take the gift. Right now. Give it to me."

Sophie grabbed his shoulder, pulling him back. "Joseph, don't be absurd! It would be no better than the bargain."

The air around Odilé pulsed. I felt it in my muscles, the rapid beating of my heart as she drew upon it.

It seemed as if the scene before me froze—Hannigan offering his hand to Odilé's lamia; Sophie watching in horror, grasping his arm—and in that moment, I was struck with a clarity that was like the cracking open of the world. The thing I had known and not let myself see—the absurd belief that my talent could have brought me fame, had Odilé not destroyed it. I understood now that she had not taken it from me. Had she not already said as much? On that street in Florence. . . . *You haven't enough talent to change the world.* I had known it then, but I had been determined to find blame for my own lack, to believe a lie that was more comfortable than the truth. Yet inspiration had returned to me, hadn't it? Sophie, and love, had given me what I'd thought was lost.

I thought of what Sophie had said about her brother, *I cannot live without him.* And I knew that was true—Odilé could not choose either of them to take her place, because the twins were too connected. There must always be *one,* she'd said. What had kept the bargain from sealing would prevent this too.

It had to be me.

If I did not take the gift, we would all die. Joseph Hannigan's talent would be gone. And Sophie's too. The words on Sophie's note settled hard within me. *I love you.*

I stepped forward. It was my first completely selfless act—it was the only thing to do to save the woman I loved, and I thought—I hoped—that perhaps it would make a difference, to take the gift not out of greed, but out of love. "They cannot be chosen. The gift belongs to me, Odilé. You know it as well as I."

Sophie cried out in a grief and dismay that tore at my heart. Her brother said, sharply, desperately, "No, Dane. For Sophie's sake, don't do this."

But it was for her sake I was.

"A man." Odilé ignored them both, as I forced myself to do. "Yes, why not? An incubus muse. It is woman's time to shine, I think."

She met my gaze. Here was the demon I'd seen crawling upon the dead. Here was every nightmare I'd ever had. But here also was the Odilé I'd loved, and I felt the bond between us— seven years of pursuit, seven years of bondage. Symmetry, as she was so fond of saying. I was ready to bring it to an end, and I think so was she.

"There must always be one," she told me, again, her coils undulating. "And you will have three years to choose each time."

"I understand," I said.

"There is a trunk in my bedroom. In it, you will find everything I know." She smiled softly. Her gaze took in Sophie and Joseph before lighting again on me. "I had thought there was nothing new in the world. How strange to find I was wrong."

I felt the weight of her regard, and with it an acknowledgment that the last seven years had not been devoid of meaning, that I had been a worthy adversary. That I had been important after all.

"Have you a knife?" she asked.

I reached into my coat pocket and took out the one I always carried. "It's quite small."

"It is large enough for this." She reached for me, gripping my arm and pulling me close, so her coils tangled about my feet— this was what I would become. It was my last chance to refuse. I glanced at Sophie, who looked stricken.

"Nicholas," she whispered.

I ignored her, and the pain in my heart.

Odilé said, "What do you most desire, Nicholas?"

"To matter," I answered.

She smiled. She whispered in my ear, "Hold to your promise. Make Joseph famous. I want the world to know my name."

"I will," I vowed.

She drew back, staring into my eyes, the gray subsumed by dark, everything we'd been to each other swirling in their depths. "Goodbye, *cheri*."

I plunged the knife into her breast and heard her little gasp of pain; I saw her relief and gratitude.

Then she went lax in my arms, and I felt the flood of the transfer, an energy greater than anything I had ever known sweeping into me, and I cried out, releasing her without meaning to, collapsing beside her on the marble floor, watching her transform into herself again, the woman I had once loved— beautiful Odilé—as I felt the monster come to life within me.

FIFTY-ONE

DECEMBER, 1879
SOPHIE

It was snowing. The marble angels of the Salute were faint and ghostly through the fog of snowflakes, and the usually translucent domes looked to be covered with the fallen wing feathers of the heavenly host trumpeting their glories. On either side of the church, the balconies and rooftops of the palazzos were sugared like iced confections. The Canal below was a deeply opaque green, as if the snow falling within it had mixed like the paints on Joseph's palette, a whisk of white into pure emerald. Gondolas were nothing more than sliding shadows. There was a quiet upon the world that one felt even through the buzz of talk in the Alvisi, as if Venice had become even more an enchanted city, one only existing in a fairy tale.

Oh, but it was that, wasn't it? Even more so now, for me.

". . . and the city took on again its everyday mask," I said to the group of listeners gathered about me, continuing the story I'd been telling for the past hour. "The oil lamps in the corner shrines were lit as they always were, the rats stealing bits of offerings left for the saints as they always did, the cats lifting their taunting tails as they slinked by. It was as if nothing had happened and nothing had changed. The veil lowered, and no one but they three knew what really lay beneath, or what strange enchantments existed beyond the sight of men."

I let my voice fall to a whisper, and for a breath—for the briefest of moments—the snowfall hush of Venice descended upon our little group, and the sounds of the conversations in the room beyond seemed to fade.

Frank Duveneck was the first to leap to his feet. "Marvelous!" he said, clapping. "My God, Miss Hannigan, you do have a way with a tale. Why, you almost make me believe such things exist as immortal succubi!"

The cartographer sitting beside him laughed. "Indeed! Hannigan, for shame! Why did you not tell us before that your sister was such a brilliant storyteller?"

We all looked over to where my brother stood beside the painting that held the place of honor in the main *sala*. Joseph smiled and winked, and my heart swelled with love for him. "Sophie's been shy. I've only just convinced her to show the rest of you what I've always known."

Duveneck's gaze went to the painting. "Did she really exist? Is the woman on your canvas really the succubus in the story?"

I wondered if I was the only one who saw the sadness in my brother's eyes as he said, "Well, that's the pleasure of a story, isn't it? Deciding for yourself how real you wish to make it."

The painting was the masterpiece Odilé had known it would be. Joseph had told me, *I want it to be worthy of her, Soph.* And it *was* worthy. It was exquisite—a woman posed at the doorway to a bedroom, looking back over her shoulder as she reached to take down her hair while demons in the darkness beyond beckoned. A ghost in a twirling chemise. A monster with glowing eyes. An angel who was sometimes a devil, depending on the light. *Odilé León, Inamorata,* he'd called it, and every night for a week critics had gathered about it, lauding him, scrawling excitedly in their notebooks. It would go to the Exhibition at the Salon of Paris next, thanks to Nicholas's connections.

"How vibrantly you've done her," Duveneck said. "I almost imagine that if I kissed that mole on her back I would feel warm skin. Such an alluring flaw!"

The cartographer said, "It's the flaws that make true beauty, don't you think, Duveneck? Symmetry is boring."

"It was the flaw that was my inspiration," Joseph said quietly, with a smile that was just for me.

"Well, if she is real, I'd give my soul to meet her. Where is she?" the cartographer asked.

"Turned to smoke and drifted away, as I just told you," I answered.

They all laughed. It was just a story, after all. Such bargains were the stuff of legends, best told on cold winter nights over glasses of wine. Spells cast in inebriation and dreams, inexplicable, impossible. Layers beneath the world, like the angel/demon in Joseph's painting, only visible in a certain light.

The cartographer said, "You'll tell us another story tomorrow? Your tales have become the sole reason I attend this salon, Miss Hannigan, so you must promise to be here."

I nodded and smiled and said that of course I would be here, where else should I be? I had to admit the attention was heady, and I loved telling the stories for an audience. It was not just Joseph and me who needed such gilding in a cruel and ugly world, and I liked that the way I colored it stayed in their hearts and minds, in their dreams.

When the others disappeared into the crowd, Joseph came up behind me, squatting at my chair to rest his chin upon my shoulder, his thick hair brushing my cheek. "They half believe it."

"Sometimes I half don't," I mused. "But then, it felt so real, didn't it?"

"Your stories always do," he said.

And it had begun to feel like a story, truly. Something I'd imagined, words formed from nothing. Odilé seemed at times like a trick of the light—her laughter, the jewels that had glinted at her throat, the serpent's coils, and the red of the blood on her breast as Nicholas withdrew the knife—flickering in and out of my sightlines like a ghost, though I had watched her leave us, and I knew she was gone. I had seen her turn to smoke the color of her eyes and drift away in a sudden breeze through the court-yard while we watched in stunned surprise, and then Nicholas had raised his head and said with a sigh, "Well, that's it then. It's done," and Joseph had followed the last of the smoke with a gaze so full of compassion I wanted to cry. Then he blinked and helped Nicholas to his feet, and they had clasped shoulders like comrades in arms, like brothers.

They'd come to me and Nicholas had taken me into his arms, and the moment he'd touched me, I felt the draw of his hunger—so pure and sweet, so tempting. The longing for it had overwhelmed me, and I realized it was what Joseph had felt with Odilé. I understood. But Nicholas had jerked away, whispering, *No. Oh no.*

I'd known it then, just as he did. I had known it as I knew the beat of my brother's heart. Nicholas had made his choice, as I had made mine. He had taken the gift to save both Joseph and me, and in so doing, he had made anything between us impossible. Because he was an incubus, and his very touch stole everything from me. Because he loved me, and because he loved my brother, and we loved him, he could get past the wall that Odilé could never broach. We could not help but let him in, and his hunger drew the talent I'd once told him I didn't have and left me weak and gasping.

Joseph murmured now, as if he knew what I was remembering, "Don't, Soph. Don't think it." The words we used to banish every ghost and hurt.

I wiped at my eyes and said, "No, I won't. I won't."

Joseph went suddenly still. Then he said softly, "He's here. He's just come."

I don't know how he knew it. Some connection between them, some understanding that had blossomed—two who had been under her spell, two she'd held prisoner—another link forged to bind the three of us forever.

I felt a shiver of anticipation, and looked up just in time to see Nicholas come into the *sala*. I saw the way others stopped and turned to watch him. He had always been handsome, but now he was beautiful, as if a light shone from within him, some angel's light, so that the world seemed dim about his center. Irresistible. Odilé in male form, casting enchantment wherever he went. He strode into the room as if he owned it. Katharine Bronson was on her chaise, and when she saw him she motioned him over. A woman sat beside her—I'd heard her name earlier— Constance Woolson. I watched as he went up to her, as he bowed over her hand, and I saw how caught she was by his spell. I imagined I felt the leap of her heart.

"Look at how good he is. She belongs to him already," I murmured, the ache in my chest growing.

Joseph kissed my cheek. "Yes. But he'll always be yours, Soph."

He was; I knew that.

I love you, Sophie, he'd said. *I always will. Whatever you ask of me is yours—except to destroy you. That I won't do.*

Nicholas glanced up. His gaze came unerringly to me. He put his fingers to his lips and blew me a kiss, and it seemed I felt it float across the air to brush my skin. A feather-light touch, unbearably warm.

Joseph's arm came around me, pulling me close. He buried his face in the crook of my neck as if he meant to breathe me in. I felt his lips move against my throat as he whispered, "Tell me you don't regret it."

I thought of what my brother had done for me, the sacrifice he'd made. I thought of how lost I'd been without him, and the truth I'd told Odilé and Nicholas—that I could not live without him. I thought of the look Nicholas had given us both before he stepped forward, before he'd said, *The gift belongs to me, Odilé. You know it as well as I,* and of the sorrow I'd felt when he said it. And the relief too. The terrible relief, most damning of all.

Some things even a fairy tale could not make beautiful.

"I don't regret it," I said to Joseph now. Echoes of other admissions, the same answer always, to Edward Roberts, to Miss Coring, to everyone who had ever come between us. And it was true. I didn't regret it. But I knew now that perhaps Odilé had been right when she'd said that Joseph and I kept the past too close, crippling even as we saved each other. Being with Nicholas had shown me that it didn't always have to be that way, that while Joseph was inextricably part of me, he did not have to be the whole part. I could have something of my own too.

I felt my brother's kiss just below my ear. Across the room, I saw Nicholas's wistful smile.

This was the beginning of another story, I realized. Another tale to follow to its end, one to add to the collection I'd invented for my brother, for me, for Odilé. And perhaps this one too would become a legend for gondoliers to tell tourists, a fairy tale to show us it was possible to defeat evil and despair, a guide to lead one across a chasm on a bridge spun of frailest gold. I thought of the stories Odilé had told, and knew mine were better—mine had made of her life something noble and fine. *You see, Odilé? I have made for you meaning after all.*

I thought I heard her answering laughter as she stepped into shadows and legend, fading like smoke into the softly falling snow.

ACKNOWLEDGMENTS

Many thanks go to Courtney Miller, Terry Goodman and my author team at Amazon, who are amazing in so many ways. I feel truly privileged to know and work with you all. Also, as always, thanks to Kim Witherspoon, Allison Hunter, Nathaniel Jacks and everyone at Inkwell, who make all of this so much easier. I owe a huge debt of gratitude to Kristin Hannah—always and forever, but for this book in particular—because she believed in it so strongly from the start, even when I was flailing. Thanks also to Suzanne Droppert and everyone at Liberty Bay Books in Poulsbo, Washington, for jumping so enthusiastically on my bandwagon; I appreciate it so much. My family has been so generous with their support and love through some very difficult times—I hope you all know how important you are to me. And of course, I could not do this without Kany, Maggie and Cleo, who make it all worthwhile.

ABOUT THE AUTHOR

CMC Levine, 2012

Megan Chance is a critically acclaimed, award-winning author of historical fiction. Her novels have been chosen for the Borders Original Voices and IndieBound's Booksense programs. A former television news photographer and graduate of Western Washington University, Chance lives in the Pacific Northwest with her husband and two daughters.

www.meganchance.com